Vampire Game

JUDAL

ALSO AVAILABLE FROM TOKYOPOP®

MANGA

.HACK//LEGEND OF THE TWILIGHT BRACELET (September 2003)
@LARGE (August 2003)
ANGELIC LAYER*
BABY BIRTH* (September 2003)
BATTLE ROYALE*
BRAIN POWERED*
BRIGADOON* (August 2003)
CARDCAPTOR SAKURA
CARDCAPTOR SAKURA: MASTER OF THE CLOW*
CHOBITS*
CHRONICLES OF THE CURSED SWORD
CLAMP SCHOOL DETECTIVES*
CLOVER
CONFIDENTIAL CONFESSIONS*
CORRECTOR YUI
COWBOY BEBOP*
COWBOY BEBOP: SHOOTING STAR*
DEMON DIARY
DIGIMON*
DRAGON HUNTER
DRAGON KNIGHTS*
DUKLYON: CLAMP SCHOOL DEFENDERS*
ERICA SAKURAZAWA*
FAKE*
FLCL* (September 2003)
FORBIDDEN DANCE* (August 2003)
GATE KEEPERS*
G GUNDAM*
GRAVITATION*
GTO*
GUNDAM WING
GUNDAM WING: BATTLEFIELD OF PACIFISTS
GUNDAM WING: ENDLESS WALTZ*
GUNDAM WING: THE LAST OUTPOST*
HAPPY MANIA*
HARLEM BEAT
I.N.V.U.
INITIAL D*
ISLAND
JING: KING OF BANDITS*
JULINE
KARE KANO*
KINDAICHI CASE FILES, THE*
KING OF HELL
KODOCHA: SANA'S STAGE*
LOVE HINA*
LUPIN III*
MAGIC KNIGHT RAYEARTH* (August 2003)
MAGIC KNIGHT RAYEARTH II* (COMING SOON)

MAN OF MANY FACES*
MARMALADE BOY*
MARS*
MIRACLE GIRLS
MIYUKI-CHAN IN WONDERLAND* (October 2003)
MONSTERS, INC.
PARADISE KISS*
PARASYTE
PEACH GIRL
PEACH GIRL: CHANGE OF HEART*
PET SHOP OF HORRORS*
PLANET LADDER*
PLANETES* (October 2003)
PRIEST
RAGNAROK
RAVE MASTER*
REALITY CHECK
REBIRTH
REBOUND*
RISING STARS OF MANGA
SABER MARIONETTE J*
SAILOR MOON
SAINT TAIL
SAMURAI DEEPER KYO*
SAMURAI GIRL: REAL BOUT HIGH SCHOOL*
SCRYED*
SHAOLIN SISTERS*
SHIRAHIME-SYO: SNOW GODDESS TALES* (Dec. 2003)
SHUTTERBOX (November 2003)
SORCERER HUNTERS
THE SKULL MAN*
THE VISION OF ESCAFLOWNE
TOKYO MEW MEW*
UNDER THE GLASS MOON
VAMPIRE GAME
WILD ACT*
WISH*
WORLD OF HARTZ (August 2003)
X-DAY* (August 2003)
ZODIAC P.I. *

*INDICATES 100% AUTHENTIC MANGA (RIGHT-TO-LEFT FORMAT)

CINE-MANGA™

CARDCAPTORS
JACKIE CHAN ADVENTURES (COMING SOON)
JIMMY NEUTRON (September 2003)
KIM POSSIBLE
LIZZIE MCGUIRE
POWER RANGERS: NINJA STORM (August 2003)
SPONGEBOB SQUAREPANTS (September 2003)
SPY KIDS 2

NOVELS

KARMA CLUB (Coming Soon)
SAILOR MOON

TOKYOPOP KIDS

STRAY SHEEP (September 2003)

ART BOOKS

CARDCAPTOR SAKURA*
MAGIC KNIGHT RAYEARTH*

ANIME GUIDES

COWBOY BEBOP ANIME GUIDES
GUNDAM TECHNICAL MANUALS
SAILOR MOON SCOUT GUIDES

4-28-03

VAMPIRE GAME

Volume 1

by

JUDAL

TOKYOPOP®

Los Angeles • Tokyo • London

Translator - Ikoi Hiroe
English Adaptation - Jason Dietrich
Associate Editor - Tim Beedle
Retouch and Lettering - Jon Ehinger
Cover Layout - Aaron Suhr

Editor - Luis Reyes
Managing Editor - Jill Freshney
Production Coordinator - Antonio DePietro
Production Manager - Jennifer Miller
Art Director - Matthew Alford
Director of Editorial - Jeremy Ross
VP of Production & Manufacturing - Ron Klamert
President & C.O.O. - John Parker
Publisher & C.E.O. - Stuart Levy

Email: editor@TOKYOPOP.com
Come visit us online at www.TOKYOPOP.com

A **TOKYOPOP** Manga
TOKYOPOP® is an imprint of Mixx Entertainment, Inc.
5900 Wilshire Blvd. Suite 2000, Los Angeles, CA 90036

ISBN: 1-59182-369-2

First TOKYOPOP® printing: June 2003

10 9 8 7 6 5 4 3 2 1
Printed in Canada

VAMPIRE GAME

This is the tale of the Vampire King Duzell and his quest for revenge against the good King Phelios, a valiant warrior who slayed the vampire a century ago. Now Duzell returns, reincarnated as a feline foe to deliver woe to... well, that's the problem. Who is the reincarnation of King Phelios?

Table of Contents

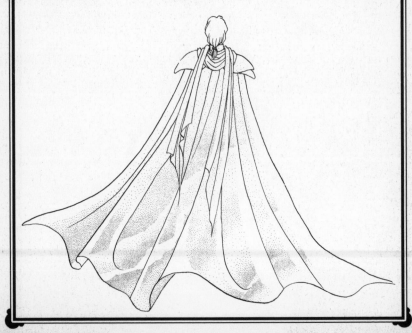

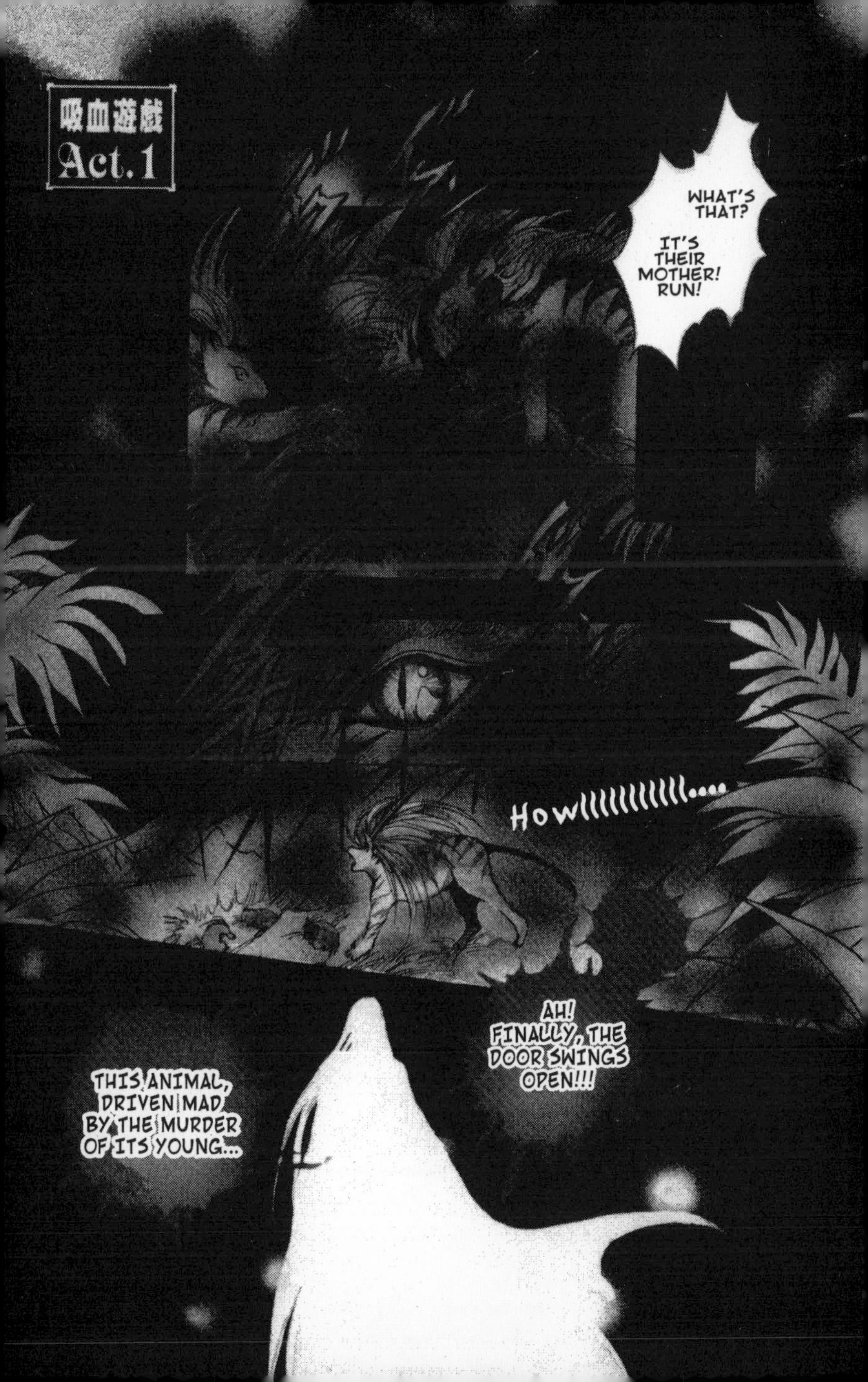
吸血遊戯
Act. 1
WHAT'S THAT?
IT'S THEIR MOTHER! RUN!
Howllllllllll....
AH! FINALLY, THE DOOR SWINGS OPEN!!!
THIS ANIMAL, DRIVEN MAD BY THE MURDER OF ITS YOUNG...

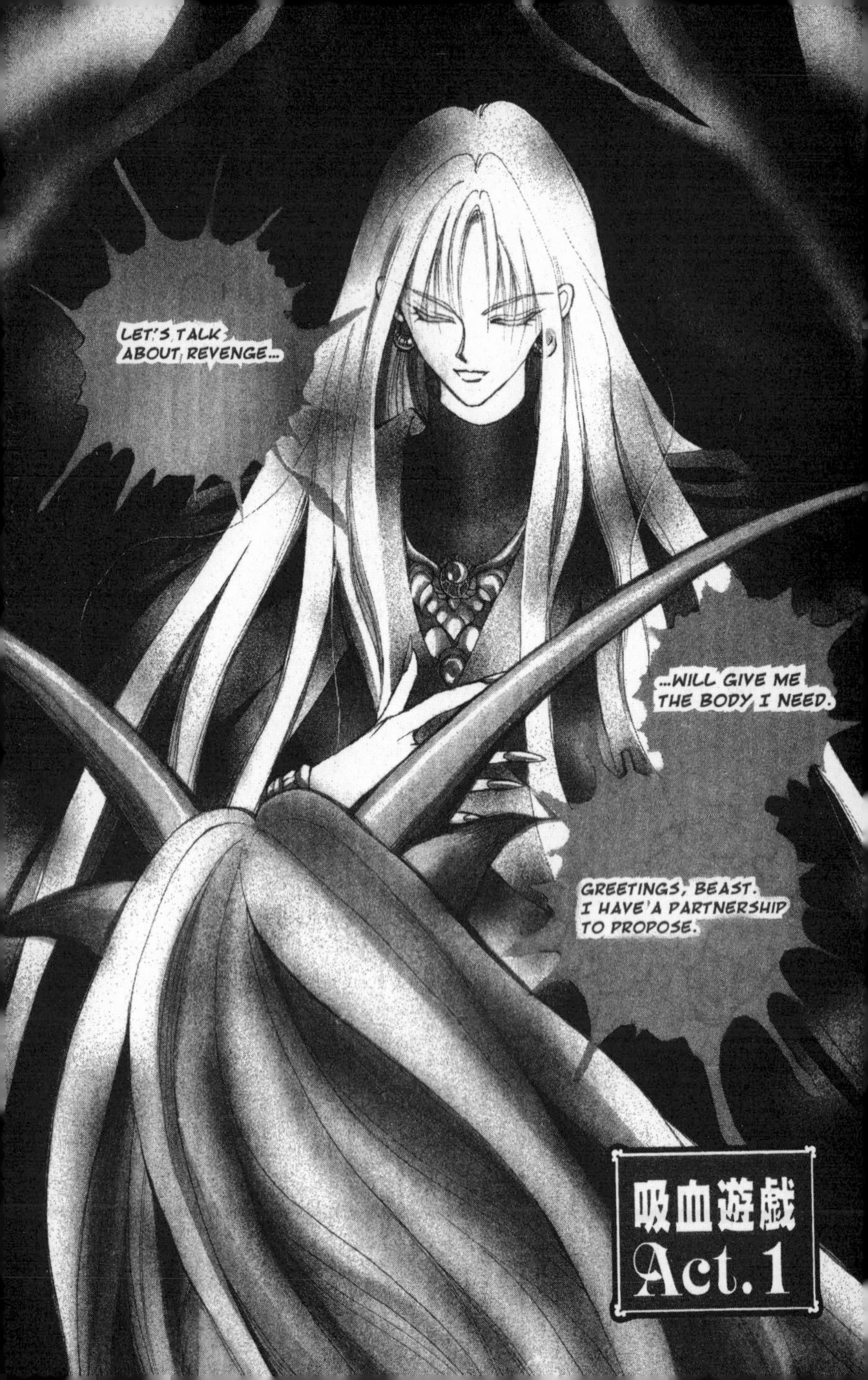
GREETINGS, BEAST. I HAVE A PARTNERSHIP TO PROPOSE.
LET'S TALK ABOUT REVENGE...
...WILL GIVE ME THE BODY I NEED.
吸血遊戯
Act. 1

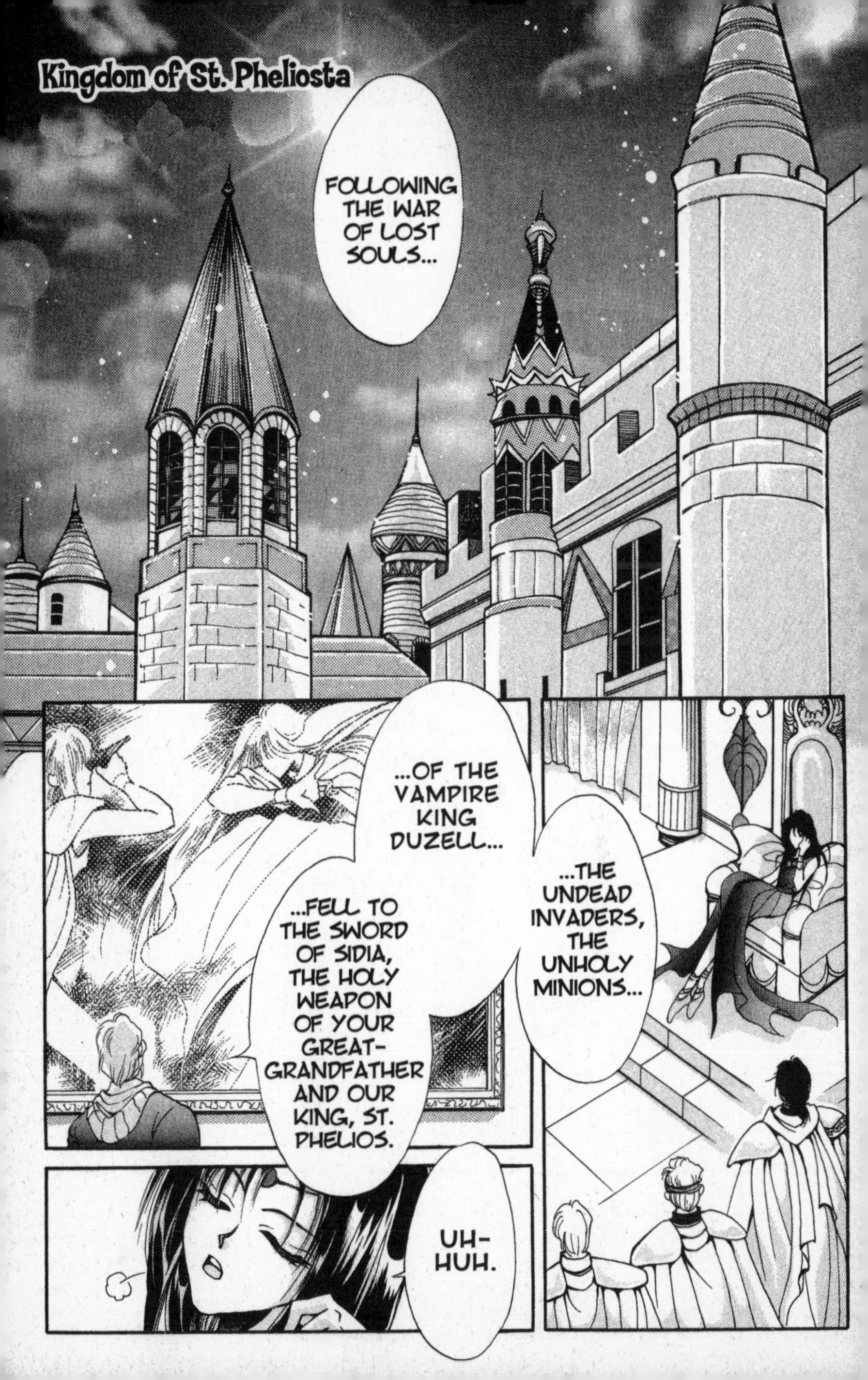
Kingdom of St. Pheliosta
FOLLOWING THE WAR OF LOST SOULS...
...THE UNDEAD INVADERS, THE UNHOLY MINIONS...
...OF THE VAMPIRE KING DUZELL...
...FELL TO THE SWORD OF SIDIA, THE HOLY WEAPON OF YOUR GREAT-GRANDFATHER AND OUR KING, ST. PHELIOS.
UH-HUH.

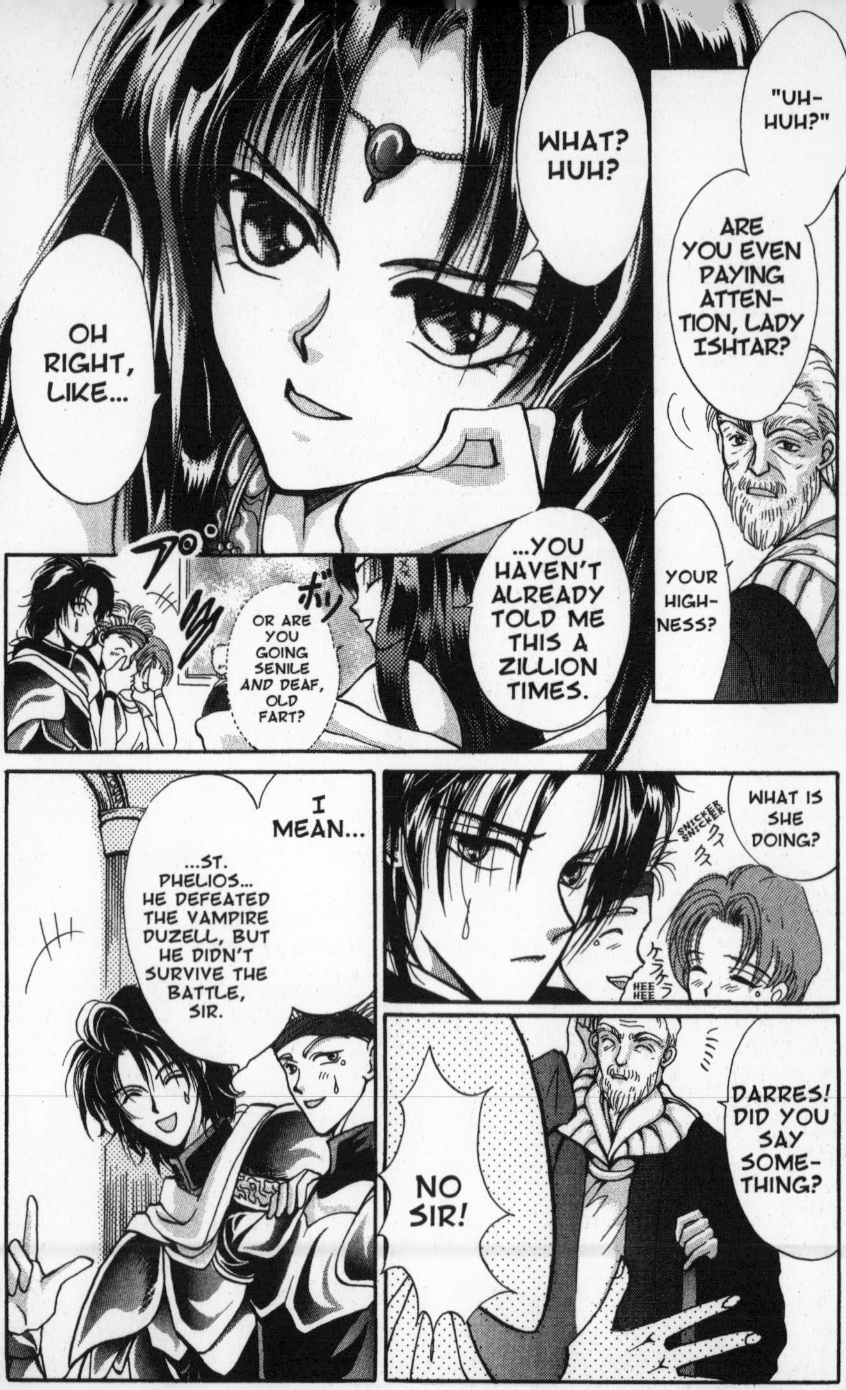
"UH-HUH?"
ARE YOU EVEN PAYING ATTENTION, LADY ISHTAR?
YOUR HIGHNESS?
WHAT? HUH?
OH RIGHT, LIKE...
...YOU HAVEN'T ALREADY TOLD ME THIS A ZILLION TIMES.
OR ARE YOU GOING SENILE AND DEAF, OLD FART?
WHAT IS SHE DOING?
SNICKER SNICKER
HEE HEE
DARRES! DID YOU SAY SOMETHING?
NO SIR!
I MEAN...
...ST. PHELIOS... HE DEFEATED THE VAMPIRE DUZELL, BUT HE DIDN'T SURVIVE THE BATTLE, SIR.

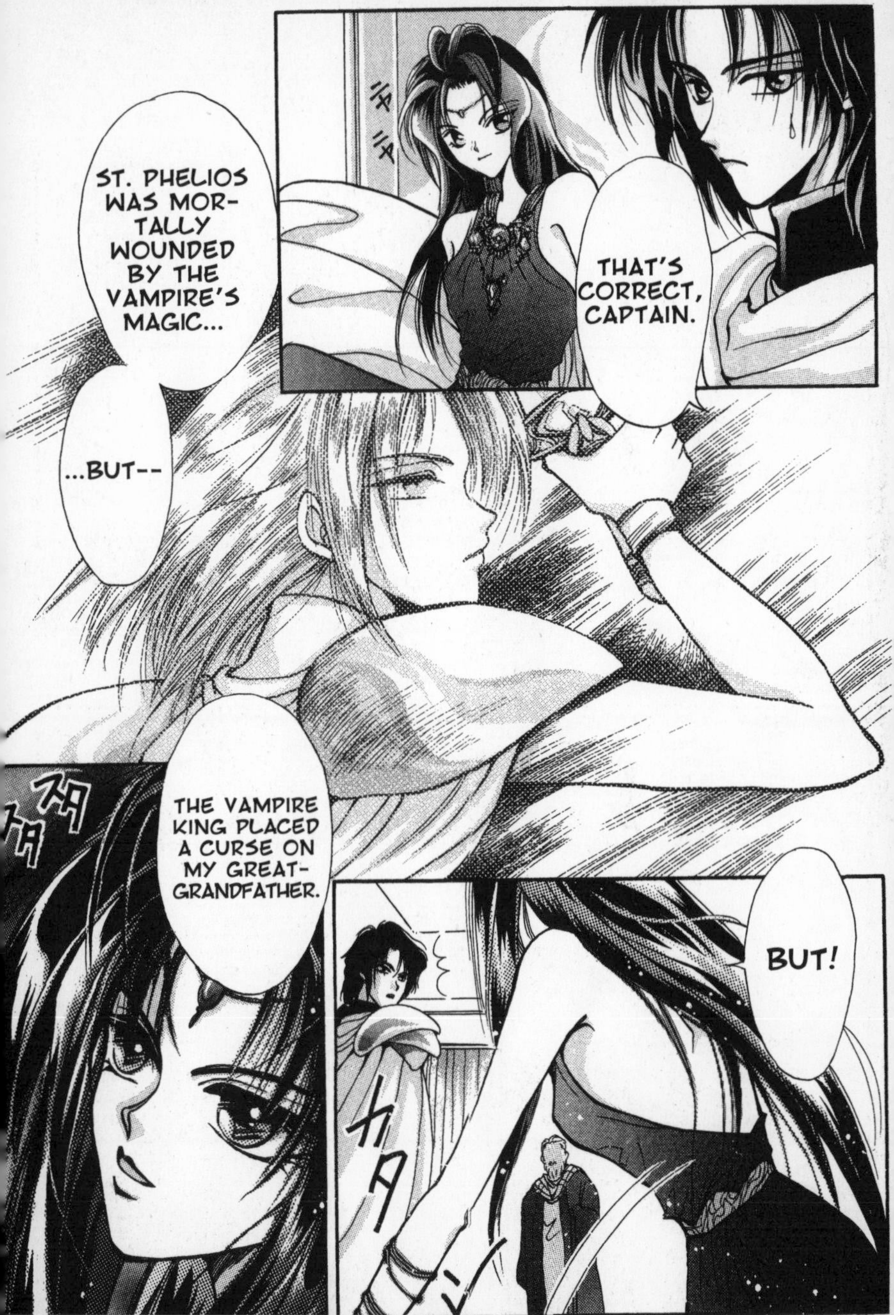
THAT'S CORRECT, CAPTAIN.
ST. PHELIOS WAS MORTALLY WOUNDED BY THE VAMPIRE'S MAGIC...
...BUT--
BUT!
THE VAMPIRE KING PLACED A CURSE ON MY GREAT-GRANDFATHER.

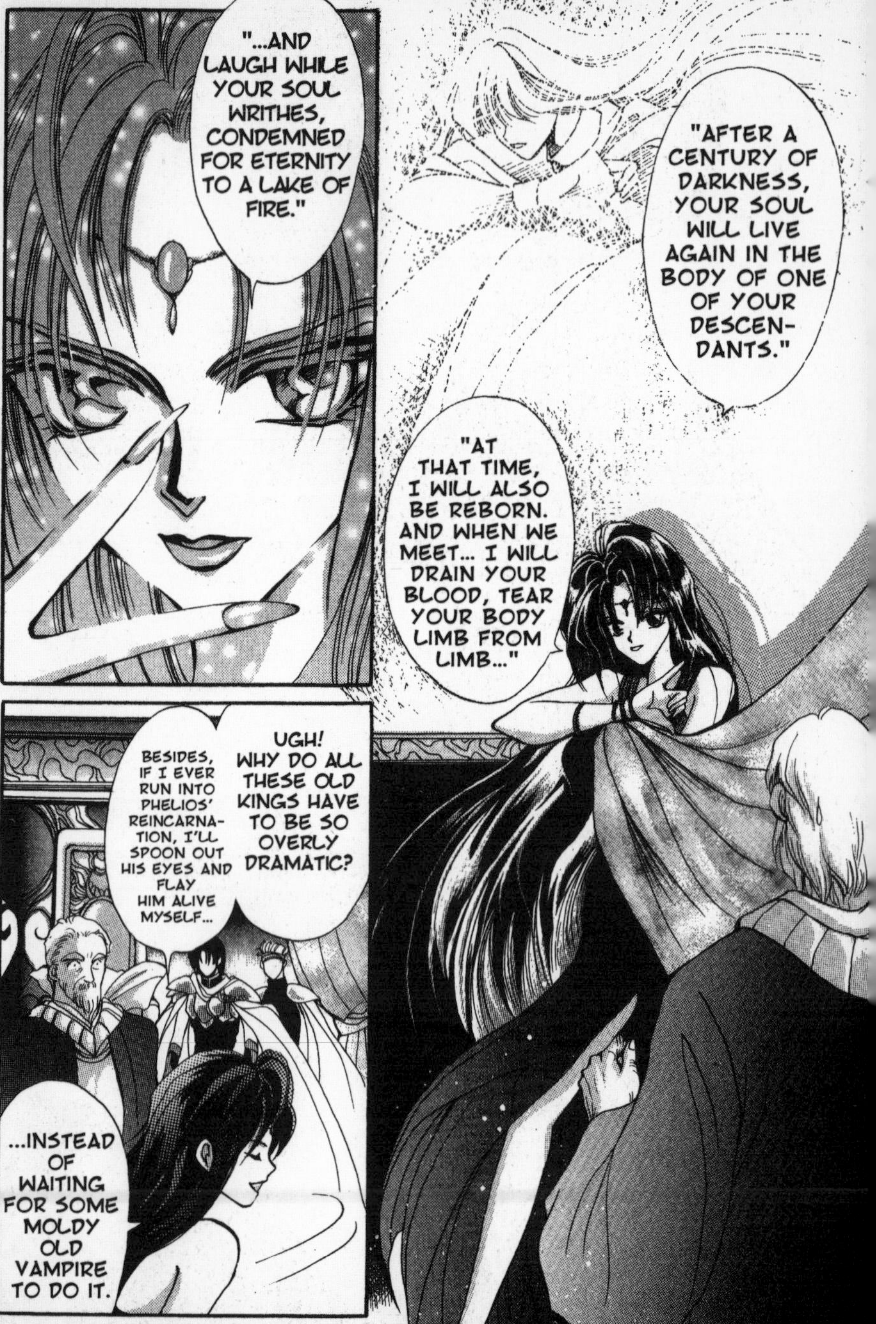
"AFTER A CENTURY OF DARKNESS, YOUR SOUL WILL LIVE AGAIN IN THE BODY OF ONE OF YOUR DESCEN-DANTS."
"AT THAT TIME, I WILL ALSO BE REBORN. AND WHEN WE MEET... I WILL DRAIN YOUR BLOOD, TEAR YOUR BODY LIMB FROM LIMB..."
"...AND LAUGH WHILE YOUR SOUL WRITHES, CONDEMNED FOR ETERNITY TO A LAKE OF FIRE."
UGH! WHY DO ALL THESE OLD KINGS HAVE TO BE SO OVERLY DRAMATIC?
BESIDES, IF I EVER RUN INTO PHELIOS' REINCARNA-TION, I'LL SPOON OUT HIS EYES AND FLAY HIM ALIVE MYSELF...
...INSTEAD OF WAITING FOR SOME MOLDY OLD VAMPIRE TO DO IT.

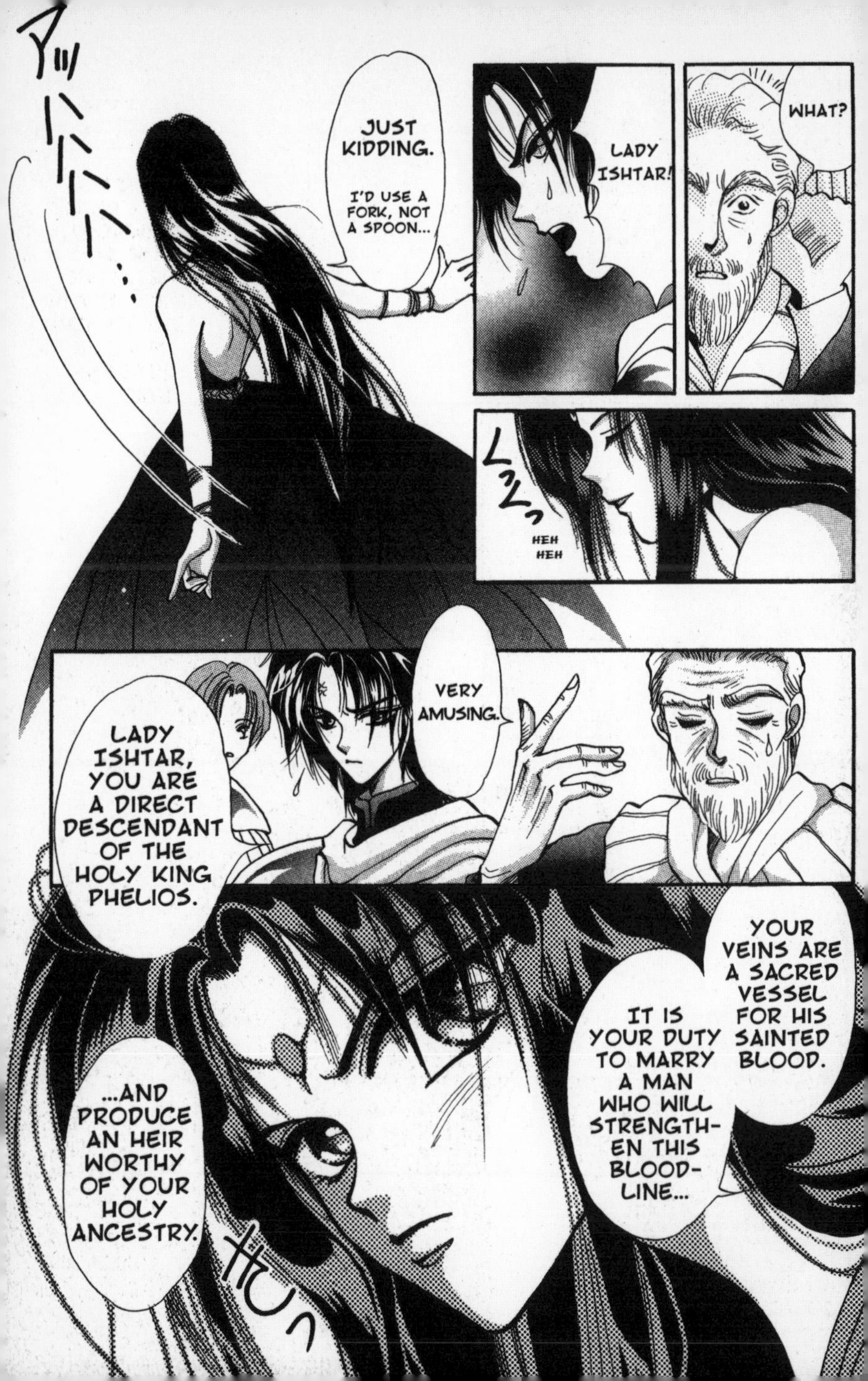
WHAT?
LADY ISHTAR!
JUST KIDDING.
I'D USE A FORK, NOT A SPOON...
HEH HEH
VERY AMUSING.
LADY ISHTAR, YOU ARE A DIRECT DESCENDANT OF THE HOLY KING PHELIOS.
YOUR VEINS ARE A SACRED VESSEL FOR HIS SAINTED BLOOD.
IT IS YOUR DUTY TO MARRY A MAN WHO WILL STRENGTH-EN THIS BLOOD-LINE...
...AND PRODUCE AN HEIR WORTHY OF YOUR HOLY ANCESTRY.

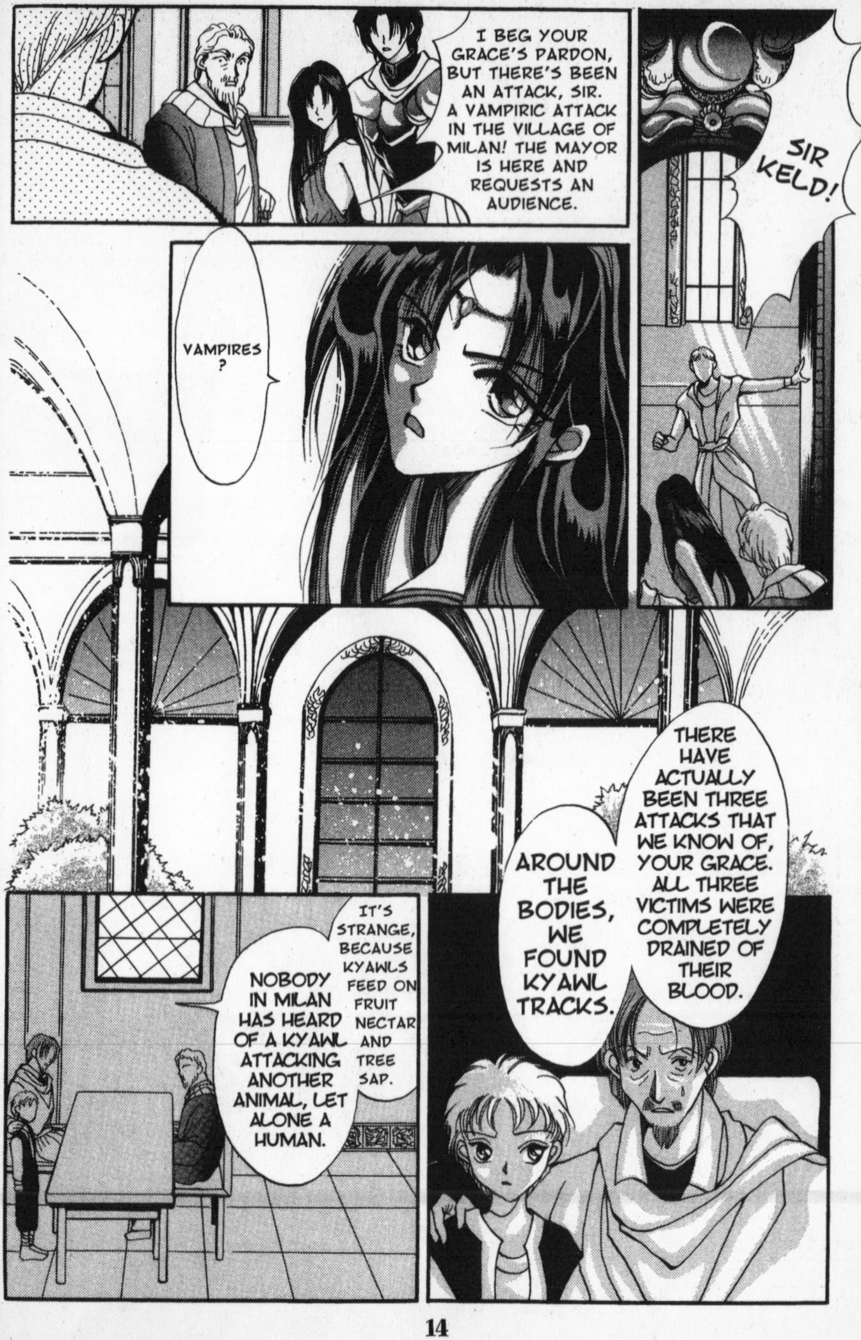
SIR KELD!
I BEG YOUR GRACE'S PARDON, BUT THERE'S BEEN AN ATTACK, SIR. A VAMPIRIC ATTACK IN THE VILLAGE OF MILAN! THE MAYOR IS HERE AND REQUESTS AN AUDIENCE.
VAMPIRES ?
THERE HAVE ACTUALLY BEEN THREE ATTACKS THAT WE KNOW OF, YOUR GRACE. ALL THREE VICTIMS WERE COMPLETELY DRAINED OF THEIR BLOOD.
AROUND THE BODIES, WE FOUND KYAWL TRACKS.
IT'S STRANGE, BECAUSE KYAWLS FEED ON FRUIT NECTAR AND TREE SAP.
NOBODY IN MILAN HAS HEARD OF A KYAWL ATTACKING ANOTHER ANIMAL, LET ALONE A HUMAN.

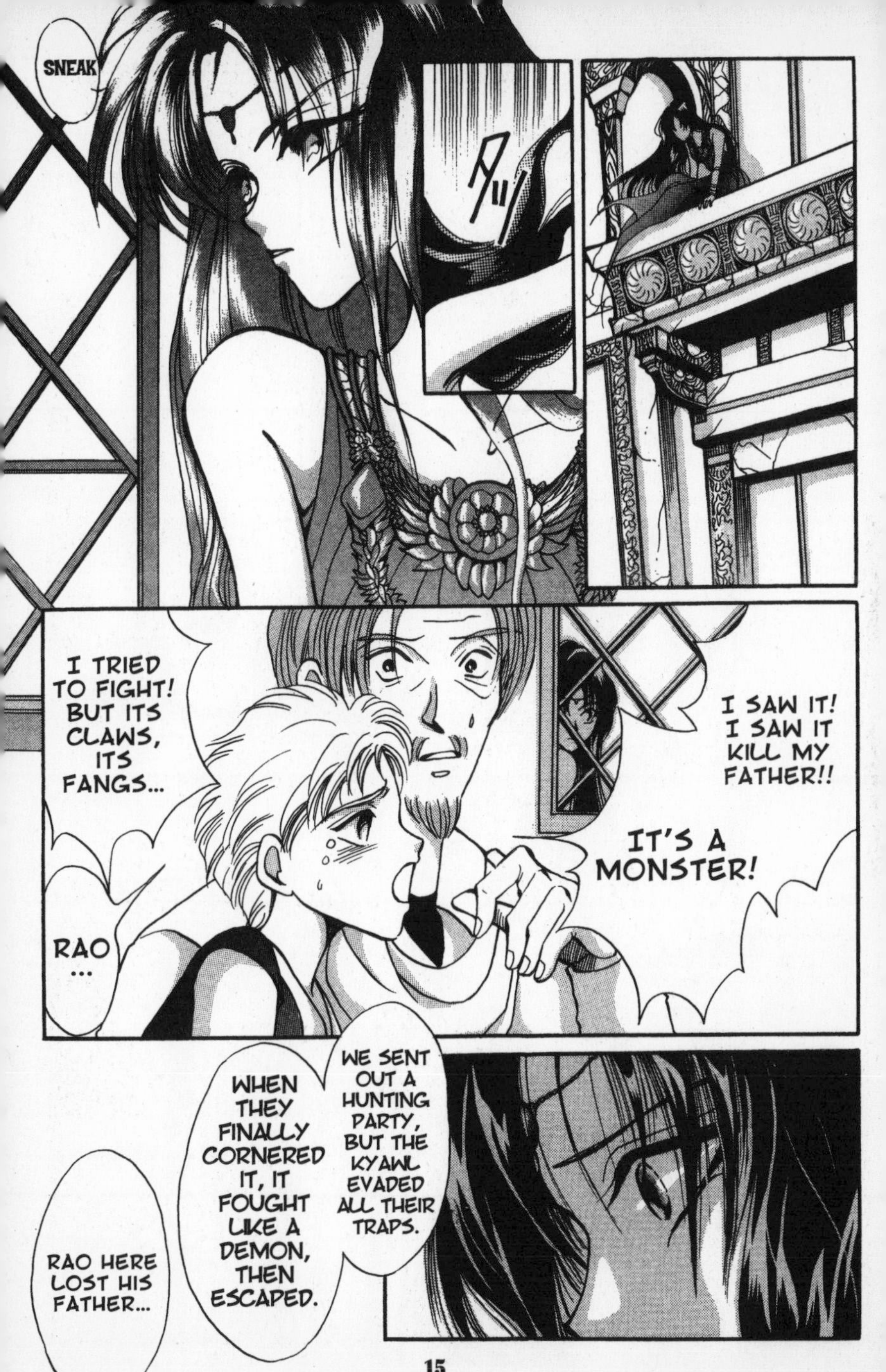
SNEAK
I SAW IT! I SAW IT KILL MY FATHER!!
IT'S A MONSTER!
I TRIED TO FIGHT! BUT ITS CLAWS, ITS FANGS...
RAO ...
WE SENT OUT A HUNTING PARTY, BUT THE KYAWL EVADED ALL THEIR TRAPS.
WHEN THEY FINALLY CORNERED IT, IT FOUGHT LIKE A DEMON, THEN ESCAPED.
RAO HERE LOST HIS FATHER...

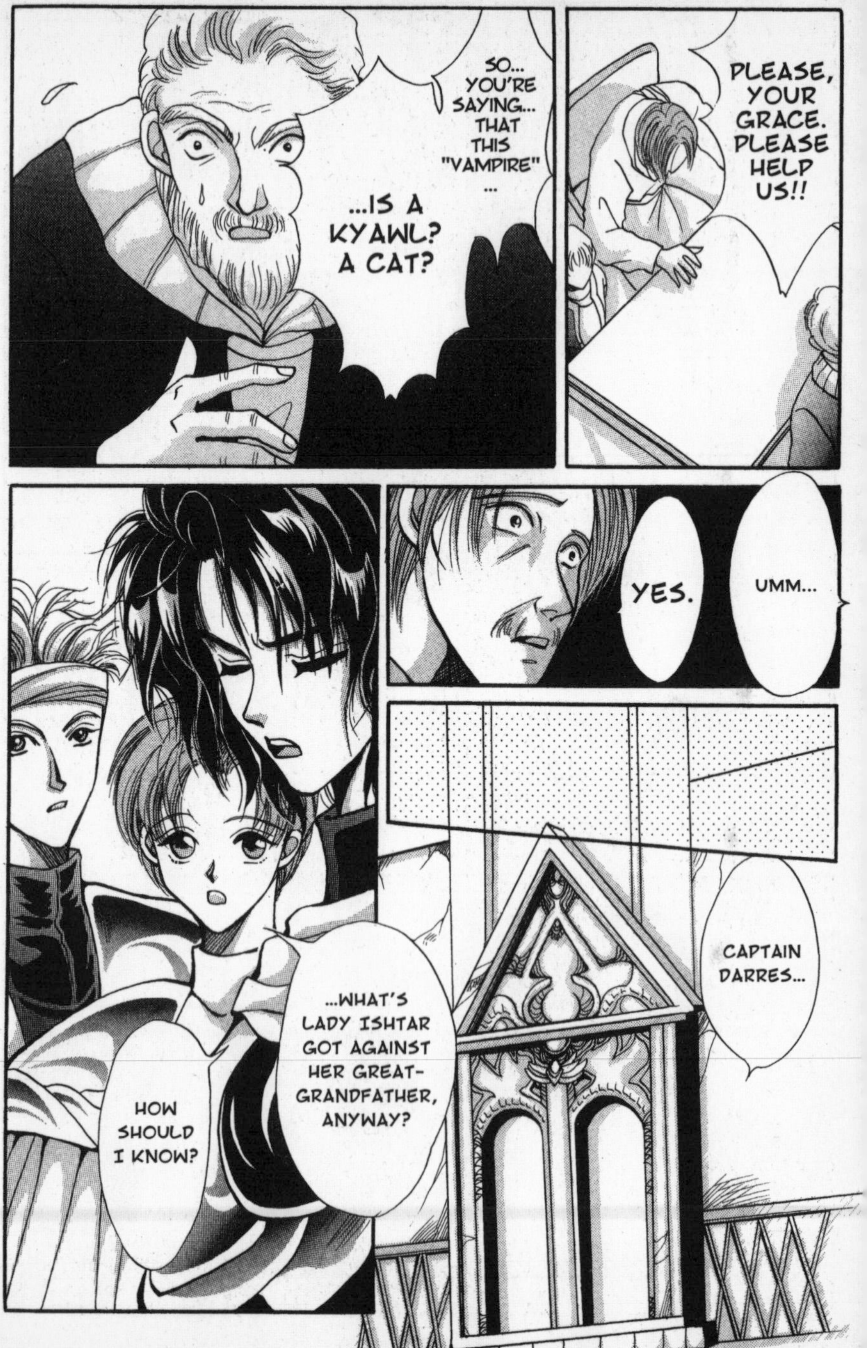
PLEASE, YOUR GRACE. PLEASE HELP US!!
SO... YOU'RE SAYING... THAT THIS "VAMPIRE" ...
...IS A KYAWL? A CAT?
UMM...
YES.
CAPTAIN DARRES...
...WHAT'S LADY ISHTAR GOT AGAINST HER GREAT-GRANDFATHER, ANYWAY?
HOW SHOULD I KNOW?

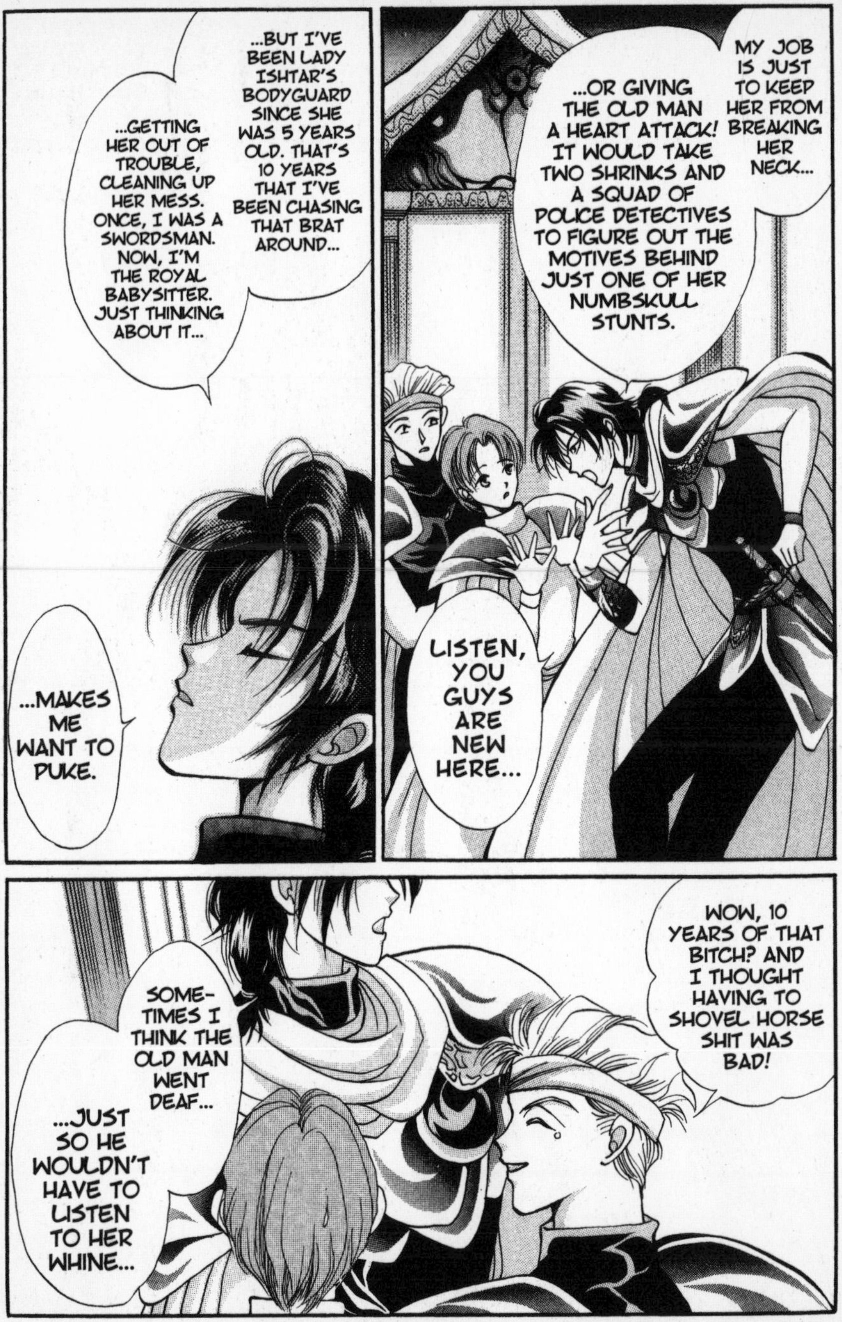
MY JOB IS JUST TO KEEP HER FROM BREAKING HER NECK...
...OR GIVING THE OLD MAN A HEART ATTACK! IT WOULD TAKE TWO SHRINKS AND A SQUAD OF POLICE DETECTIVES TO FIGURE OUT THE MOTIVES BEHIND JUST ONE OF HER NUMBSKULL STUNTS.
LISTEN, YOU GUYS ARE NEW HERE...
...BUT I'VE BEEN LADY ISHTAR'S BODYGUARD SINCE SHE WAS 5 YEARS OLD. THAT'S 10 YEARS THAT I'VE BEEN CHASING THAT BRAT AROUND...
...GETTING HER OUT OF TROUBLE, CLEANING UP HER MESS. ONCE, I WAS A SWORDSMAN. NOW, I'M THE ROYAL BABYSITTER. JUST THINKING ABOUT IT...
...MAKES ME WANT TO PUKE.
WOW, 10 YEARS OF THAT BITCH? AND I THOUGHT HAVING TO SHOVEL HORSE SHIT WAS BAD!
SOME-TIMES I THINK THE OLD MAN WENT DEAF...
...JUST SO HE WOULDN'T HAVE TO LISTEN TO HER WHINE...

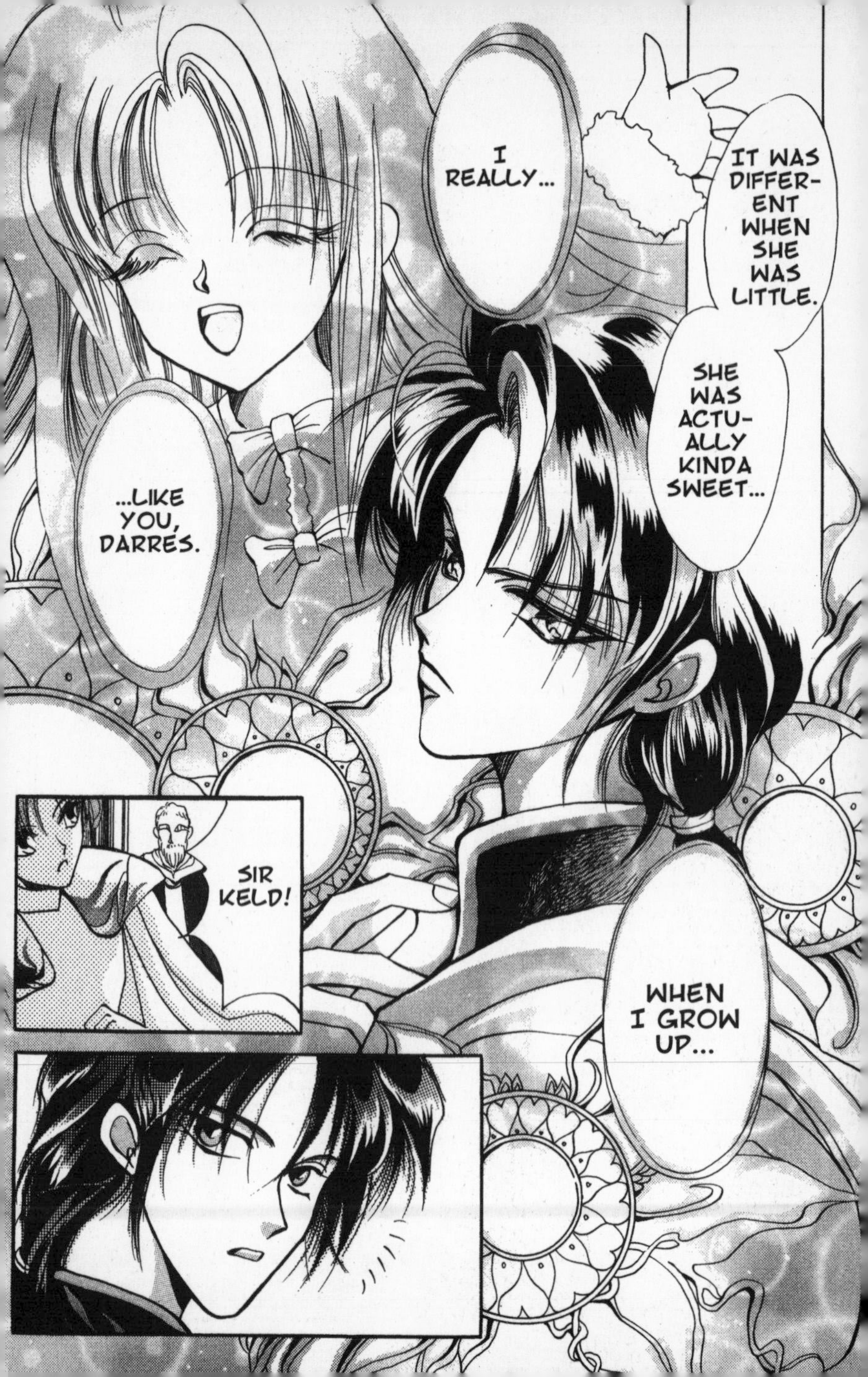
IT WAS DIFFERENT WHEN SHE WAS LITTLE.
SHE WAS ACTUALLY KINDA SWEET...
WHEN I GROW UP...
I REALLY...
...LIKE YOU, DARRES.
SIR KELD!

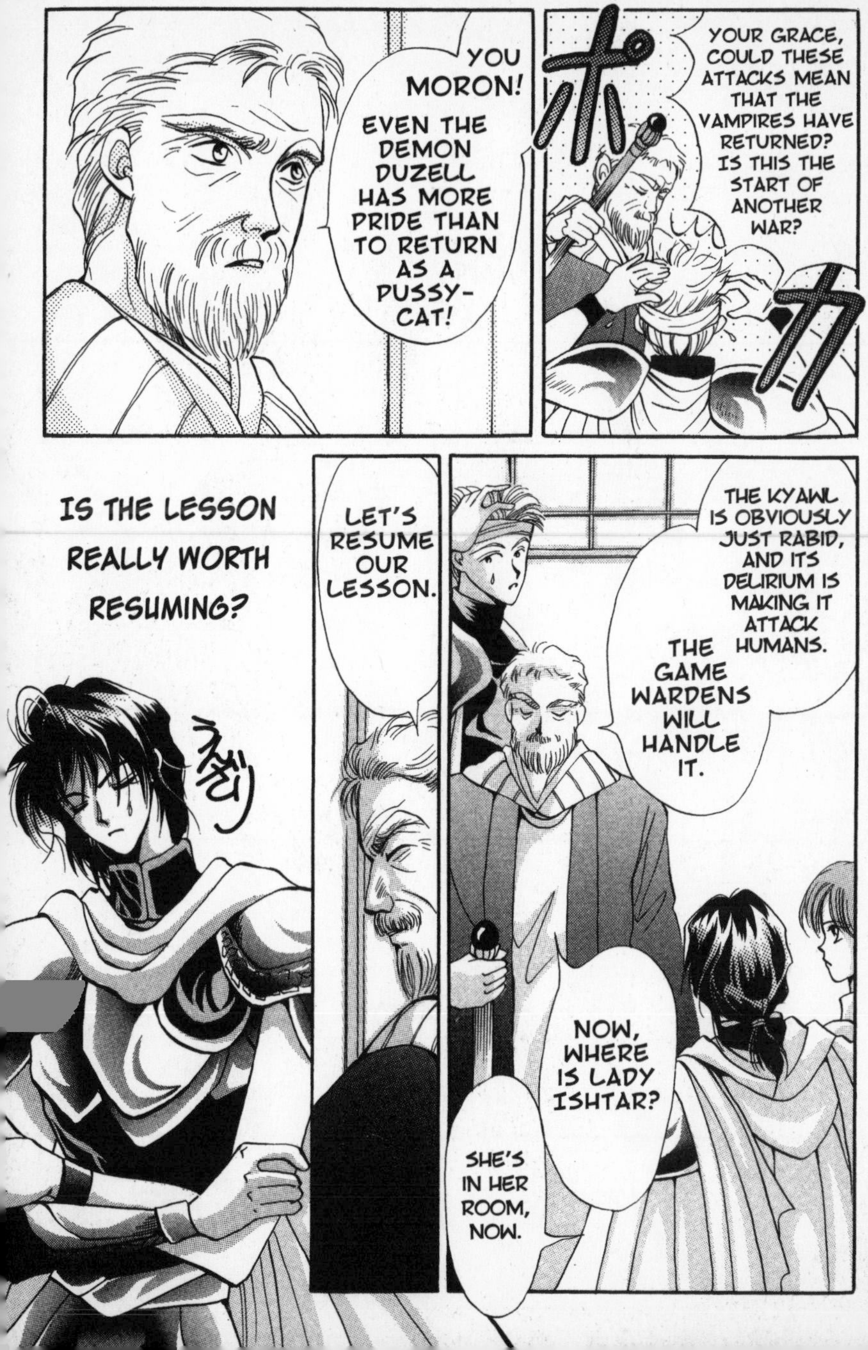
YOUR GRACE, COULD THESE ATTACKS MEAN THAT THE VAMPIRES HAVE RETURNED? IS THIS THE START OF ANOTHER WAR?
ポ
カ
YOU MORON!
EVEN THE DEMON DUZELL HAS MORE PRIDE THAN TO RETURN AS A PUSSY-CAT!
THE KYAWL IS OBVIOUSLY JUST RABID, AND ITS DELIRIUM IS MAKING IT ATTACK HUMANS.
THE GAME WARDENS WILL HANDLE IT.
NOW, WHERE IS LADY ISHTAR?
SHE'S IN HER ROOM, NOW.
LET'S RESUME OUR LESSON.
IS THE LESSON REALLY WORTH RESUMING?

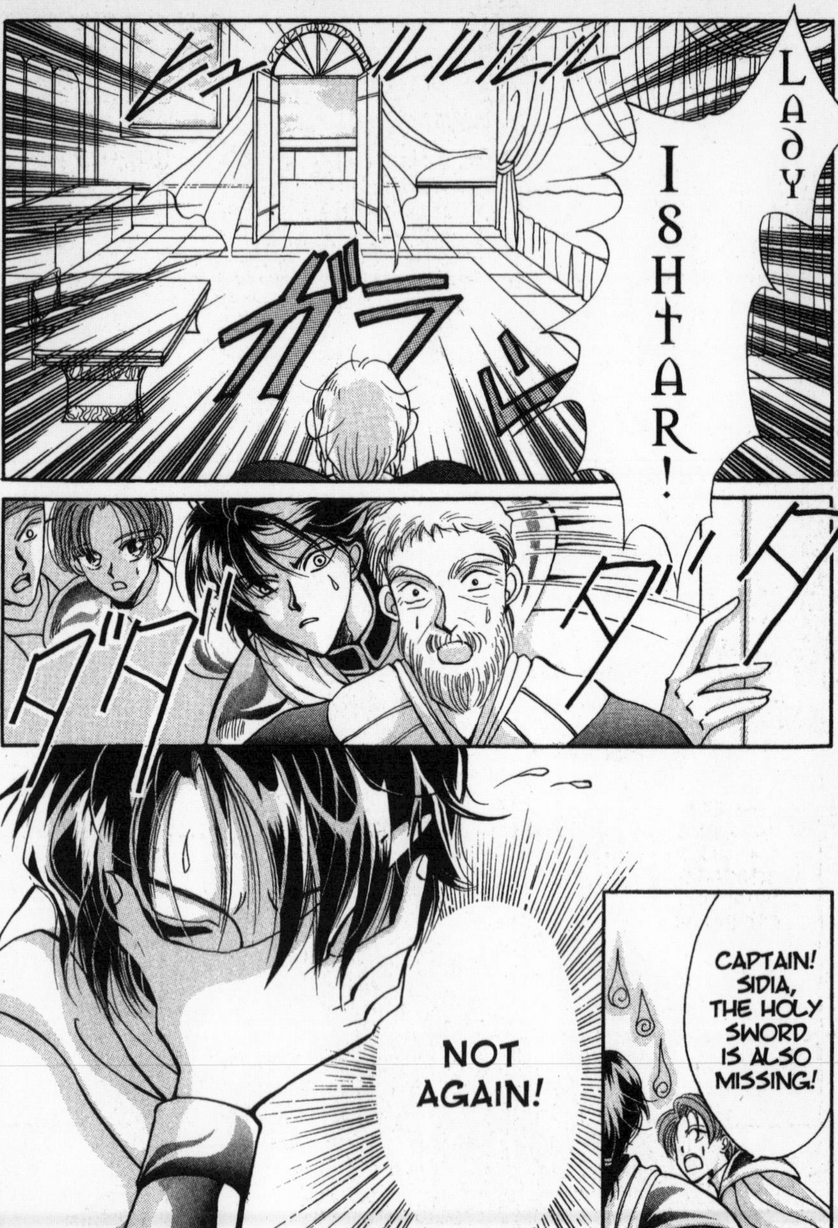
LADY ISHTAR!
CAPTAIN! SIDIA, THE HOLY SWORD IS ALSO MISSING!
NOT AGAIN!

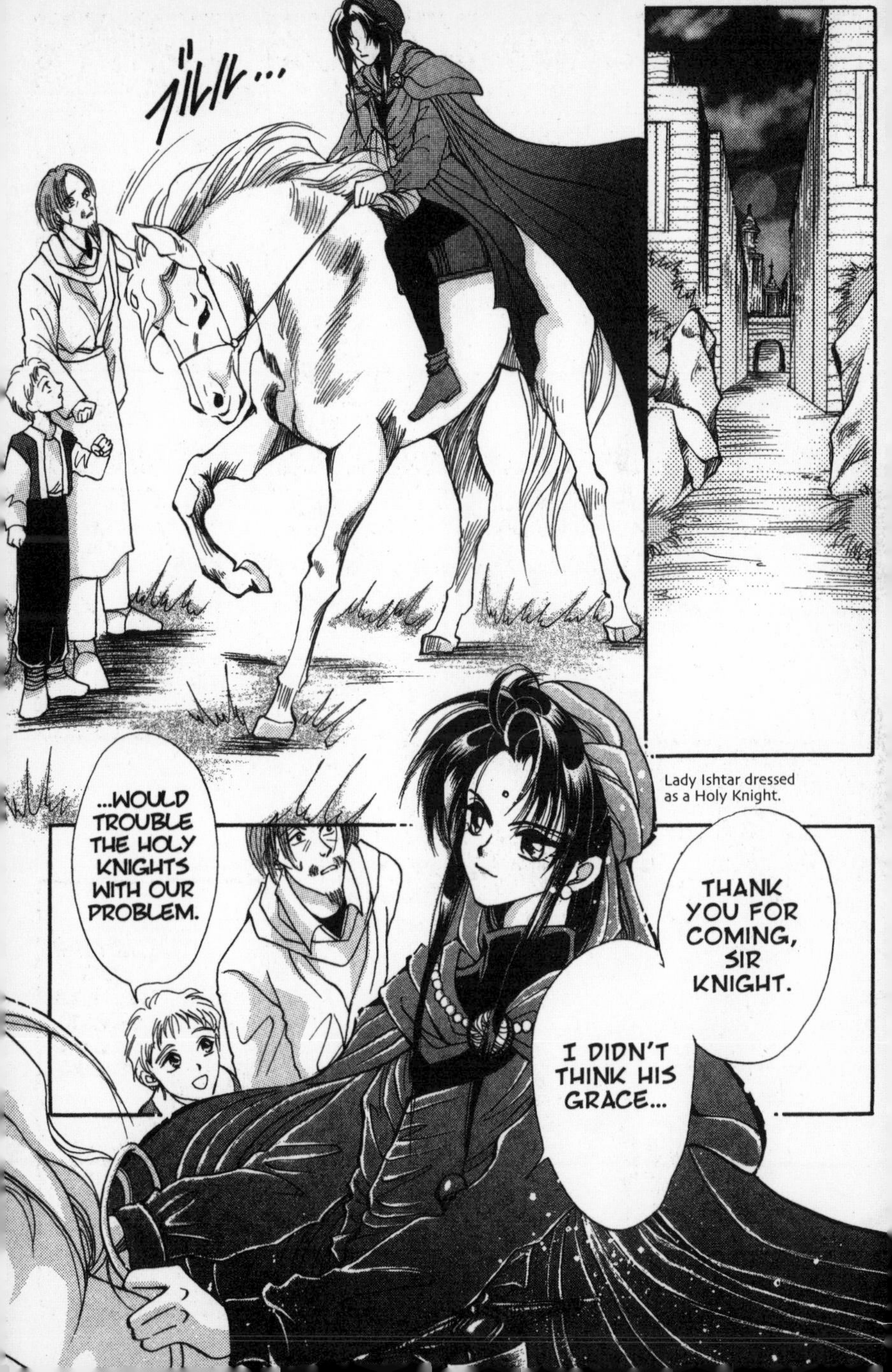
ブルル...
Lady Ishtar dressed as a Holy Knight.
THANK YOU FOR COMING, SIR KNIGHT.
I DIDN'T THINK HIS GRACE...
...WOULD TROUBLE THE HOLY KNIGHTS WITH OUR PROBLEM.

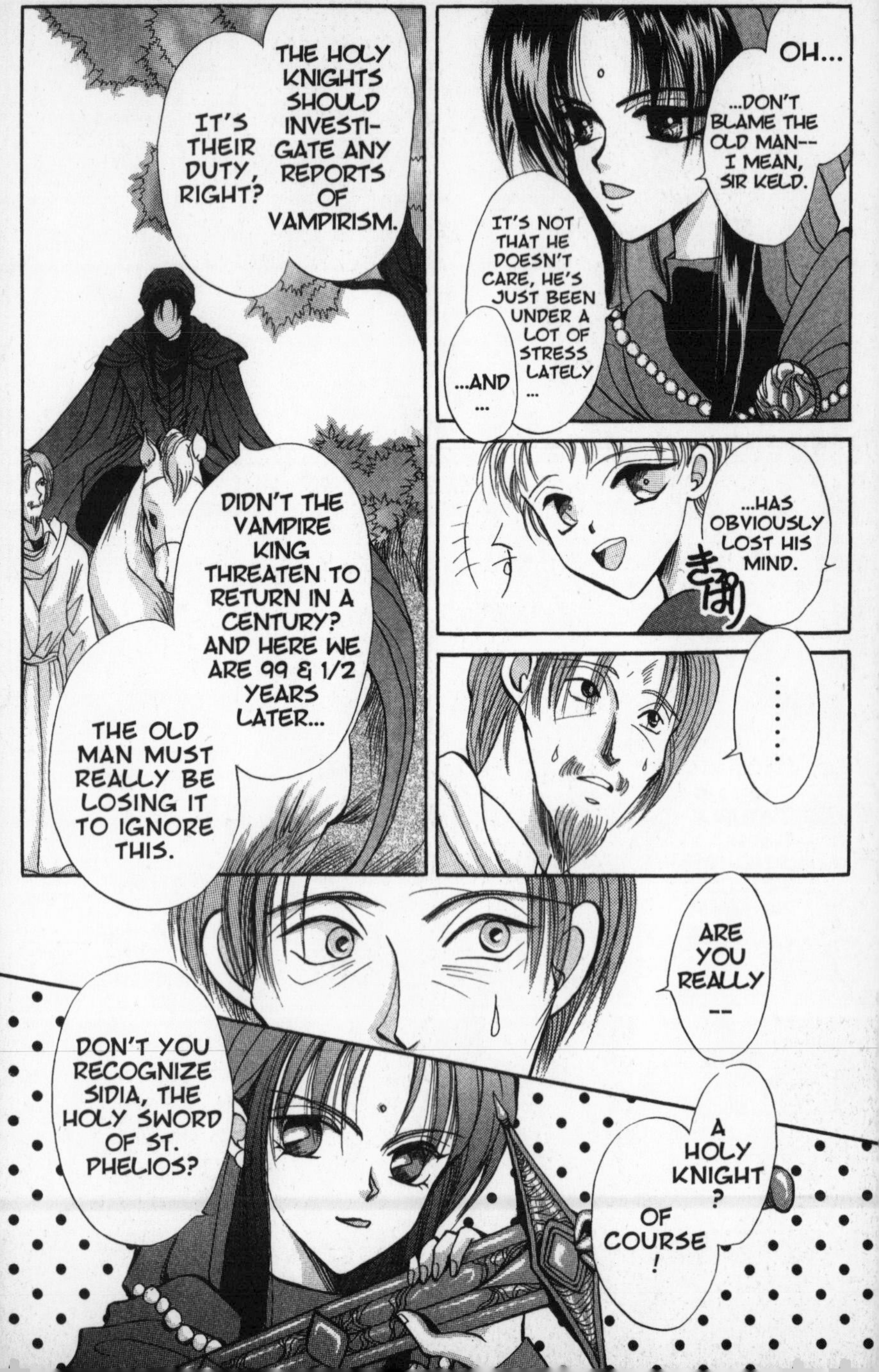
OH...
...DON'T BLAME THE OLD MAN-- I MEAN, SIR KELD.
IT'S NOT THAT HE DOESN'T CARE, HE'S JUST BEEN UNDER A LOT OF STRESS LATELY...
...AND...
...HAS OBVIOUSLY LOST HIS MIND.
きっぱり
......
THE HOLY KNIGHTS SHOULD INVESTIGATE ANY REPORTS OF VAMPIRISM.
IT'S THEIR DUTY, RIGHT?
DIDN'T THE VAMPIRE KING THREATEN TO RETURN IN A CENTURY? AND HERE WE ARE 99 & 1/2 YEARS LATER...
THE OLD MAN MUST REALLY BE LOSING IT TO IGNORE THIS.
ARE YOU REALLY--
A HOLY KNIGHT?
OF COURSE!
DON'T YOU RECOGNIZE SIDIA, THE HOLY SWORD OF ST. PHELIOS?

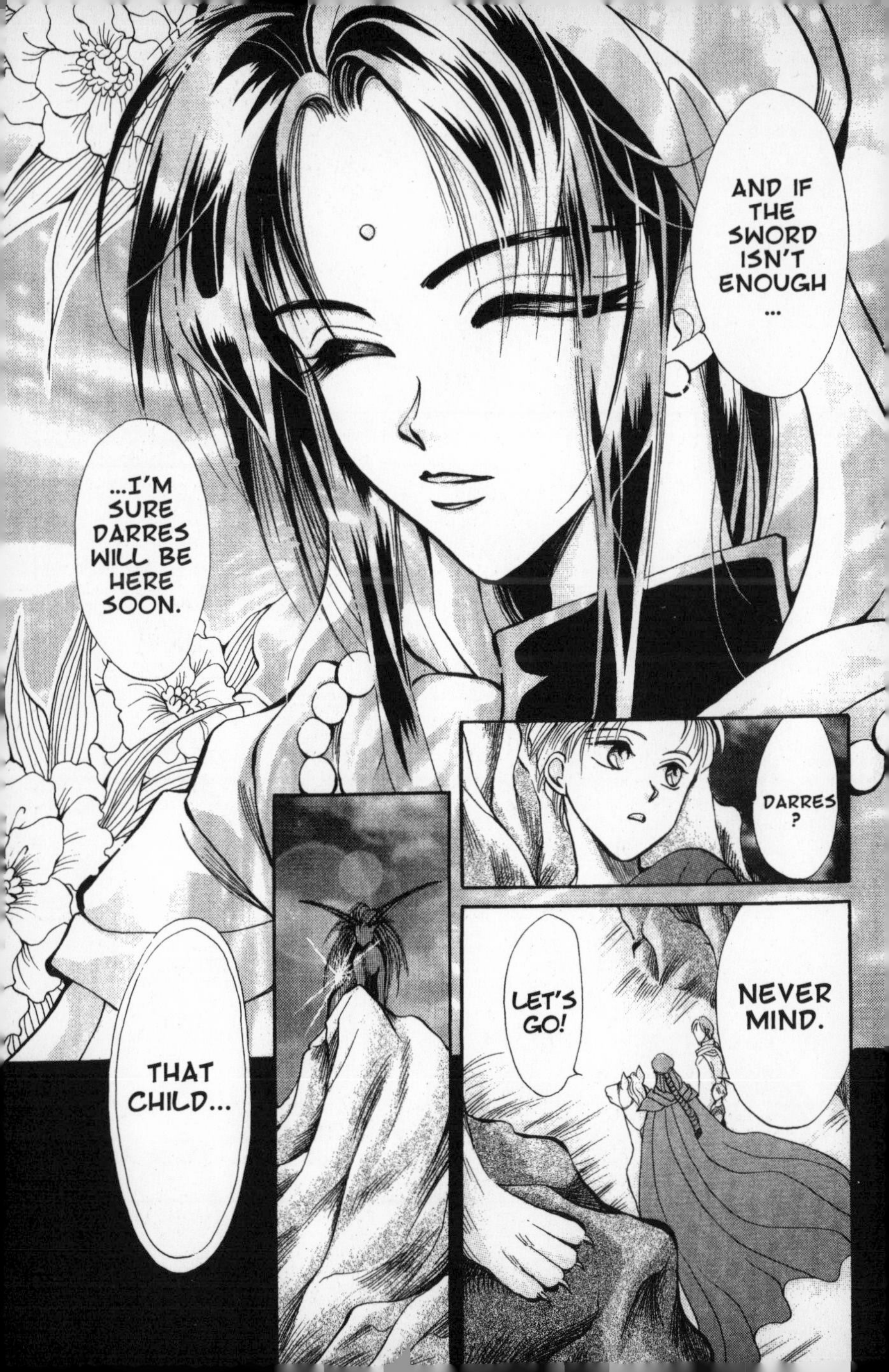
AND IF THE SWORD ISN'T ENOUGH...
...I'M SURE DARRES WILL BE HERE SOON.
DARRES?
NEVER MIND.
LET'S GO!
THAT CHILD...

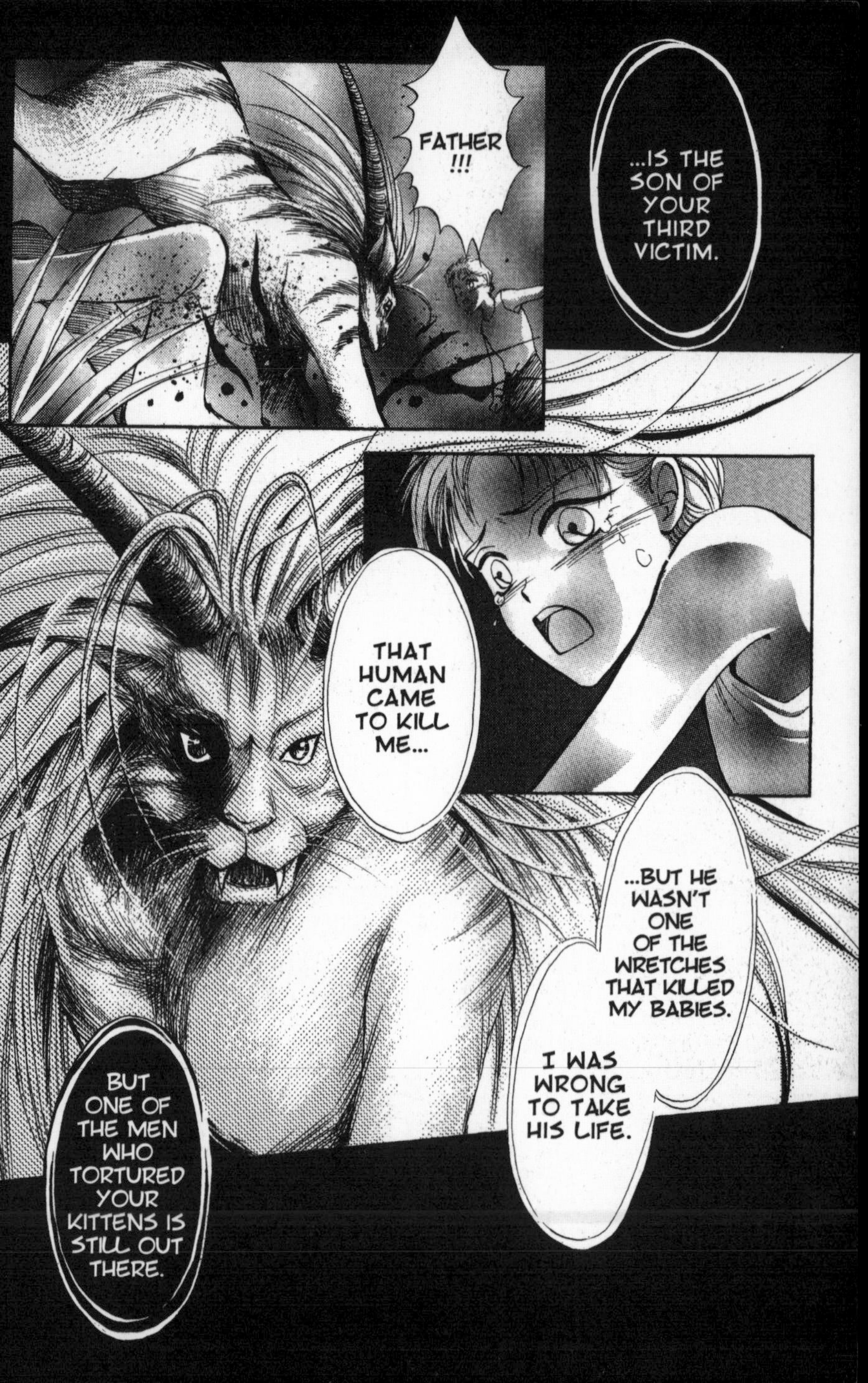
...IS THE SON OF YOUR THIRD VICTIM.
FATHER !!!
THAT HUMAN CAME TO KILL ME...
...BUT HE WASN'T ONE OF THE WRETCHES THAT KILLED MY BABIES.
I WAS WRONG TO TAKE HIS LIFE.
BUT ONE OF THE MEN WHO TORTURED YOUR KITTENS IS STILL OUT THERE.

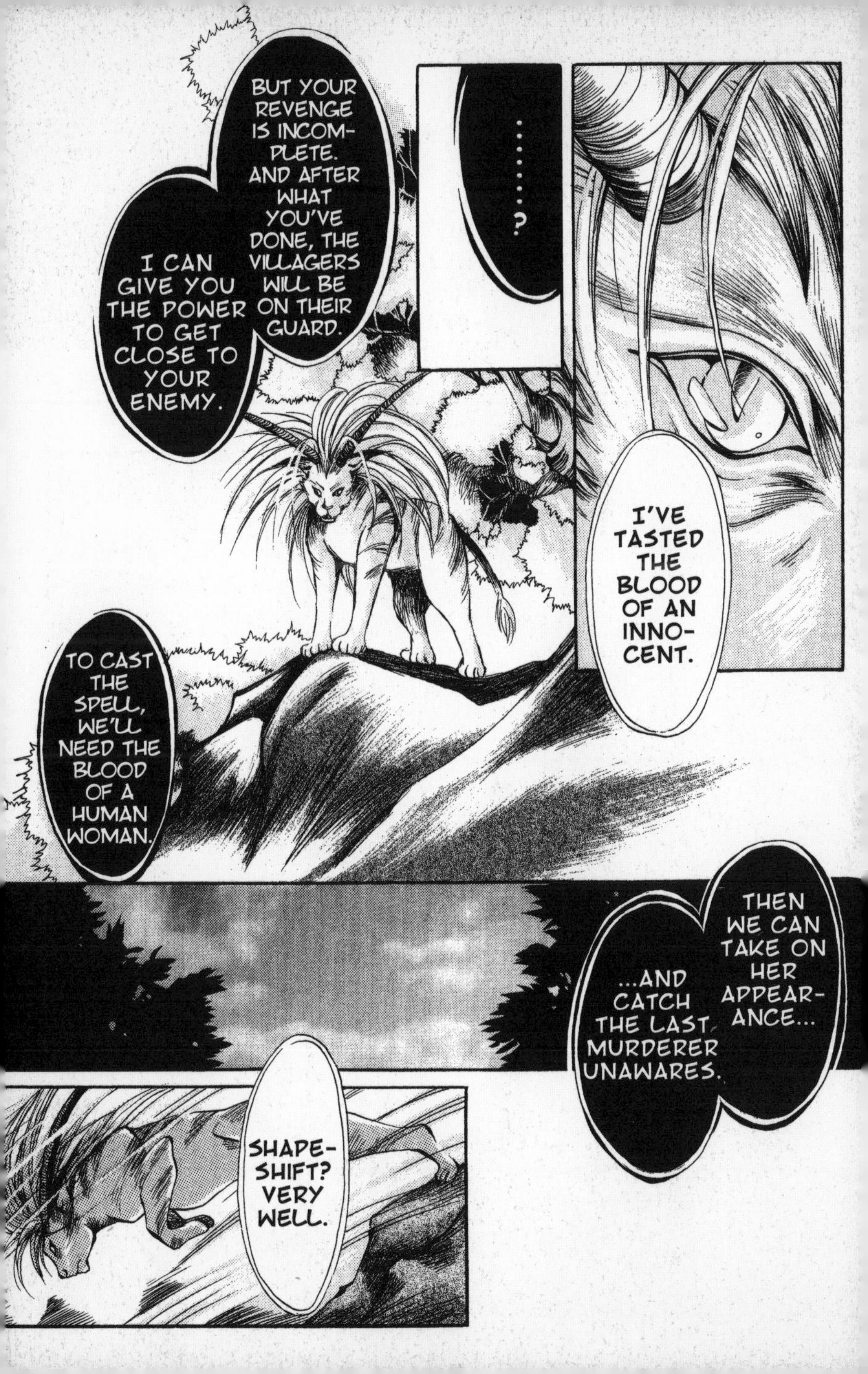
BUT YOUR REVENGE IS INCOMPLETE. AND AFTER WHAT YOU'VE DONE, THE VILLAGERS WILL BE ON THEIR GUARD.
I CAN GIVE YOU THE POWER TO GET CLOSE TO YOUR ENEMY.
......?
TO CAST THE SPELL, WE'LL NEED THE BLOOD OF A HUMAN WOMAN.
I'VE TASTED THE BLOOD OF AN INNOCENT.
THEN WE CAN TAKE ON HER APPEARANCE...
...AND CATCH THE LAST MURDERER UNAWARES.
SHAPE-SHIFT? VERY WELL.

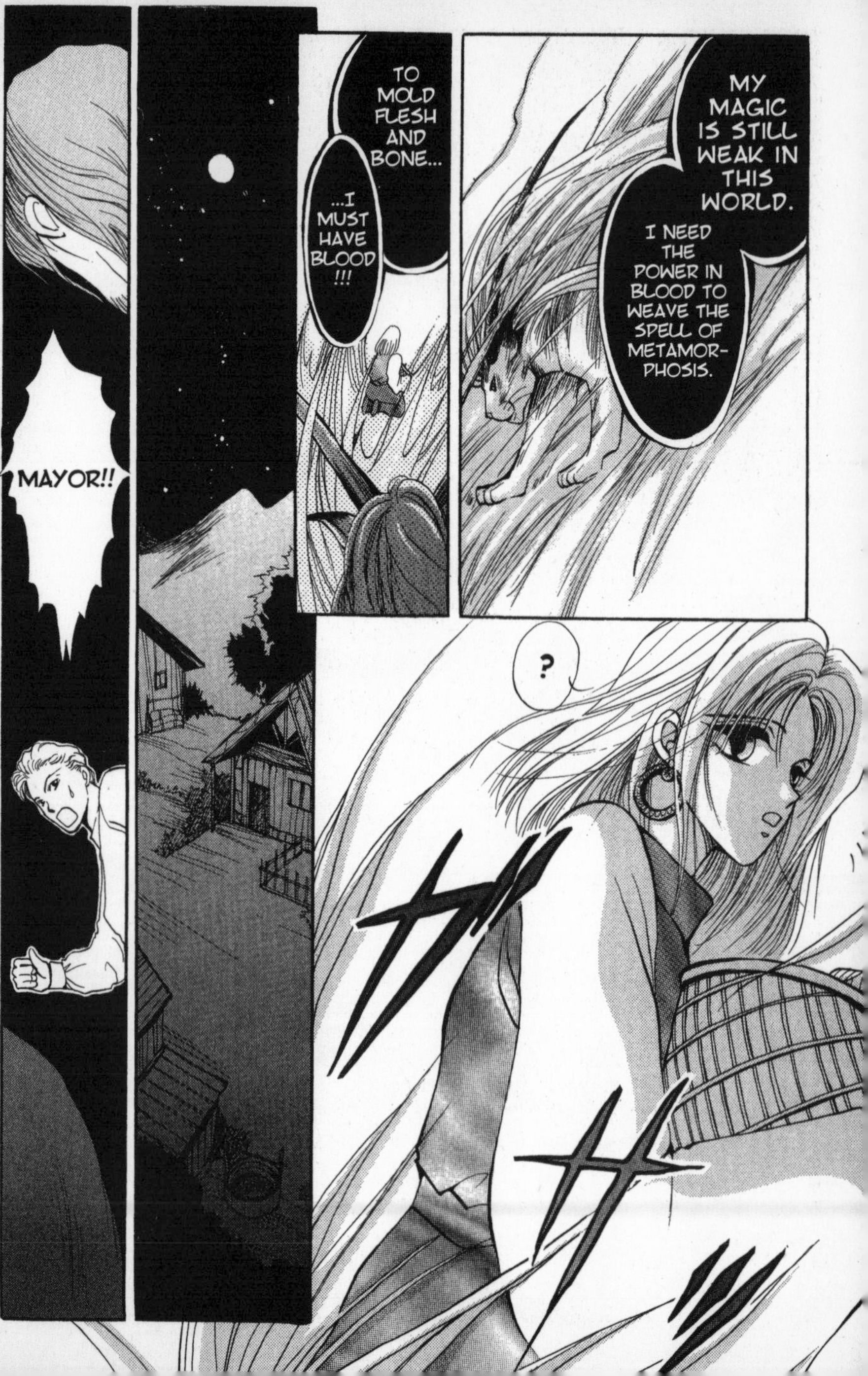
MY MAGIC IS STILL WEAK IN THIS WORLD.
I NEED THE POWER IN BLOOD TO WEAVE THE SPELL OF METAMORPHOSIS.
TO MOLD FLESH AND BONE...
...I MUST HAVE BLOOD!!!
?
MAYOR!!

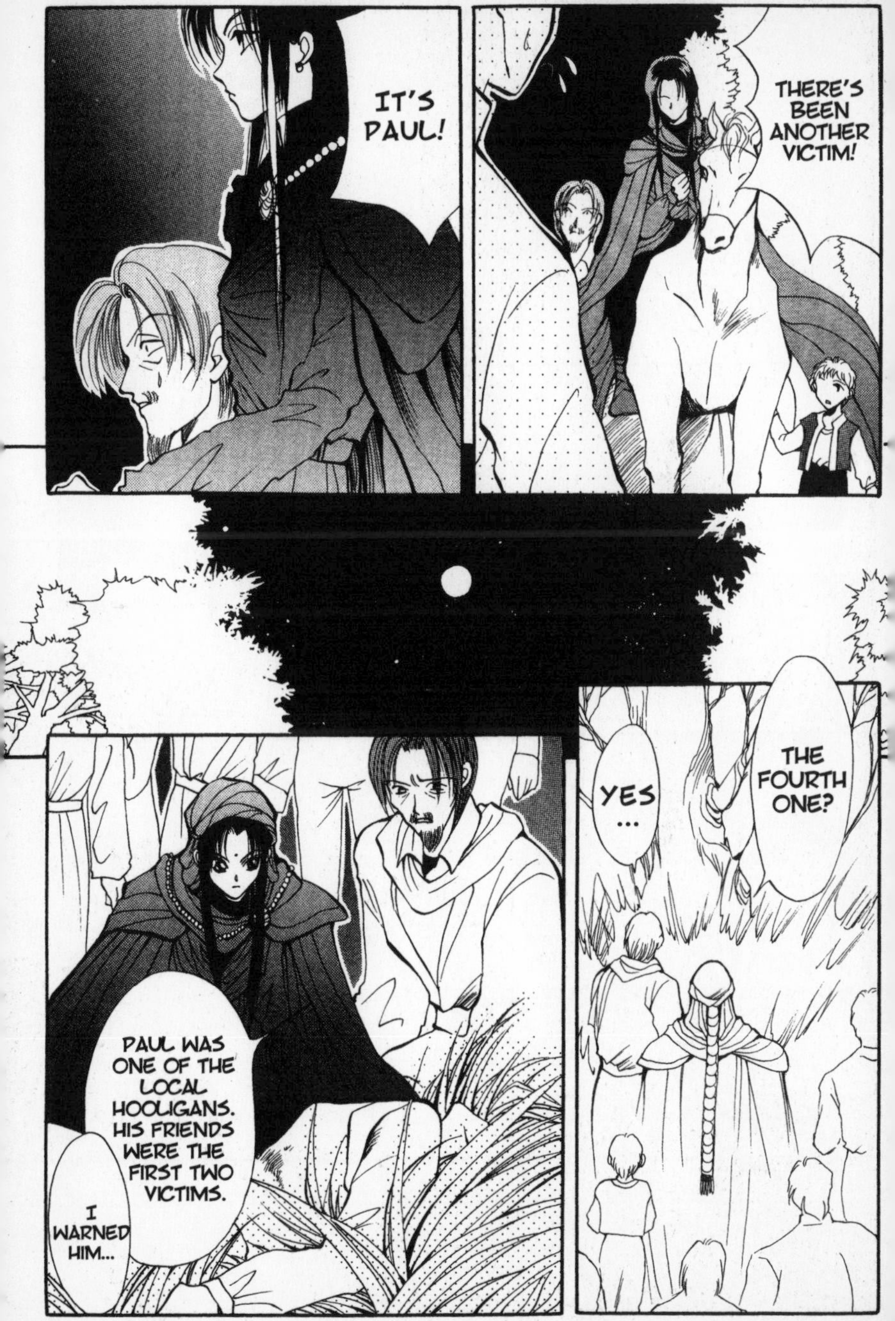
THERE'S BEEN ANOTHER VICTIM!
IT'S PAUL!
THE FOURTH ONE?
YES ...
PAUL WAS ONE OF THE LOCAL HOOLIGANS. HIS FRIENDS WERE THE FIRST TWO VICTIMS.
I WARNED HIM...

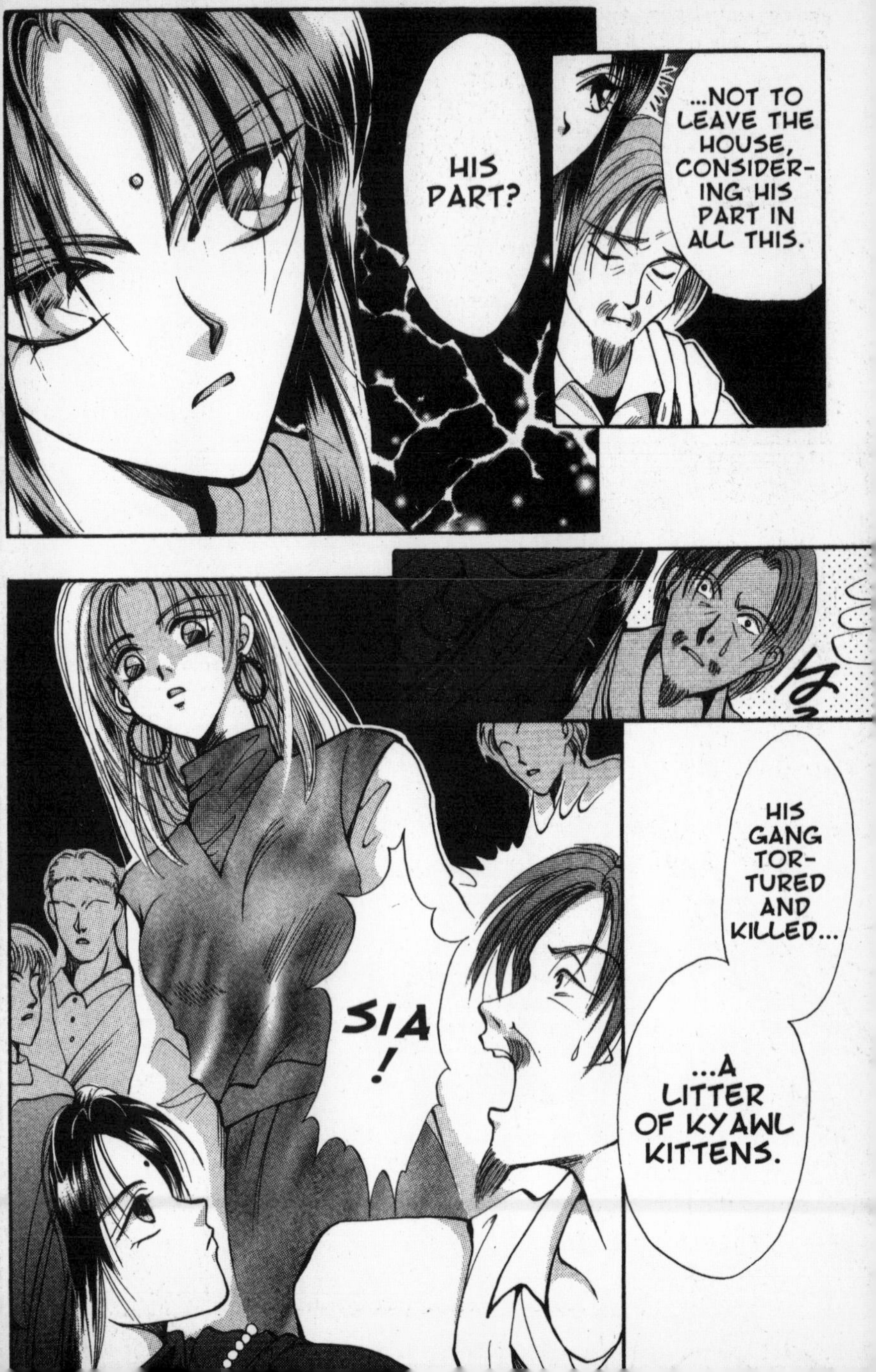
...NOT TO LEAVE THE HOUSE, CONSIDERING HIS PART IN ALL THIS.
HIS PART?
HIS GANG TORTURED AND KILLED...
...A LITTER OF KYAWL KITTENS.
SIA!

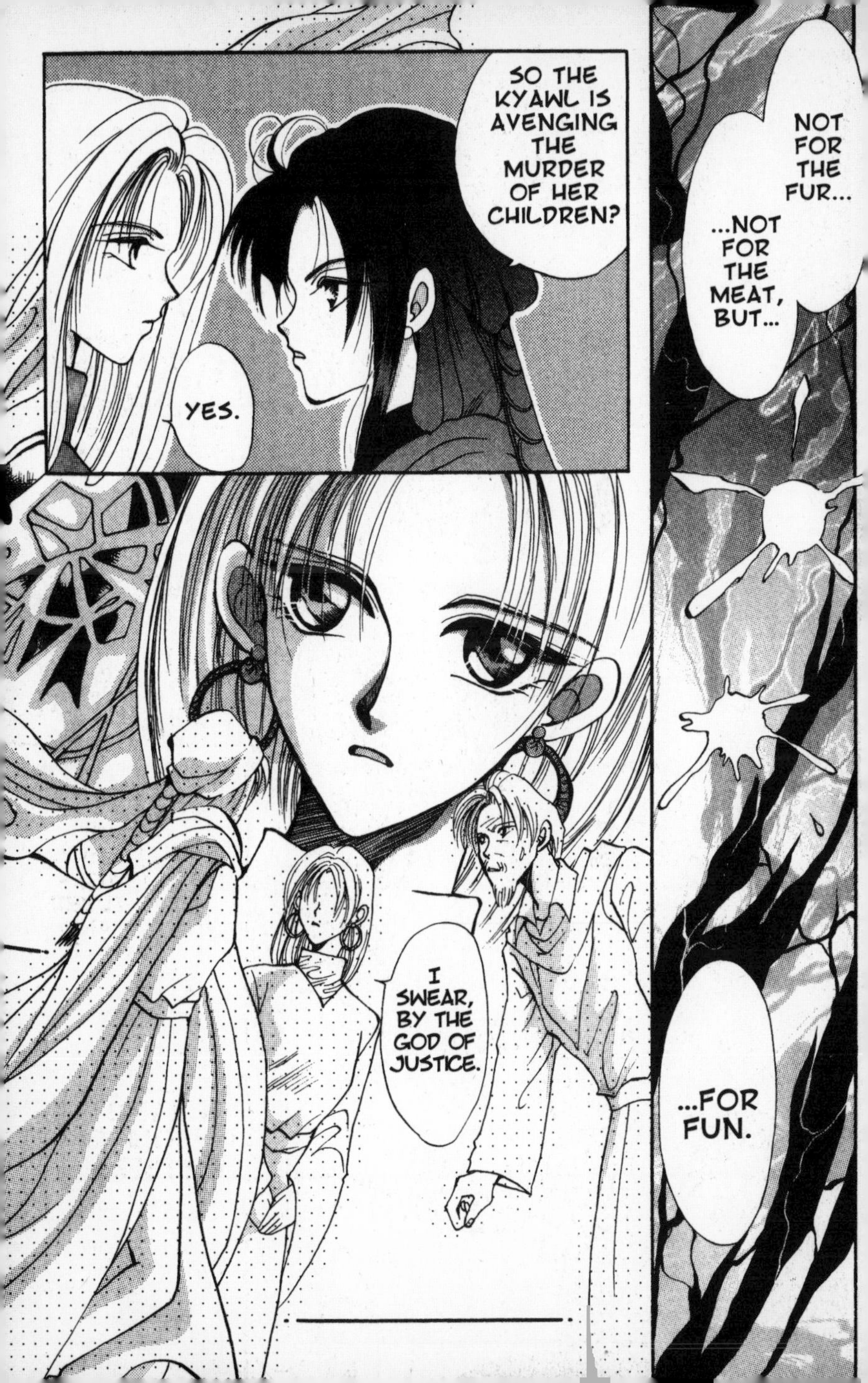
NOT FOR THE FUR...
...NOT FOR THE MEAT, BUT...
...FOR FUN.
SO THE KYAWL IS AVENGING THE MURDER OF HER CHILDREN?
YES.
I SWEAR, BY THE GOD OF JUSTICE.

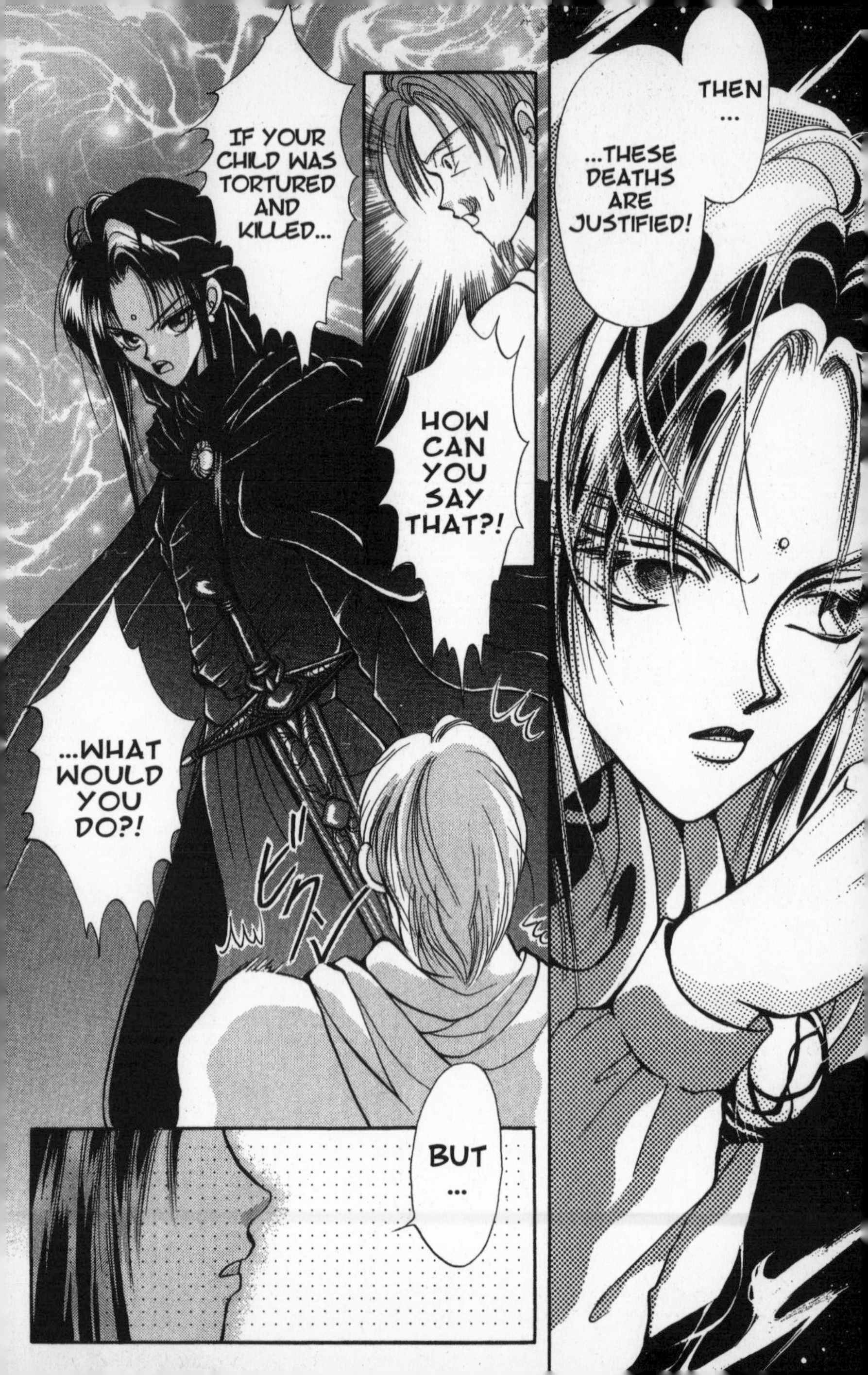
THEN ...
...THESE DEATHS ARE JUSTIFIED!
IF YOUR CHILD WAS TORTURED AND KILLED...
HOW CAN YOU SAY THAT?!
...WHAT WOULD YOU DO?!
BUT ...

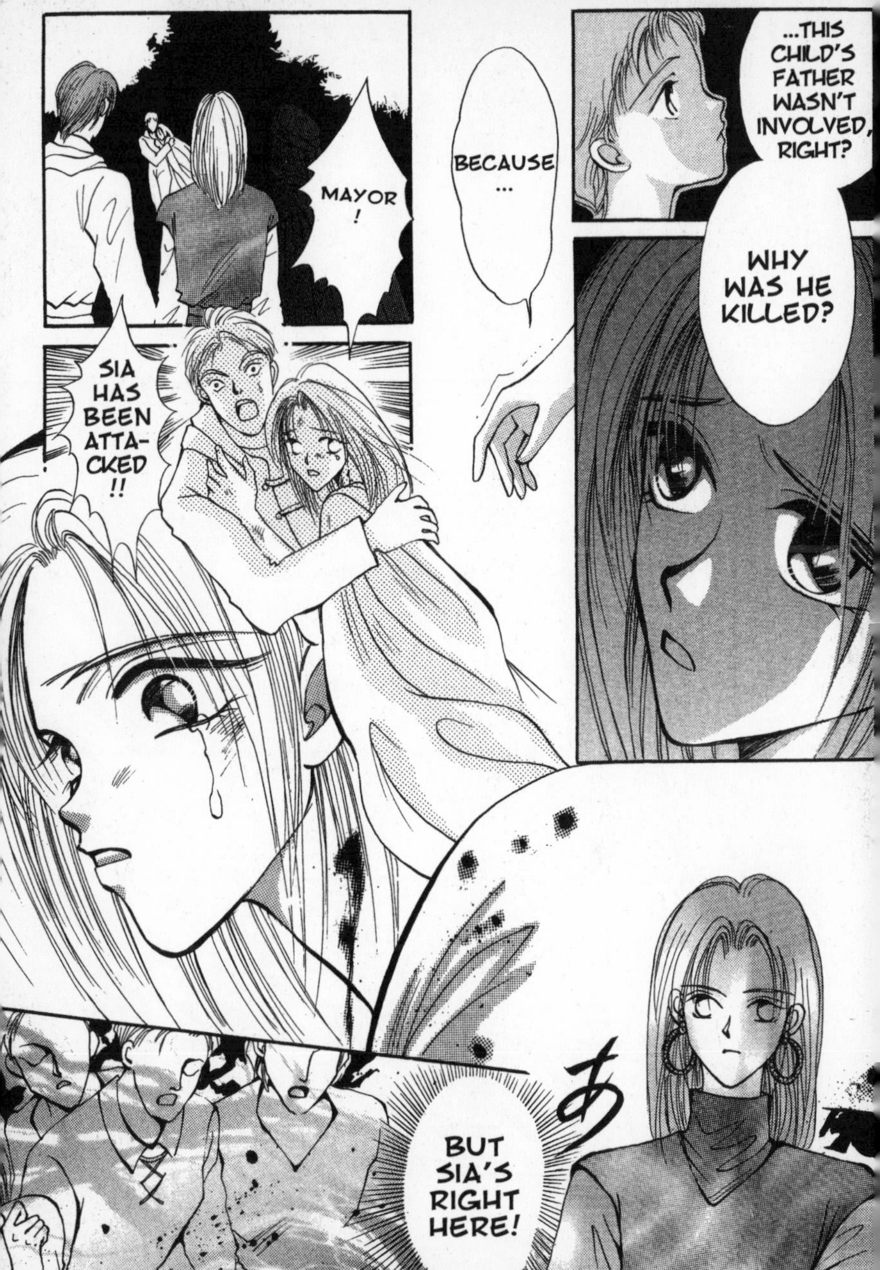
...THIS CHILD'S FATHER WASN'T INVOLVED, RIGHT?
WHY WAS HE KILLED?
BECAUSE ...
MAYOR!
SIA HAS BEEN ATTA-CKED!!
あ
BUT SIA'S RIGHT HERE!

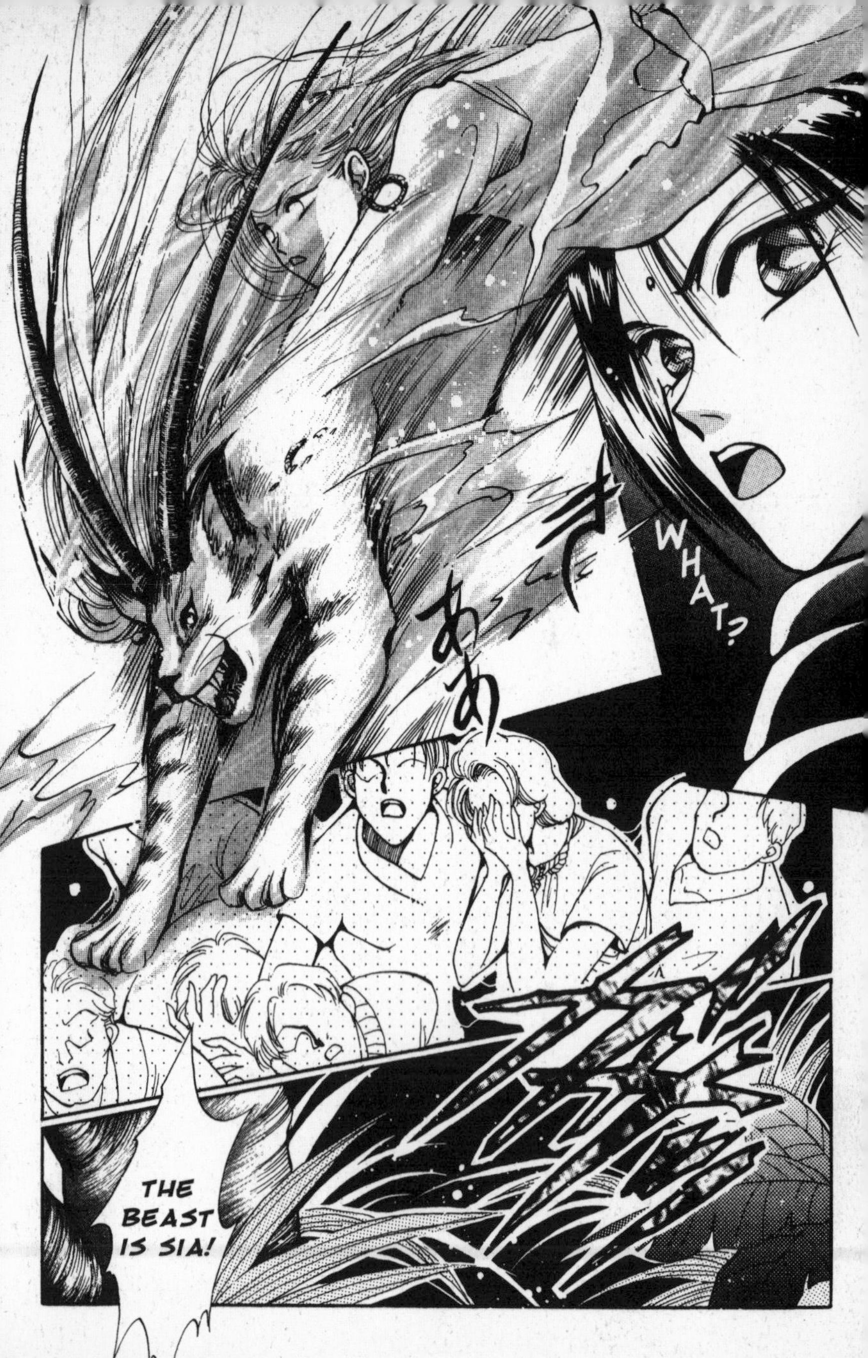
WHAT?
THE BEAST IS SIA!

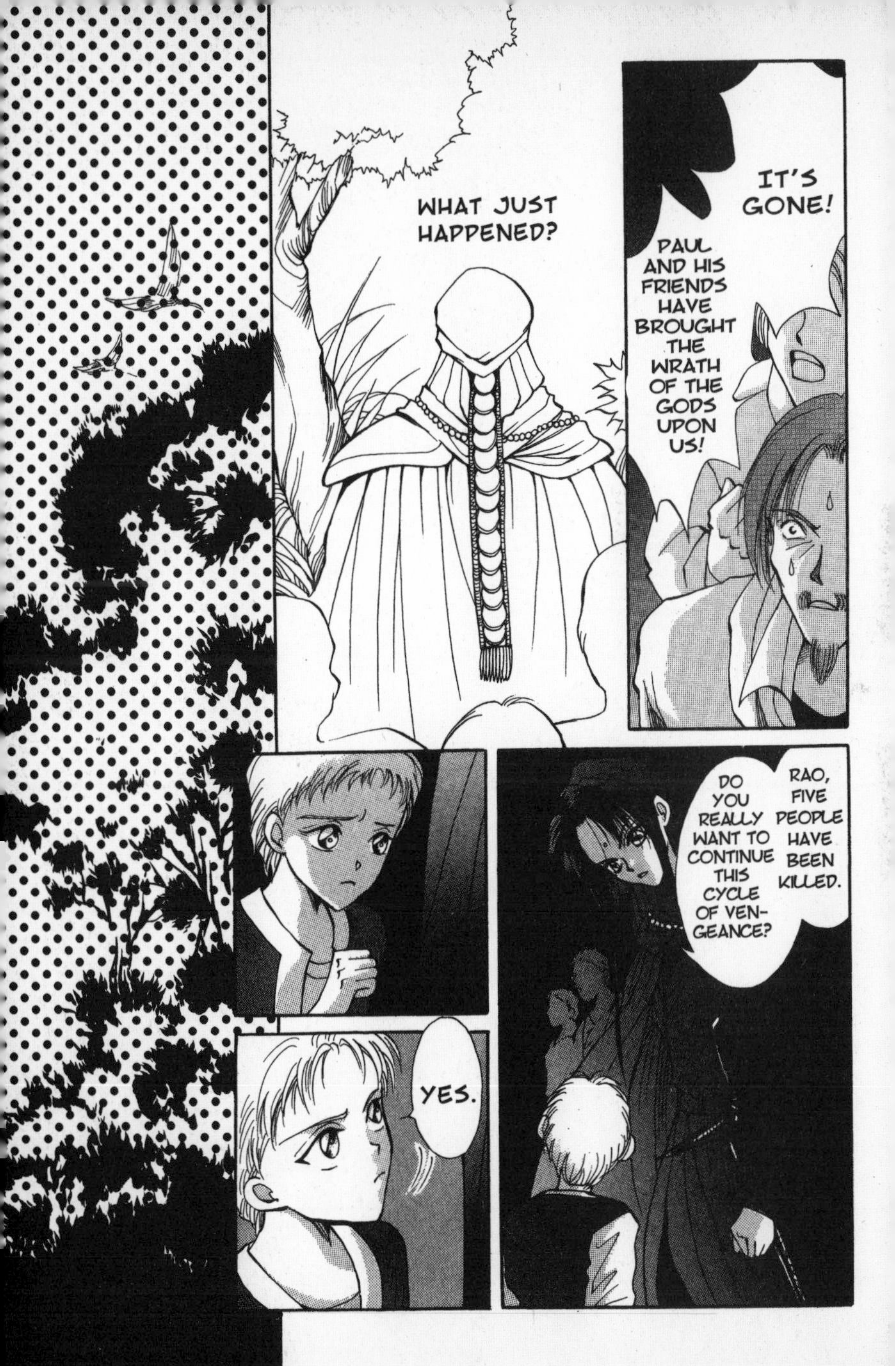
IT'S GONE!
PAUL AND HIS FRIENDS HAVE BROUGHT THE WRATH OF THE GODS UPON US!
WHAT JUST HAPPENED?
RAO, FIVE PEOPLE HAVE BEEN KILLED.
DO YOU REALLY WANT TO CONTINUE THIS CYCLE OF VEN-GEANCE?
...
YES.

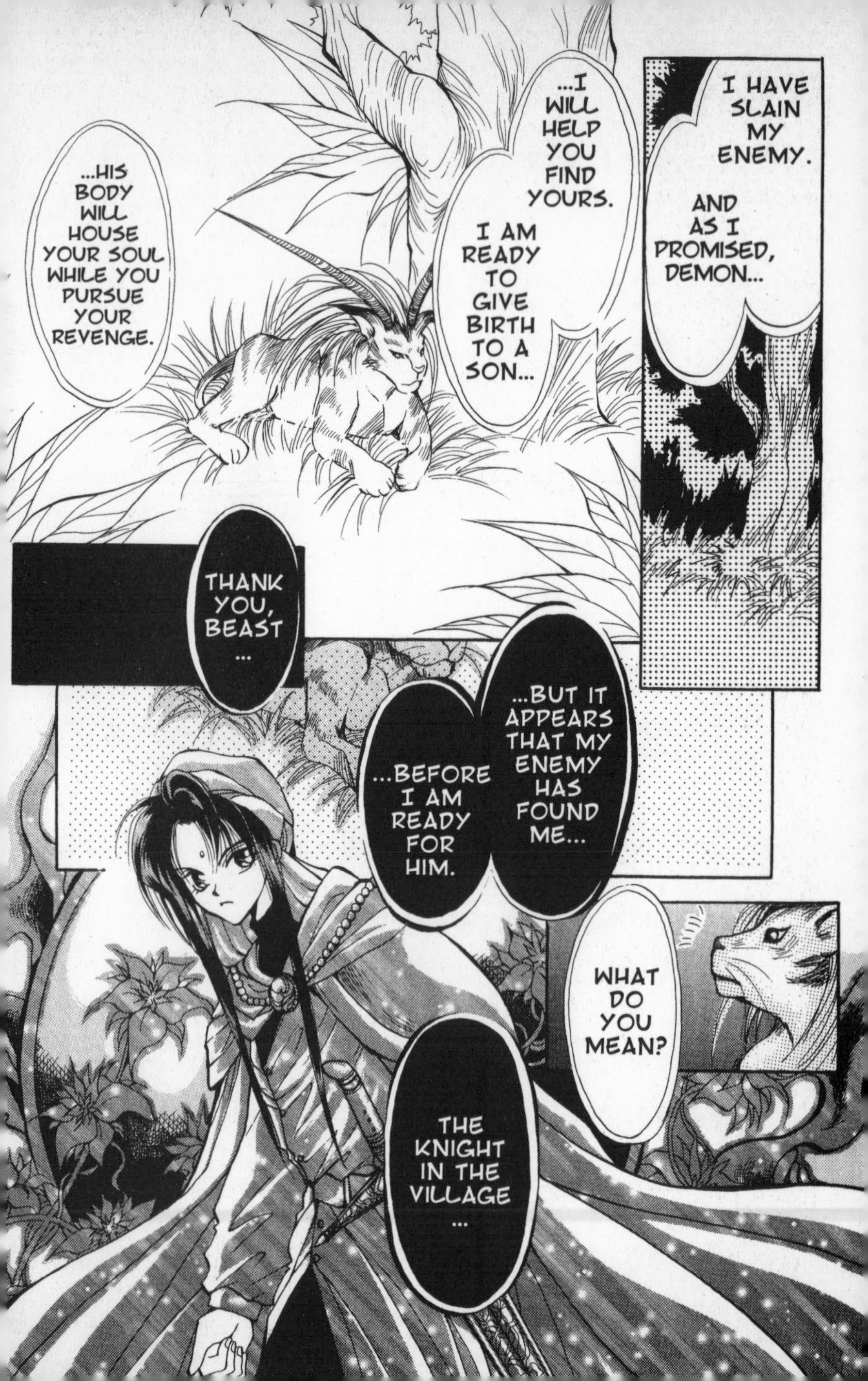
I HAVE SLAIN MY ENEMY.
AND AS I PROMISED, DEMON...
...I WILL HELP YOU FIND YOURS.
I AM READY TO GIVE BIRTH TO A SON...
...HIS BODY WILL HOUSE YOUR SOUL WHILE YOU PURSUE YOUR REVENGE.
THANK YOU, BEAST ...
...BUT IT APPEARS THAT MY ENEMY HAS FOUND ME...
...BEFORE I AM READY FOR HIM.
WHAT DO YOU MEAN?
THE KNIGHT IN THE VILLAGE ...

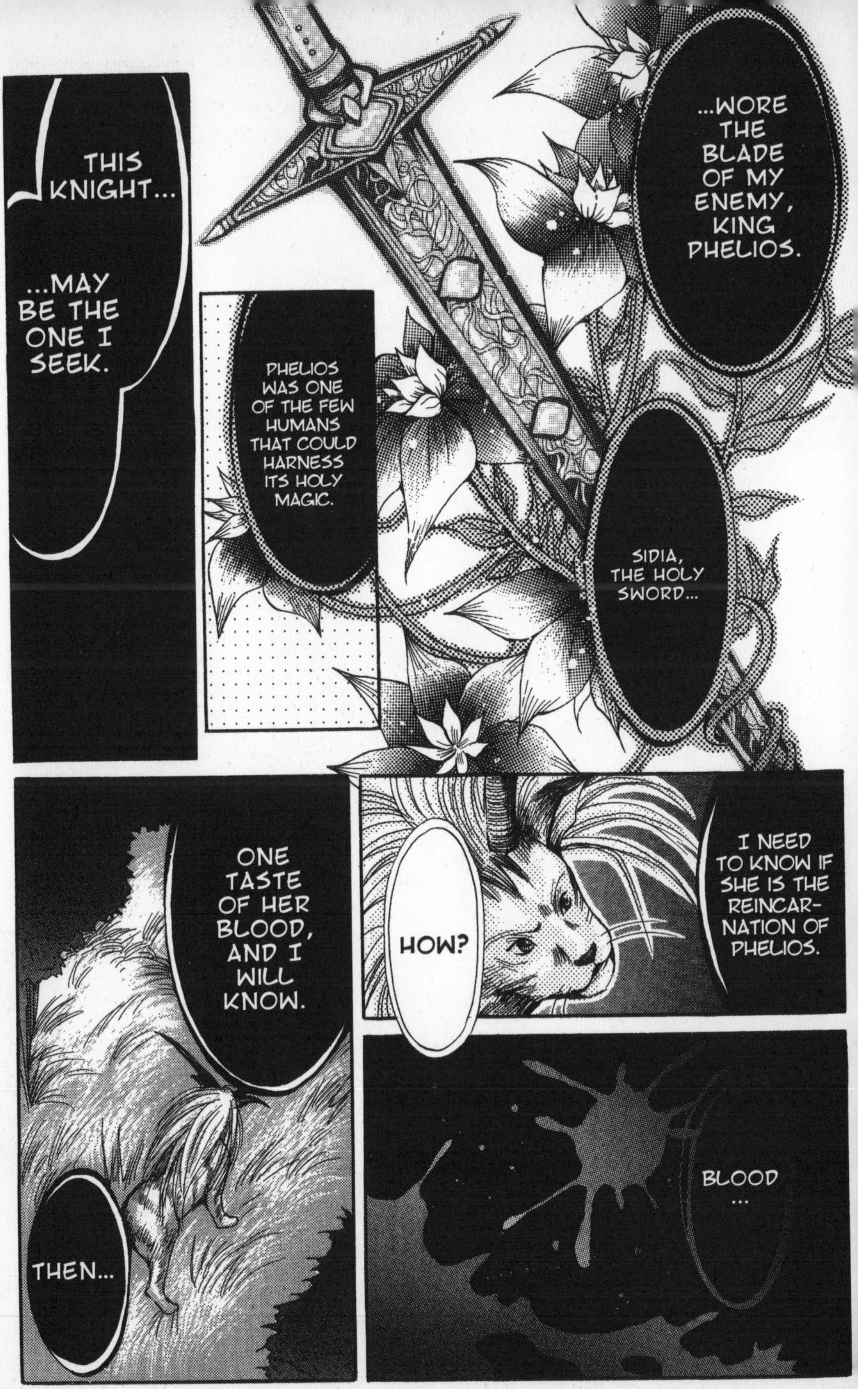
...WORE THE BLADE OF MY ENEMY, KING PHELIOS.
SIDIA, THE HOLY SWORD...
PHELIOS WAS ONE OF THE FEW HUMANS THAT COULD HARNESS ITS HOLY MAGIC.
THIS KNIGHT...
...MAY BE THE ONE I SEEK.
I NEED TO KNOW IF SHE IS THE REINCAR-NATION OF PHELIOS.
HOW?
BLOOD ...
ONE TASTE OF HER BLOOD, AND I WILL KNOW.
THEN...

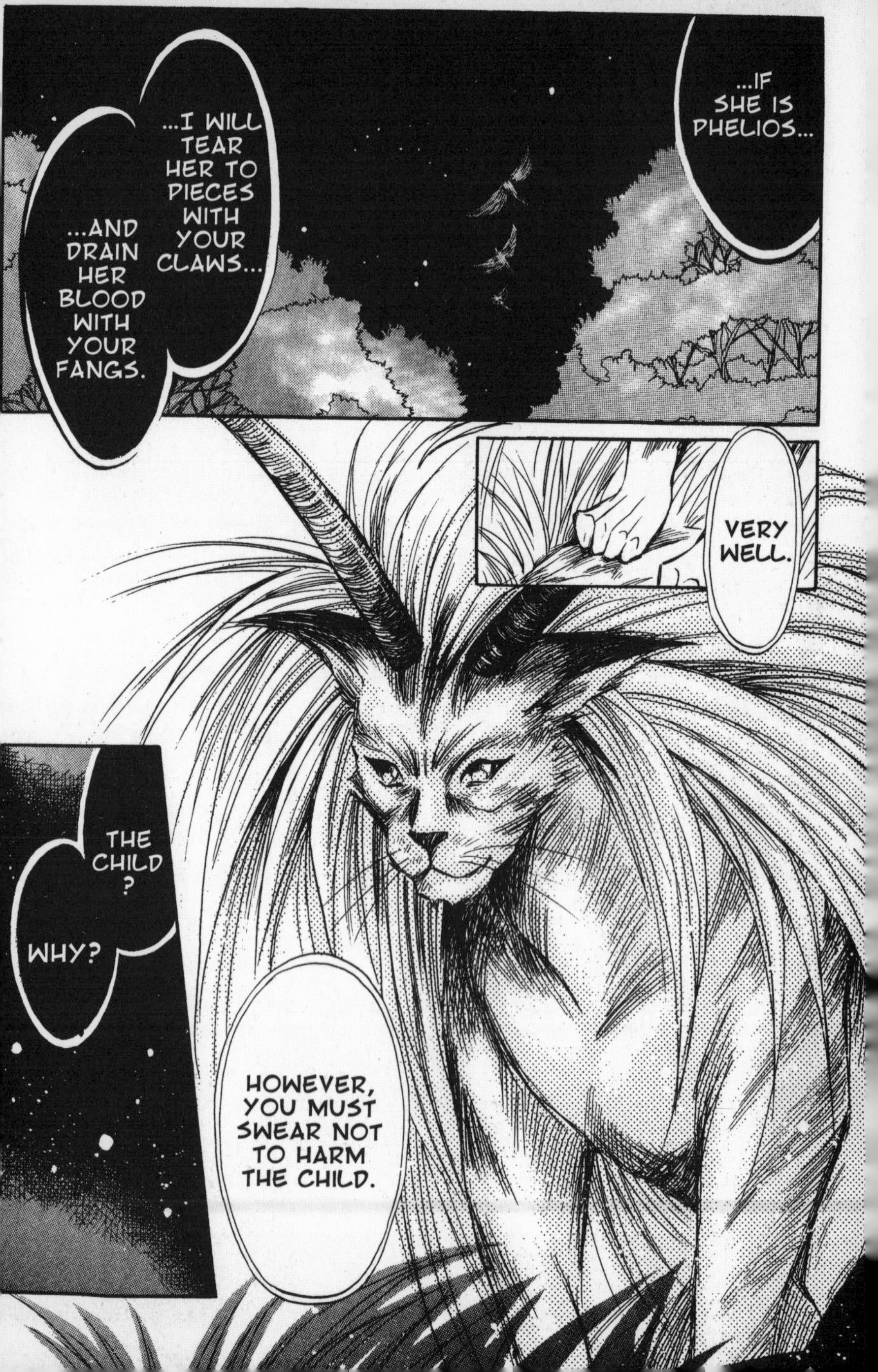
...IF SHE IS PHELIOS...
...I WILL TEAR HER TO PIECES WITH YOUR CLAWS...
...AND DRAIN HER BLOOD WITH YOUR FANGS.
VERY WELL.
HOWEVER, YOU MUST SWEAR NOT TO HARM THE CHILD.
THE CHILD?
WHY?

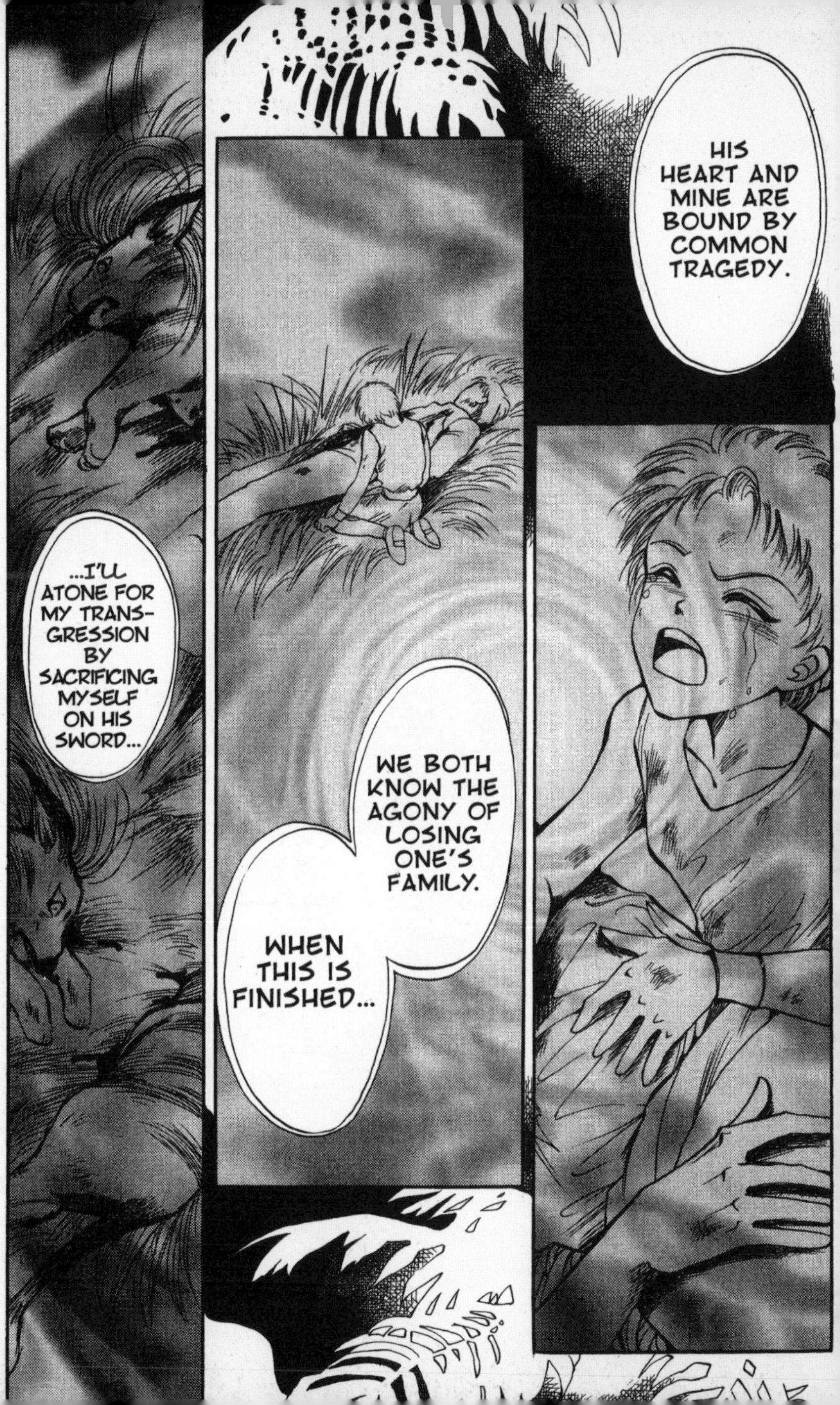
HIS HEART AND MINE ARE BOUND BY COMMON TRAGEDY.
WE BOTH KNOW THE AGONY OF LOSING ONE'S FAMILY.
WHEN THIS IS FINISHED...
...I'LL ATONE FOR MY TRANS-GRESSION BY SACRIFICING MYSELF ON HIS SWORD...

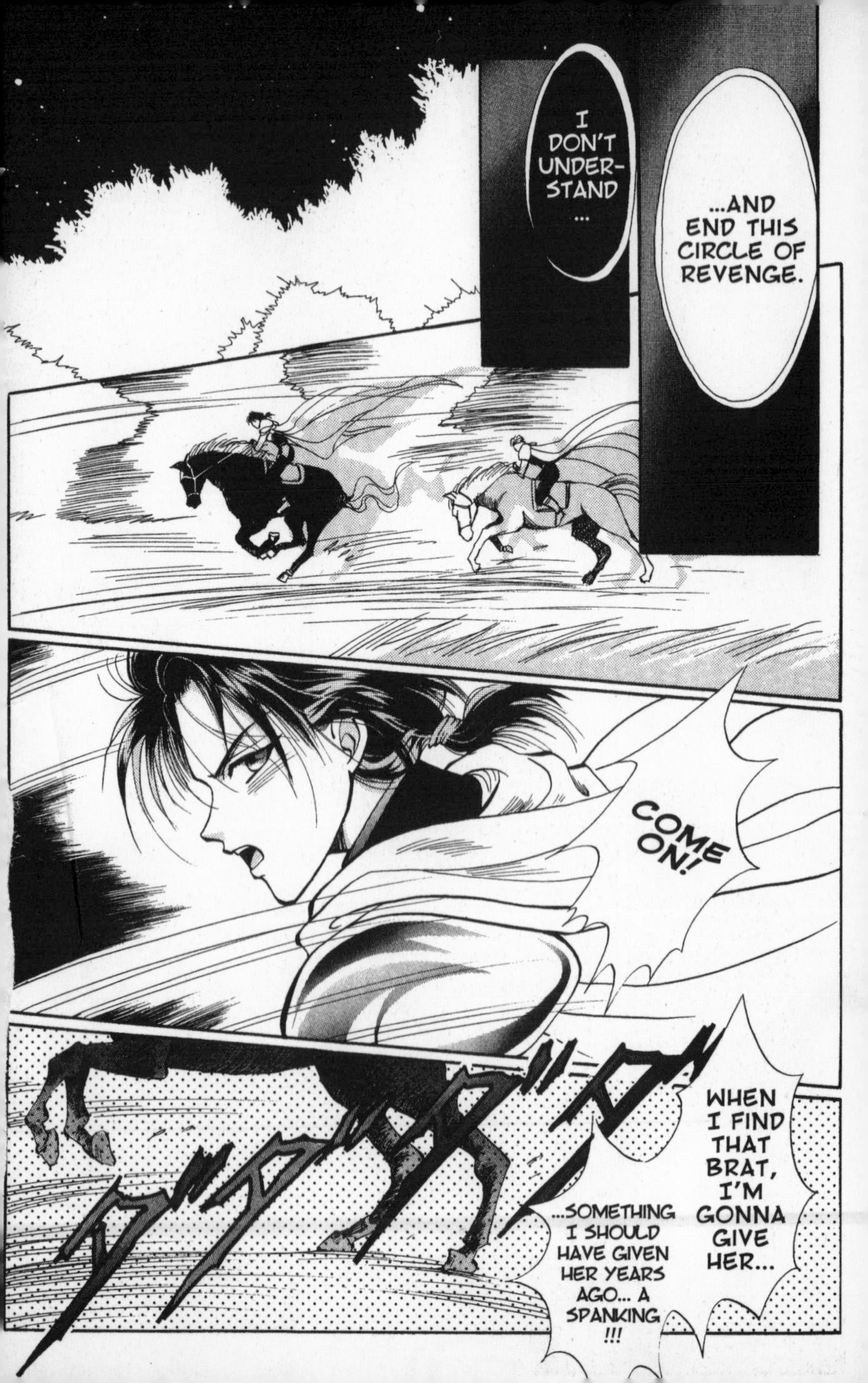
...AND END THIS CIRCLE OF REVENGE.
I DON'T UNDER-STAND...
COME ON!
WHEN I FIND THAT BRAT, I'M GONNA GIVE HER...
...SOMETHING I SHOULD HAVE GIVEN HER YEARS AGO... A SPANKING!!!

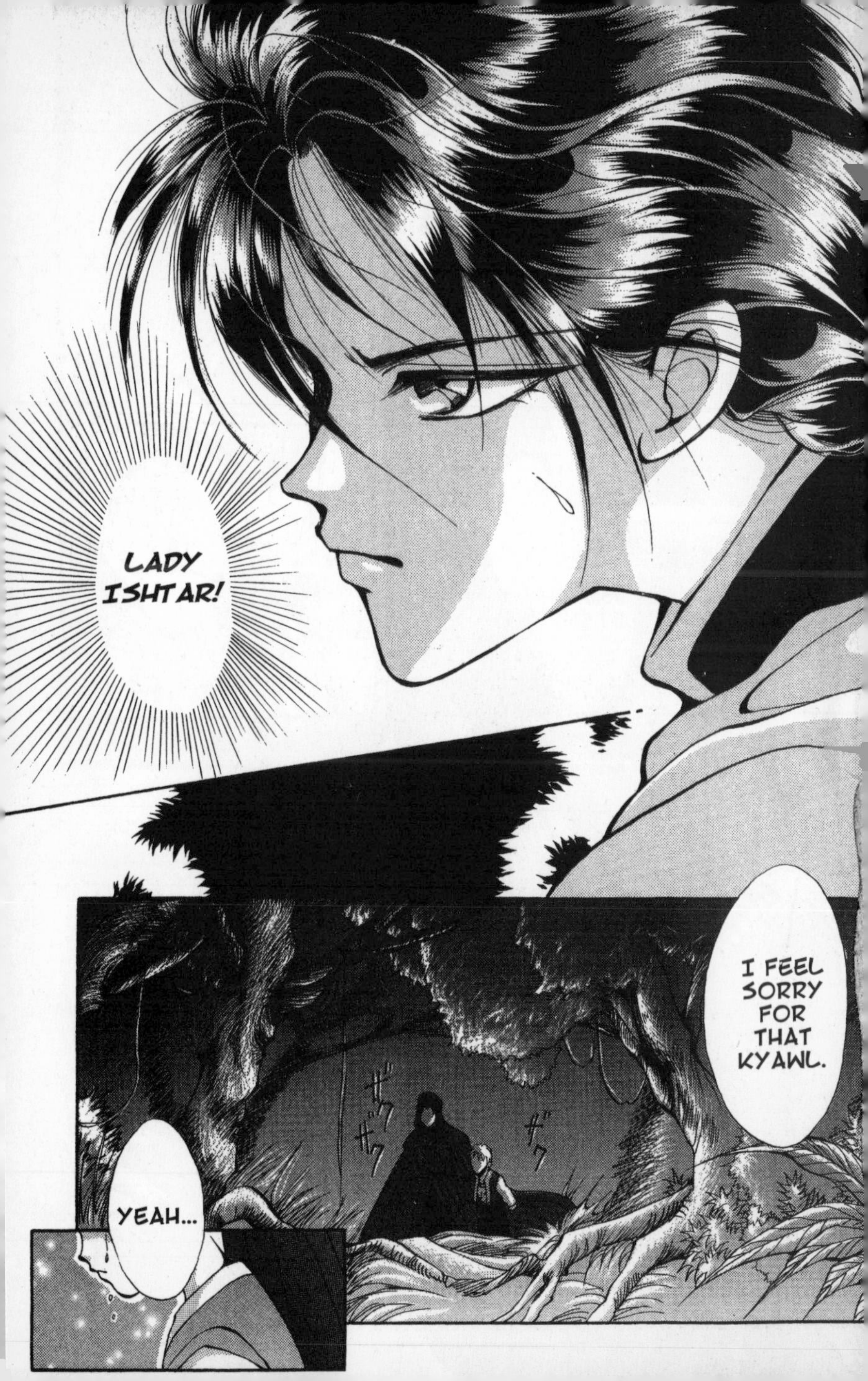
LADY ISHTAR!
I FEEL SORRY FOR THAT KYAWL.
YEAH...

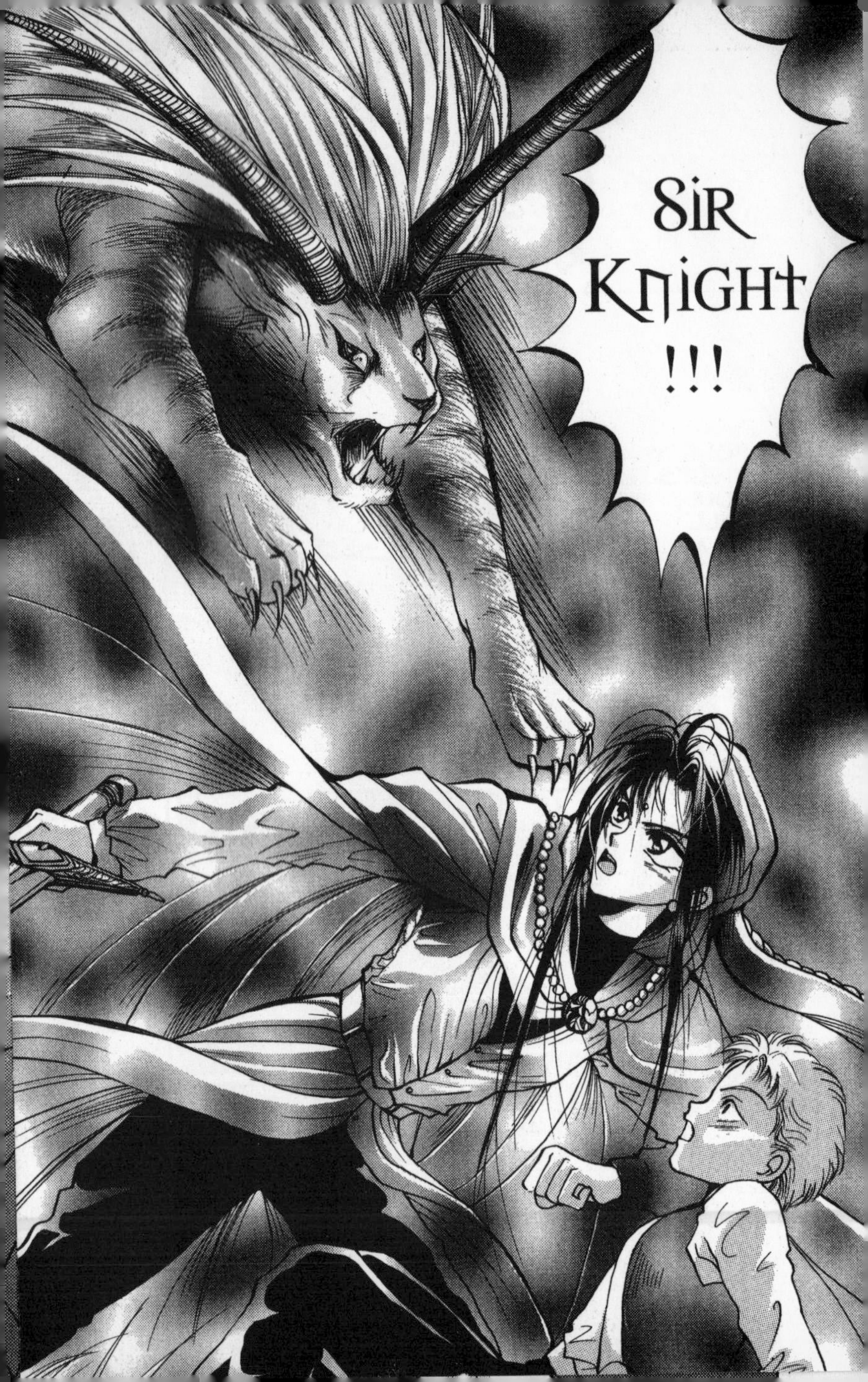
SIR KNIGHT !!!

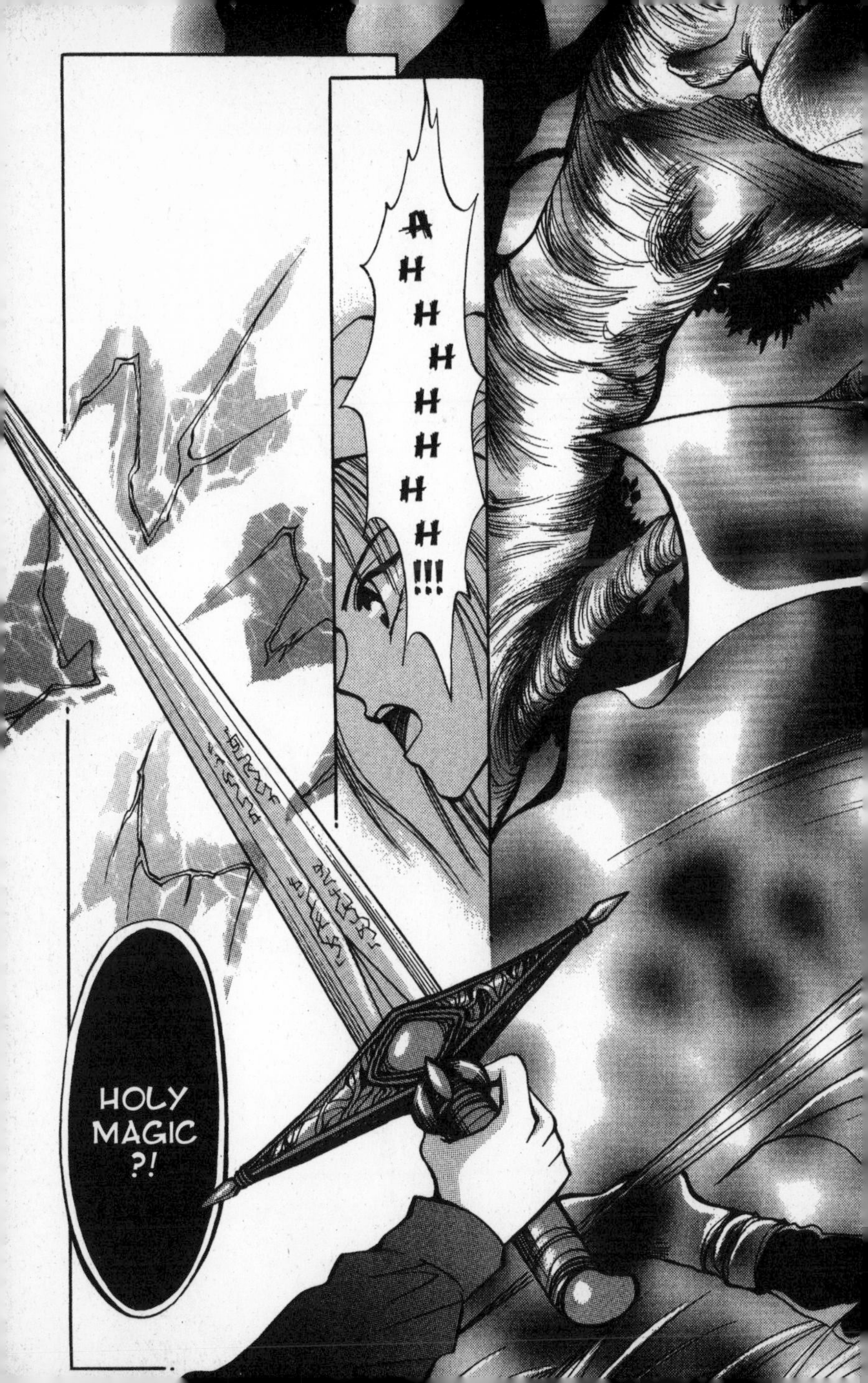
AHHHHHHH!!!
HOLY MAGIC?!

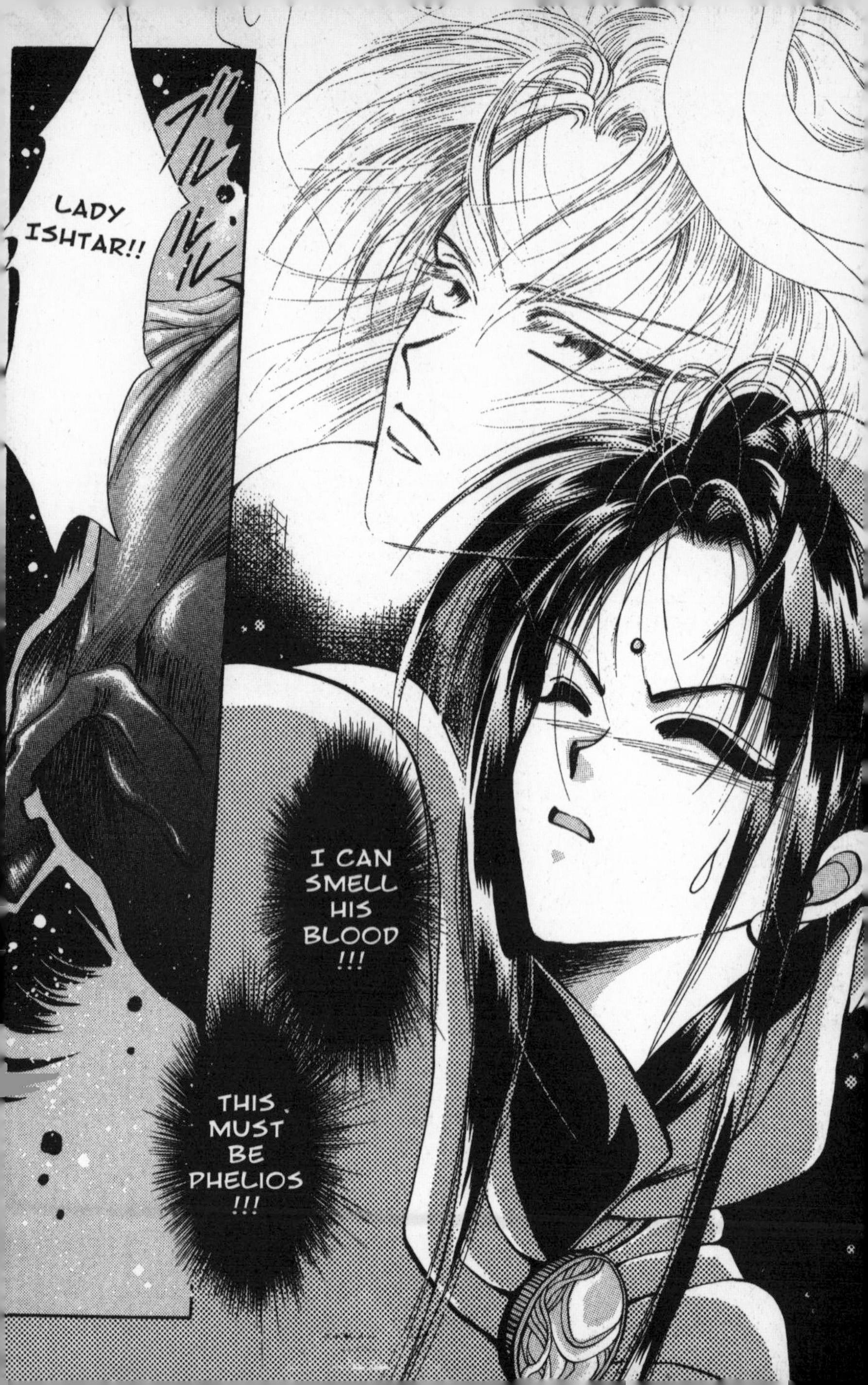
I CAN SMELL HIS BLOOD !!!
THIS MUST BE PHELIOS !!!
LADY ISHTAR!!

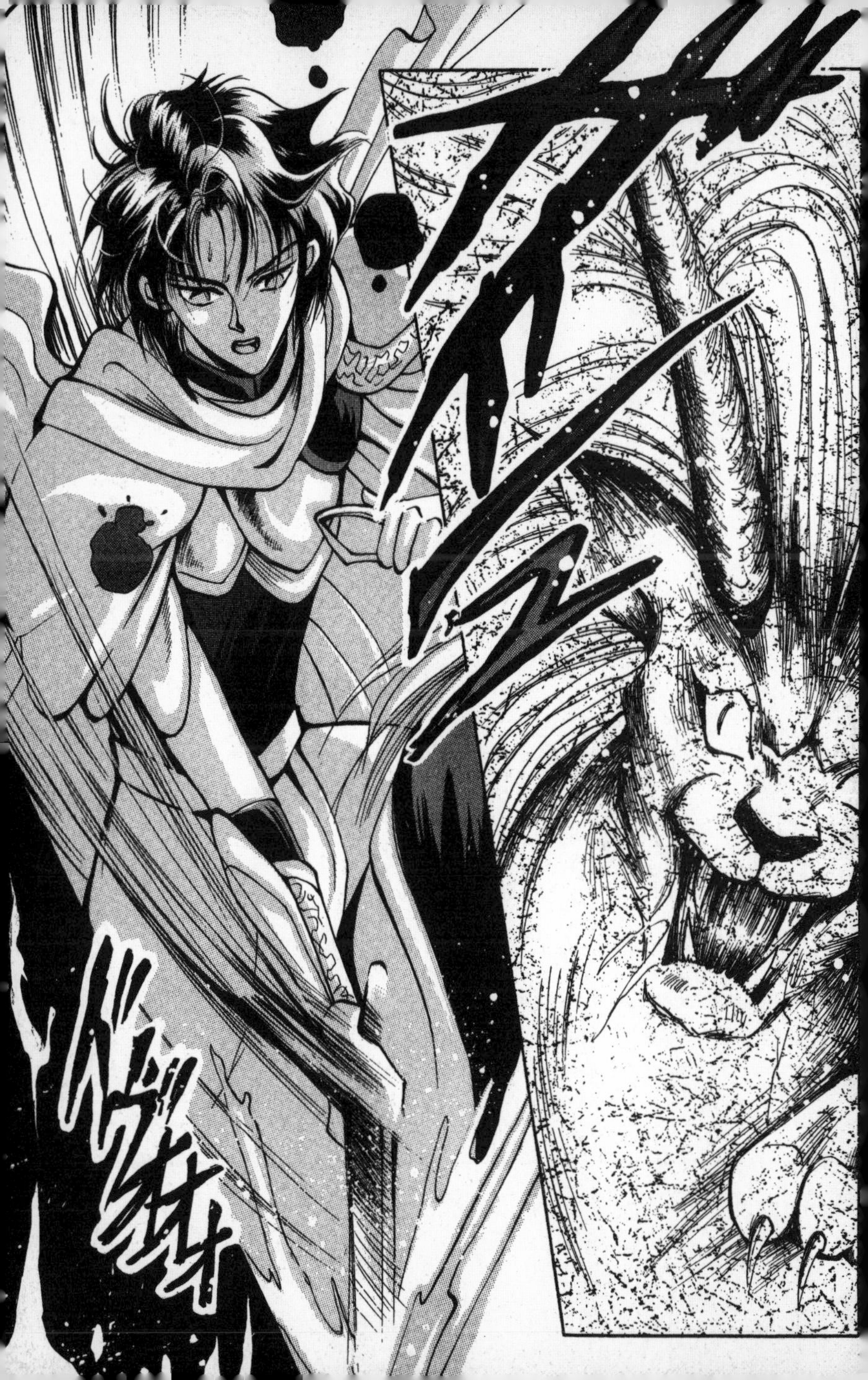

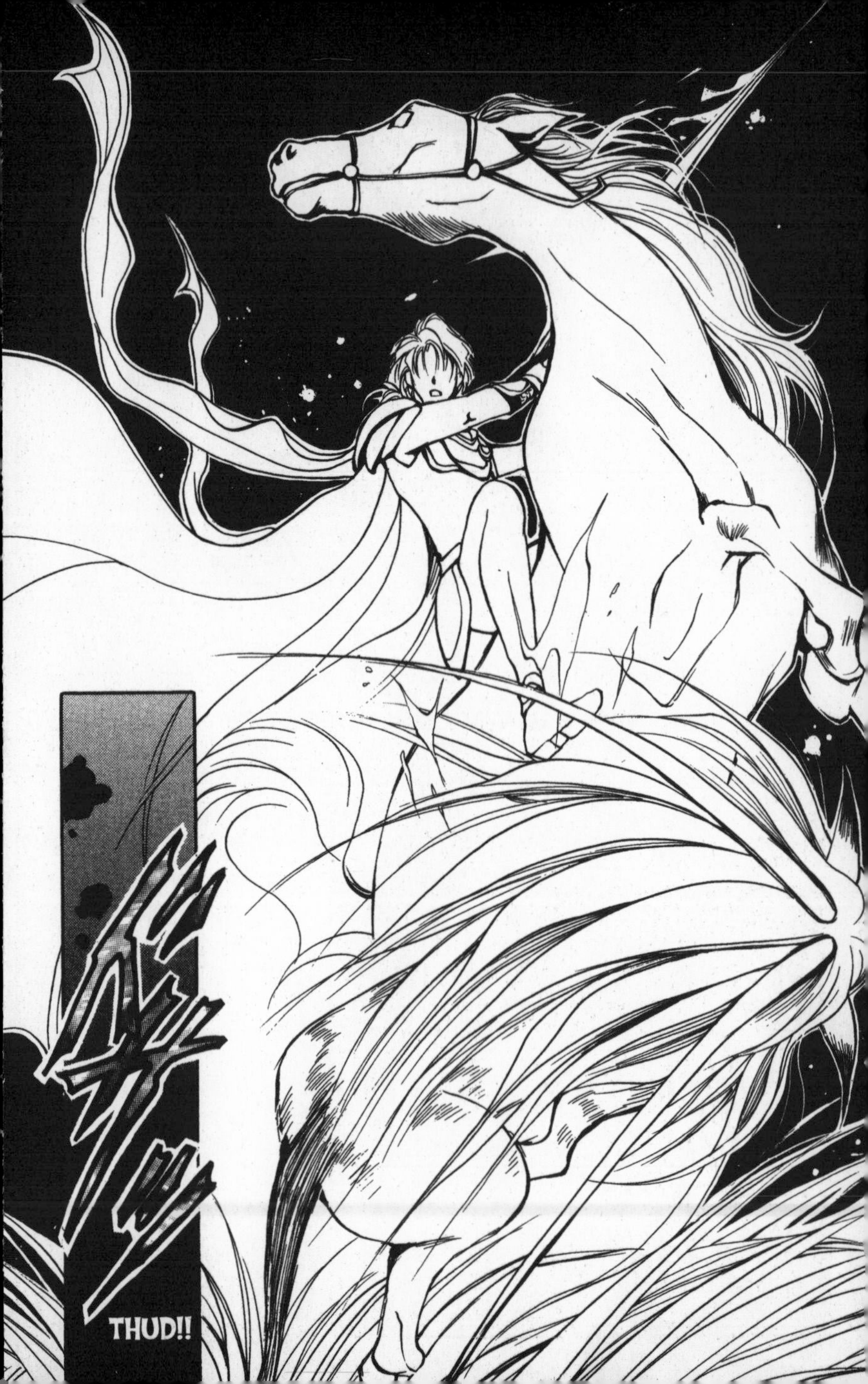
THUD!!

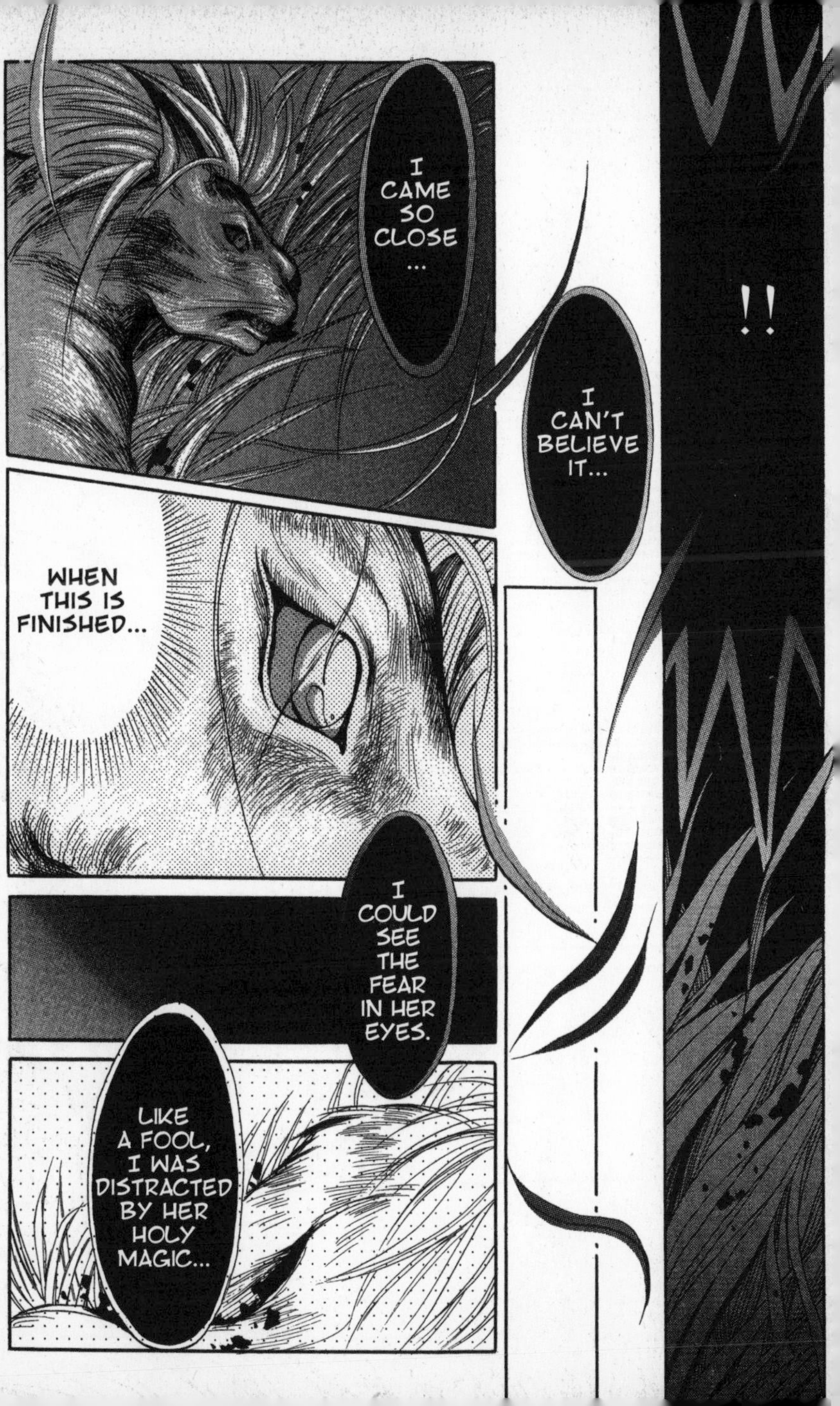
!!
I CAME SO CLOSE...
I CAN'T BELIEVE IT...
WHEN THIS IS FINISHED...
I COULD SEE THE FEAR IN HER EYES.
LIKE A FOOL, I WAS DISTRACTED BY HER HOLY MAGIC...

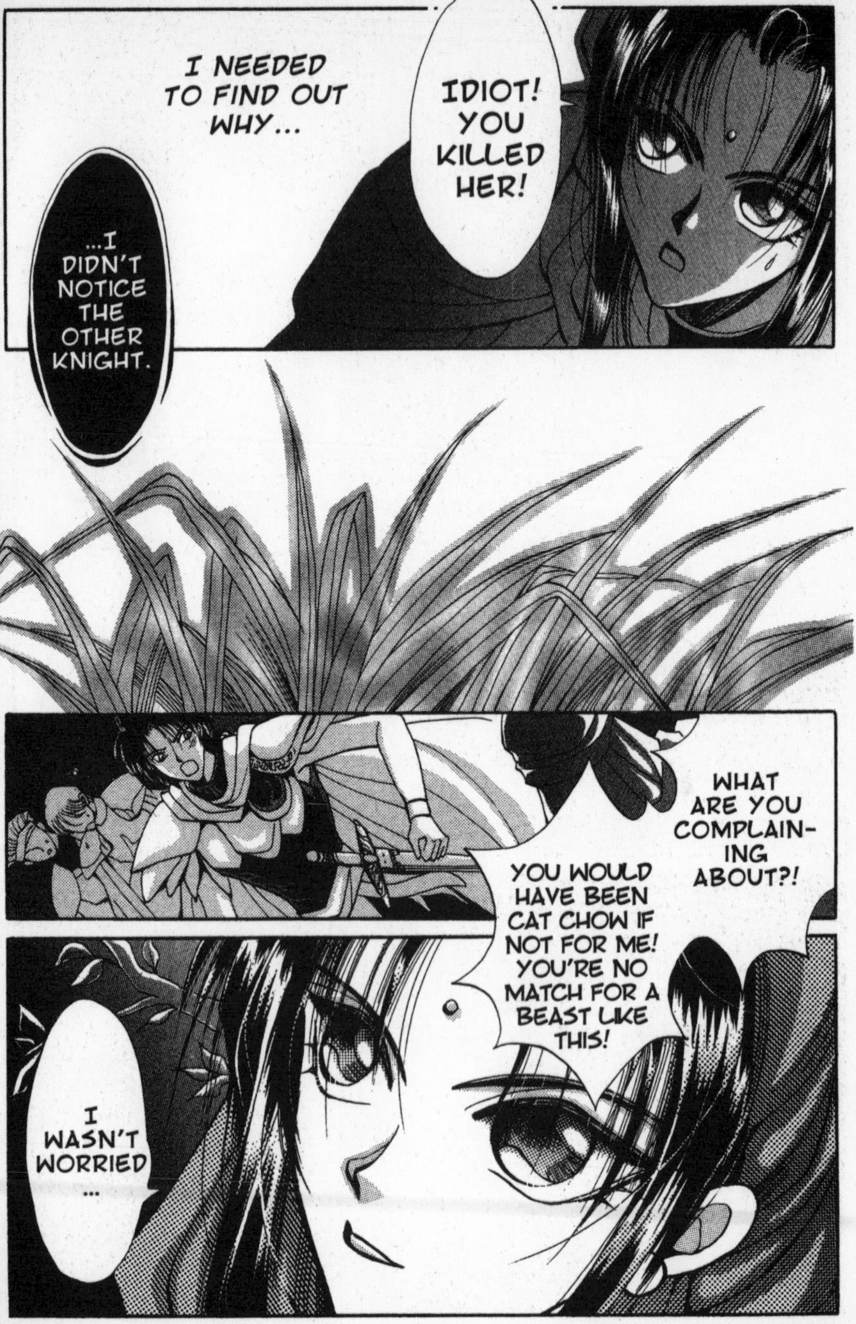
IDIOT! YOU KILLED HER!
I NEEDED TO FIND OUT WHY...
...I DIDN'T NOTICE THE OTHER KNIGHT.
WHAT ARE YOU COMPLAIN-ING ABOUT?!
YOU WOULD HAVE BEEN CAT CHOW IF NOT FOR ME! YOU'RE NO MATCH FOR A BEAST LIKE THIS!
I WASN'T WORRIED ...

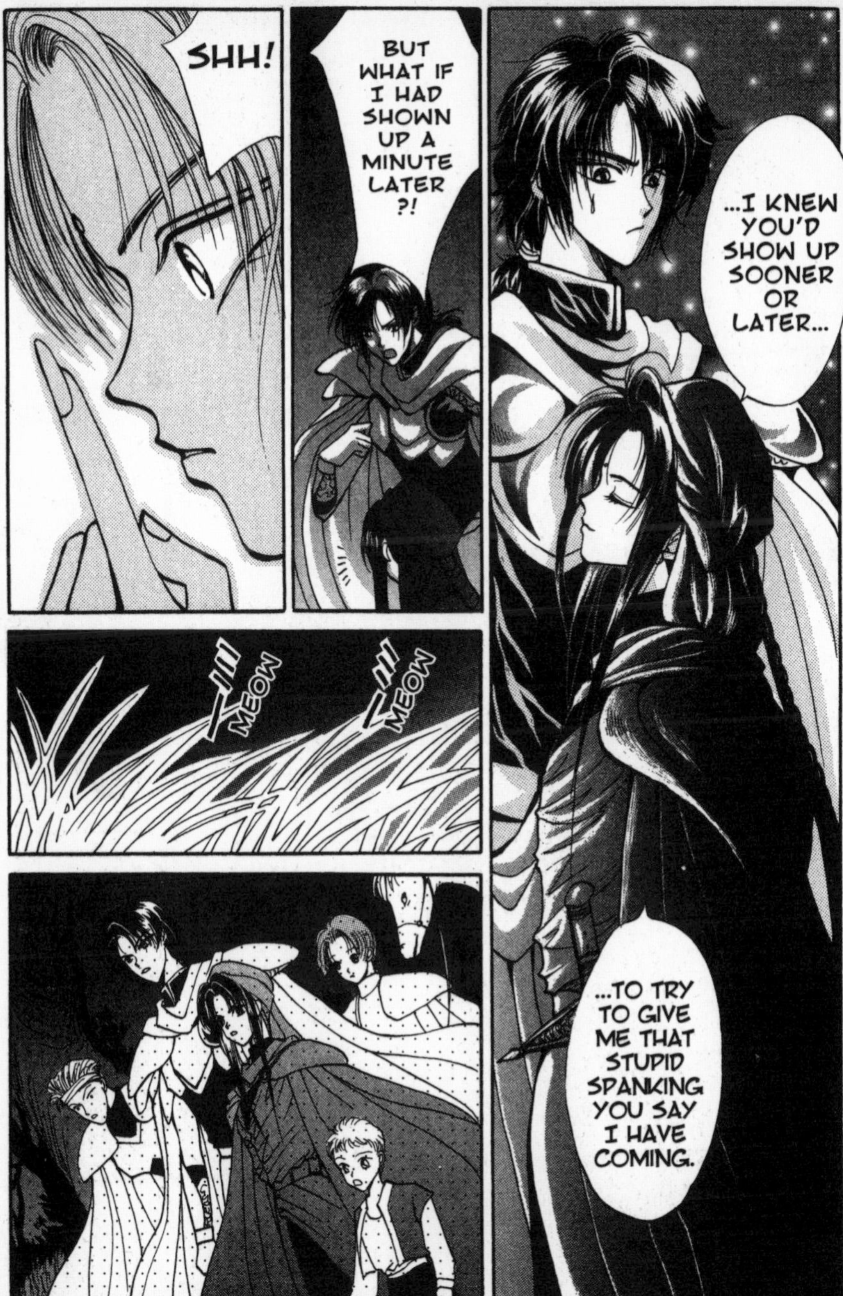
...I KNEW YOU'D SHOW UP SOONER OR LATER...
...TO TRY TO GIVE ME THAT STUPID SPANKING YOU SAY I HAVE COMING.
BUT WHAT IF I HAD SHOWN UP A MINUTE LATER ?!
SHH!
MEOW
MEOW

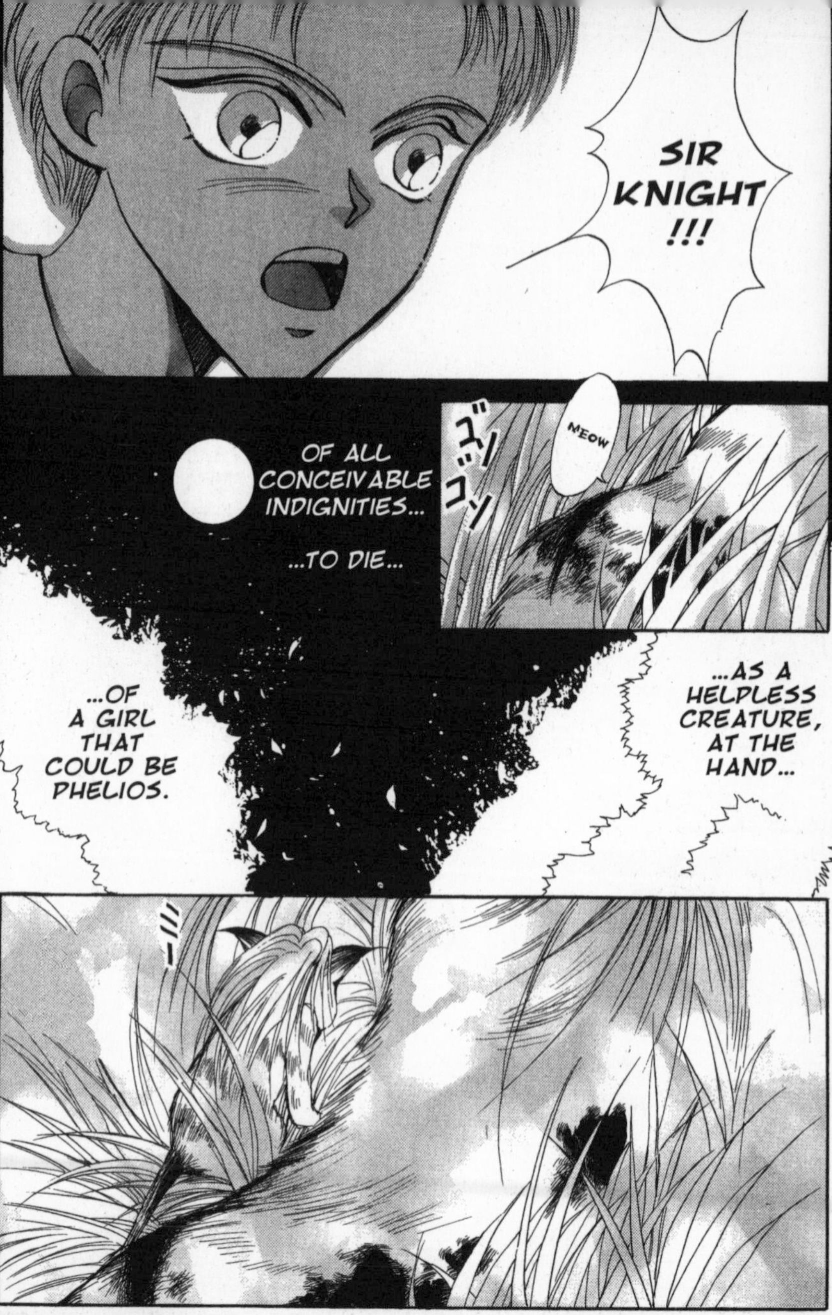
SIR KNIGHT!!!
MEOW
OF ALL CONCEIVABLE INDIGNITIES...
...TO DIE...
...AS A HELPLESS CREATURE, AT THE HAND...
...OF A GIRL THAT COULD BE PHELIOS.

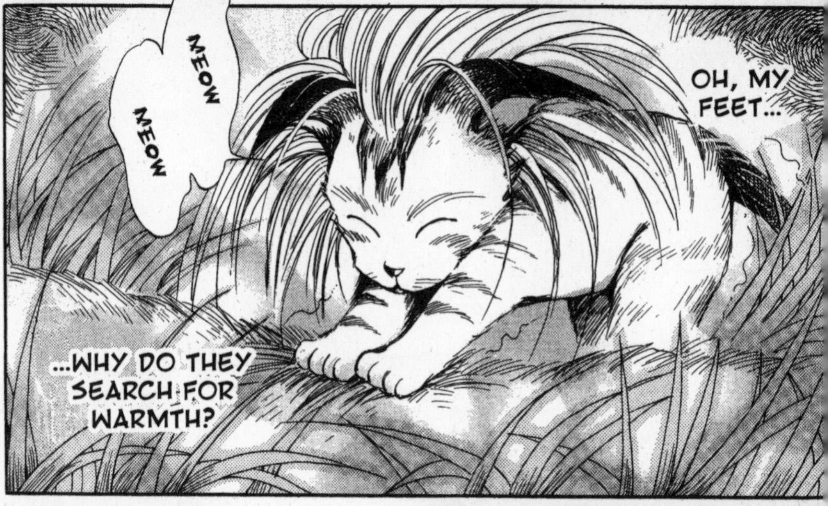
OH, MY FEET...
MEOW MEOW
...WHY DO THEY SEARCH FOR WARMTH?
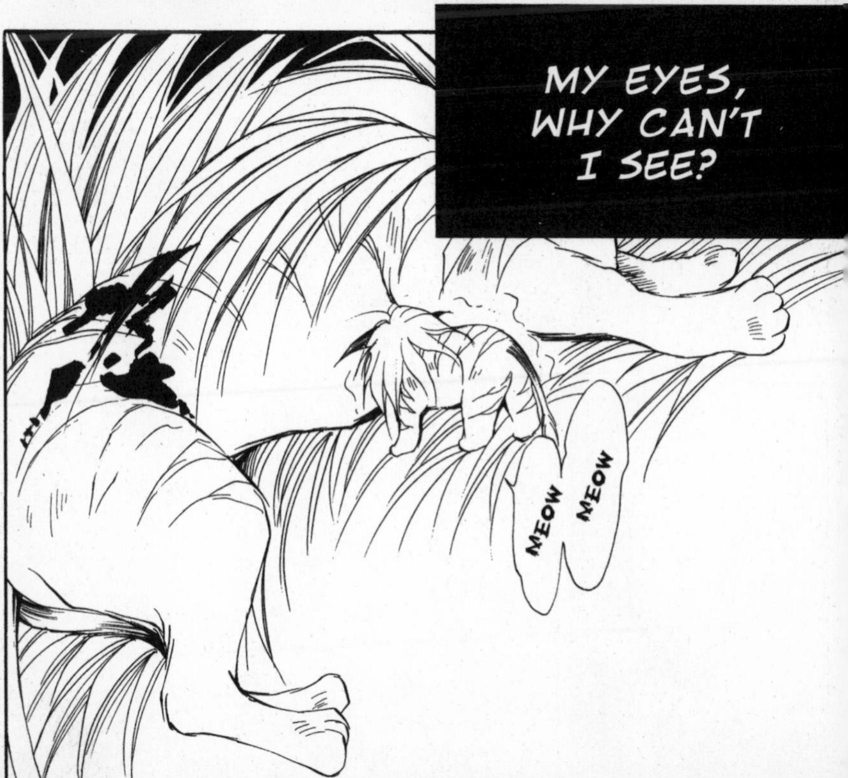
MY EYES, WHY CAN'T I SEE?
MEOW MEOW

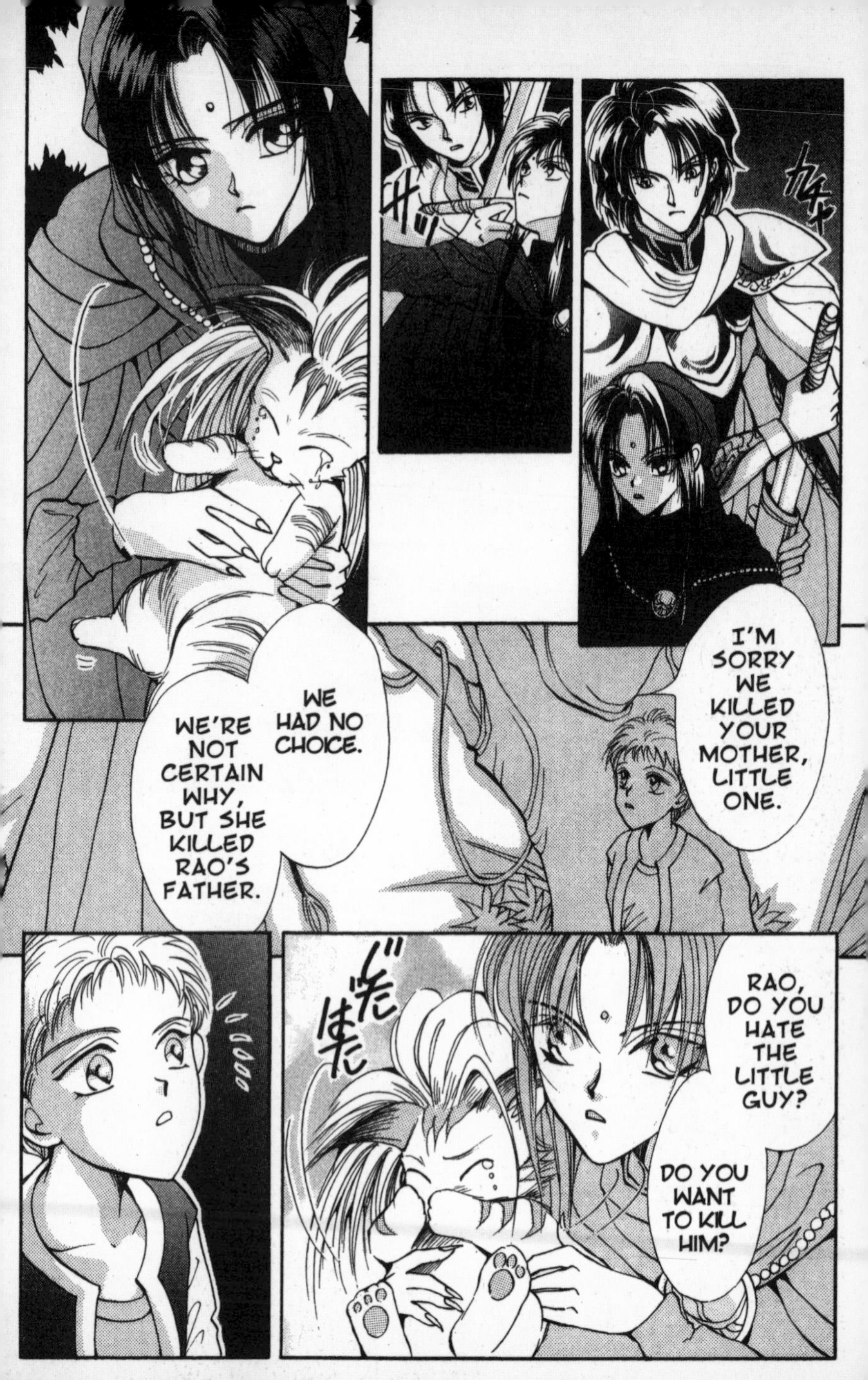
I'M SORRY WE KILLED YOUR MOTHER, LITTLE ONE.
WE HAD NO CHOICE.
WE'RE NOT CERTAIN WHY, BUT SHE KILLED RAO'S FATHER.
RAO, DO YOU HATE THE LITTLE GUY?
DO YOU WANT TO KILL HIM?

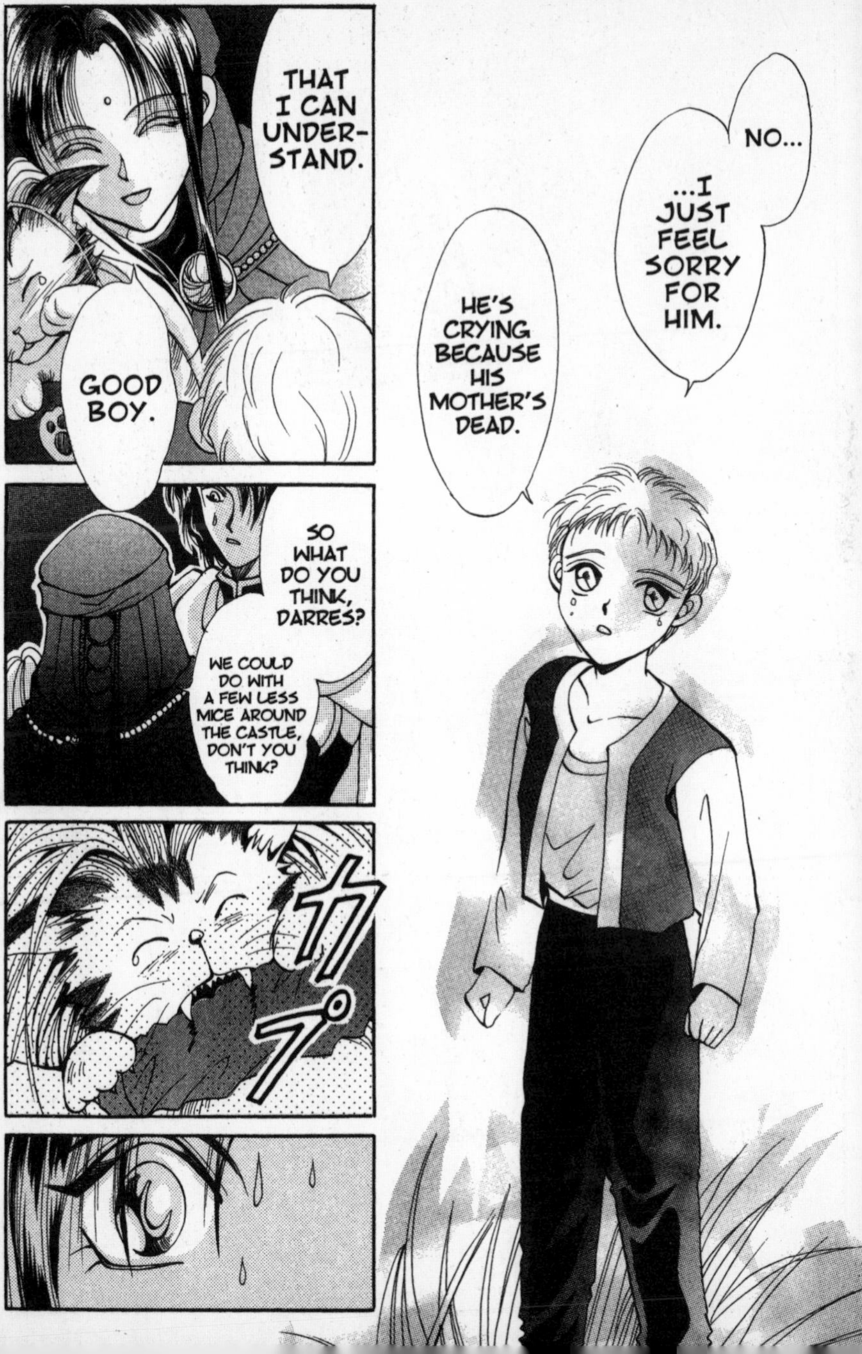
NO...
...I JUST FEEL SORRY FOR HIM.
HE'S CRYING BECAUSE HIS MOTHER'S DEAD.
THAT I CAN UNDER-STAND.
GOOD BOY.
SO WHAT DO YOU THINK, DARRES?
WE COULD DO WITH A FEW LESS MICE AROUND THE CASTLE, DON'T YOU THINK?
カプ

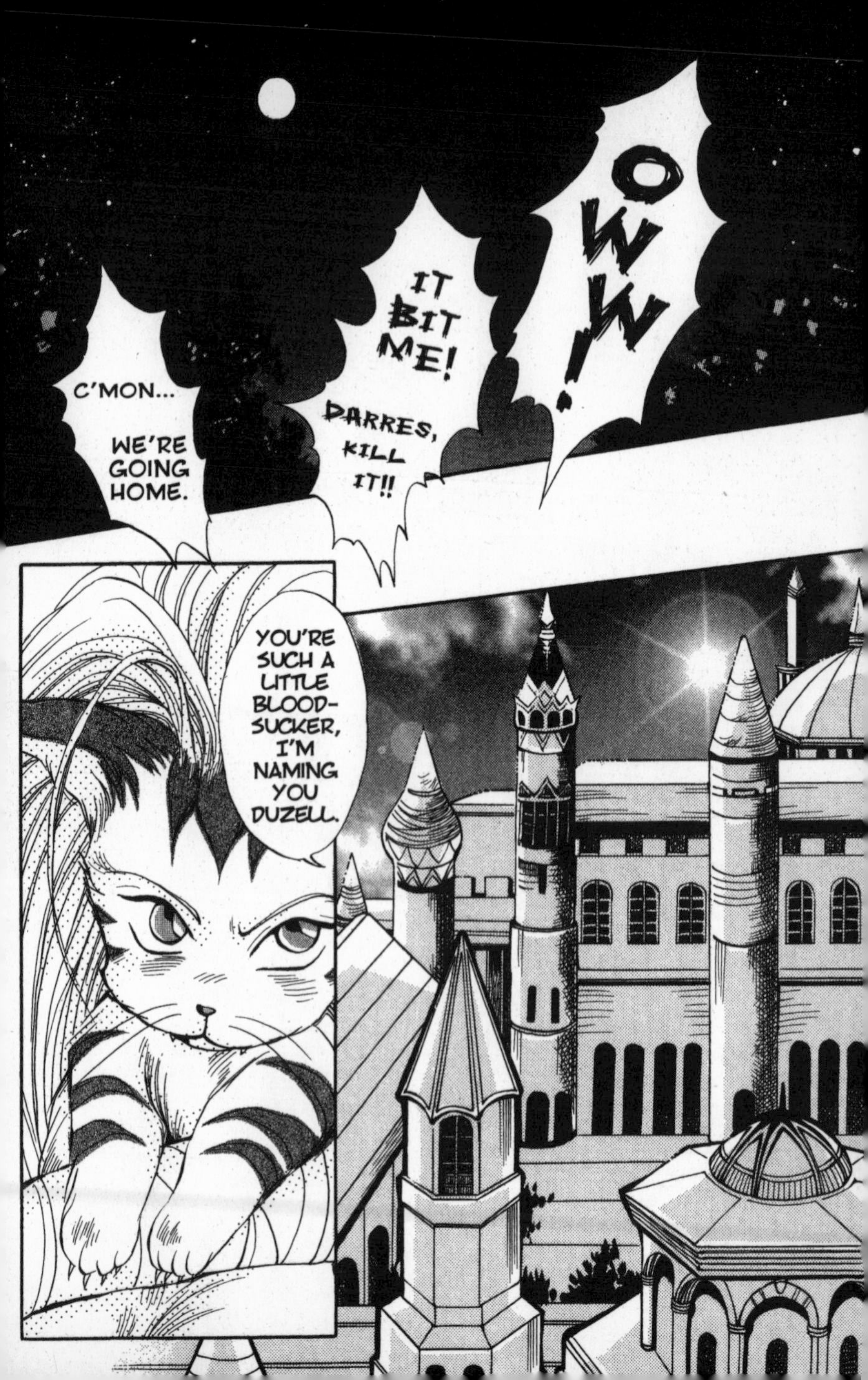
OWW!
IT BIT ME!
DARRES, KILL IT!!
C'MON...
WE'RE GOING HOME.
YOU'RE SUCH A LITTLE BLOOD-SUCKER, I'M NAMING YOU DUZELL.

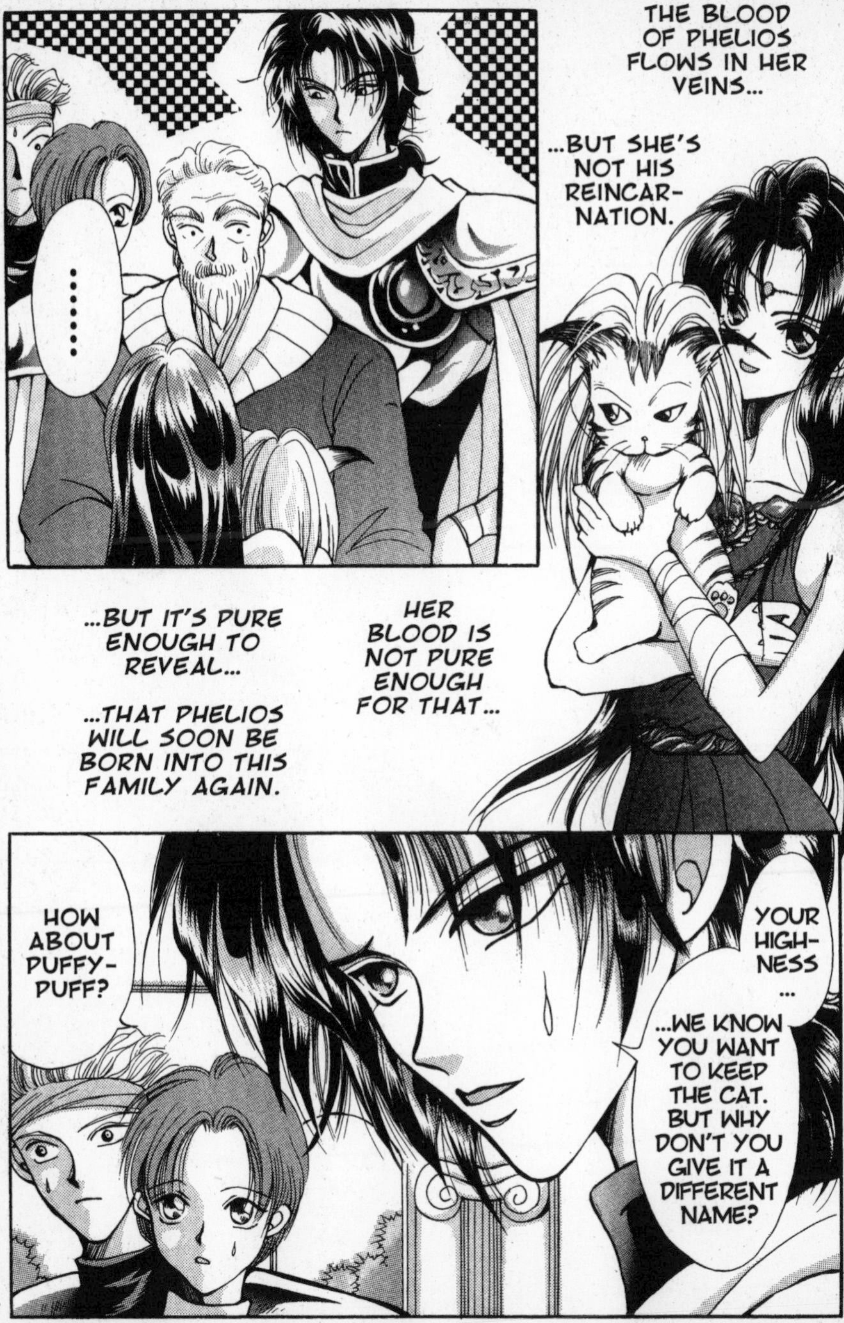
THE BLOOD OF PHELIOS FLOWS IN HER VEINS...
...BUT SHE'S NOT HIS REINCARNATION.
HER BLOOD IS NOT PURE ENOUGH FOR THAT...
...BUT IT'S PURE ENOUGH TO REVEAL...
...THAT PHELIOS WILL SOON BE BORN INTO THIS FAMILY AGAIN.
......
YOUR HIGHNESS...
...WE KNOW YOU WANT TO KEEP THE CAT. BUT WHY DON'T YOU GIVE IT A DIFFERENT NAME?
HOW ABOUT PUFFY-PUFF?

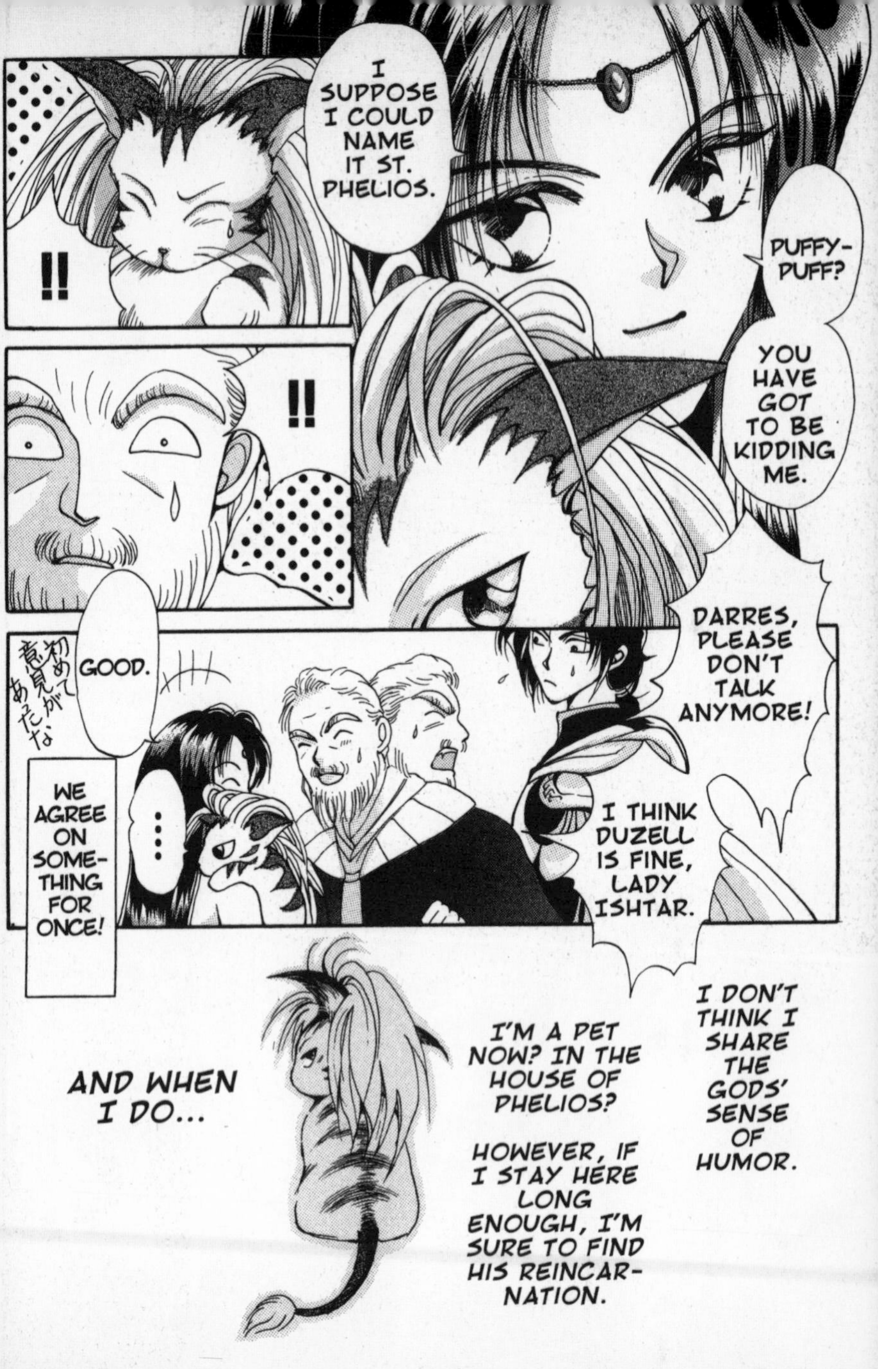
PUFFY-PUFF?
YOU HAVE GOT TO BE KIDDING ME.
I SUPPOSE I COULD NAME IT ST. PHELIOS.
!!
!!
DARRES, PLEASE DON'T TALK ANYMORE!
I THINK DUZELL IS FINE, LADY ISHTAR.
GOOD.
初めて意見があったな
WE AGREE ON SOME-THING FOR ONCE!
....
I DON'T THINK I SHARE THE GODS' SENSE OF HUMOR.
I'M A PET NOW? IN THE HOUSE OF PHELIOS?
HOWEVER, IF I STAY HERE LONG ENOUGH, I'M SURE TO FIND HIS REINCAR-NATION.
AND WHEN I DO...

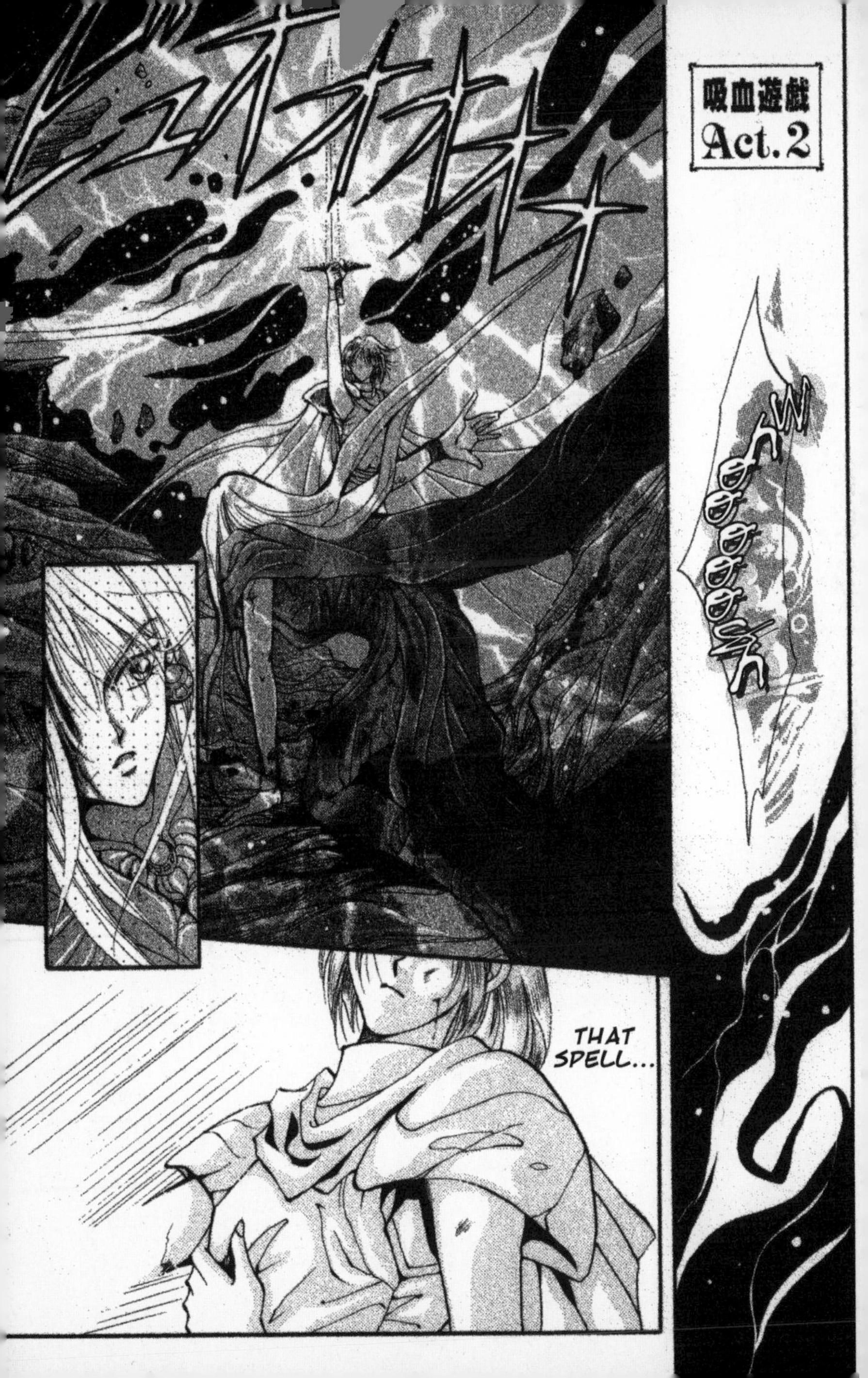
吸血遊戯
Act.2
WHOOOOOSH
THAT SPELL...

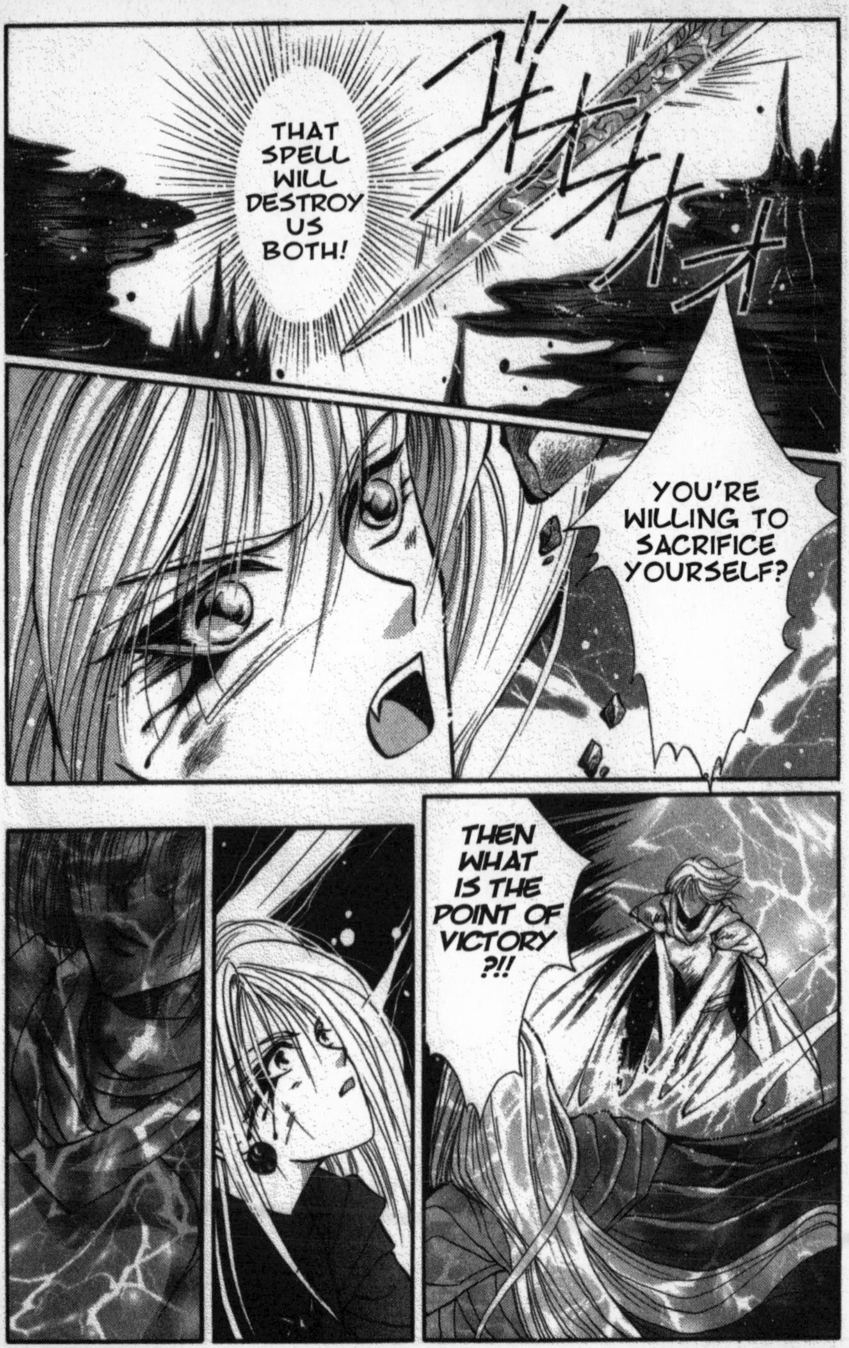
THAT SPELL WILL DESTROY US BOTH!
YOU'RE WILLING TO SACRIFICE YOURSELF?
THEN WHAT IS THE POINT OF VICTORY ?!!

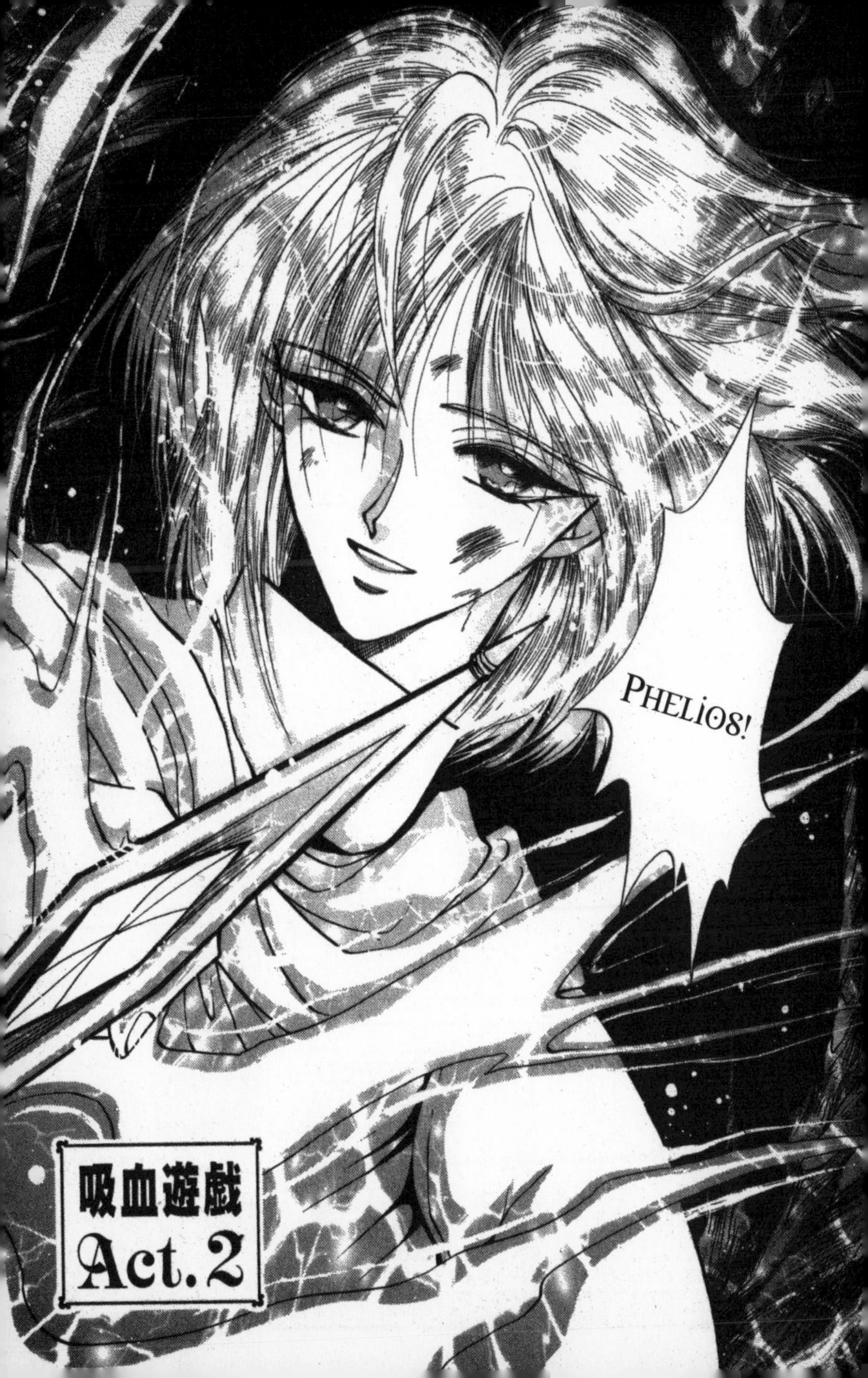
PHELIOS!
吸血遊戯
Act. 2

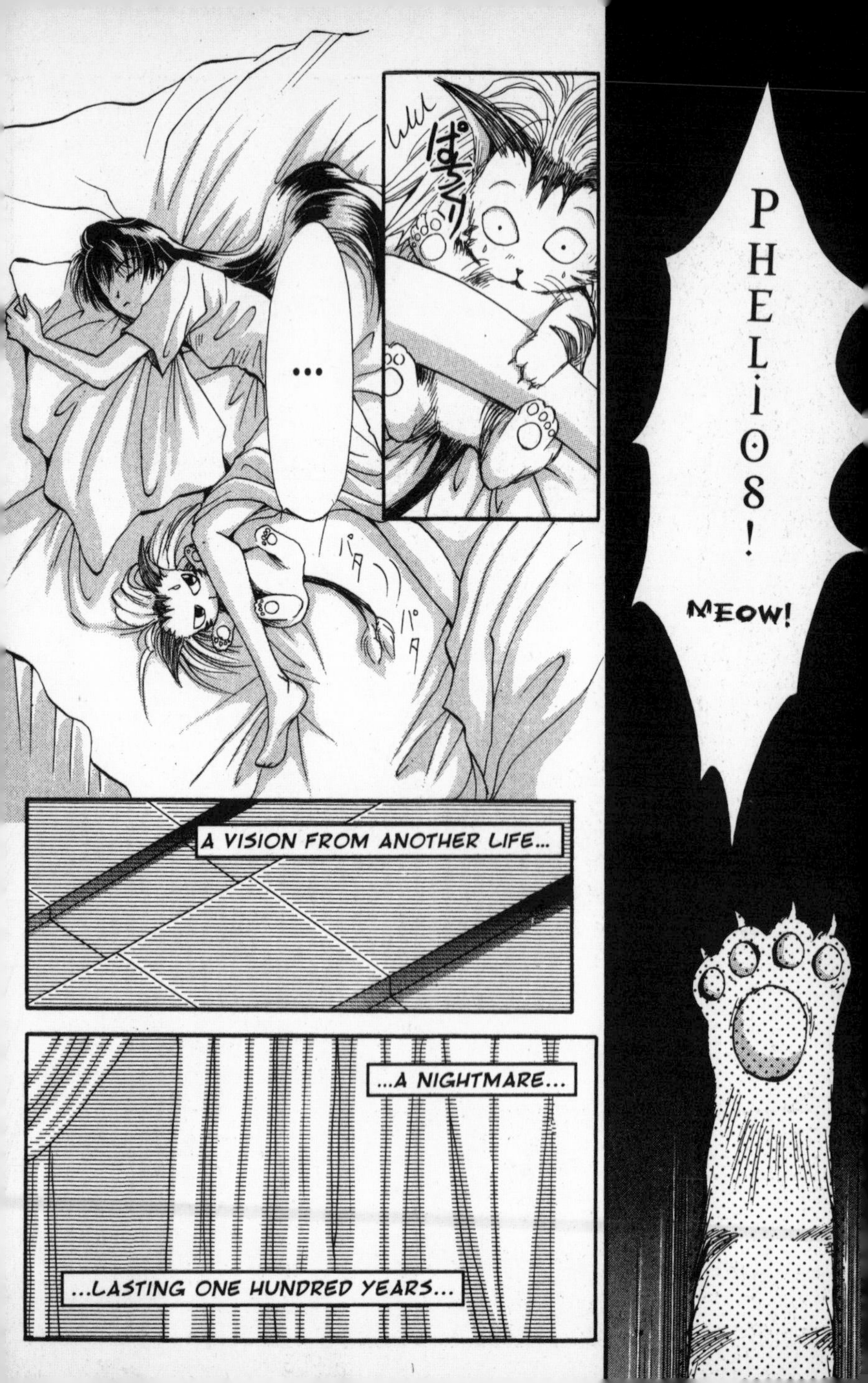
PHELIOS!
MEOW!
ぱちくり
...
パタ
パタ
A VISION FROM ANOTHER LIFE...
...A NIGHTMARE...
...LASTING ONE HUNDRED YEARS...

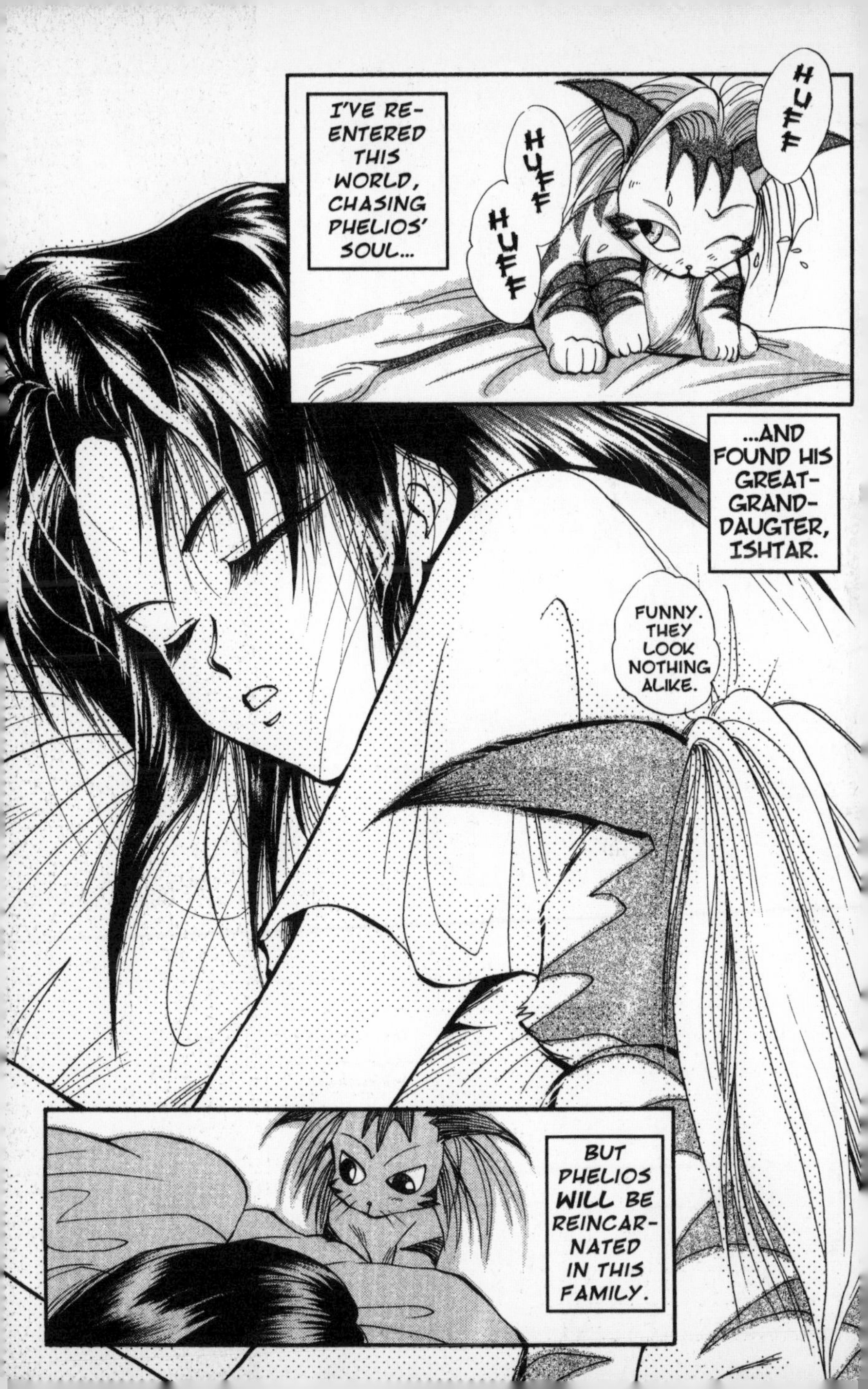
HUFF
HUFF HUFF
I'VE RE-ENTERED THIS WORLD, CHASING PHELIOS' SOUL...
...AND FOUND HIS GREAT-GRAND-DAUGTER, ISHTAR.
FUNNY. THEY LOOK NOTHING ALIKE.
BUT PHELIOS WILL BE REINCAR-NATED IN THIS FAMILY.

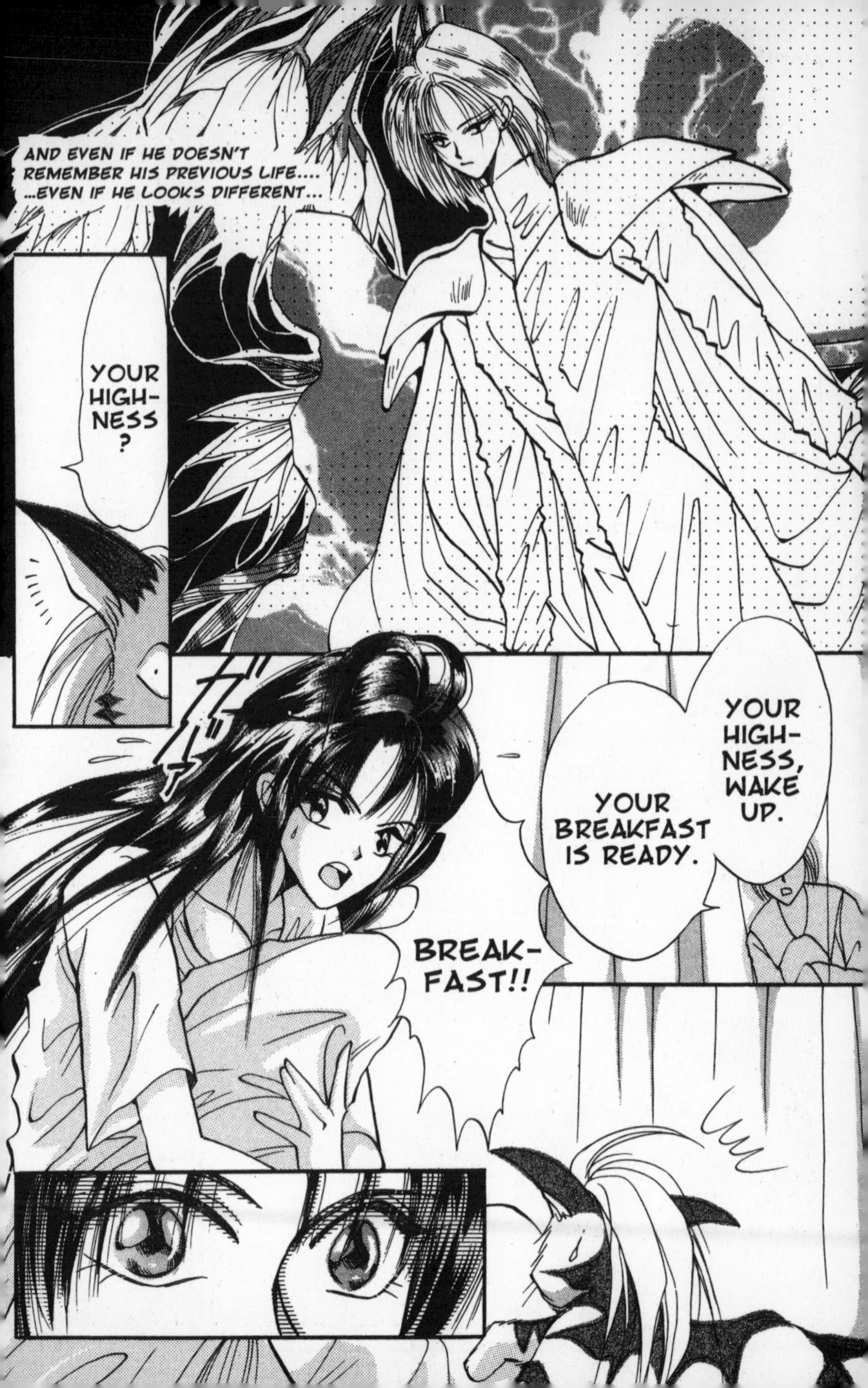
AND EVEN IF HE DOESN'T REMEMBER HIS PREVIOUS LIFE.... ...EVEN IF HE LOOKS DIFFERENT...
YOUR HIGH-NESS ?
YOUR HIGH-NESS, WAKE UP.
YOUR BREAKFAST IS READY.
BREAK-FAST!!

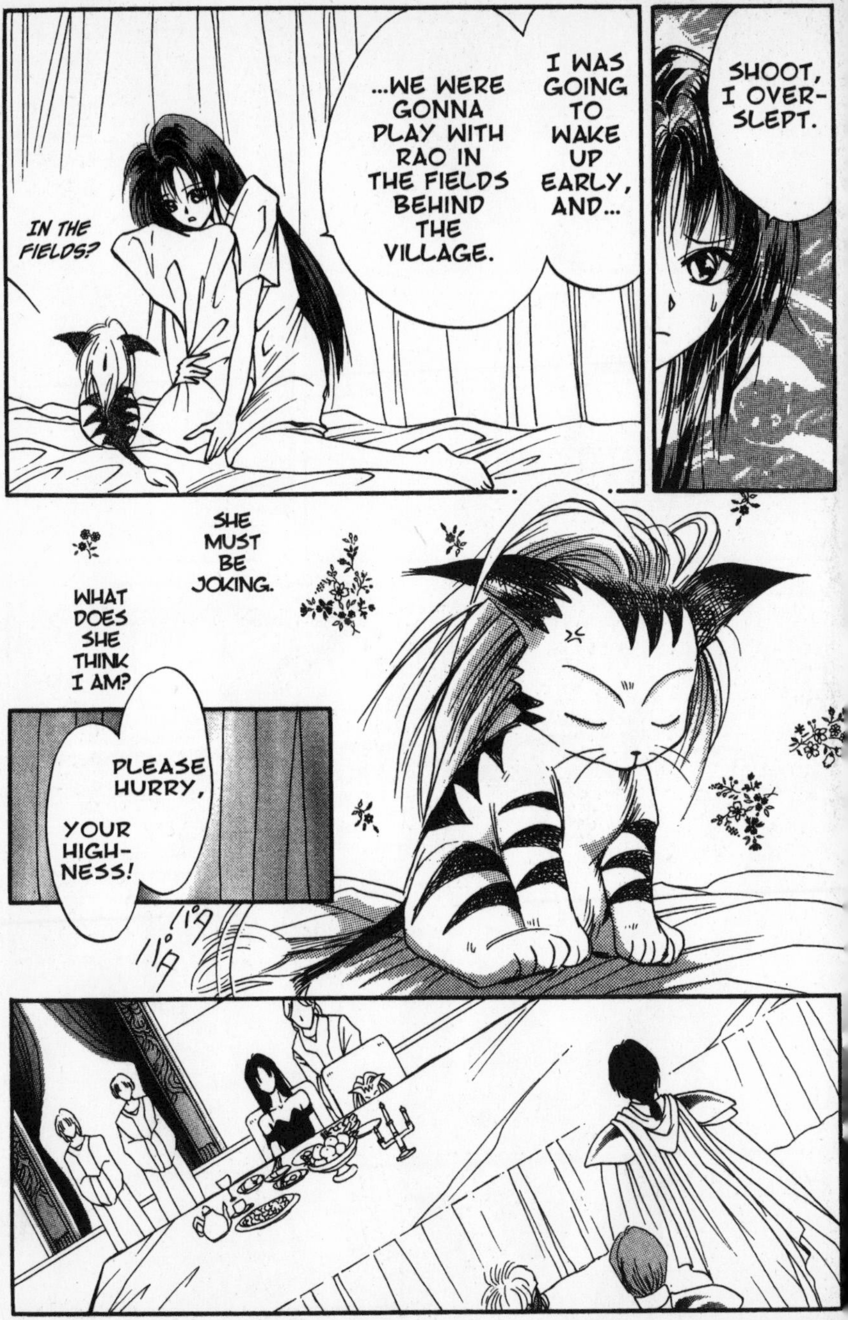
SHOOT, I OVER-SLEPT.
I WAS GOING TO WAKE UP EARLY, AND...
...WE WERE GONNA PLAY WITH RAO IN THE FIELDS BEHIND THE VILLAGE.
IN THE FIELDS?
SHE MUST BE JOKING.
WHAT DOES SHE THINK I AM?
PLEASE HURRY,
YOUR HIGH-NESS!
パタ パタ

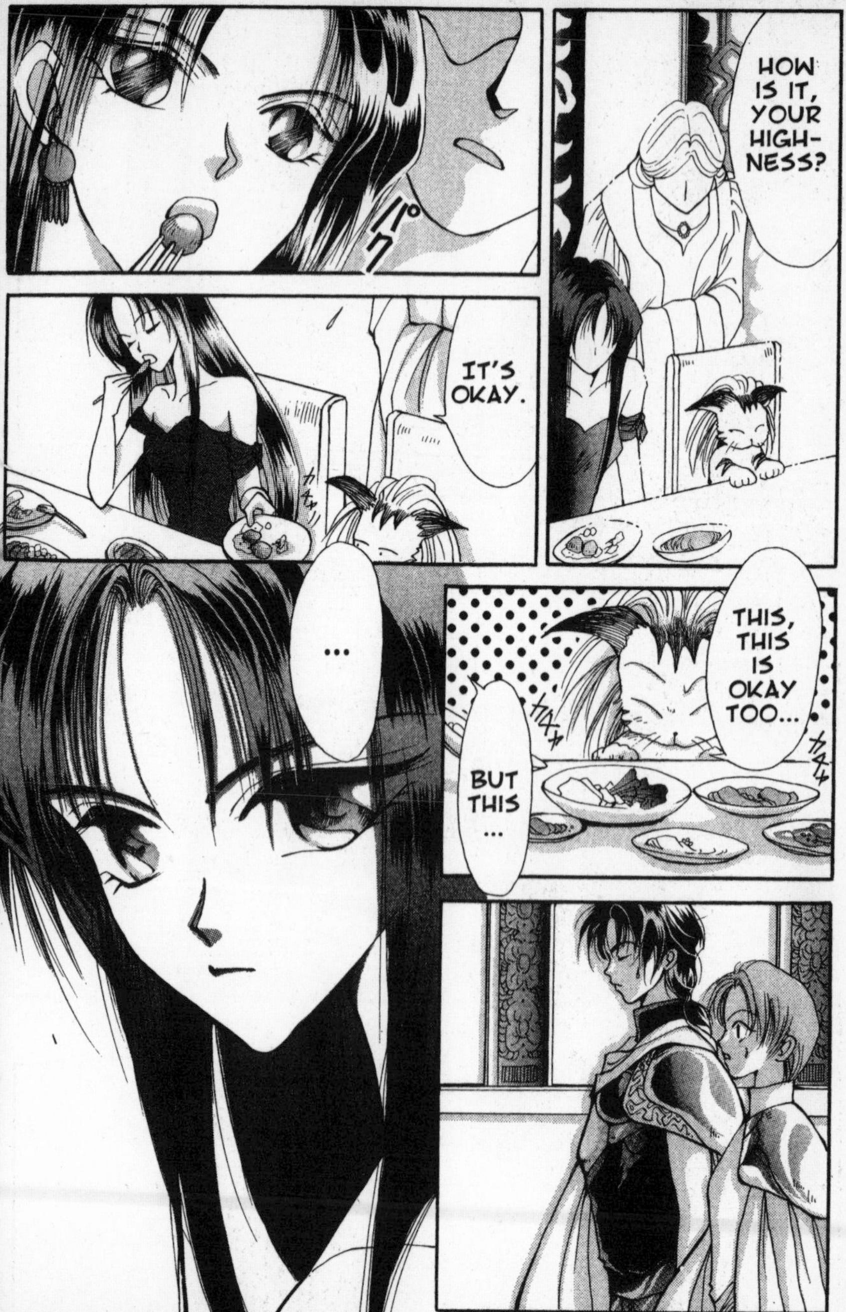
HOW IS IT, YOUR HIGHNESS?
パク
IT'S OKAY.
THIS, THIS IS OKAY TOO...
BUT THIS ...
...

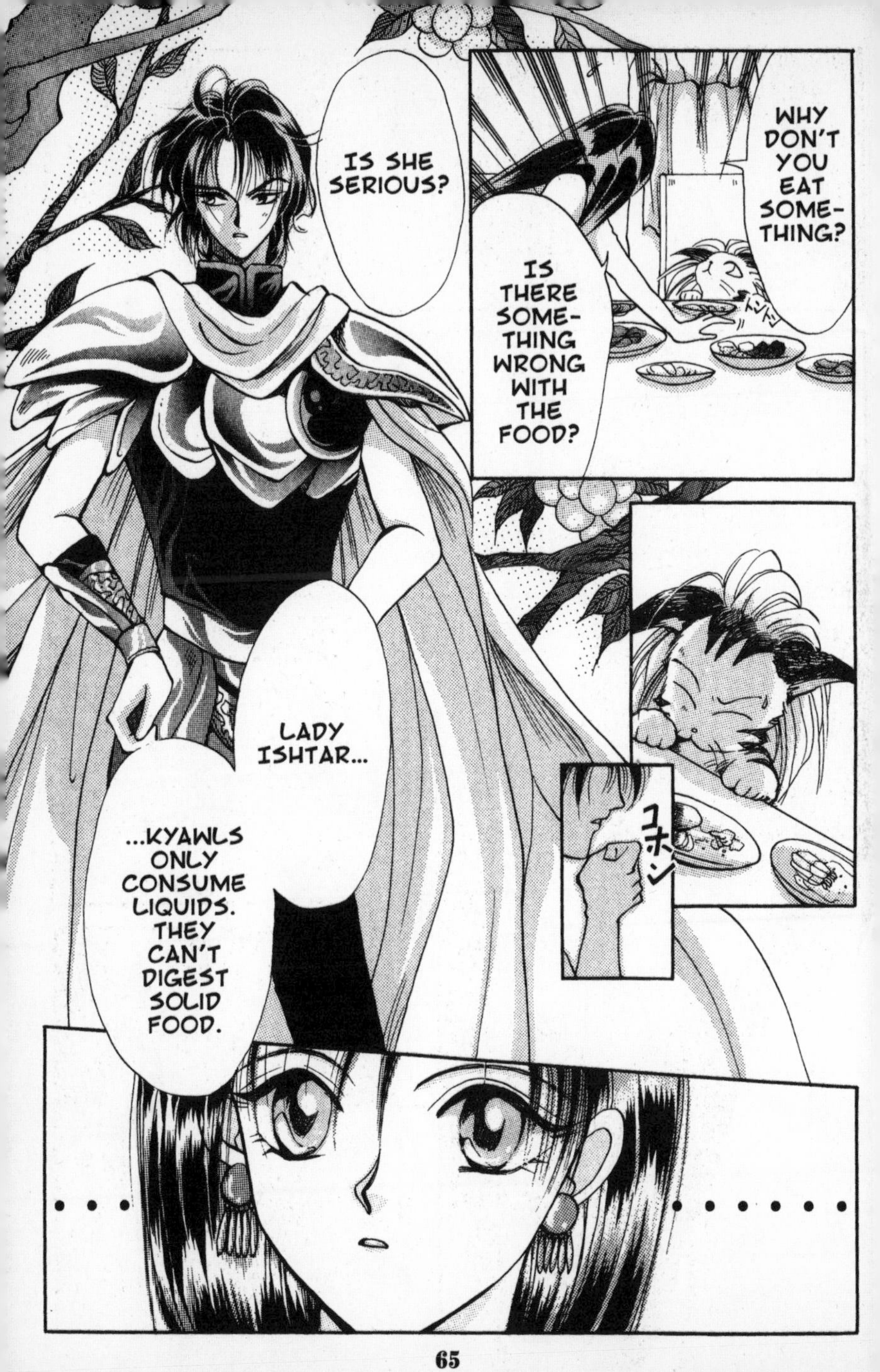
WHY DON'T YOU EAT SOME-THING?
IS THERE SOME-THING WRONG WITH THE FOOD?
コホン
IS SHE SERIOUS?
LADY ISHTAR...
...KYAWLS ONLY CONSUME LIQUIDS. THEY CAN'T DIGEST SOLID FOOD.
• • • • • • • •

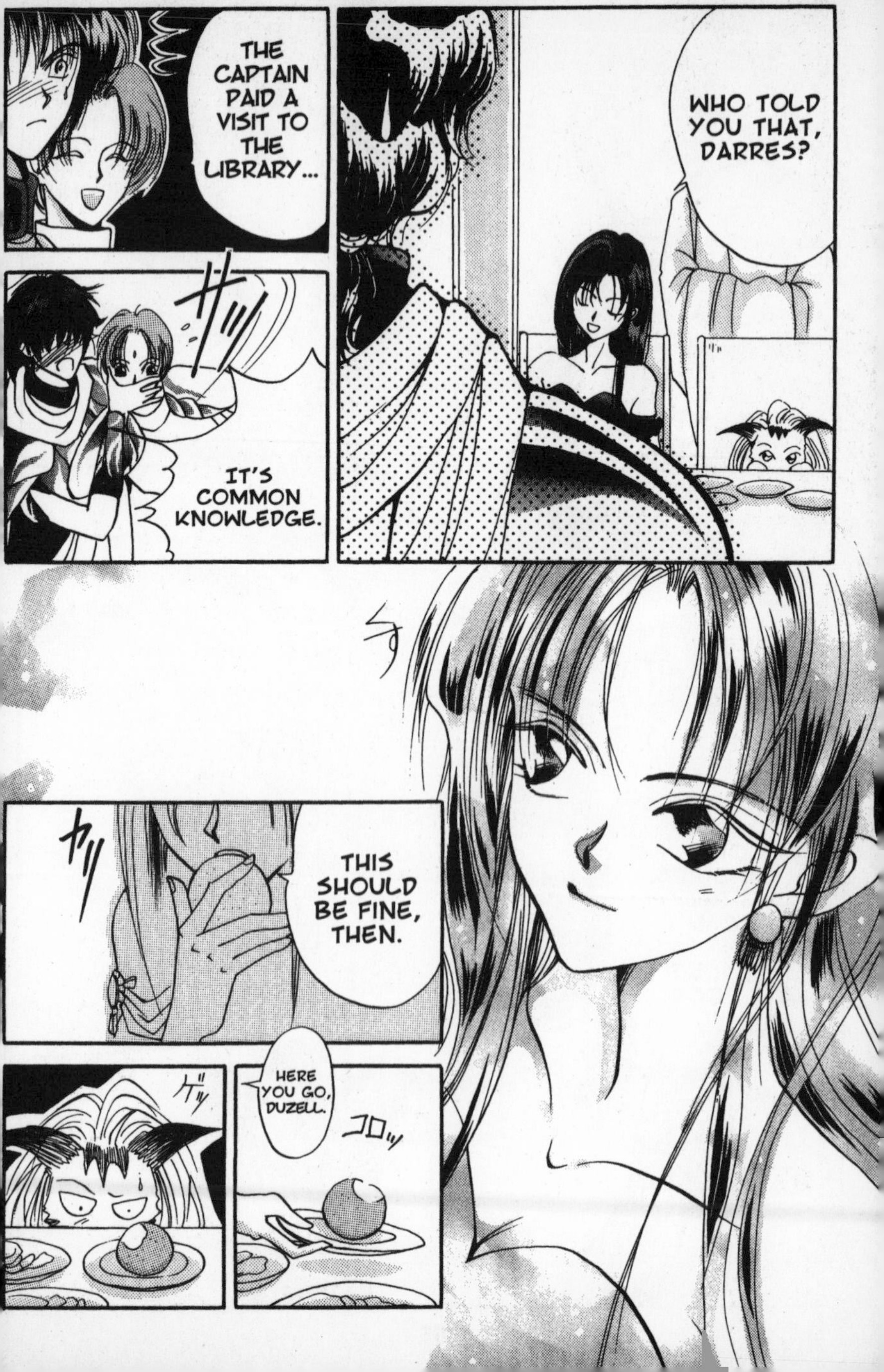
WHO TOLD YOU THAT, DARRES?
THE CAPTAIN PAID A VISIT TO THE LIBRARY...
IT'S COMMON KNOWLEDGE.
THIS SHOULD BE FINE, THEN.
HERE YOU GO, DUZELL.

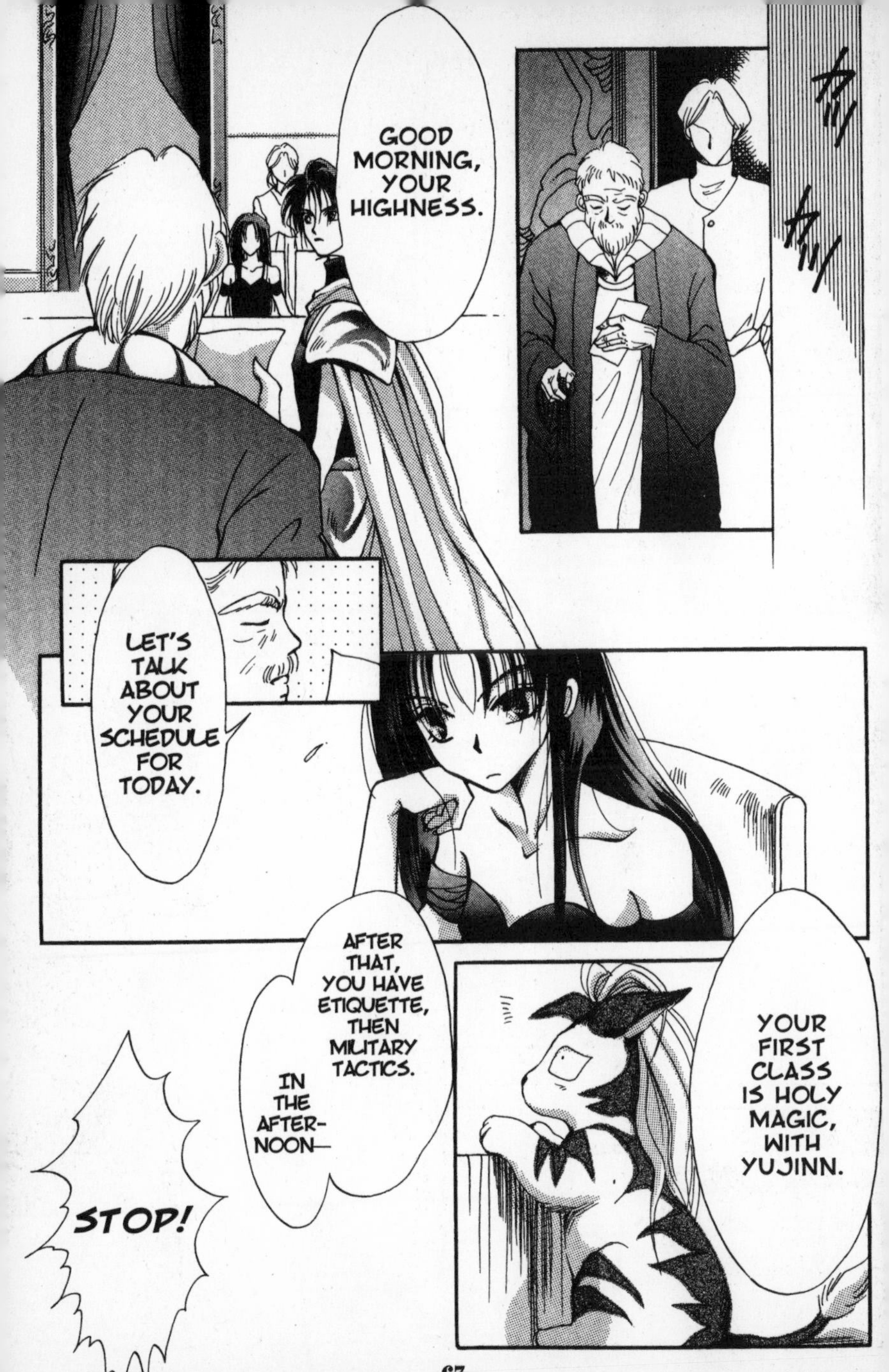
GOOD MORNING, YOUR HIGHNESS.
LET'S TALK ABOUT YOUR SCHEDULE FOR TODAY.
YOUR FIRST CLASS IS HOLY MAGIC, WITH YUJINN.
AFTER THAT, YOU HAVE ETIQUETTE, THEN MILITARY TACTICS.
IN THE AFTER-NOON—
STOP!

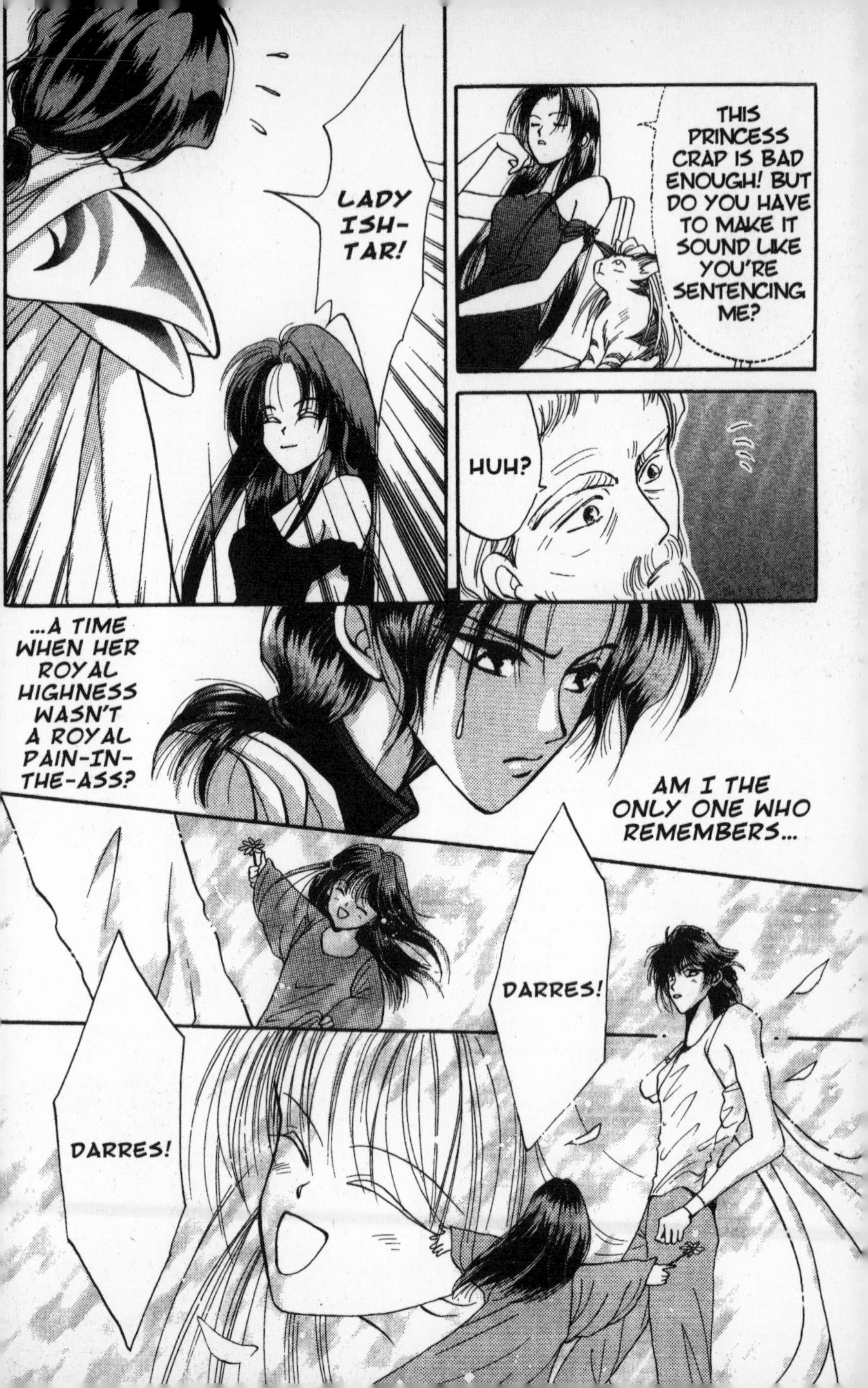
THIS PRINCESS CRAP IS BAD ENOUGH! BUT DO YOU HAVE TO MAKE IT SOUND LIKE YOU'RE SENTENCING ME?
HUH?
LADY ISH-TAR!
AM I THE ONLY ONE WHO REMEMBERS...
...A TIME WHEN HER ROYAL HIGHNESS WASN'T A ROYAL PAIN-IN-THE-ASS?
DARRES!
DARRES!

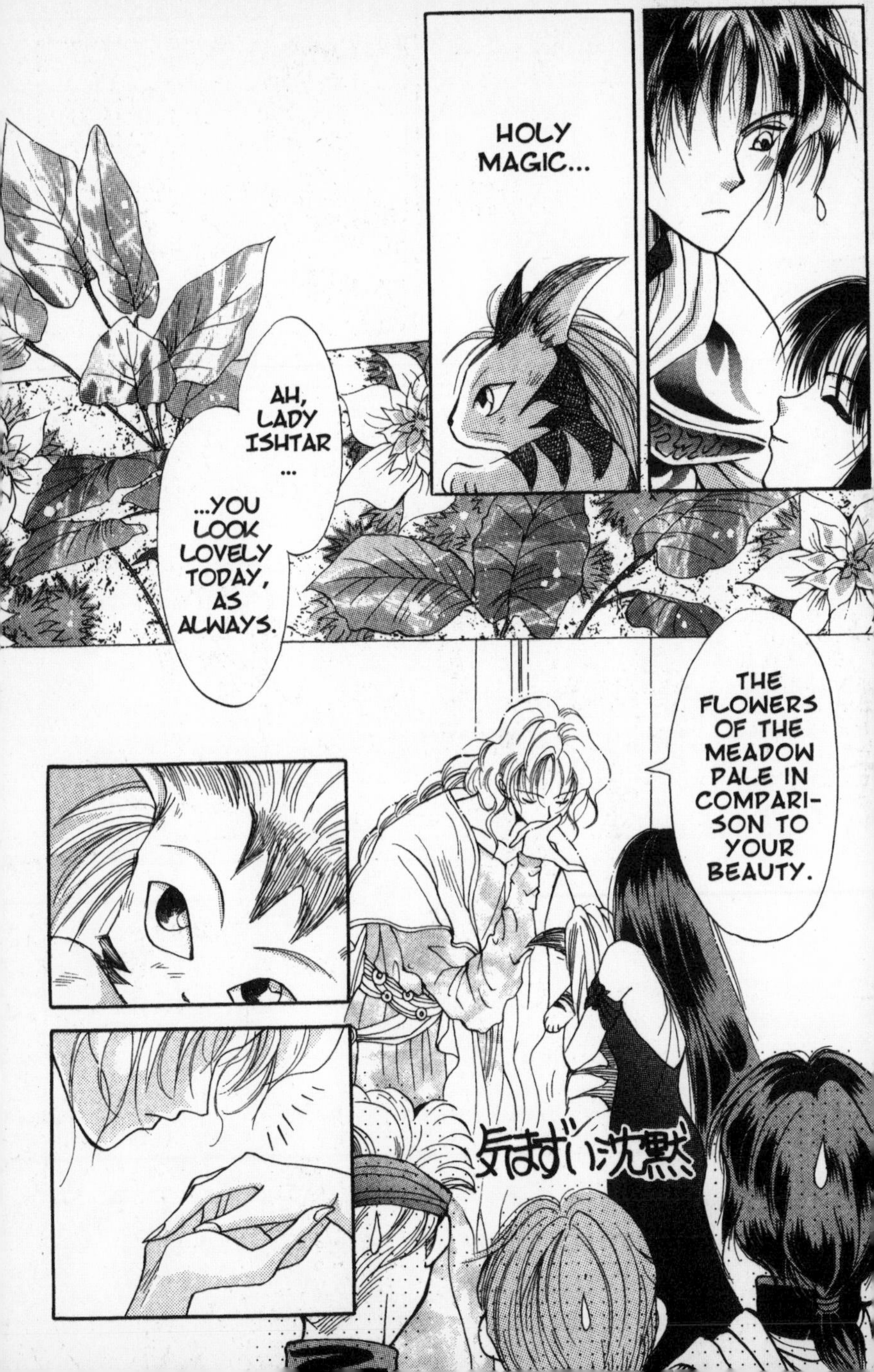
HOLY MAGIC...
AH, LADY ISHTAR ...
...YOU LOOK LOVELY TODAY, AS ALWAYS.
THE FLOWERS OF THE MEADOW PALE IN COMPARI-SON TO YOUR BEAUTY.
気まずい沈黙

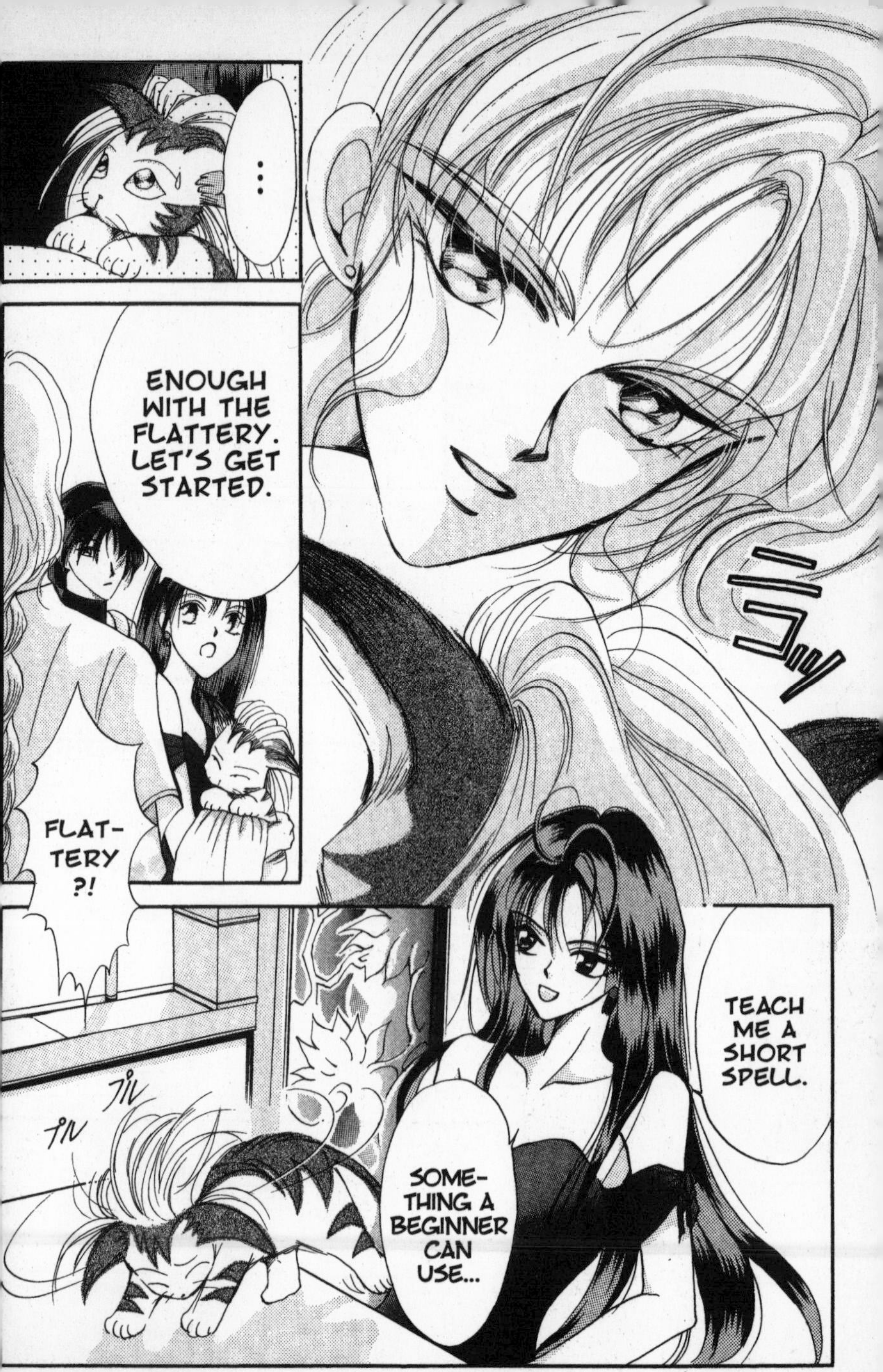
ニコッ
...
ENOUGH WITH THE FLATTERY. LET'S GET STARTED.
FLAT-TERY?!
TEACH ME A SHORT SPELL.
SOME-THING A BEGINNER CAN USE...
プル
プル

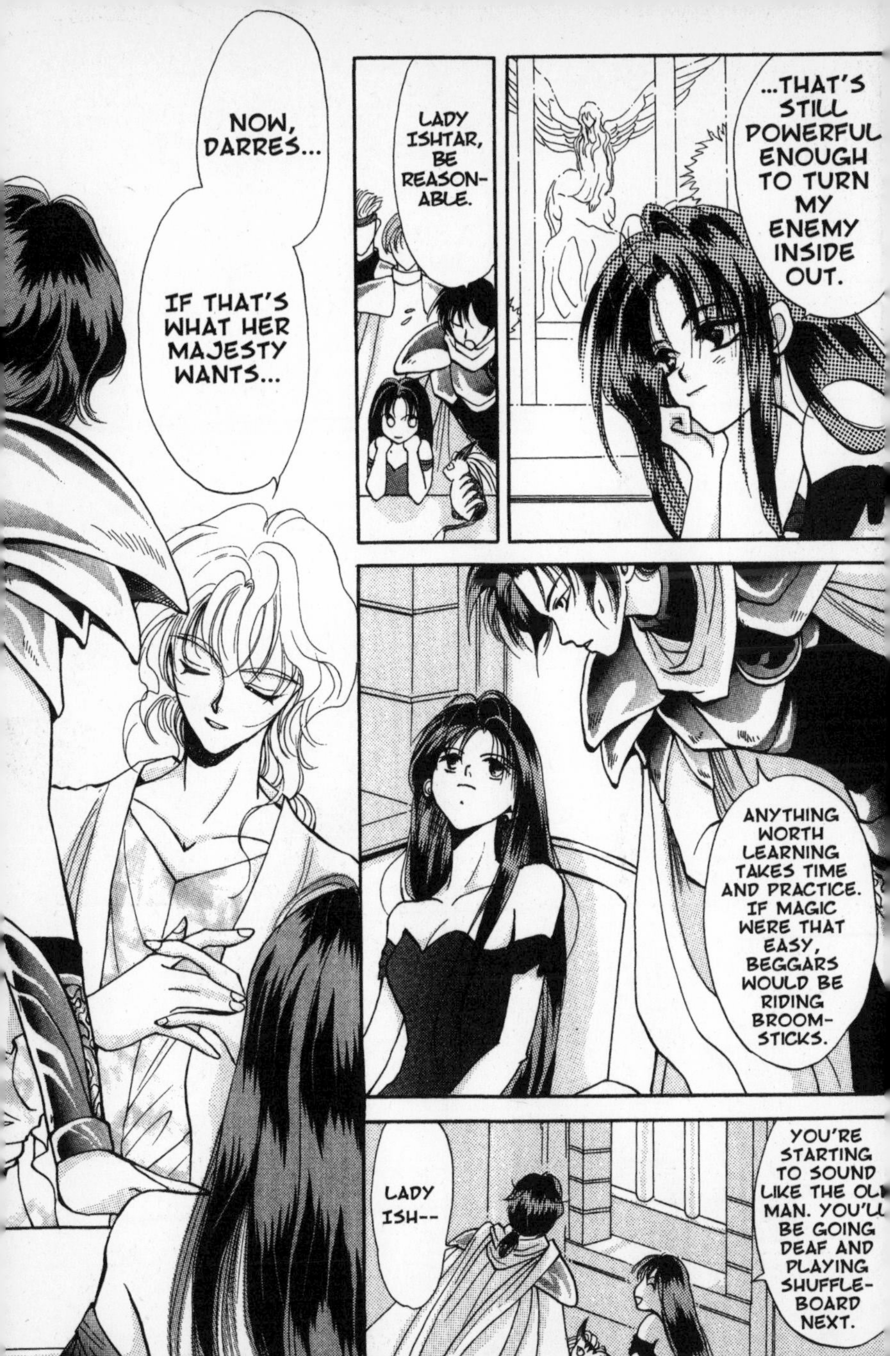
...THAT'S STILL POWERFUL ENOUGH TO TURN MY ENEMY INSIDE OUT.
LADY ISHTAR, BE REASONABLE.
ANYTHING WORTH LEARNING TAKES TIME AND PRACTICE. IF MAGIC WERE THAT EASY, BEGGARS WOULD BE RIDING BROOMSTICKS.
YOU'RE STARTING TO SOUND LIKE THE OL MAN. YOU'L BE GOING DEAF AND PLAYING SHUFFLEBOARD NEXT.
LADY ISH--
NOW, DARRES...
IF THAT'S WHAT HER MAJESTY WANTS...

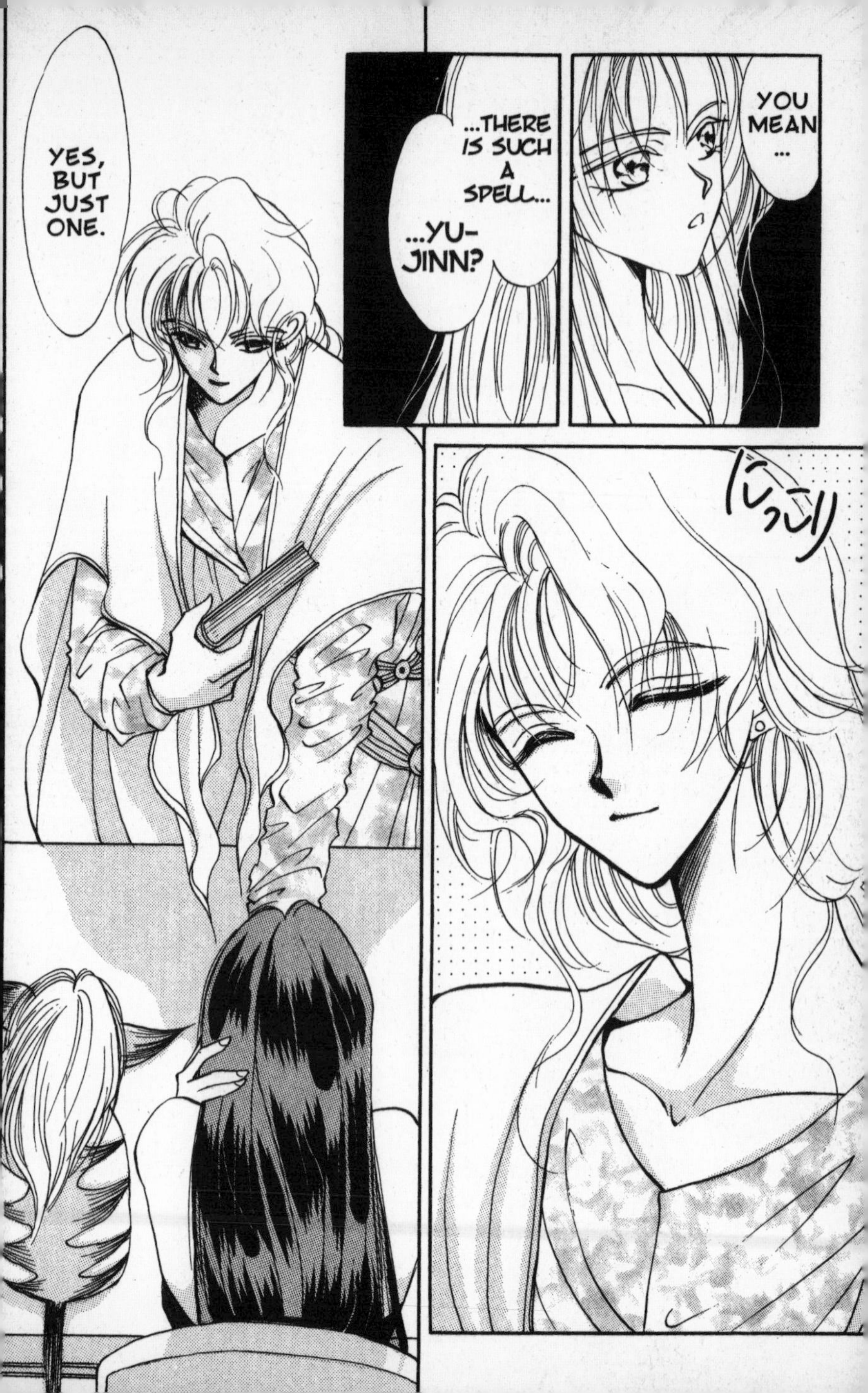
YOU MEAN ...
...THERE IS SUCH A SPELL...
...YU-JINN?
YES, BUT JUST ONE.

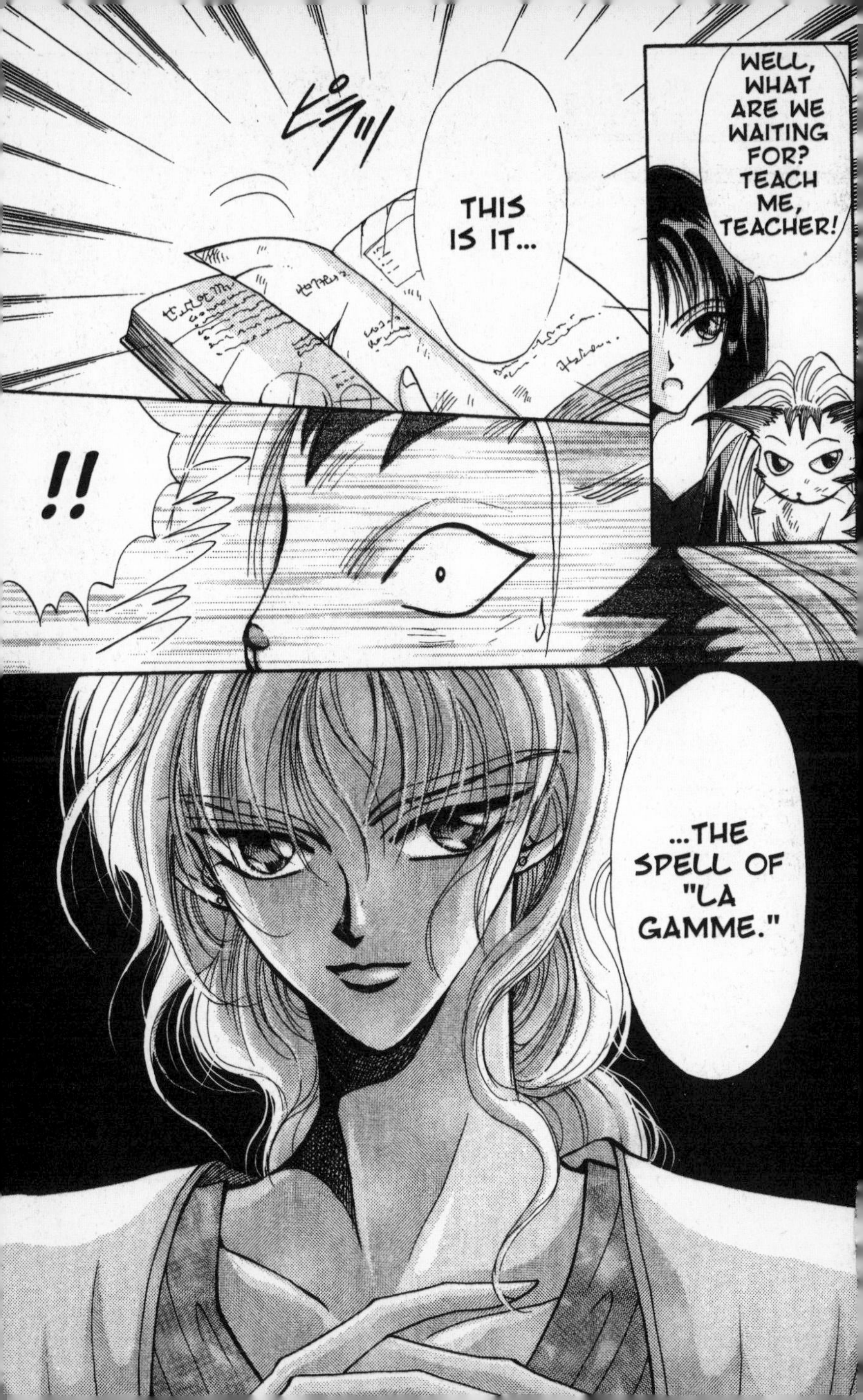
WELL, WHAT ARE WE WAITING FOR? TEACH ME, TEACHER!
ピラッ
THIS IS IT...
!!
...THE SPELL OF "LA GAMME."

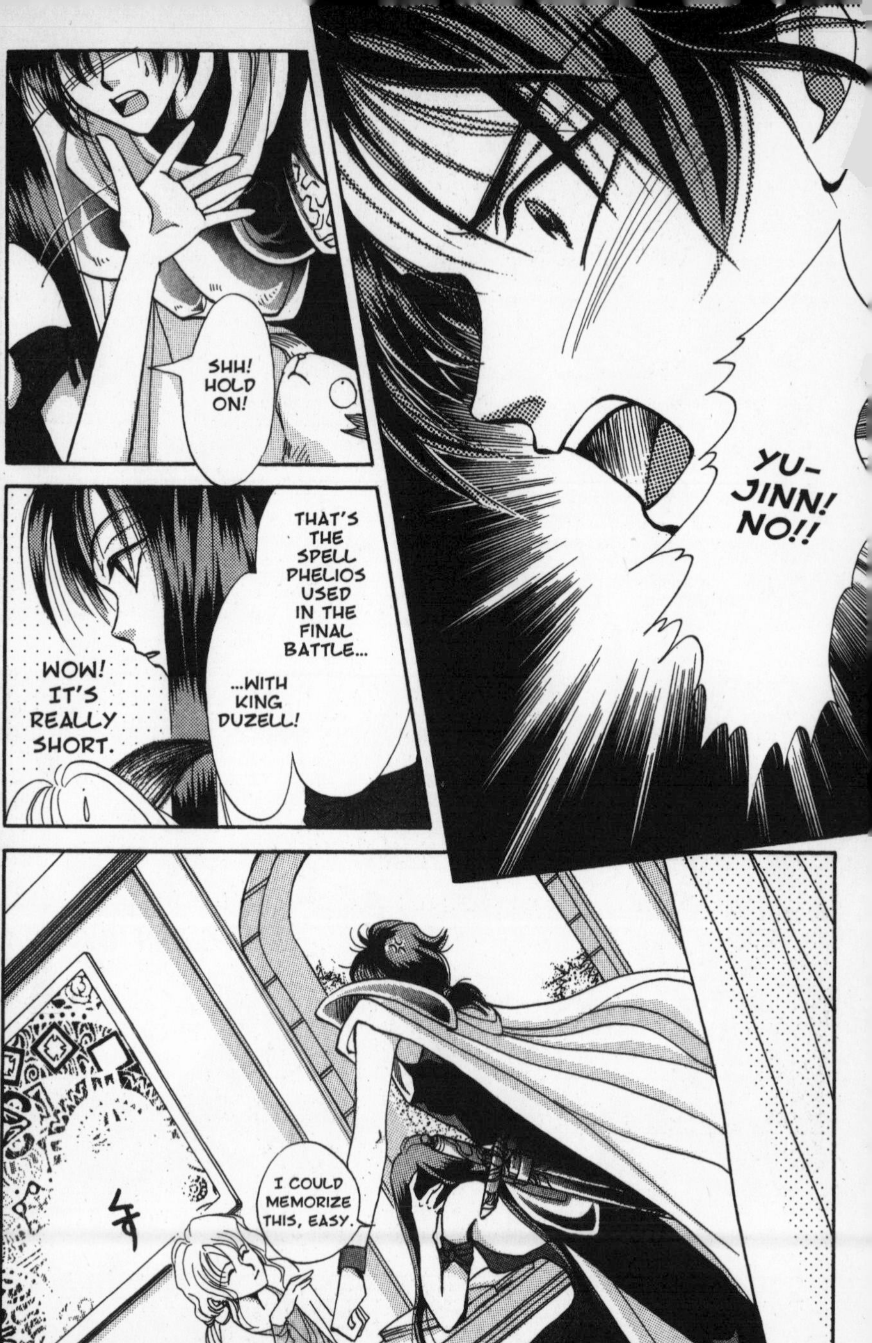
YU-JINN! NO!!
SHH! HOLD ON!
THAT'S THE SPELL PHELIOS USED IN THE FINAL BATTLE...
...WITH KING DUZELL!
WOW! IT'S REALLY SHORT.
I COULD MEMORIZE THIS, EASY.
くす

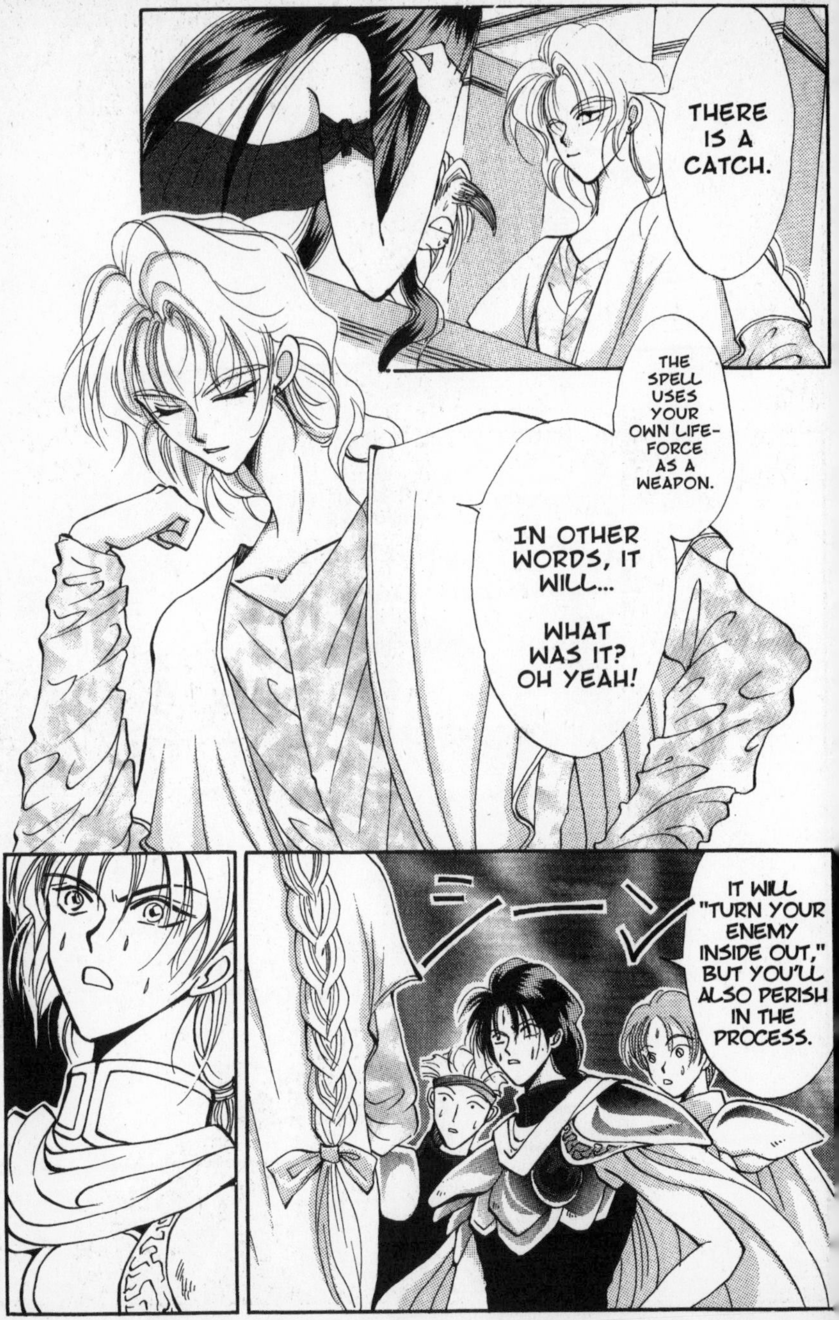
THERE IS A CATCH.
THE SPELL USES YOUR OWN LIFE-FORCE AS A WEAPON.
IN OTHER WORDS, IT WILL...
WHAT WAS IT? OH YEAH!
IT WILL "TURN YOUR ENEMY INSIDE OUT," BUT YOU'LL ALSO PERISH IN THE PROCESS.

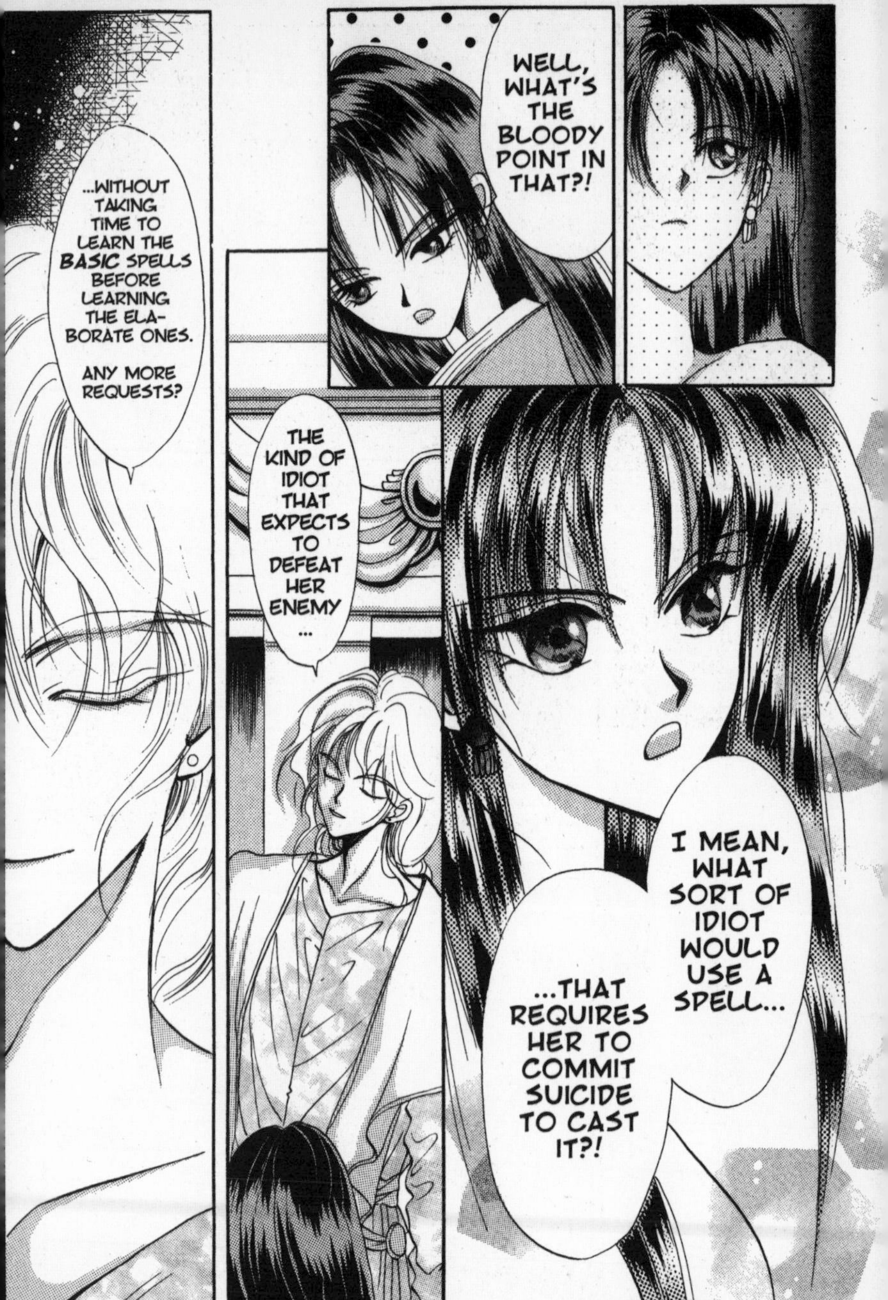

WELL, WHAT'S THE BLOODY POINT IN THAT?!
I MEAN, WHAT SORT OF IDIOT WOULD USE A SPELL...
...THAT REQUIRES HER TO COMMIT SUICIDE TO CAST IT?!
THE KIND OF IDIOT THAT EXPECTS TO DEFEAT HER ENEMY ...
...WITHOUT TAKING TIME TO LEARN THE BASIC SPELLS BEFORE LEARNING THE ELABORATE ONES.
ANY MORE REQUESTS?

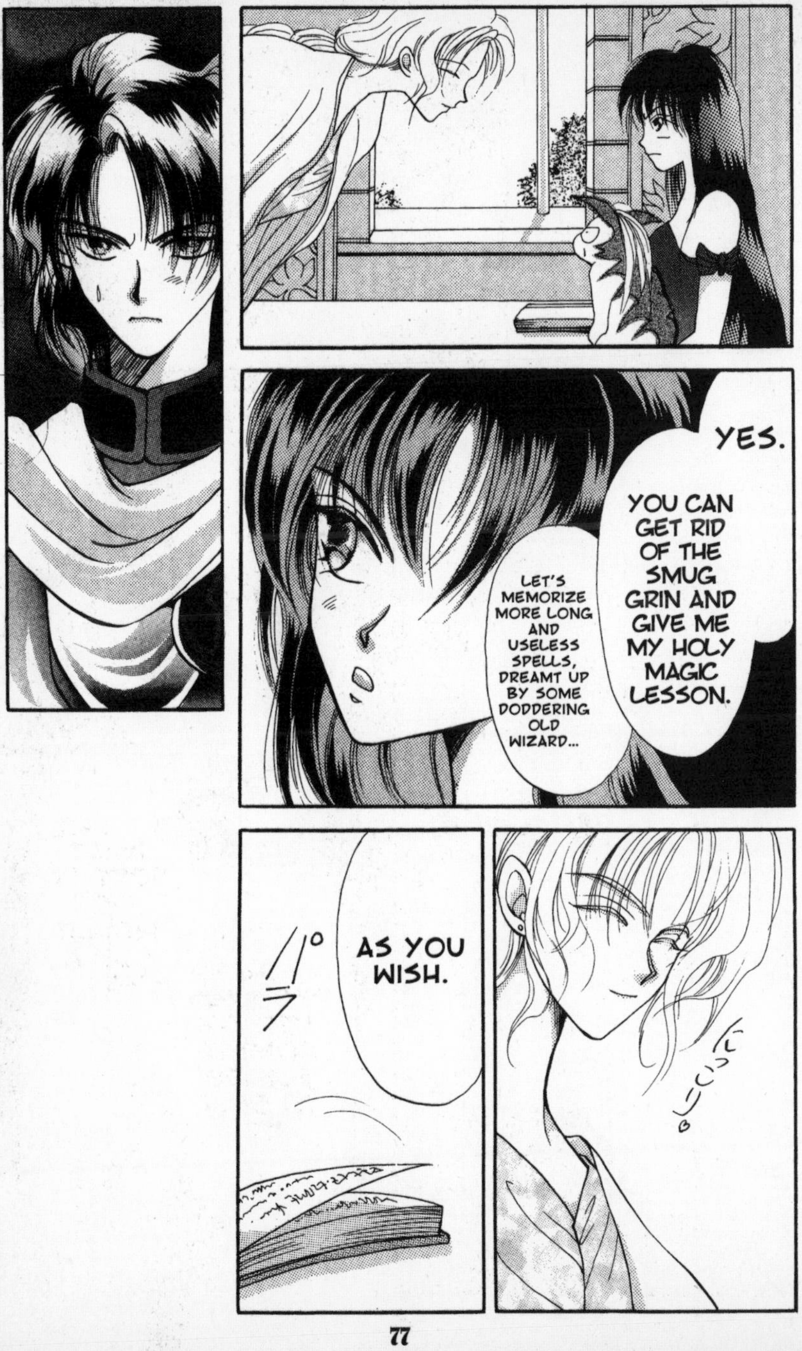
YES.
YOU CAN GET RID OF THE SMUG GRIN AND GIVE ME MY HOLY MAGIC LESSON.
LET'S MEMORIZE MORE LONG AND USELESS SPELLS, DREAMT UP BY SOME DODDERING OLD WIZARD...
AS YOU WISH.

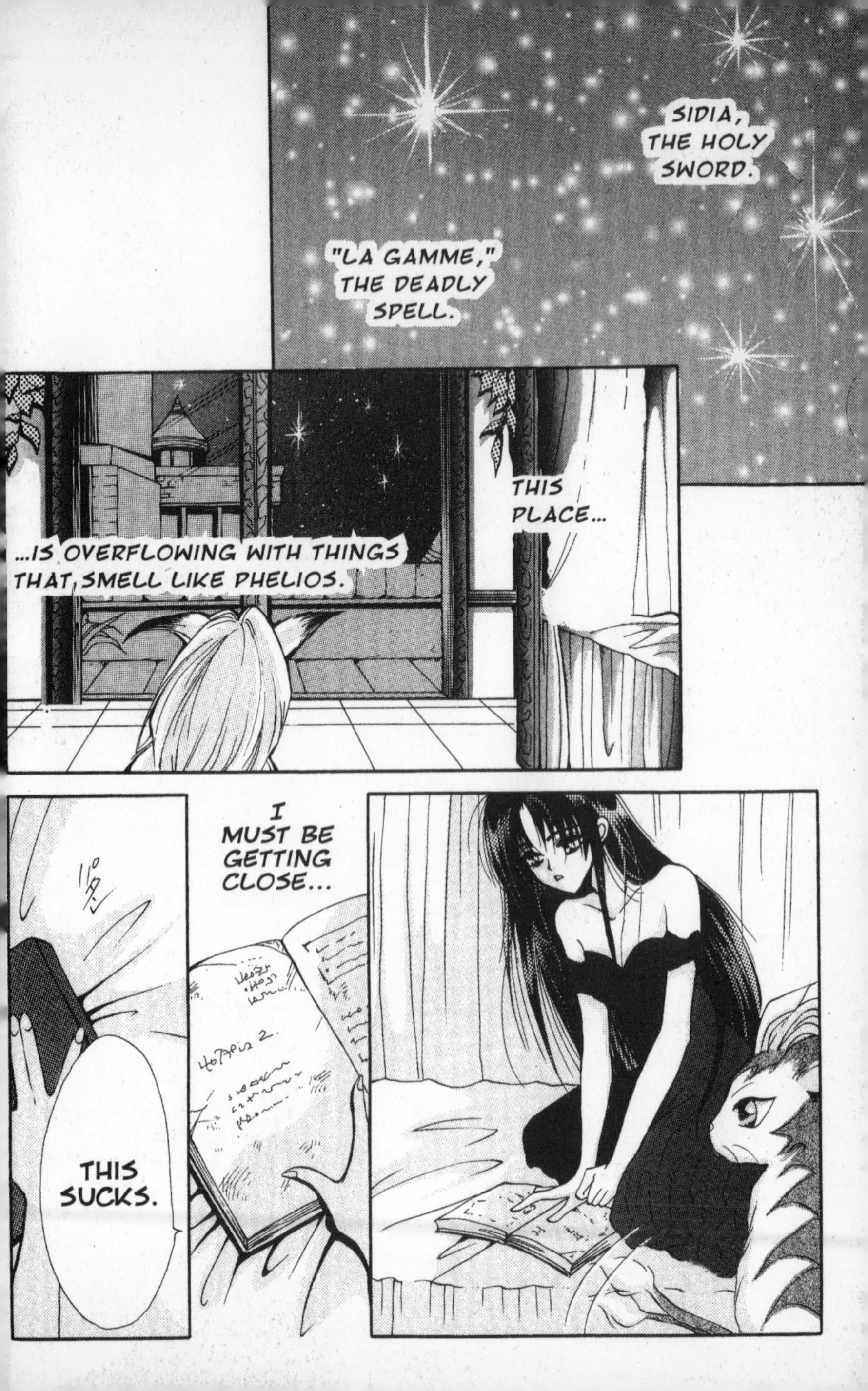
SIDIA, THE HOLY SWORD.
"LA GAMME," THE DEADLY SPELL.
THIS PLACE...
...IS OVERFLOWING WITH THINGS THAT SMELL LIKE PHELIOS.
I MUST BE GETTING CLOSE...
パタン
THIS SUCKS.

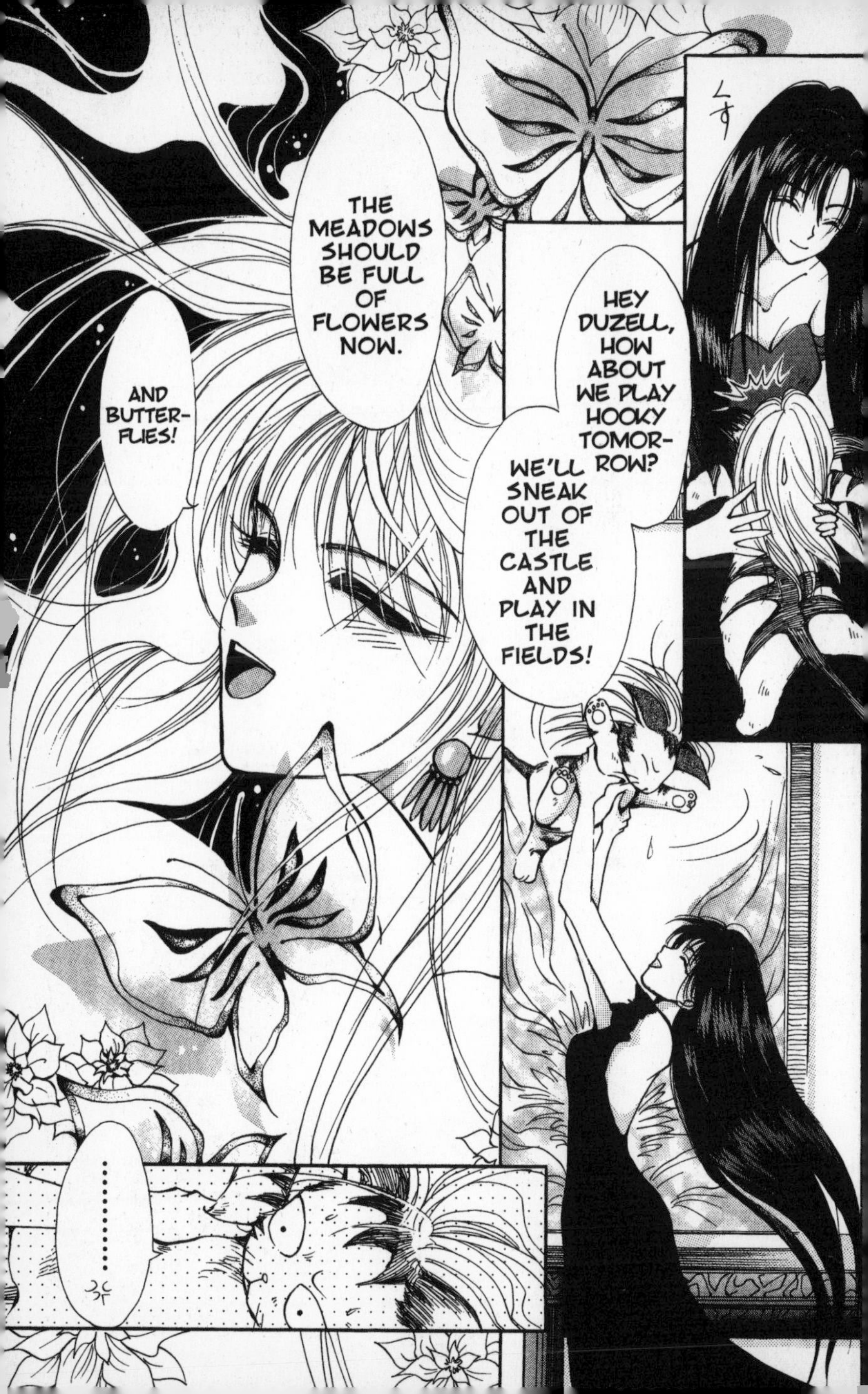
くす
HEY DUZELL, HOW ABOUT WE PLAY HOOKY TOMORROW?
WE'LL SNEAK OUT OF THE CASTLE AND PLAY IN THE FIELDS!
THE MEADOWS SHOULD BE FULL OF FLOWERS NOW.
AND BUTTERFLIES!
....

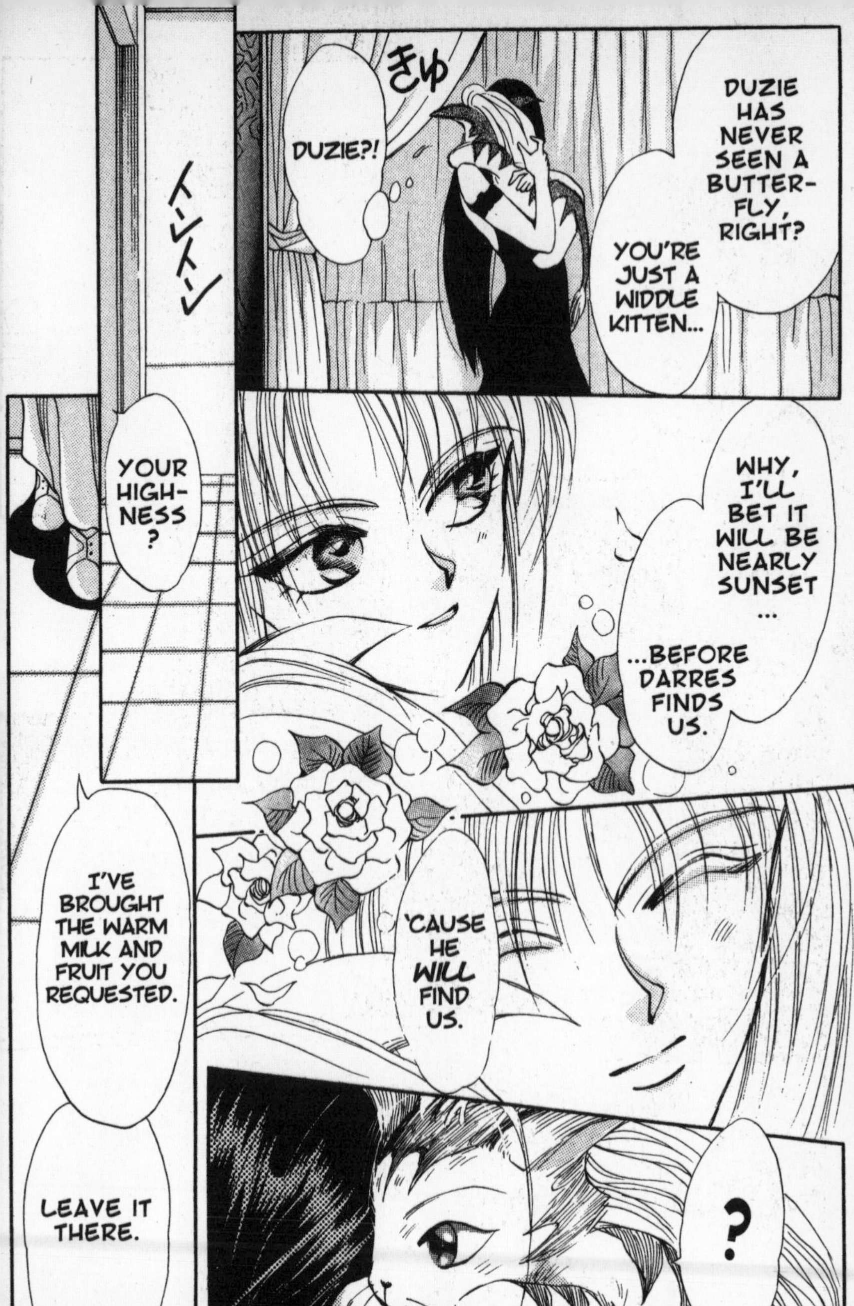
DUZIE HAS NEVER SEEN A BUTTER-FLY, RIGHT?
YOU'RE JUST A WIDDLE KITTEN...
きゅ
DUZIE?!
トントン
WHY, I'LL BET IT WILL BE NEARLY SUNSET...
...BEFORE DARRES FINDS US.
YOUR HIGH-NESS?
'CAUSE HE WILL FIND US.
I'VE BROUGHT THE WARM MILK AND FRUIT YOU REQUESTED.
?
LEAVE IT THERE.

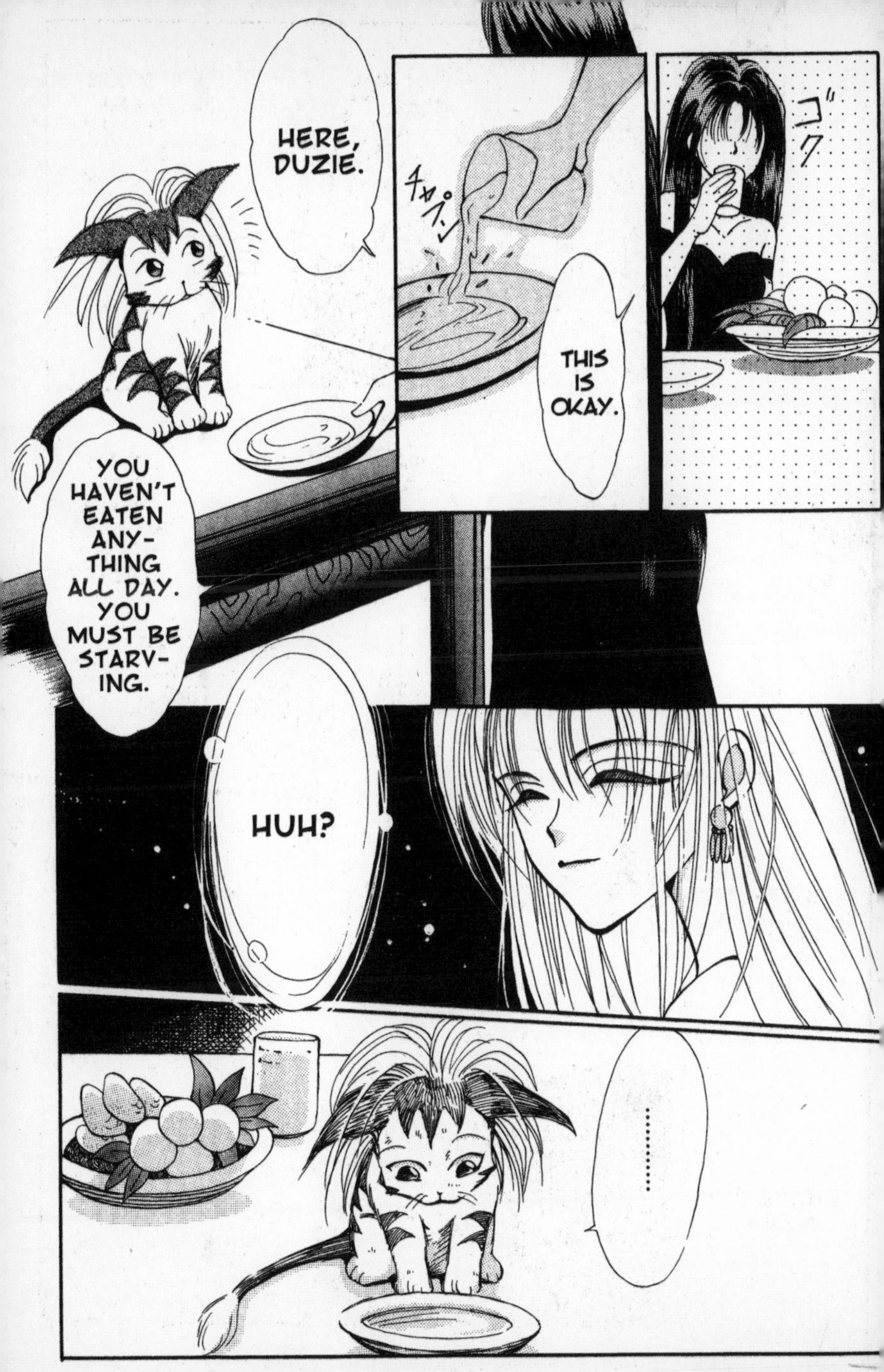
ゴク
チャプン
THIS IS OKAY.
HERE, DUZIE.
YOU HAVEN'T EATEN ANYTHING ALL DAY. YOU MUST BE STARVING.
HUH?
......

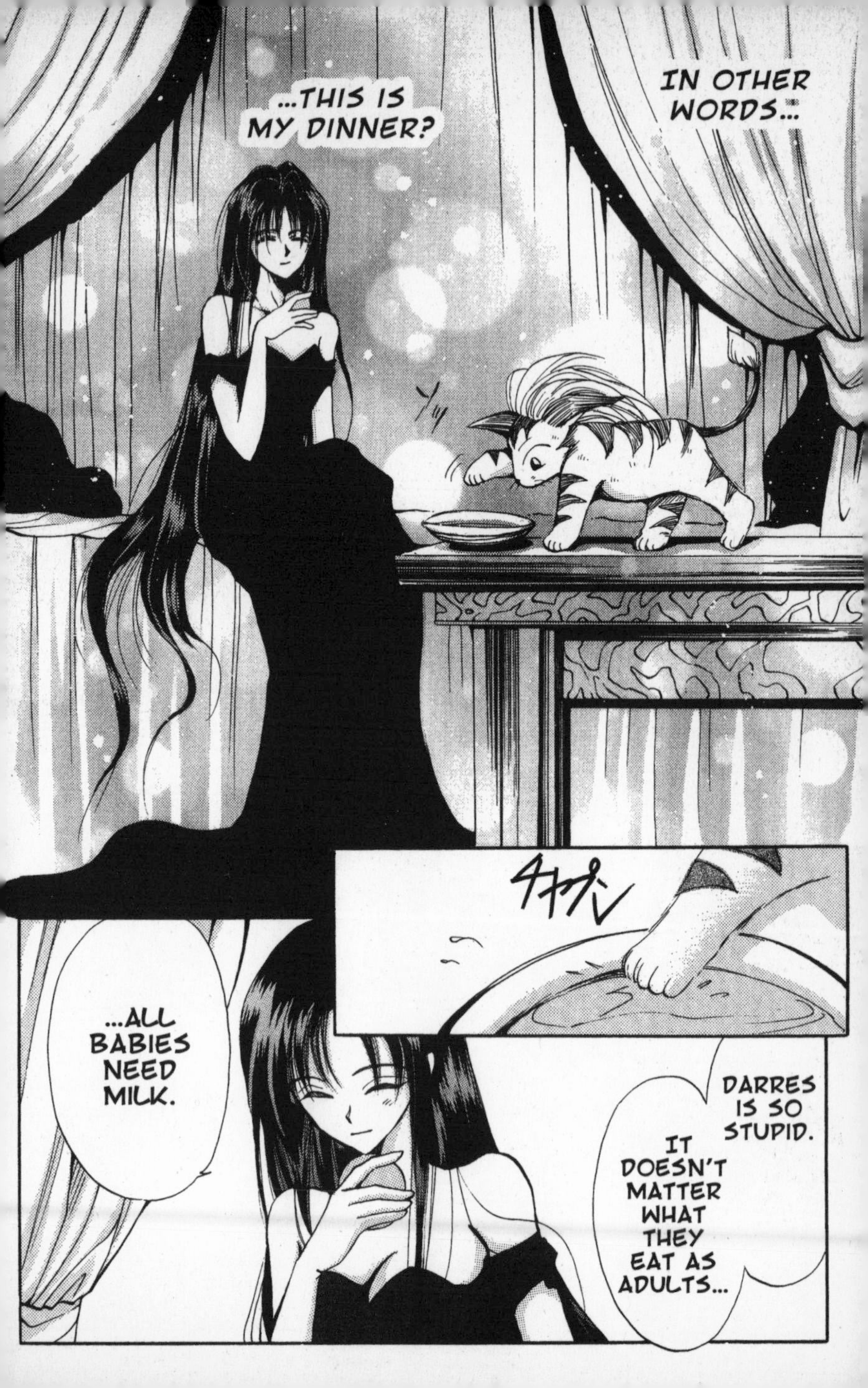
IN OTHER WORDS...
...THIS IS MY DINNER?
ソッ
チャプン
DARRES IS SO STUPID.
IT DOESN'T MATTER WHAT THEY EAT AS ADULTS...
...ALL BABIES NEED MILK.

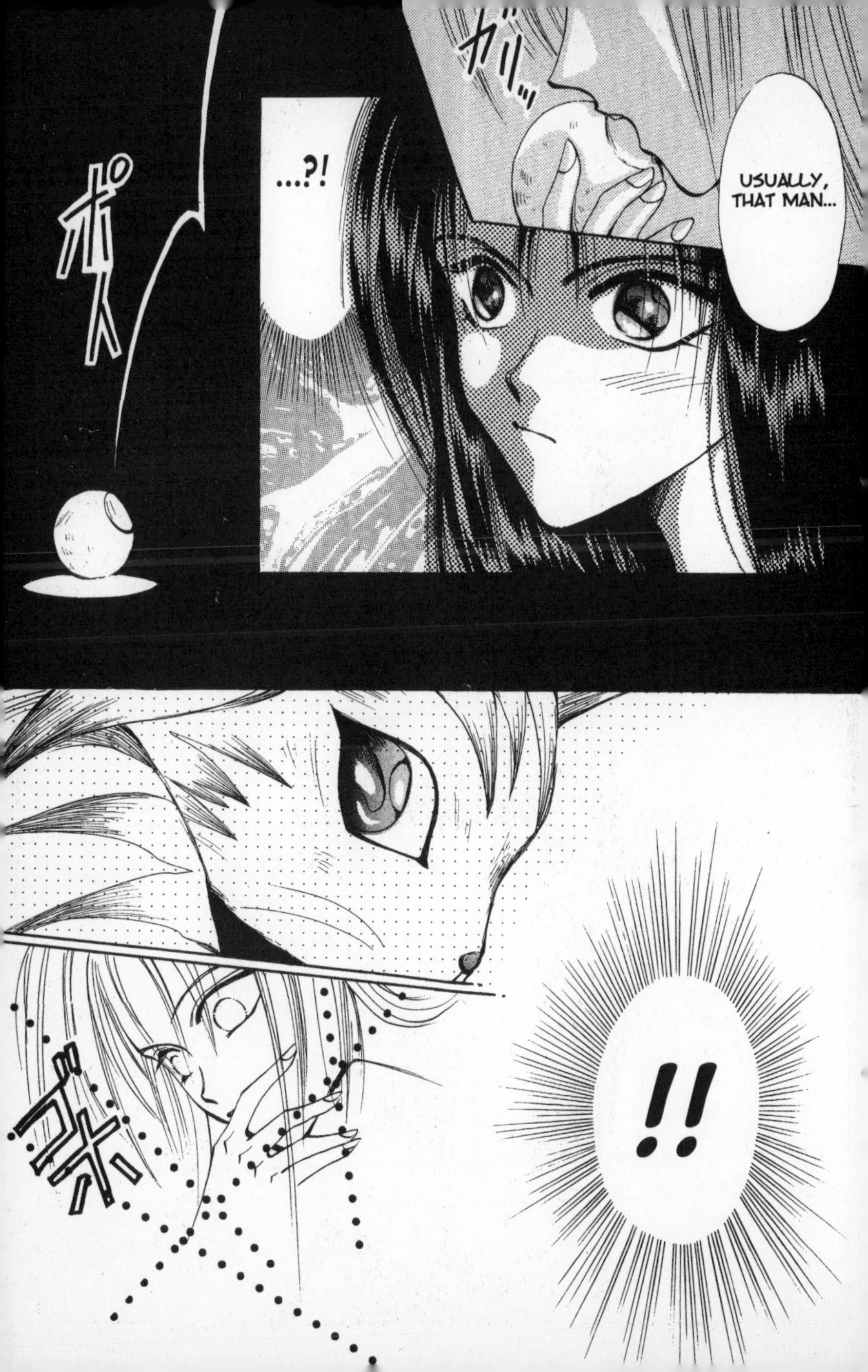
ガリッ
USUALLY, THAT MAN...
...?!
ポイ
!!

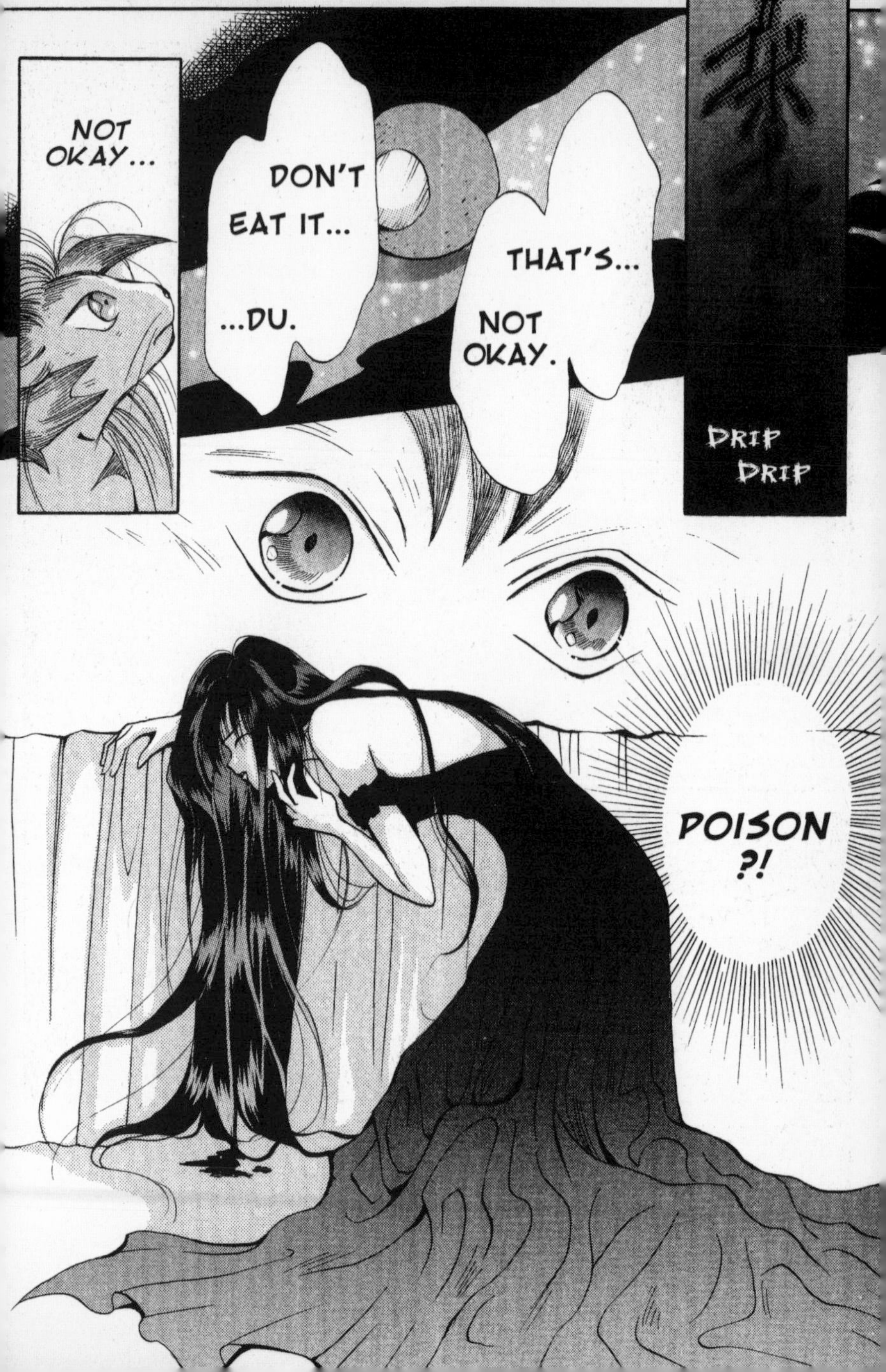
DRIP DRIP
THAT'S... NOT OKAY.
DON'T EAT IT... ...DU.
NOT OKAY...
POISON ?!

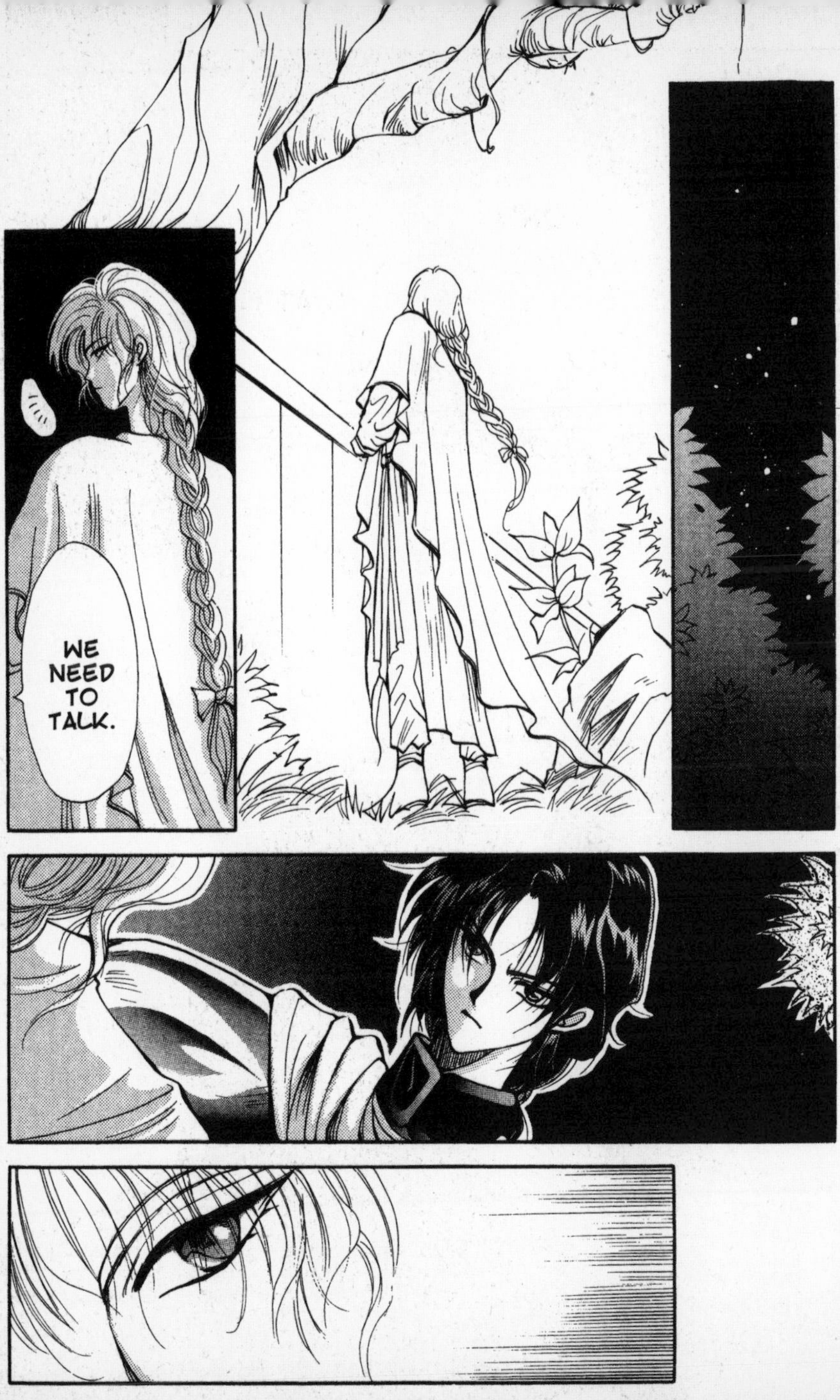
...
WE NEED TO TALK.

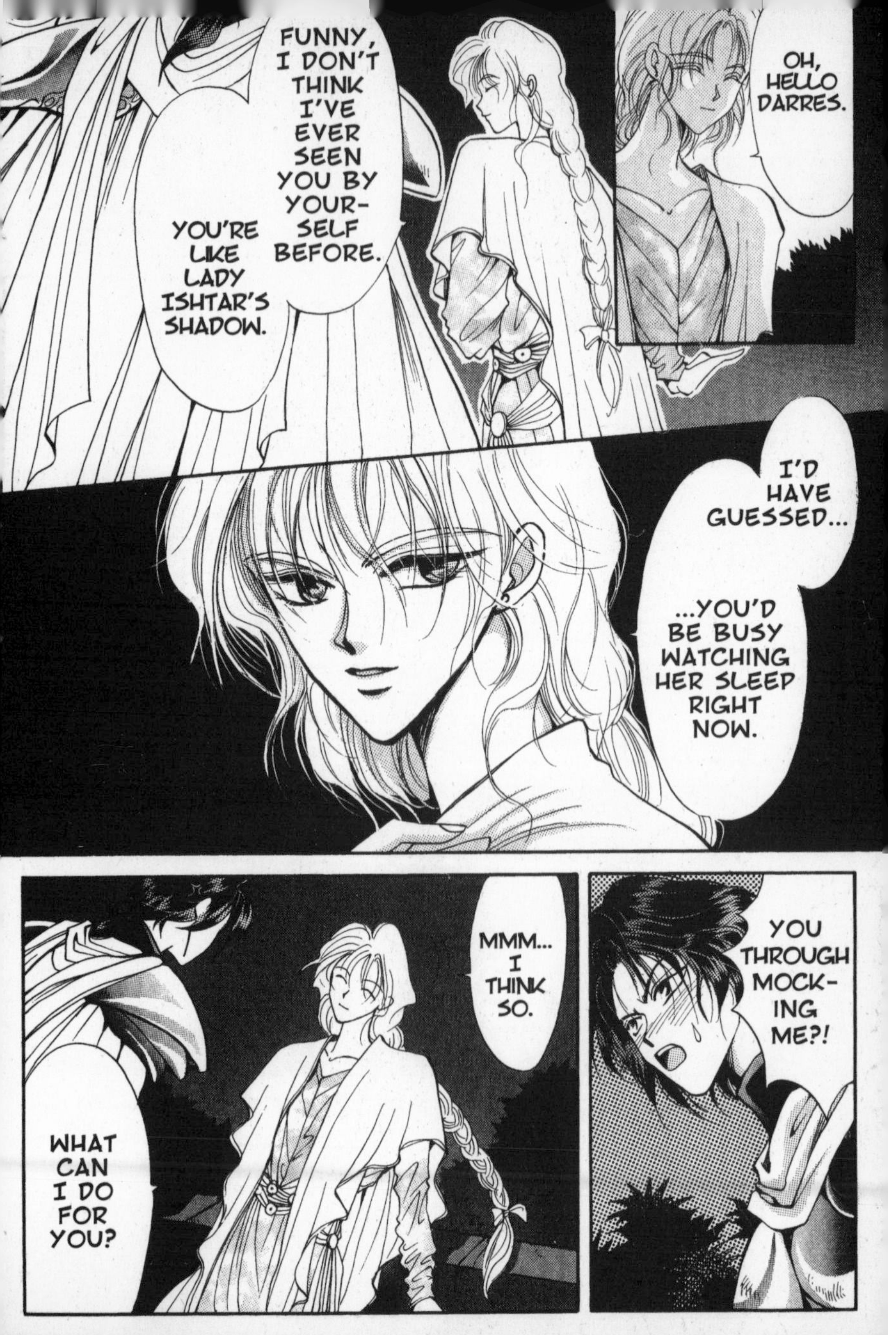
OH, HELLO DARRES.
FUNNY, I DON'T THINK I'VE EVER SEEN YOU BY YOUR-SELF BEFORE.
YOU'RE LIKE LADY ISHTAR'S SHADOW.
I'D HAVE GUESSED...
...YOU'D BE BUSY WATCHING HER SLEEP RIGHT NOW.
YOU THROUGH MOCK-ING ME?!
MMM... I THINK SO.
WHAT CAN I DO FOR YOU?

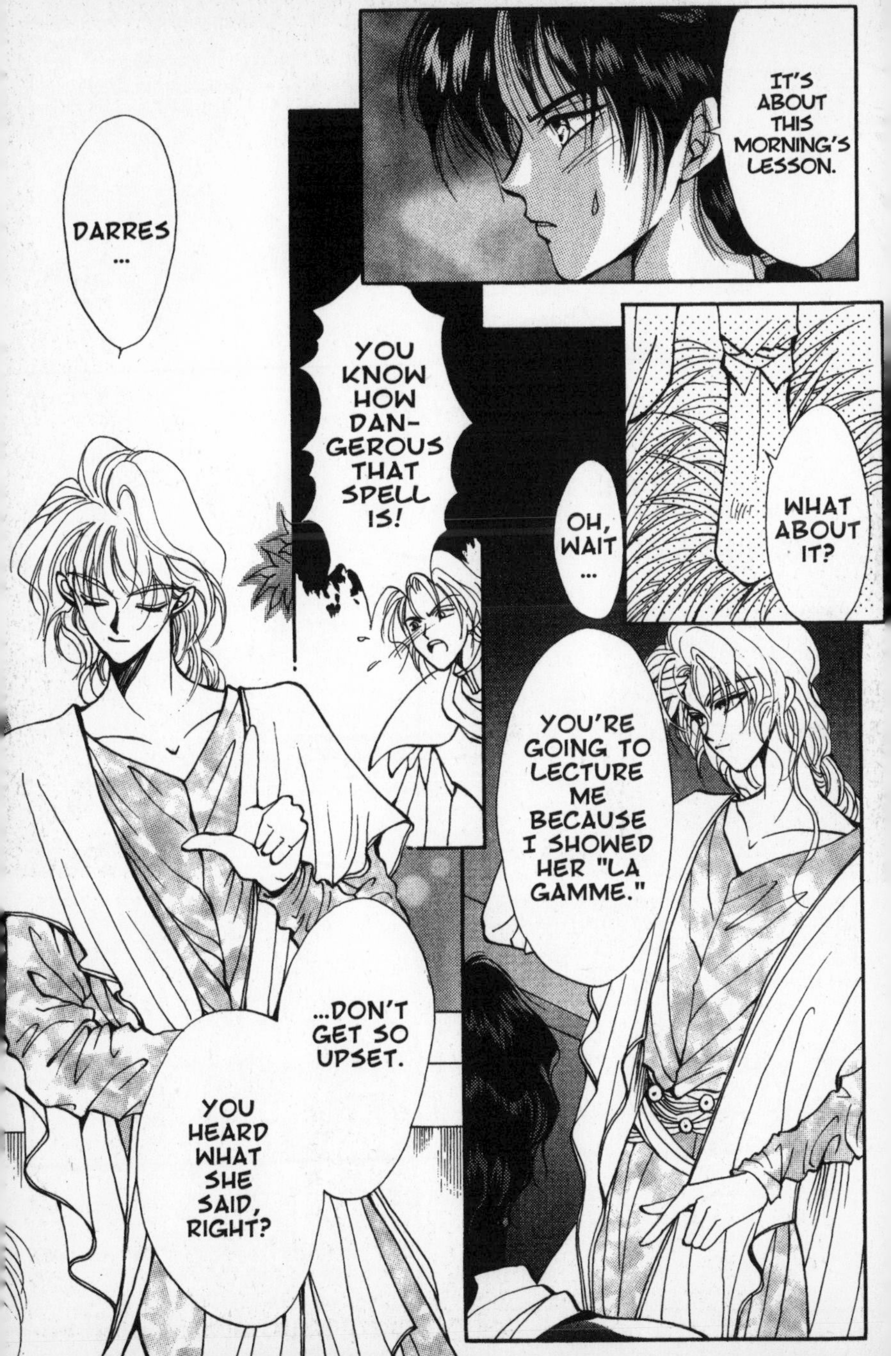
IT'S ABOUT THIS MORNING'S LESSON.
WHAT ABOUT IT?
OH, WAIT ...
YOU KNOW HOW DAN-GEROUS THAT SPELL IS!
YOU'RE GOING TO LECTURE ME BECAUSE I SHOWED HER "LA GAMME."
DARRES ...
...DON'T GET SO UPSET.
YOU HEARD WHAT SHE SAID, RIGHT?

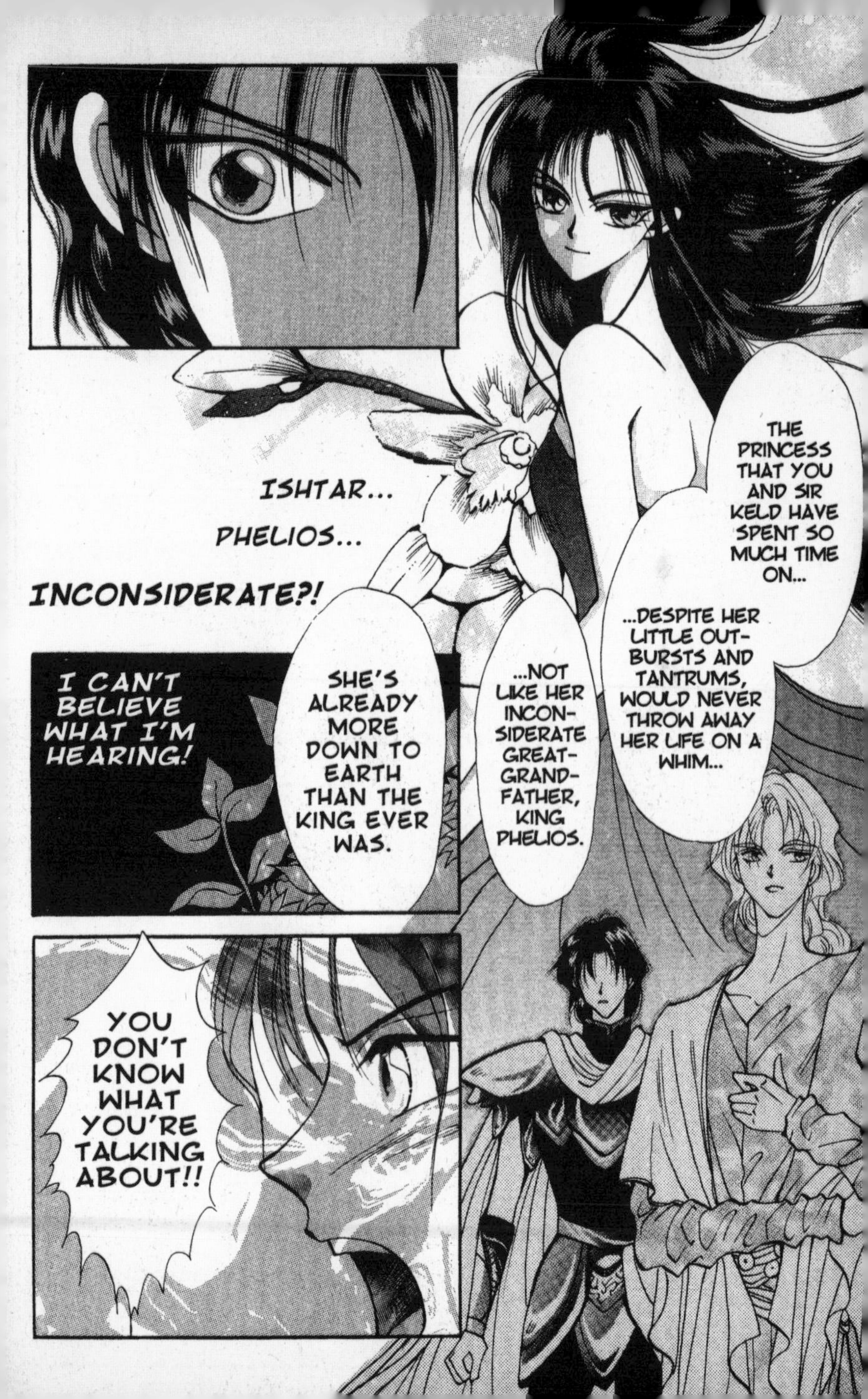
THE PRINCESS THAT YOU AND SIR KELD HAVE SPENT SO MUCH TIME ON...
...DESPITE HER LITTLE OUT-BURSTS AND TANTRUMS, WOULD NEVER THROW AWAY HER LIFE ON A WHIM...
...NOT LIKE HER INCON-SIDERATE GREAT-GRAND-FATHER, KING PHELIOS.
SHE'S ALREADY MORE DOWN TO EARTH THAN THE KING EVER WAS.
ISHTAR...
PHELIOS...
INCONSIDERATE?!
I CAN'T BELIEVE WHAT I'M HEARING!
YOU DON'T KNOW WHAT YOU'RE TALKING ABOUT!!

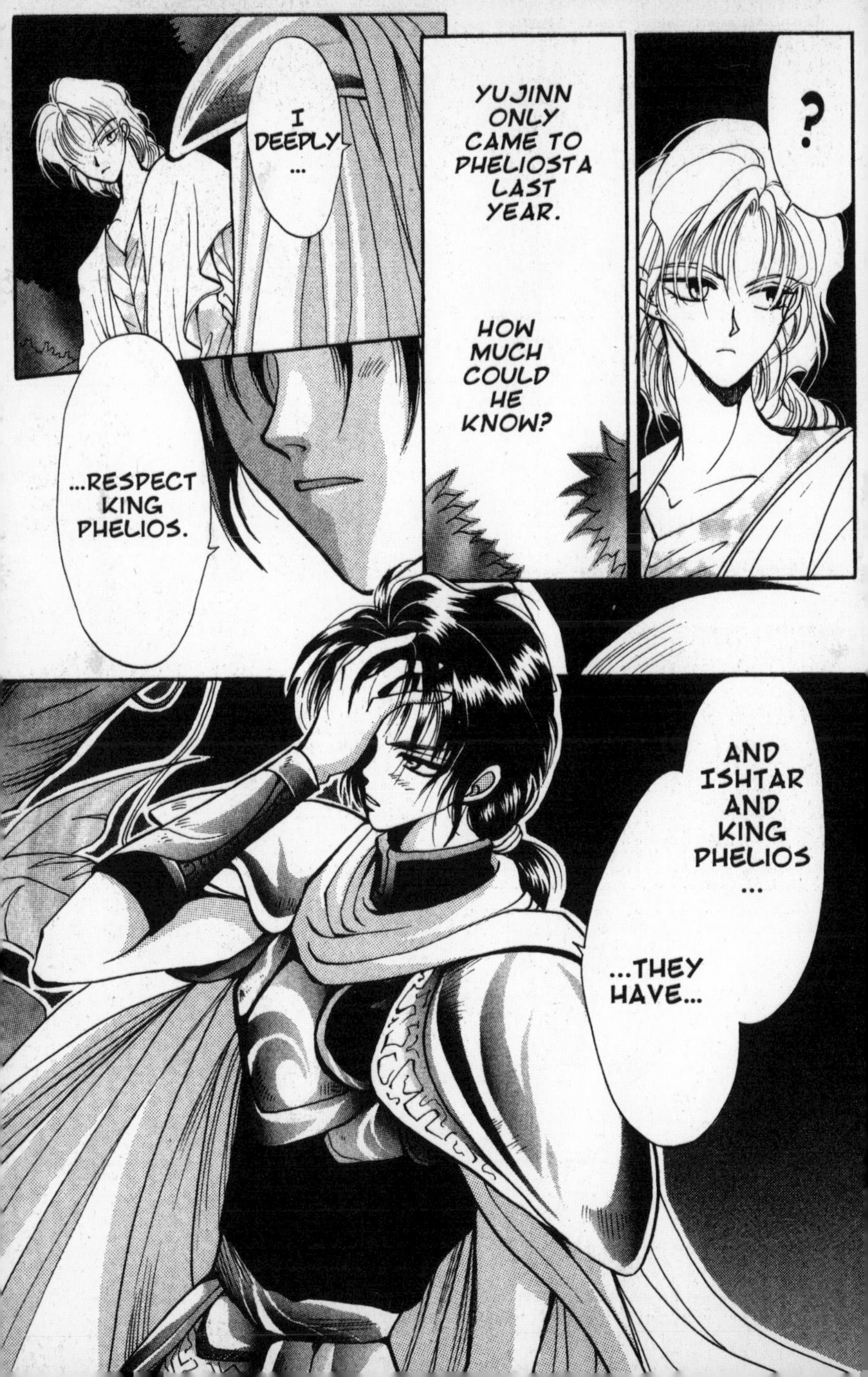
?
YUJINN ONLY CAME TO PHELIOSTA LAST YEAR.
HOW MUCH COULD HE KNOW?
I DEEPLY...
...RESPECT KING PHELIOS.
AND ISHTAR AND KING PHELIOS...
...THEY HAVE...

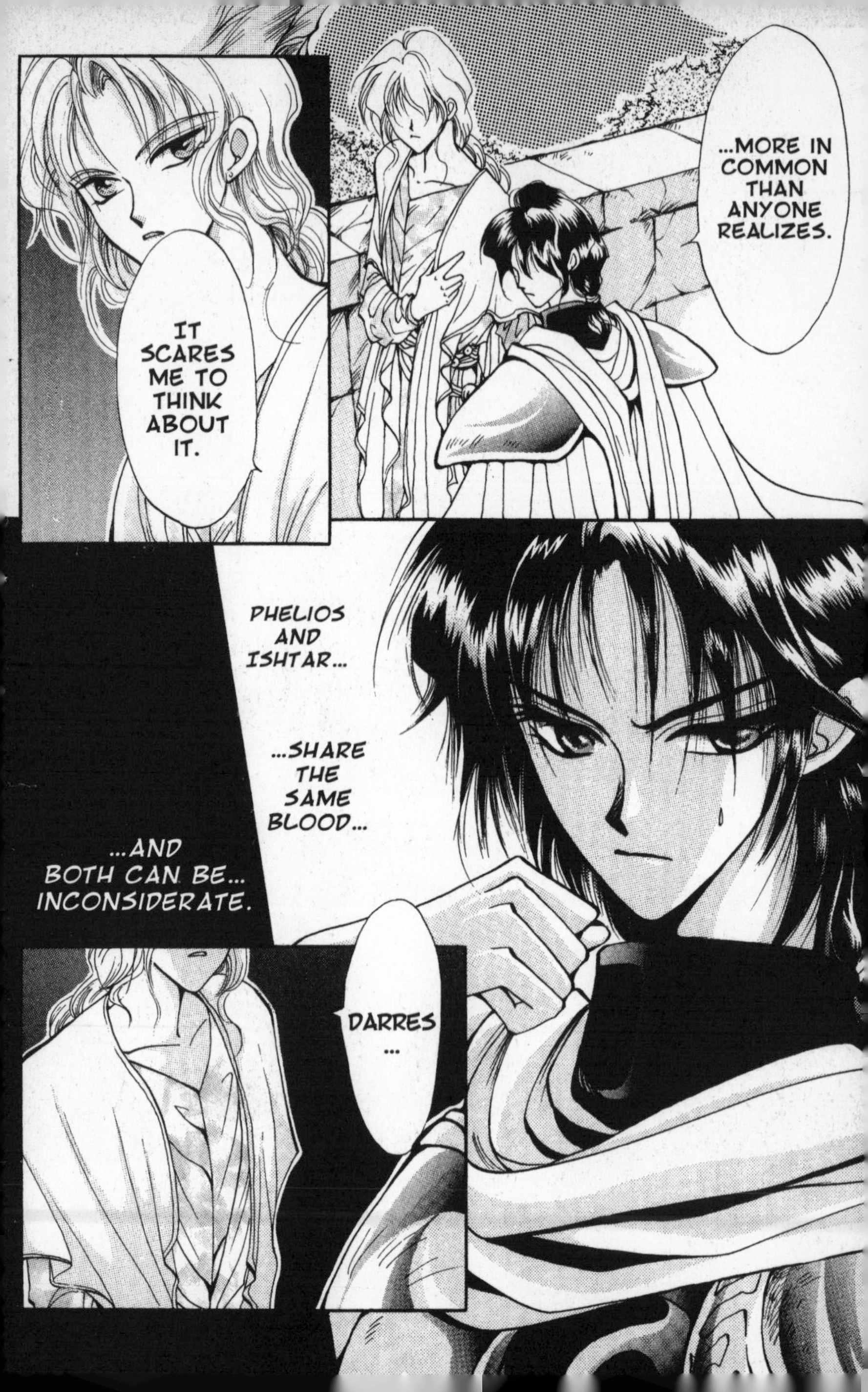
...MORE IN COMMON THAN ANYONE REALIZES.
IT SCARES ME TO THINK ABOUT IT.
PHELIOS AND ISHTAR...
...SHARE THE SAME BLOOD...
...AND BOTH CAN BE... INCONSIDERATE.
DARRES ...

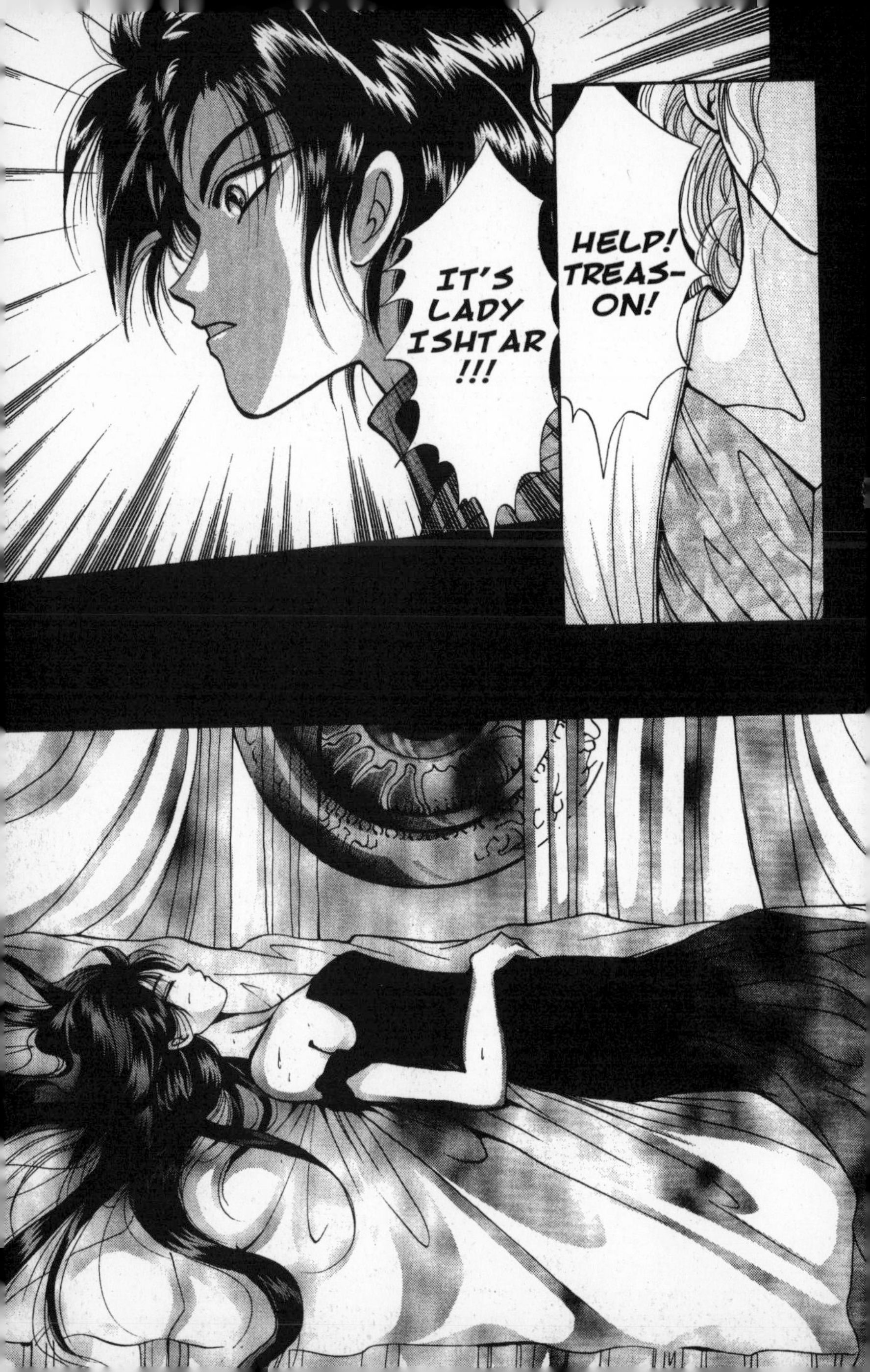
HELP! TREAS-ON!
IT'S LADY ISHTAR!!!

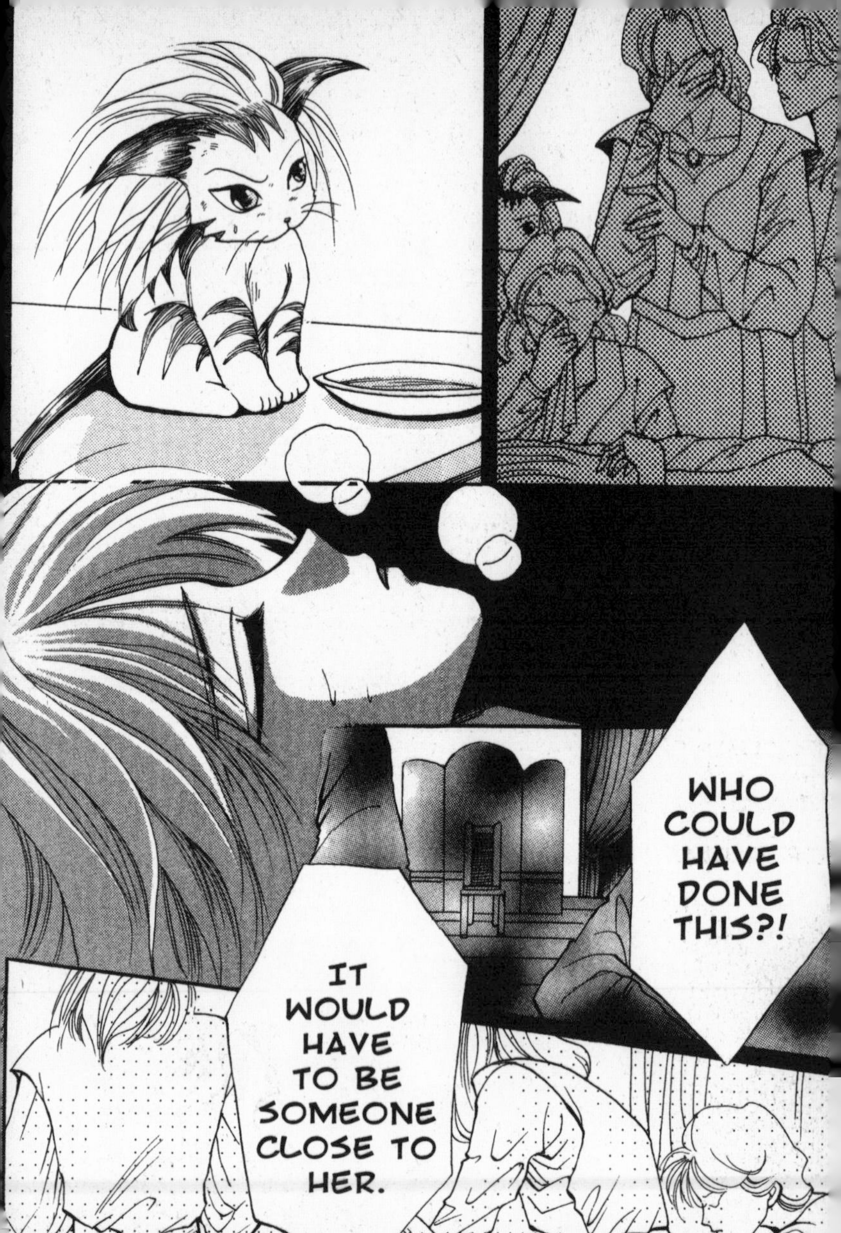
WHO COULD HAVE DONE THIS?!
IT WOULD HAVE TO BE SOMEONE CLOSE TO HER.

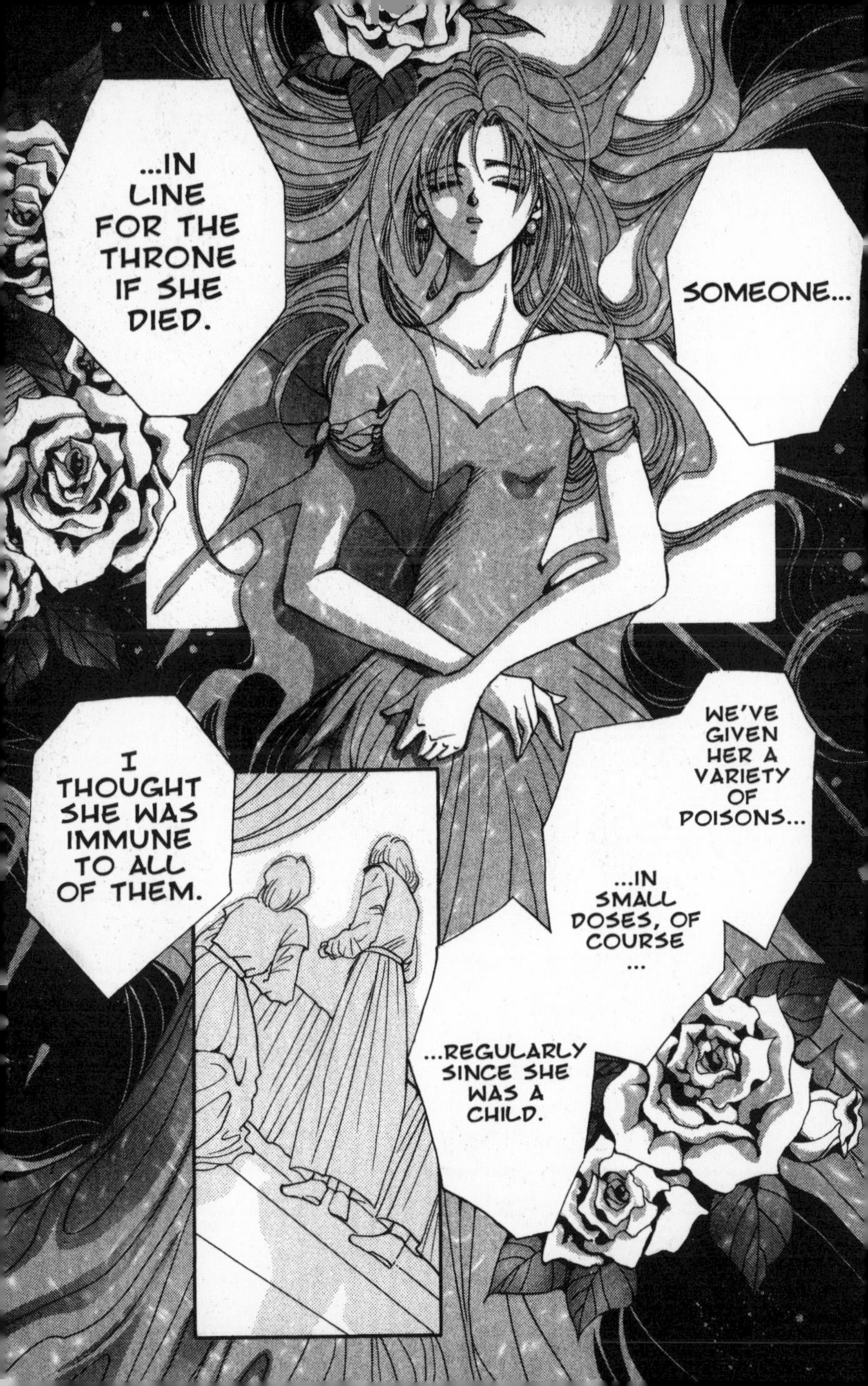
SOMEONE...
...IN LINE FOR THE THRONE IF SHE DIED.
WE'VE GIVEN HER A VARIETY OF POISONS...
...IN SMALL DOSES, OF COURSE ...
...REGULARLY SINCE SHE WAS A CHILD.
I THOUGHT SHE WAS IMMUNE TO ALL OF THEM.

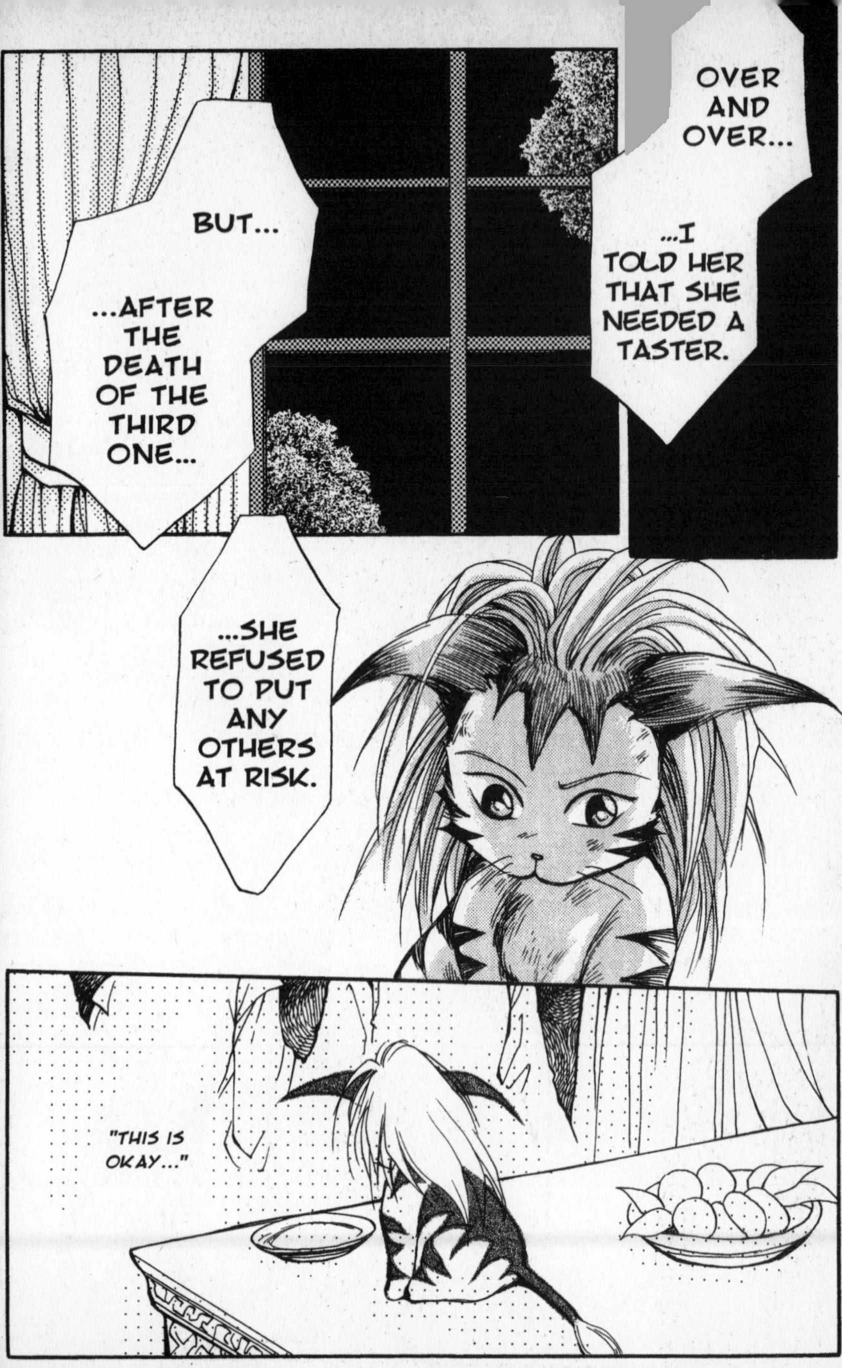
OVER AND OVER...
...I TOLD HER THAT SHE NEEDED A TASTER.
BUT...
...AFTER THE DEATH OF THE THIRD ONE...
...SHE REFUSED TO PUT ANY OTHERS AT RISK.
"THIS IS OKAY..."

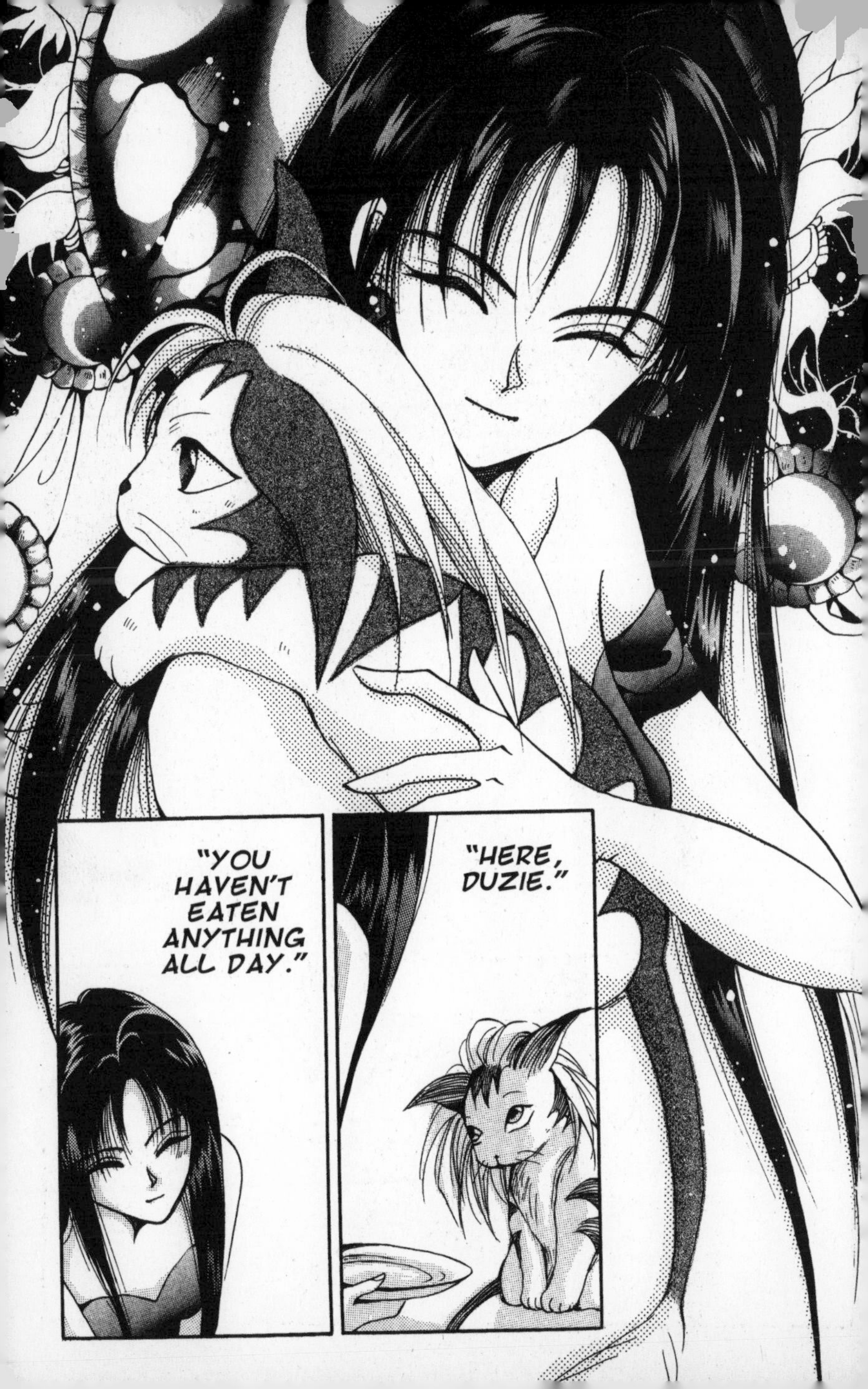
"HERE, DUZIE."
"YOU HAVEN'T EATEN ANYTHING ALL DAY."

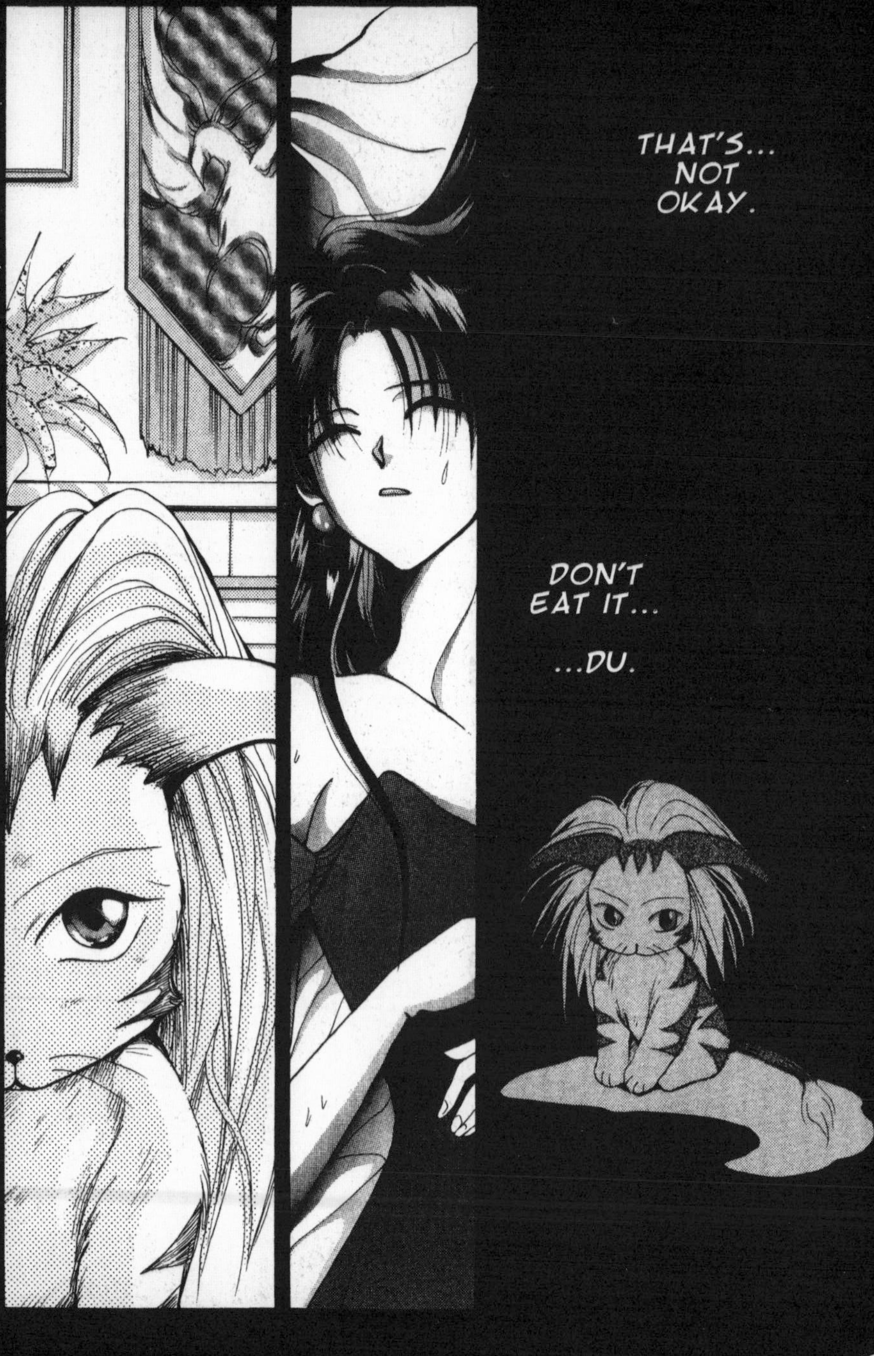
THAT'S... NOT OKAY.
DON'T EAT IT...
...DU.

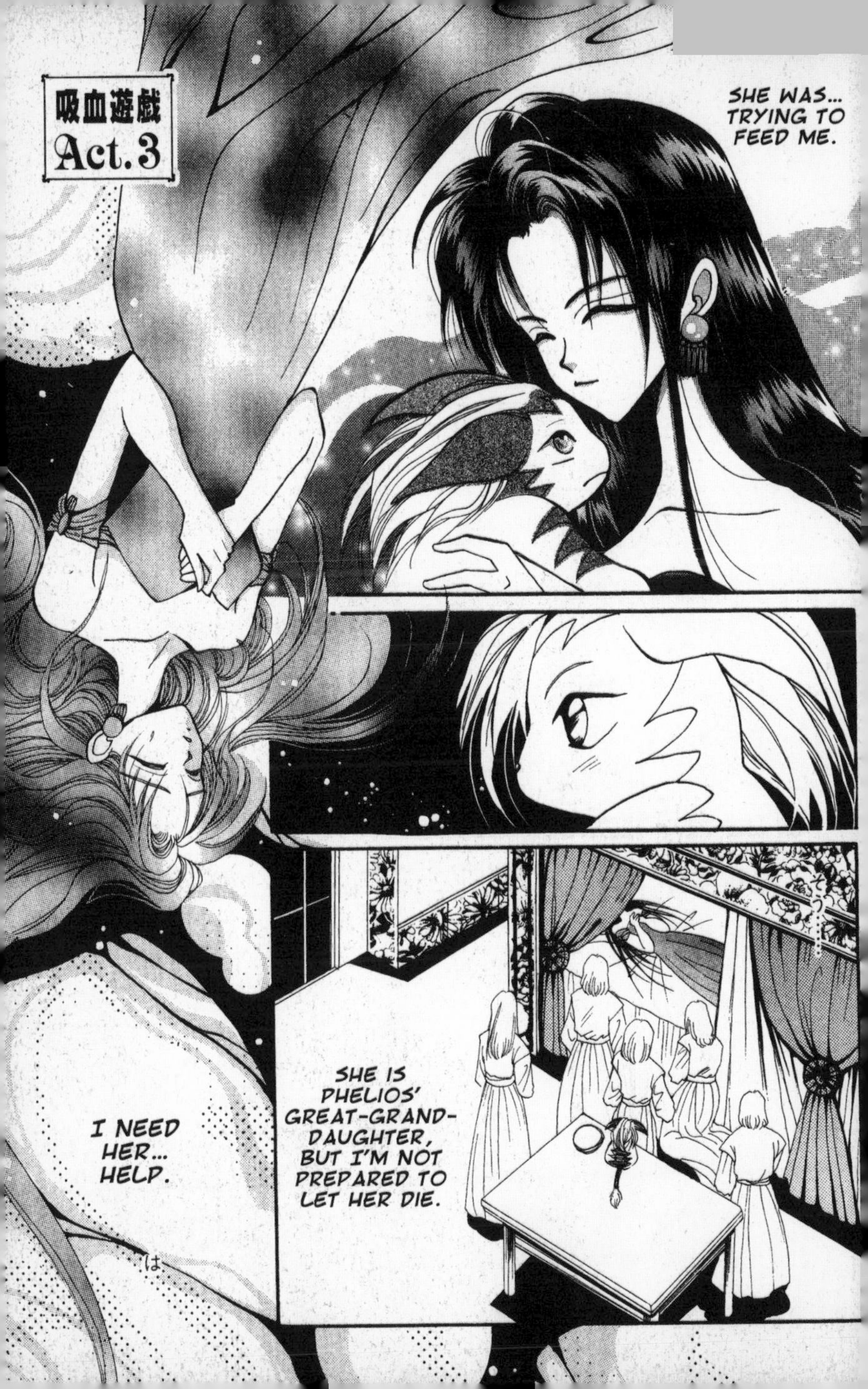
SHE WAS... TRYING TO FEED ME.
そう…
SHE IS PHELIOS' GREAT-GRAND-DAUGHTER, BUT I'M NOT PREPARED TO LET HER DIE.
吸血遊戯
Act.3
I NEED HER... HELP.
は

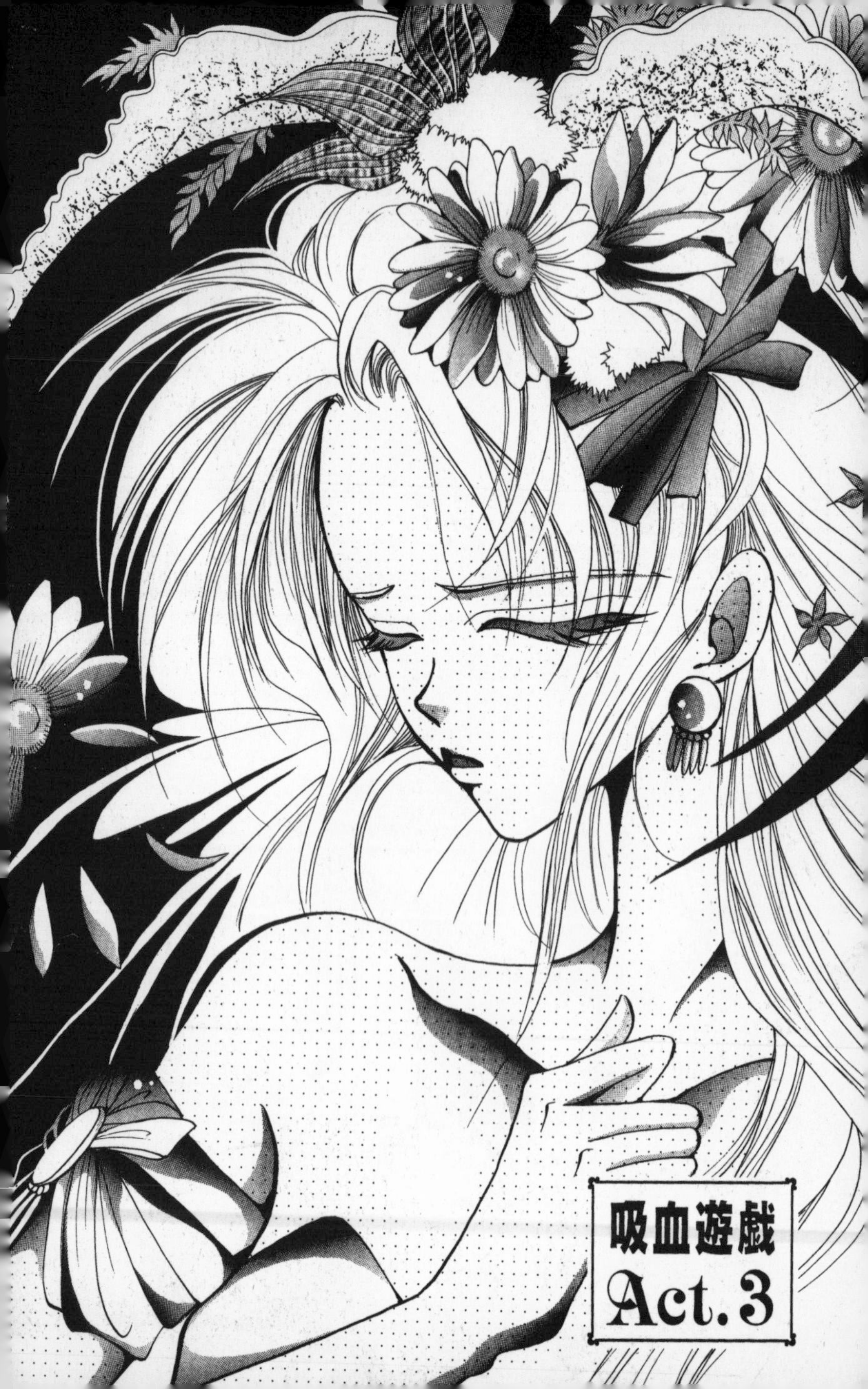
吸血遊戯
Act. 3

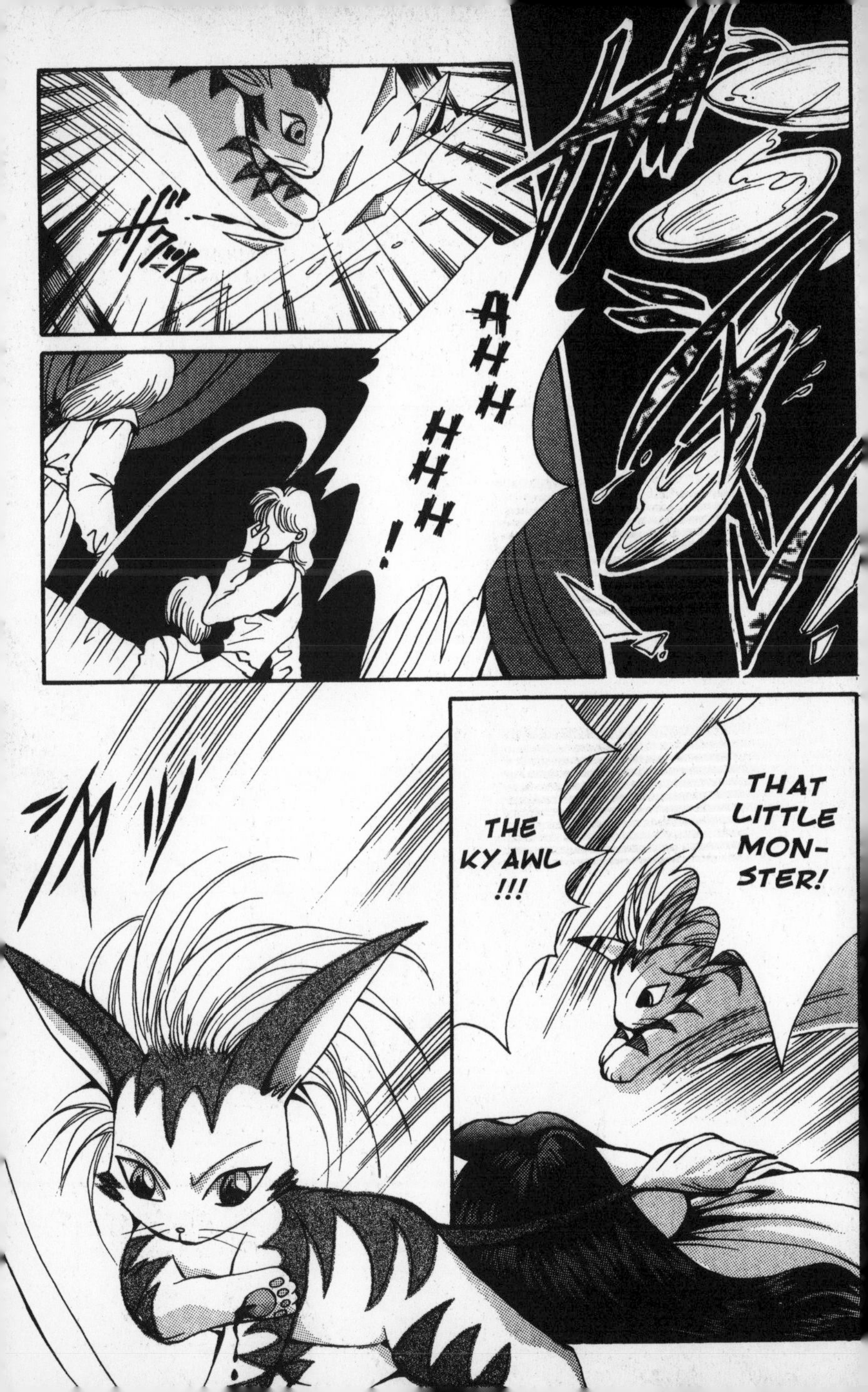
AHHHHHHH!
THAT LITTLE MON-STER!
THE KYAWL!!!

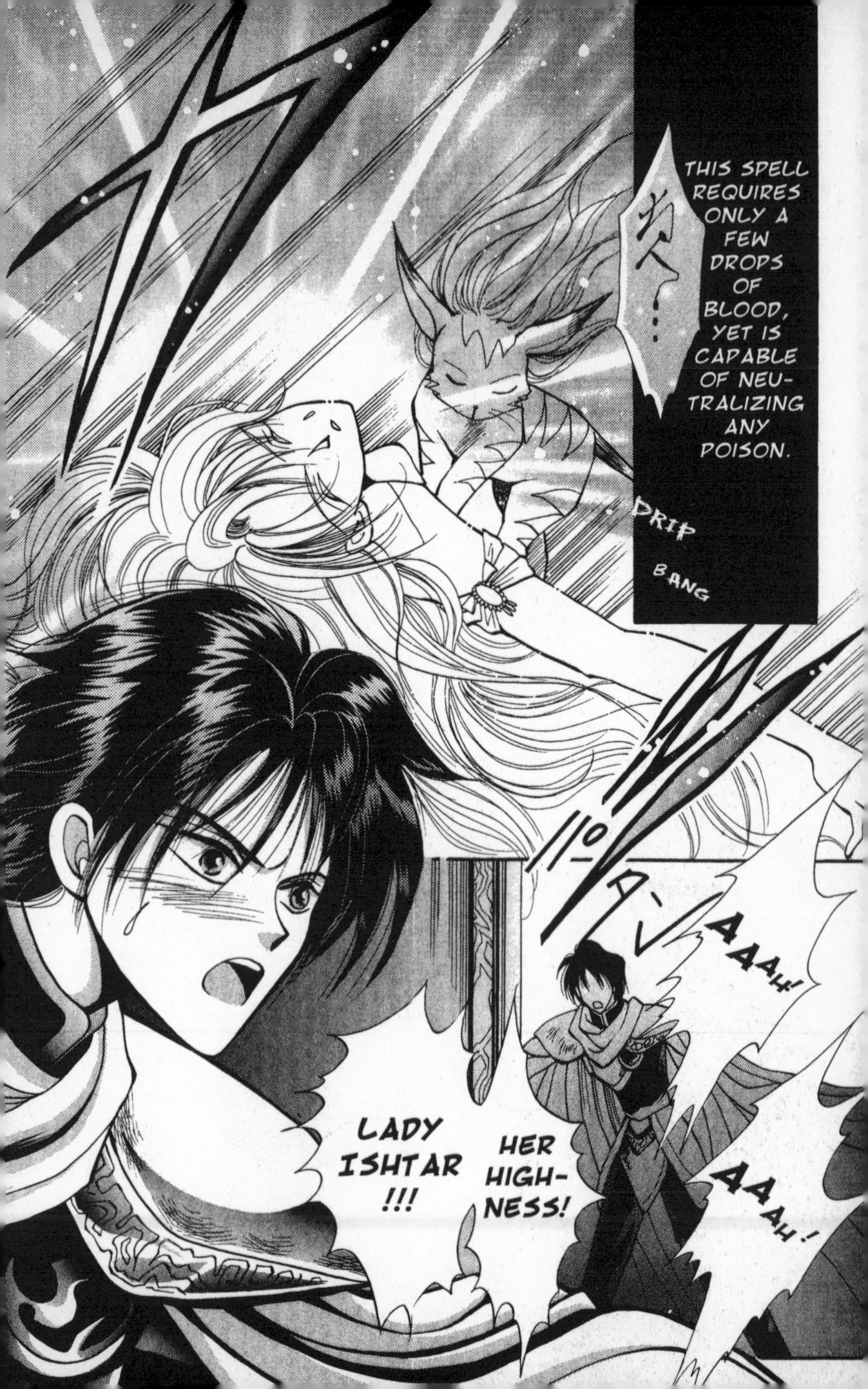
THIS SPELL REQUIRES ONLY A FEW DROPS OF BLOOD, YET IS CAPABLE OF NEU-TRALIZING ANY POISON.
DRIP
BANG
AAAAH!
AAAAH!
HER HIGH-NESS!
LADY ISHTAR !!!

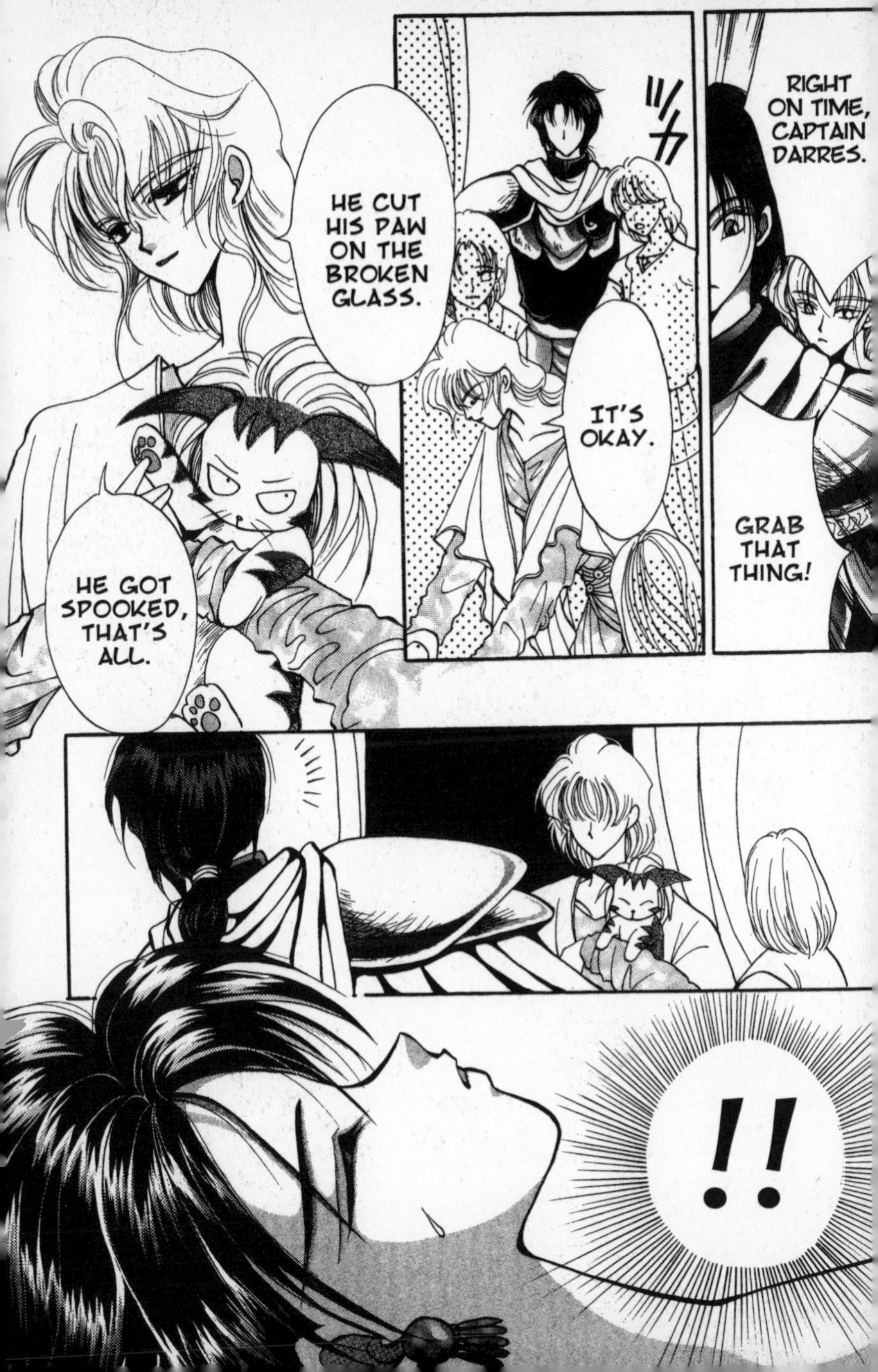
RIGHT ON TIME, CAPTAIN DARRES.
GRAB THAT THING!
IT'S OKAY.
HE CUT HIS PAW ON THE BROKEN GLASS.
HE GOT SPOOKED, THAT'S ALL.
!!

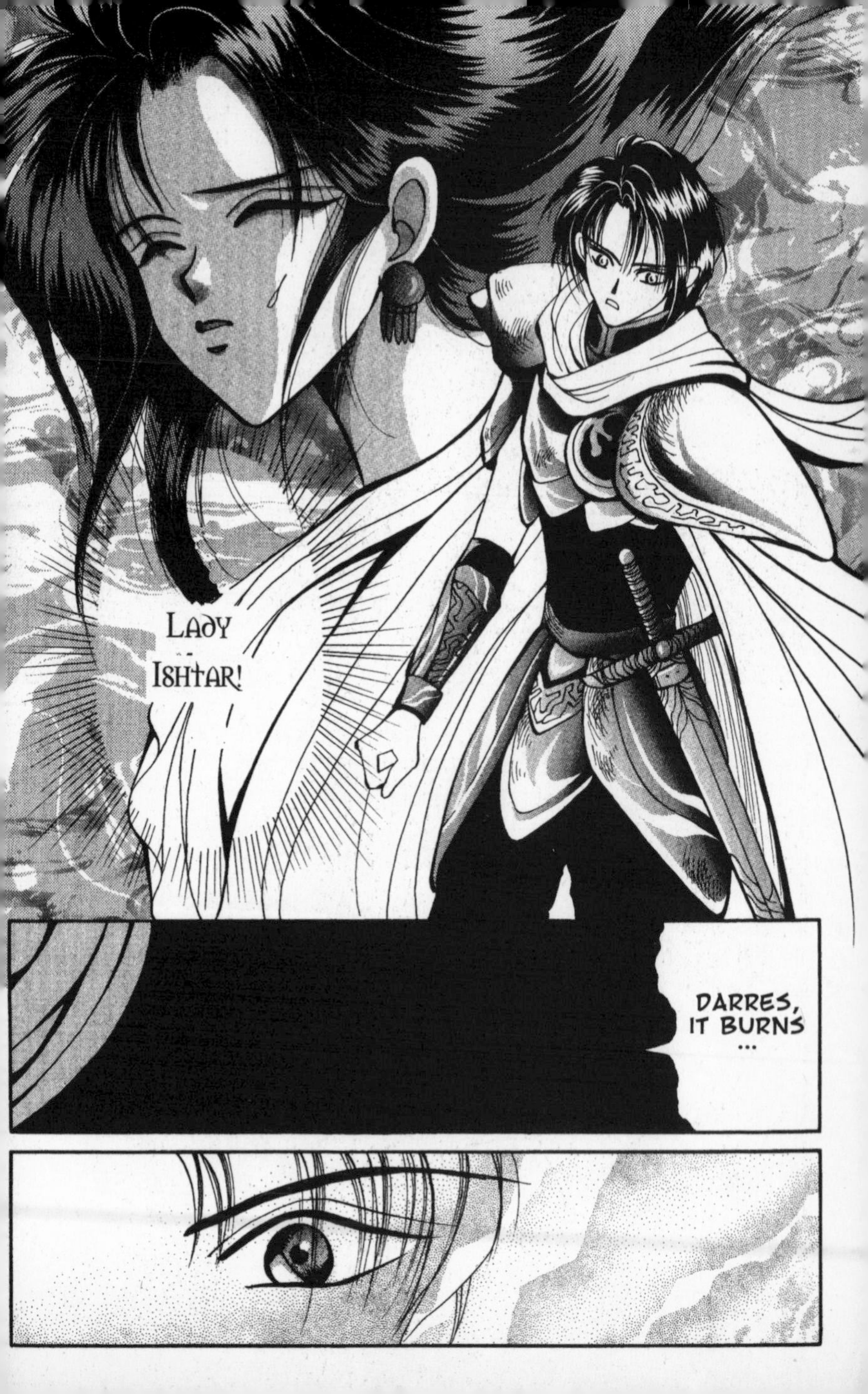
Lady -- Ishtar!
Darres, it burns ...

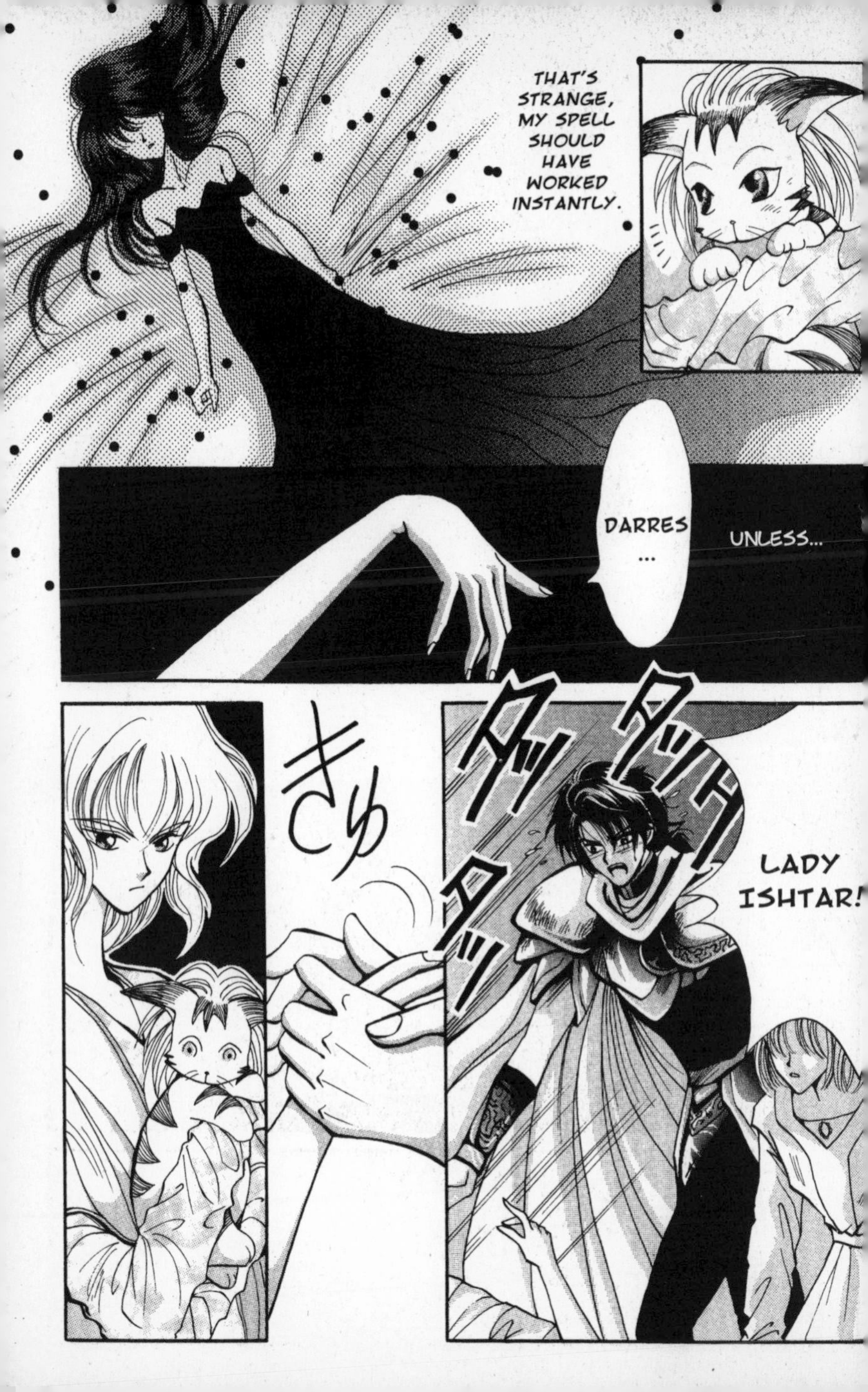
THAT'S STRANGE, MY SPELL SHOULD HAVE WORKED INSTANTLY.
UNLESS...
DARRES...
LADY ISHTAR!
タッ
タッ
タッ
きゅ

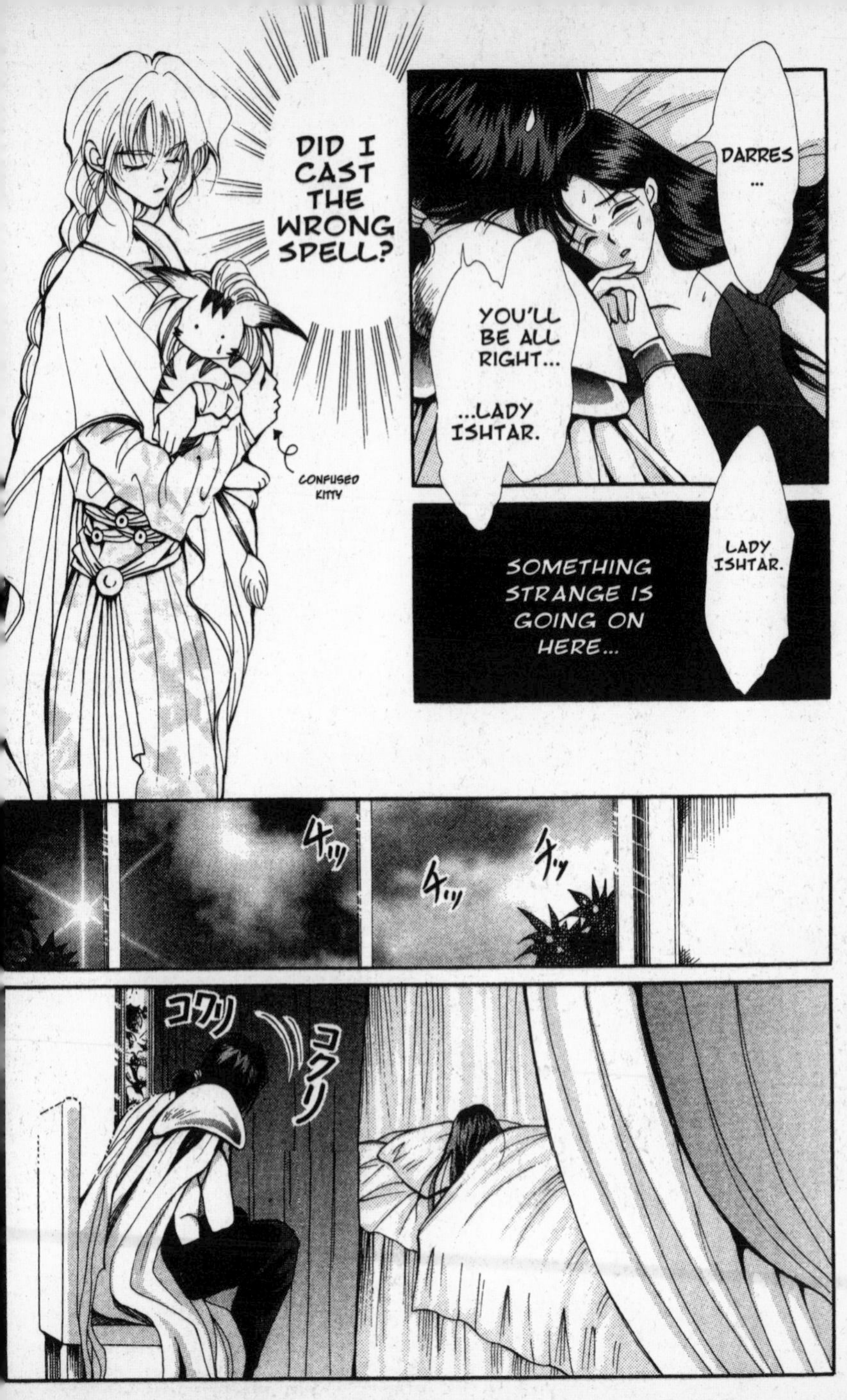
DARRES ...
YOU'LL BE ALL RIGHT...
...LADY ISHTAR.
LADY ISHTAR.
SOMETHING STRANGE IS GOING ON HERE...
DID I CAST THE WRONG SPELL?
CONFUSED KITTY
コクリ
コクリ

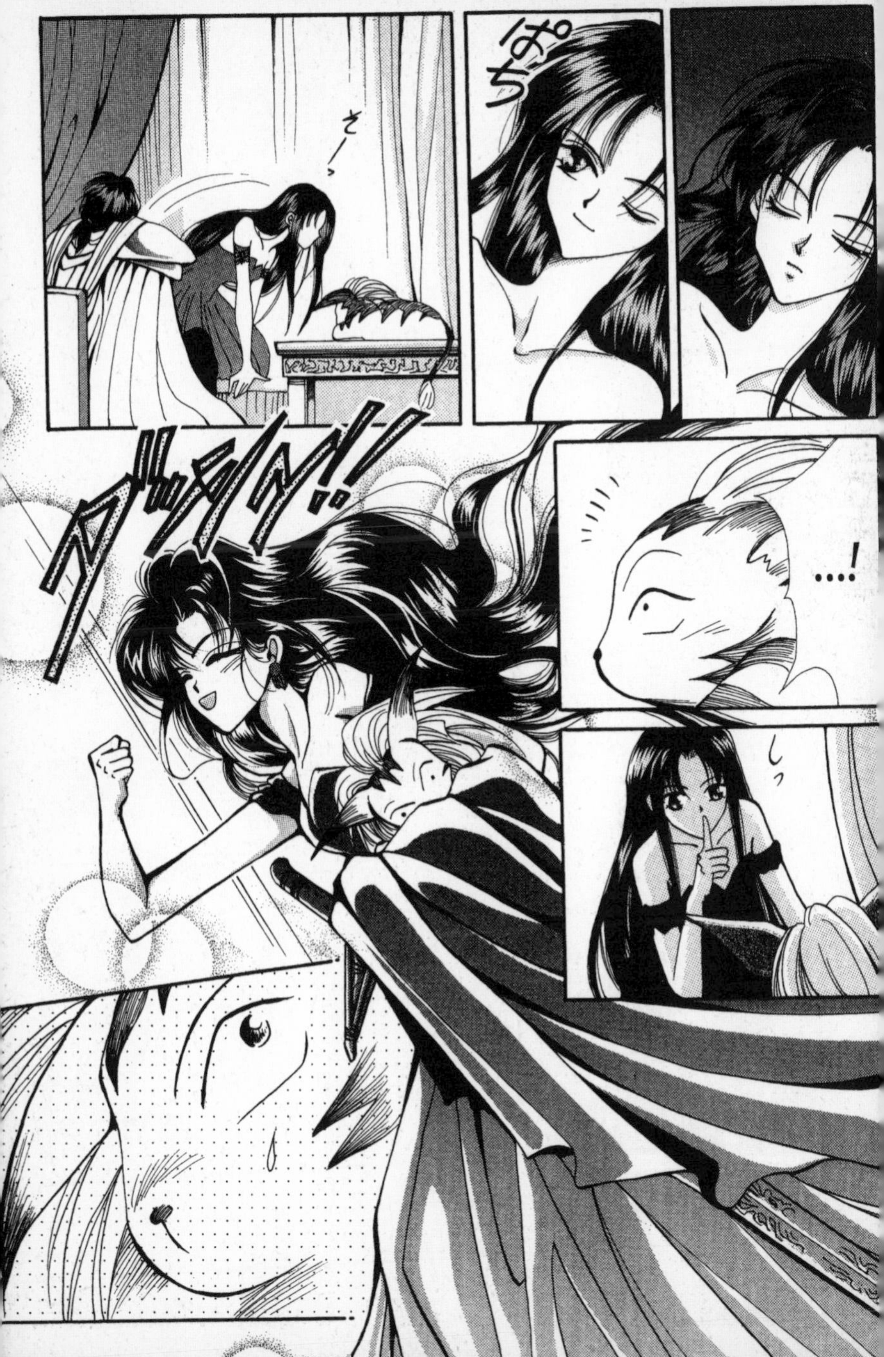
ぱち
さーっ
…!
しっ
ガッキン!!

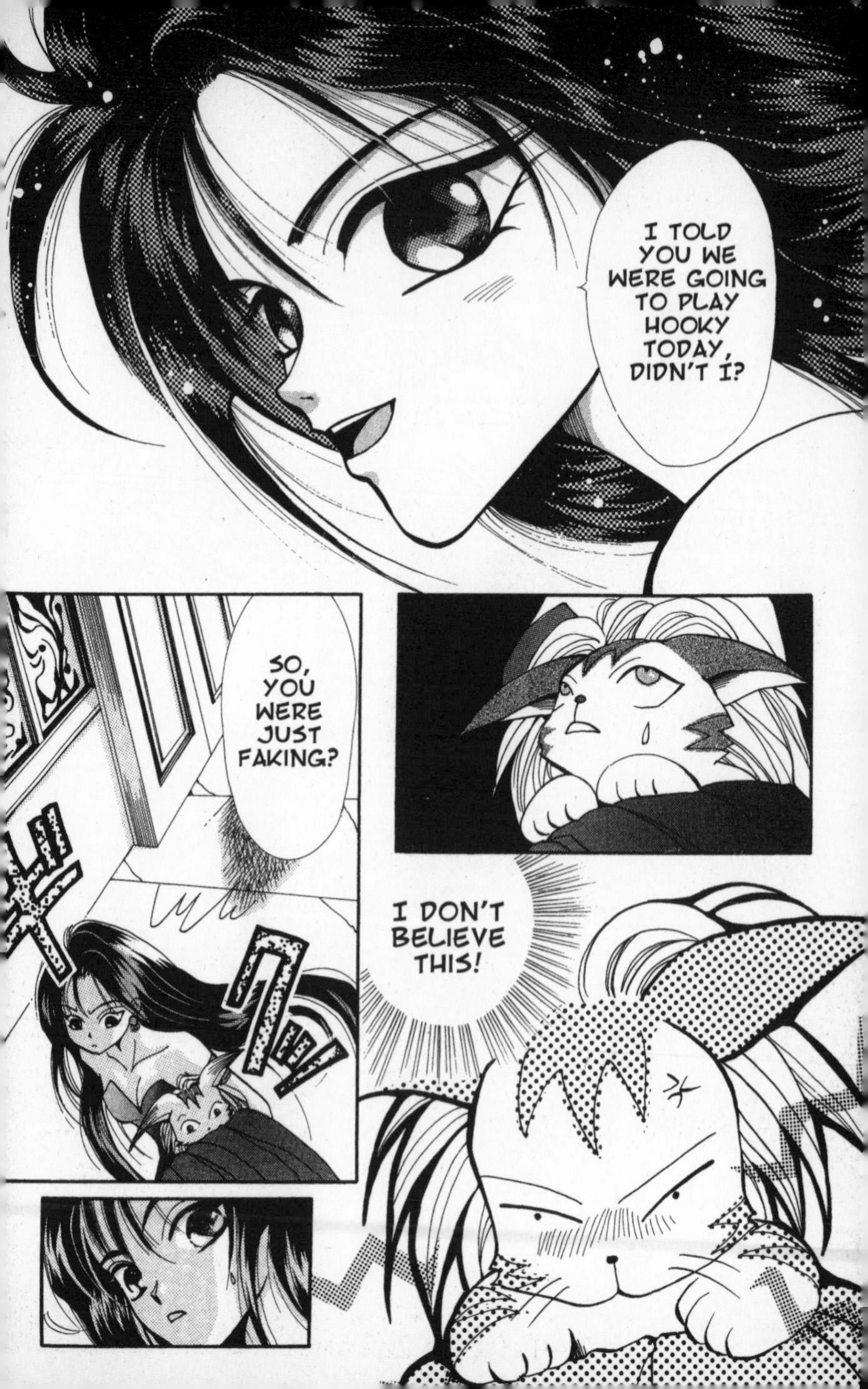
I TOLD YOU WE WERE GOING TO PLAY HOOKY TODAY, DIDN'T I?
SO, YOU WERE JUST FAKING?
I DON'T BELIEVE THIS!

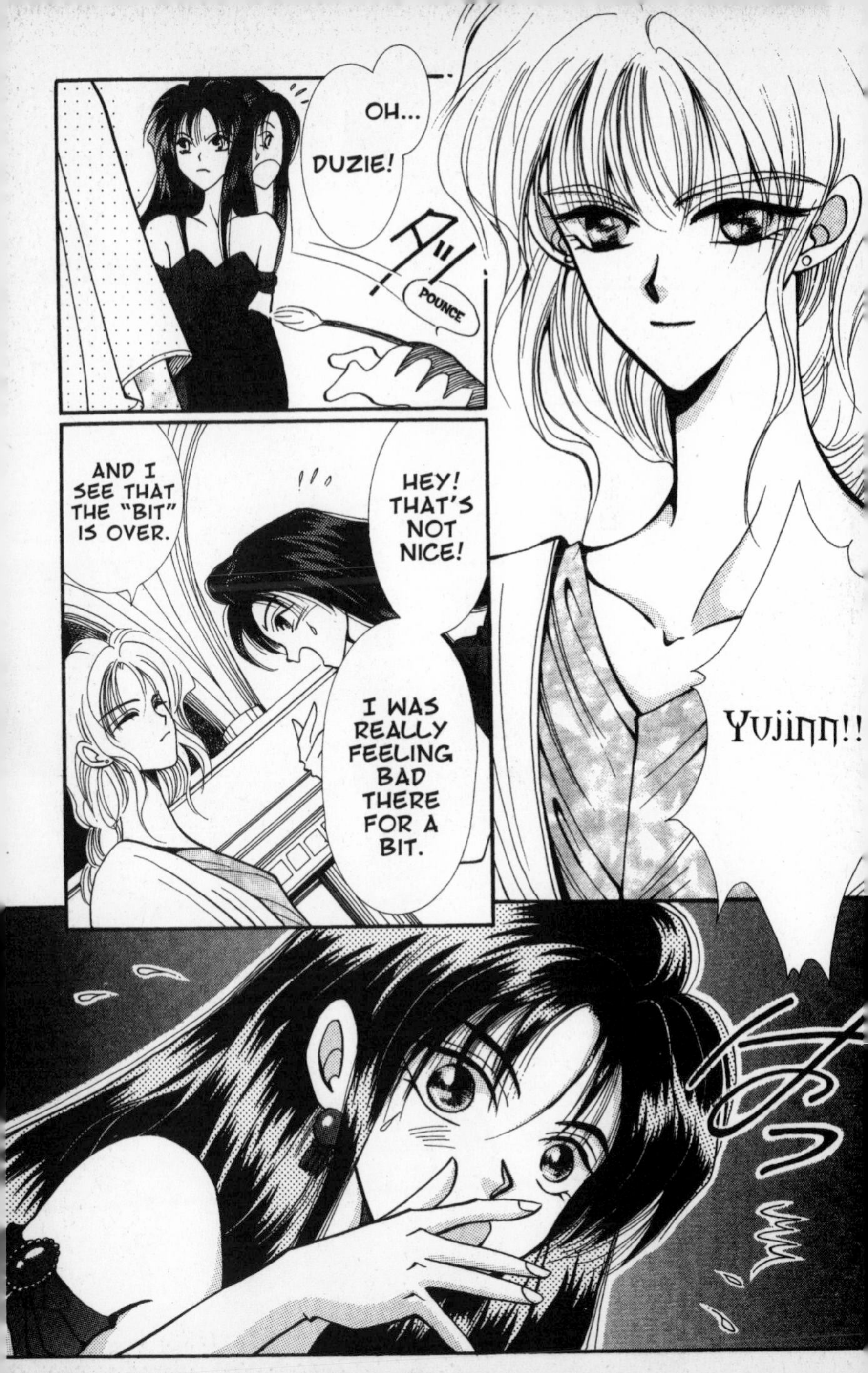
YUJINN!!
OH...
DUZIE!
POUNCE
HEY! THAT'S NOT NICE!
I WAS REALLY FEELING BAD THERE FOR A BIT.
AND I SEE THAT THE "BIT" IS OVER.

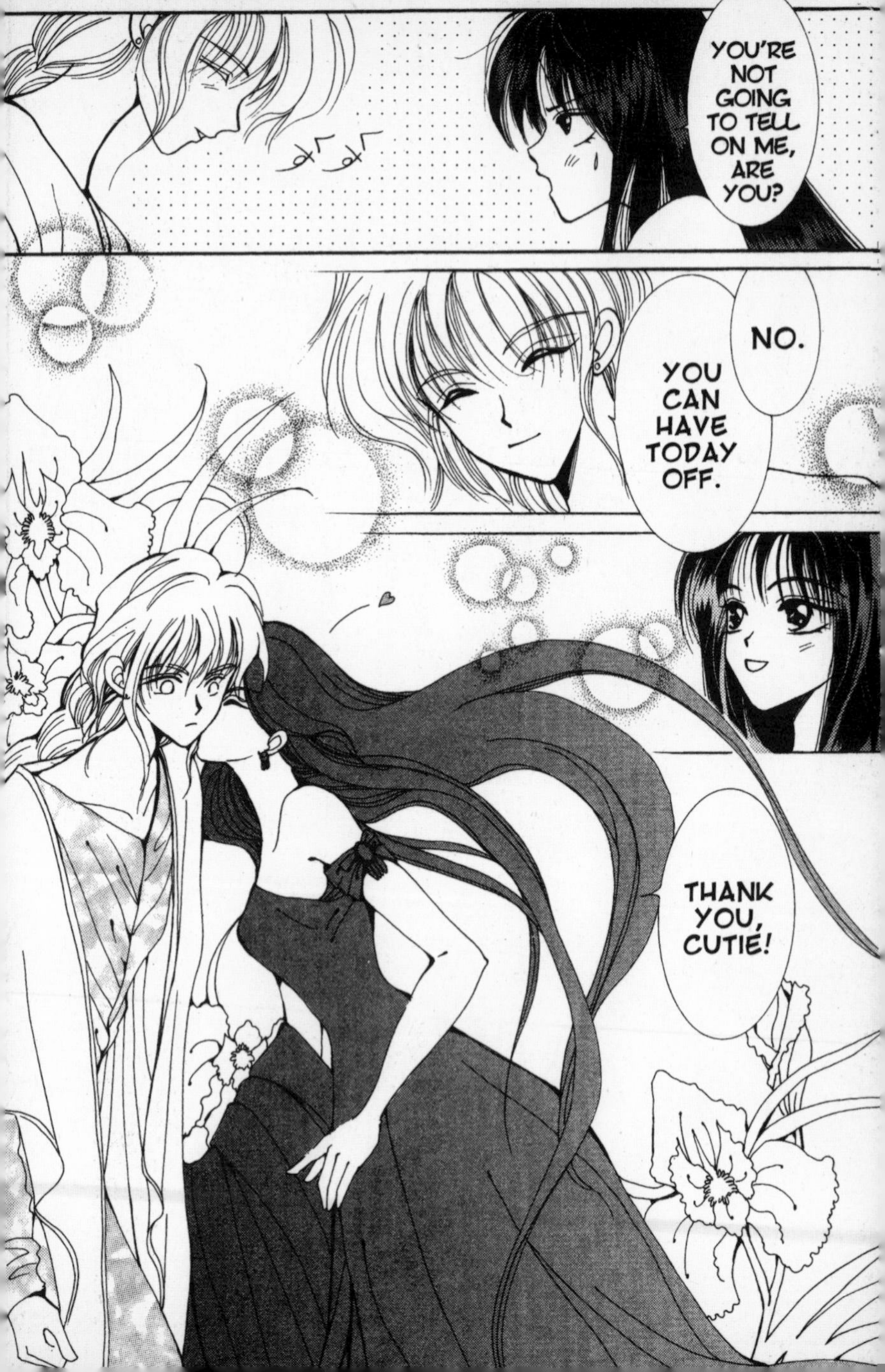
YOU'RE NOT GOING TO TELL ON ME, ARE YOU?
NO.
YOU CAN HAVE TODAY OFF.
THANK YOU, CUTIE!

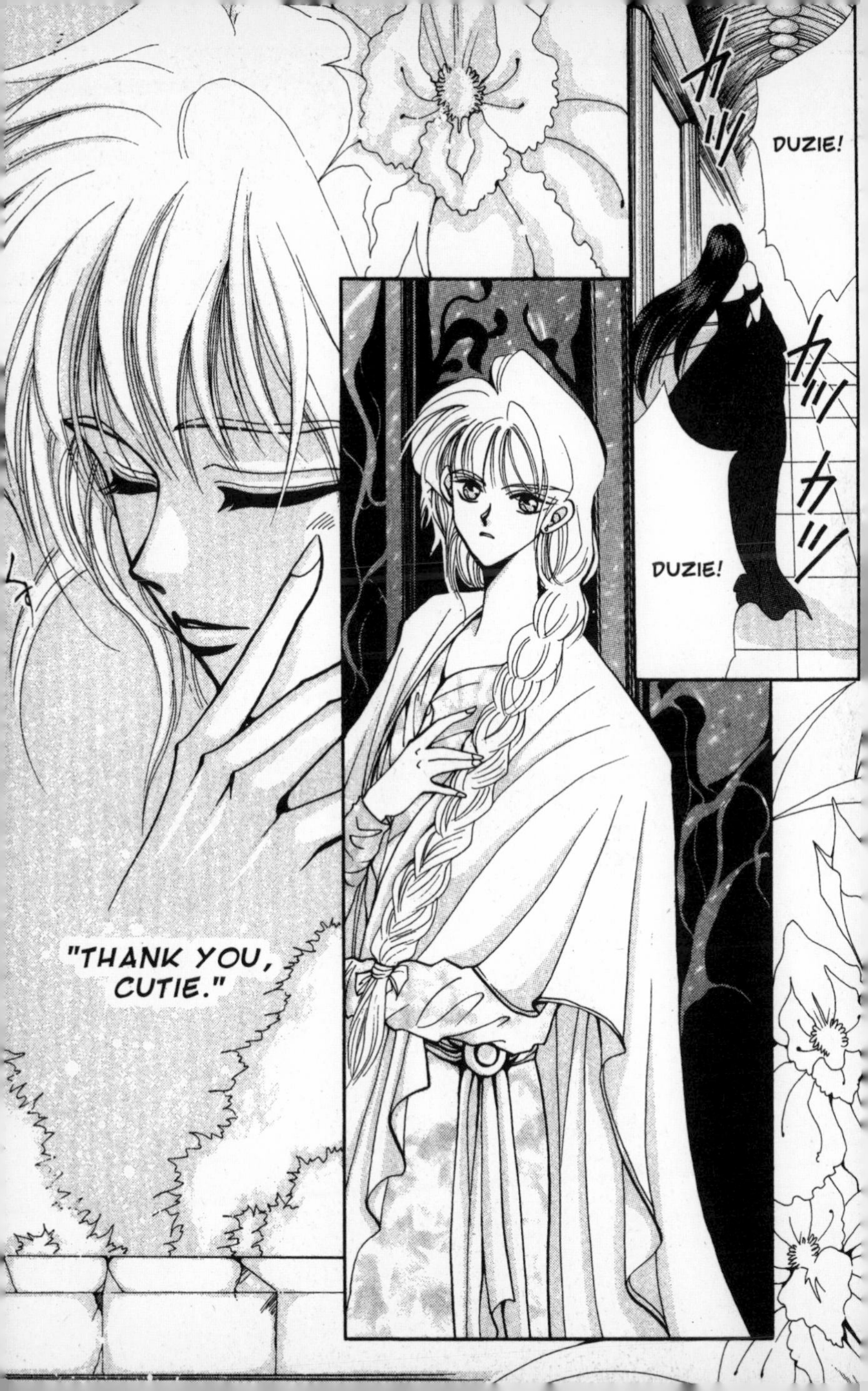
DUZIE!
DUZIE!
"THANK YOU, CUTIE."

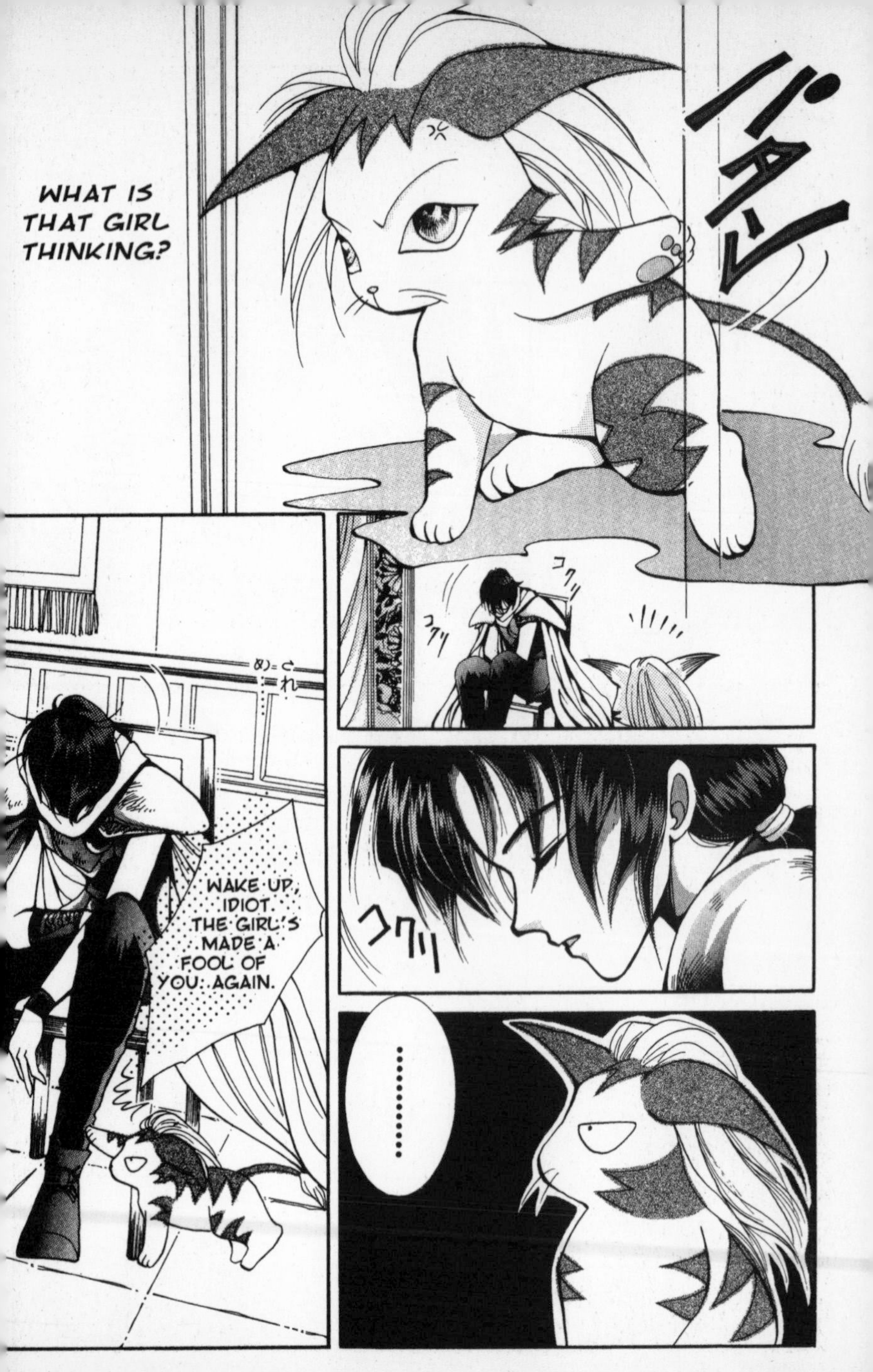
パタン
WHAT IS THAT GIRL THINKING?
コクリ
コクリ
コクリ
……………
WAKE UP, IDIOT. THE GIRL'S MADE A FOOL OF YOU. AGAIN.

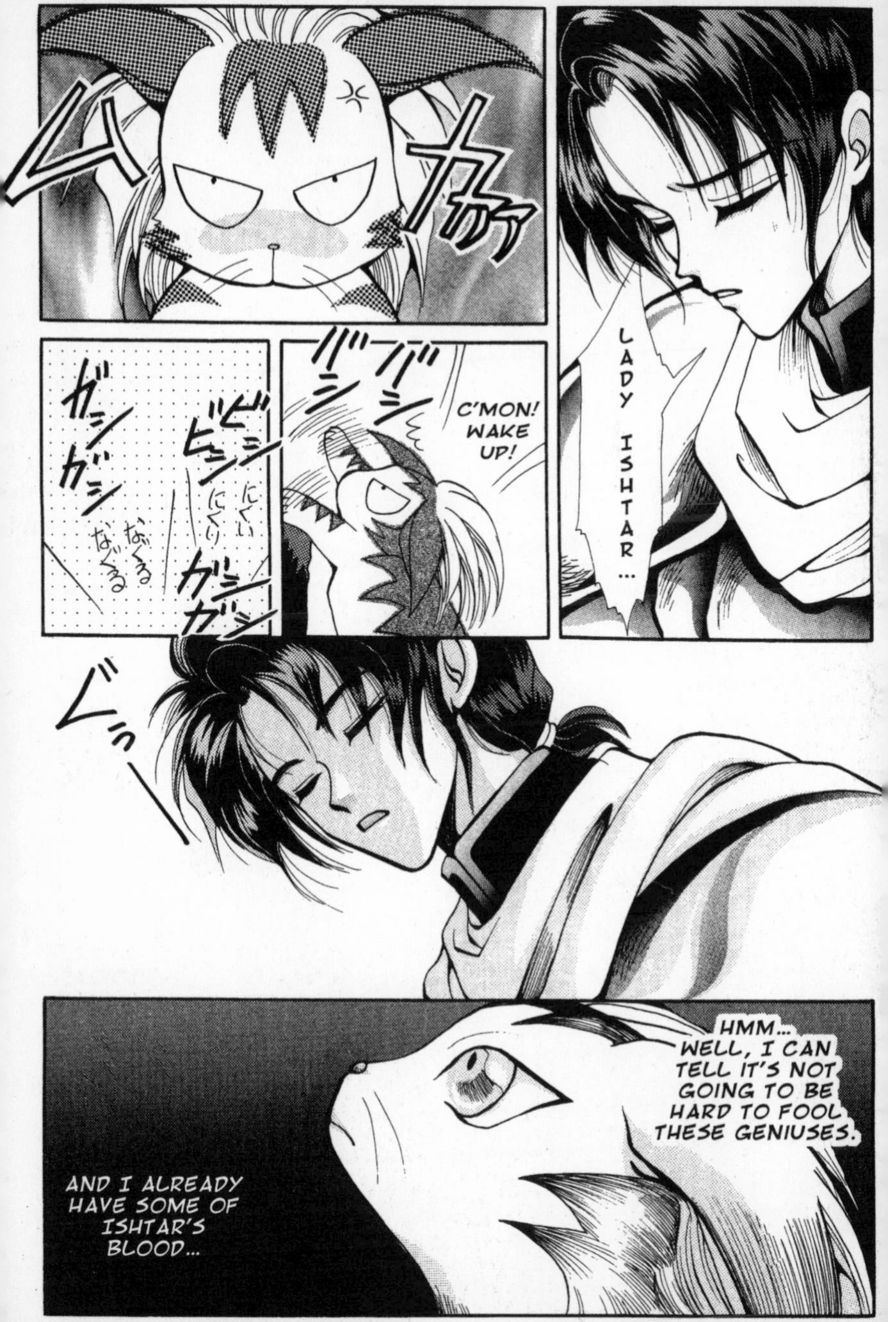
LADY ISHTAR...
C'MON! WAKE UP!
HMM... WELL, I CAN TELL IT'S NOT GOING TO BE HARD TO FOOL THESE GENIUSES.
AND I ALREADY HAVE SOME OF ISHTAR'S BLOOD...

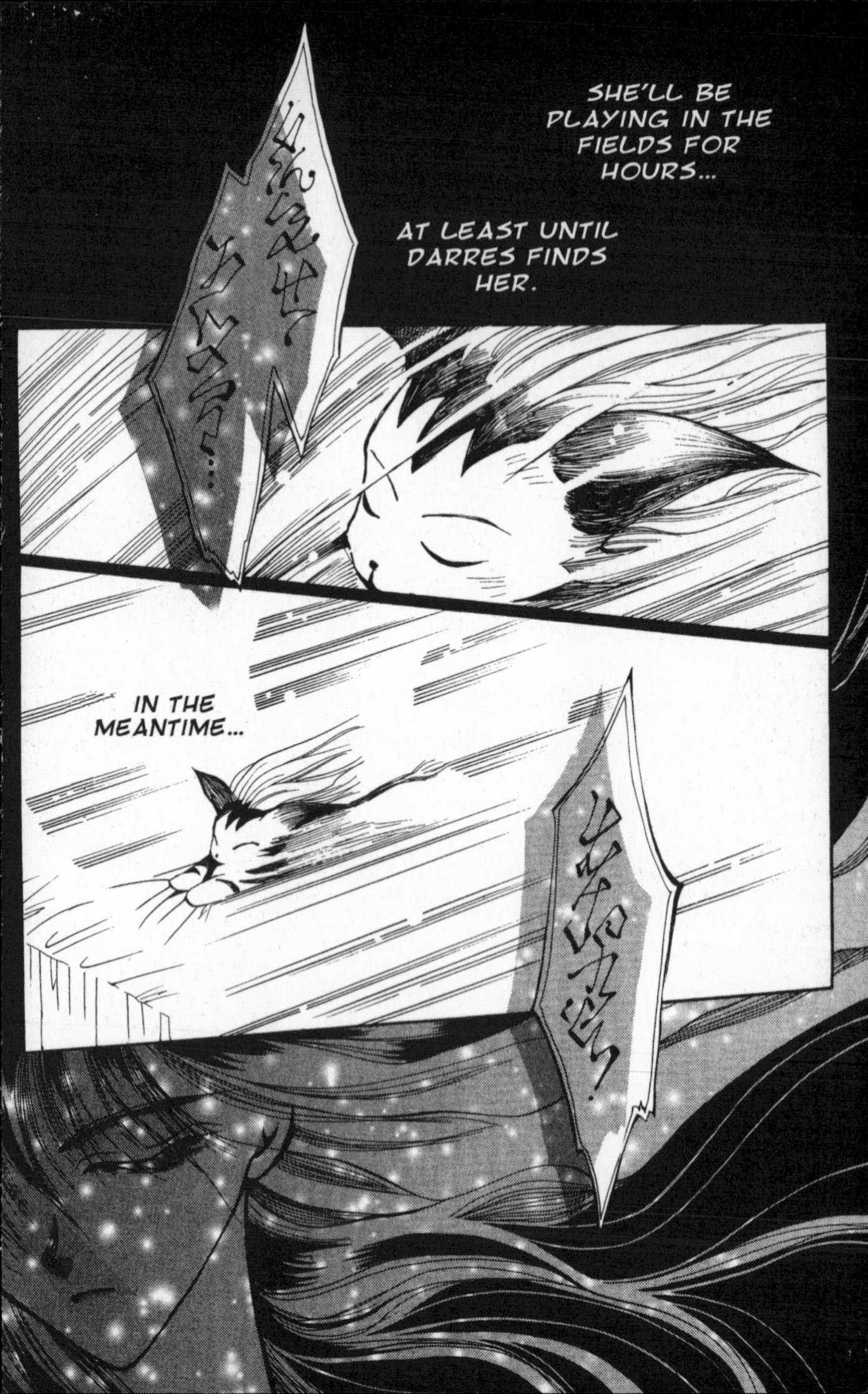
SHE'LL BE PLAYING IN THE FIELDS FOR HOURS...
AT LEAST UNTIL DARRES FINDS HER.
IN THE MEANTIME...

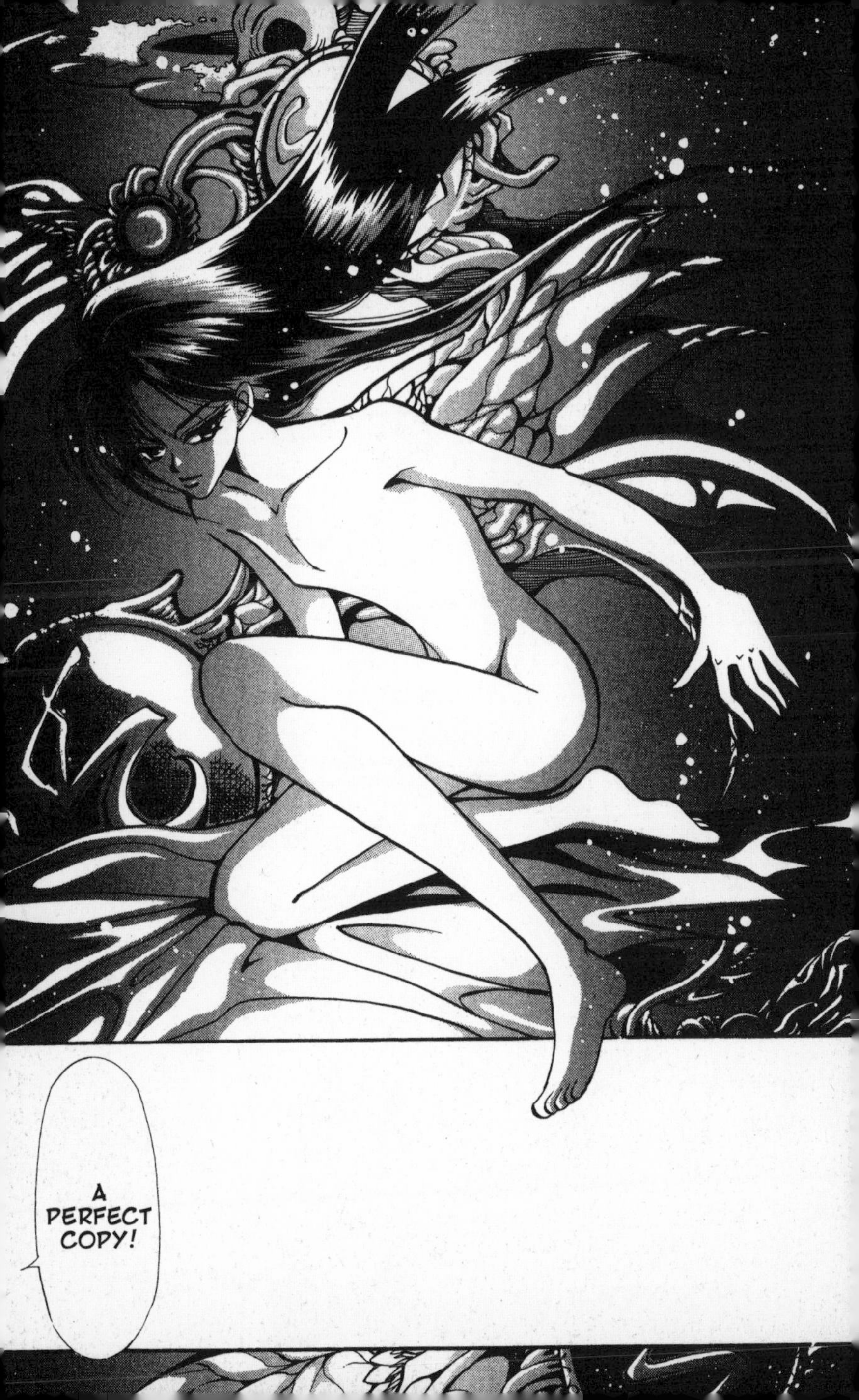
A PERFECT COPY!

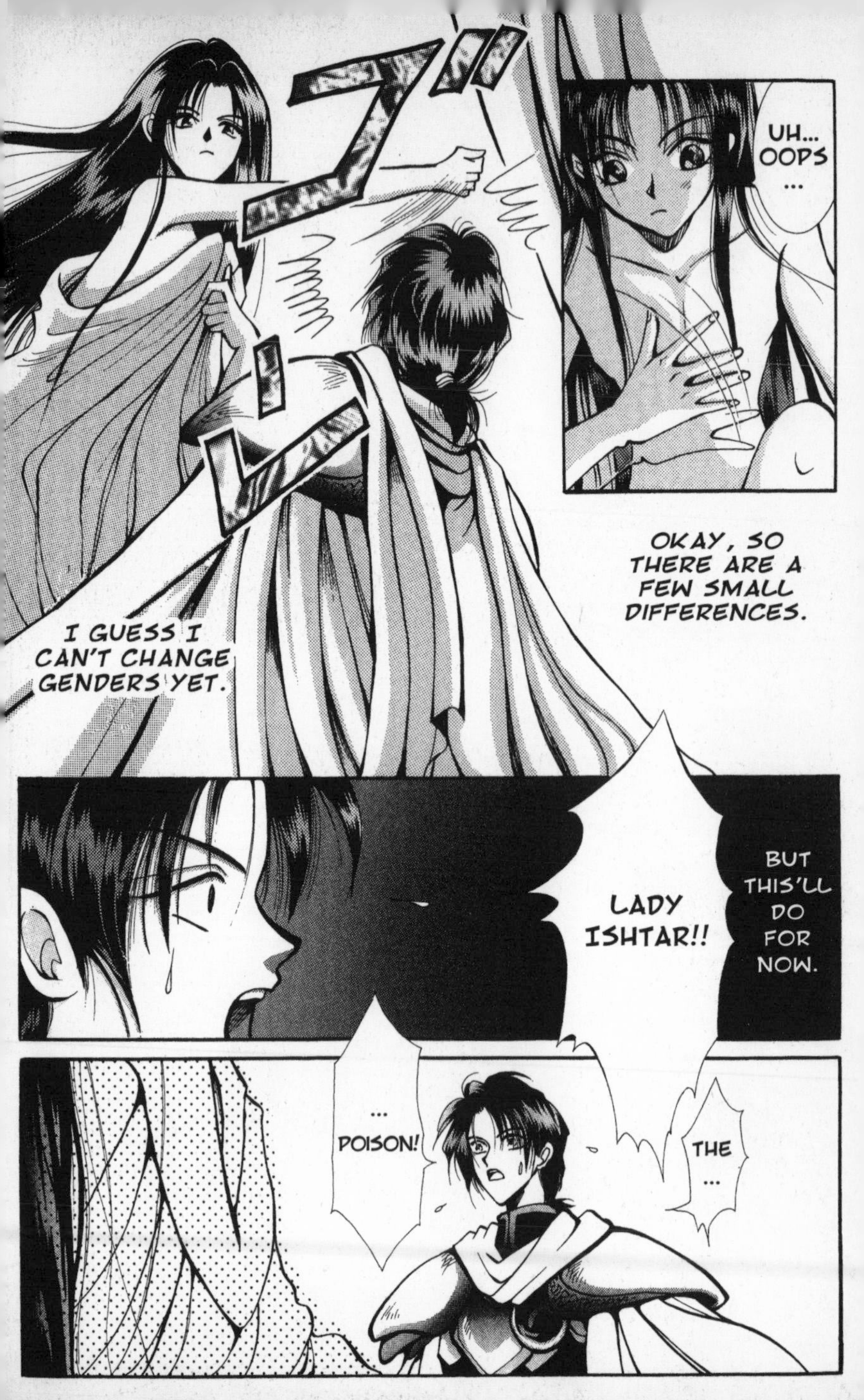
UH... OOPS ...
OKAY, SO THERE ARE A FEW SMALL DIFFERENCES.
I GUESS I CAN'T CHANGE GENDERS YET.
BUT THIS'LL DO FOR NOW.
LADY ISHTAR!!
THE ...
... POISON!

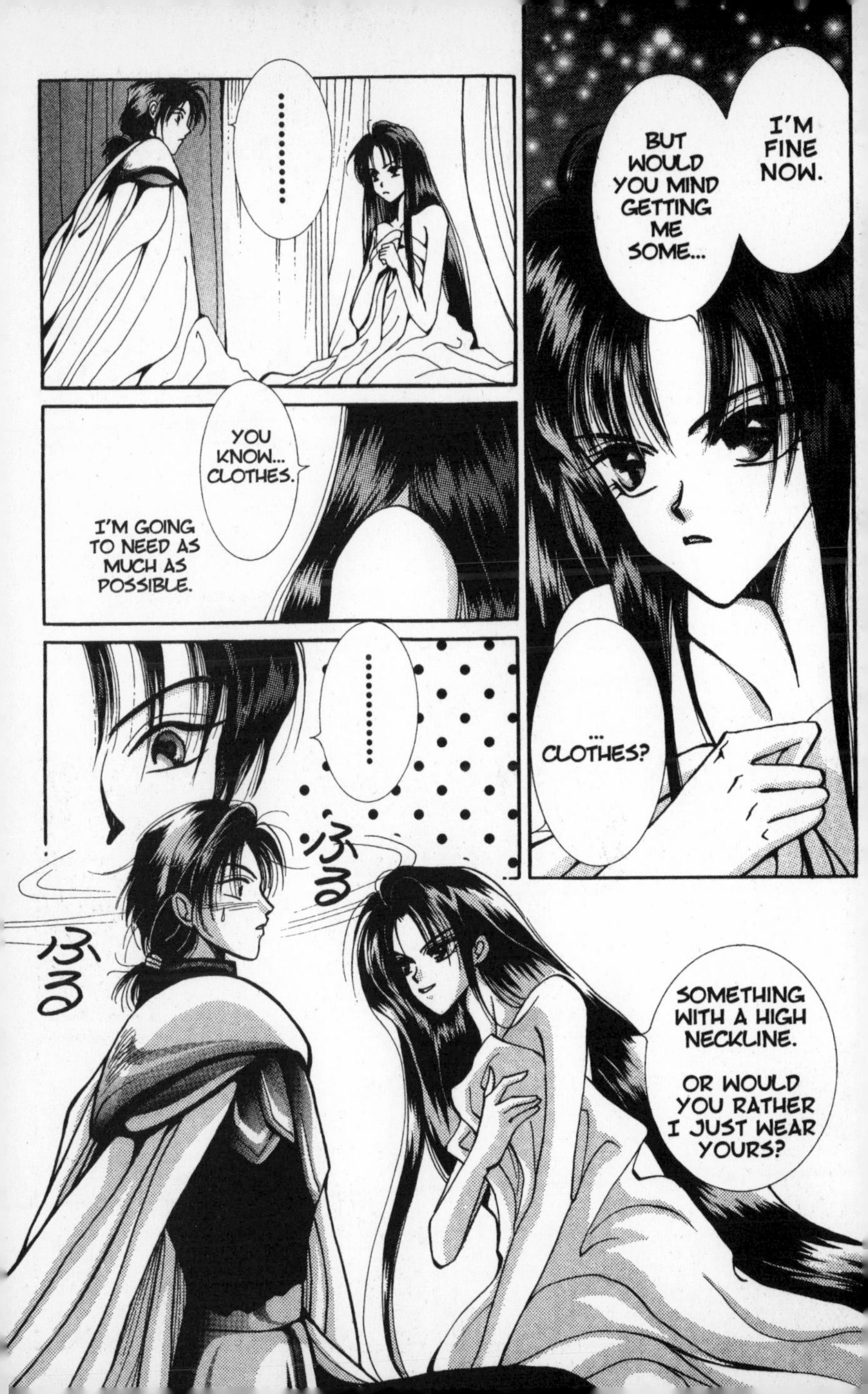

I'M FINE NOW.
BUT WOULD YOU MIND GETTING ME SOME...
...CLOTHES?
......
YOU KNOW... CLOTHES.
I'M GOING TO NEED AS MUCH AS POSSIBLE.
......
ふる
ふる
SOMETHING WITH A HIGH NECKLINE.
OR WOULD YOU RATHER I JUST WEAR YOURS?

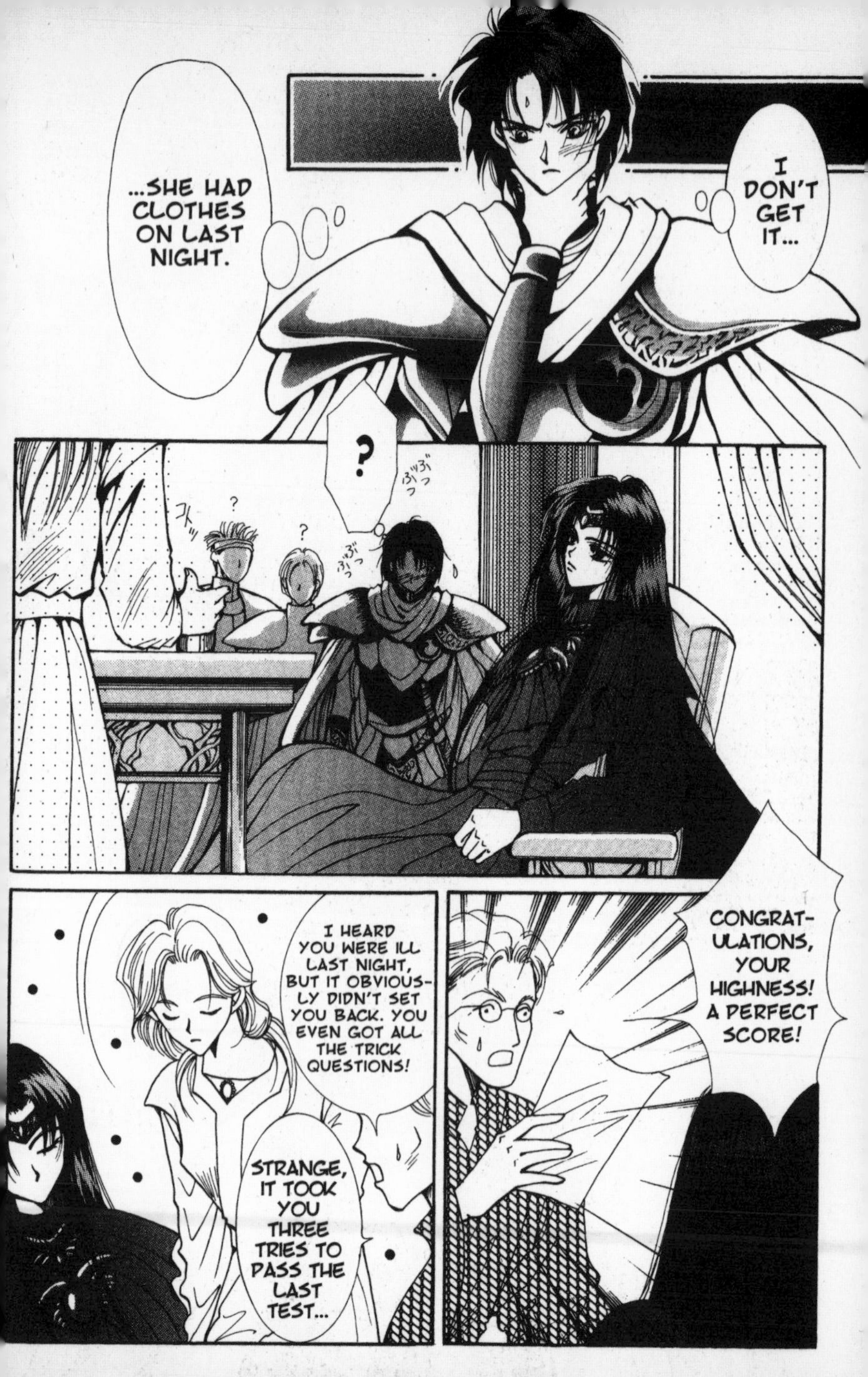
I DON'T GET IT...
...SHE HAD CLOTHES ON LAST NIGHT.
?
CONGRAT-ULATIONS, YOUR HIGHNESS! A PERFECT SCORE!
I HEARD YOU WERE ILL LAST NIGHT, BUT IT OBVIOUS-LY DIDN'T SET YOU BACK. YOU EVEN GOT ALL THE TRICK QUESTIONS!
STRANGE, IT TOOK YOU THREE TRIES TO PASS THE LAST TEST...

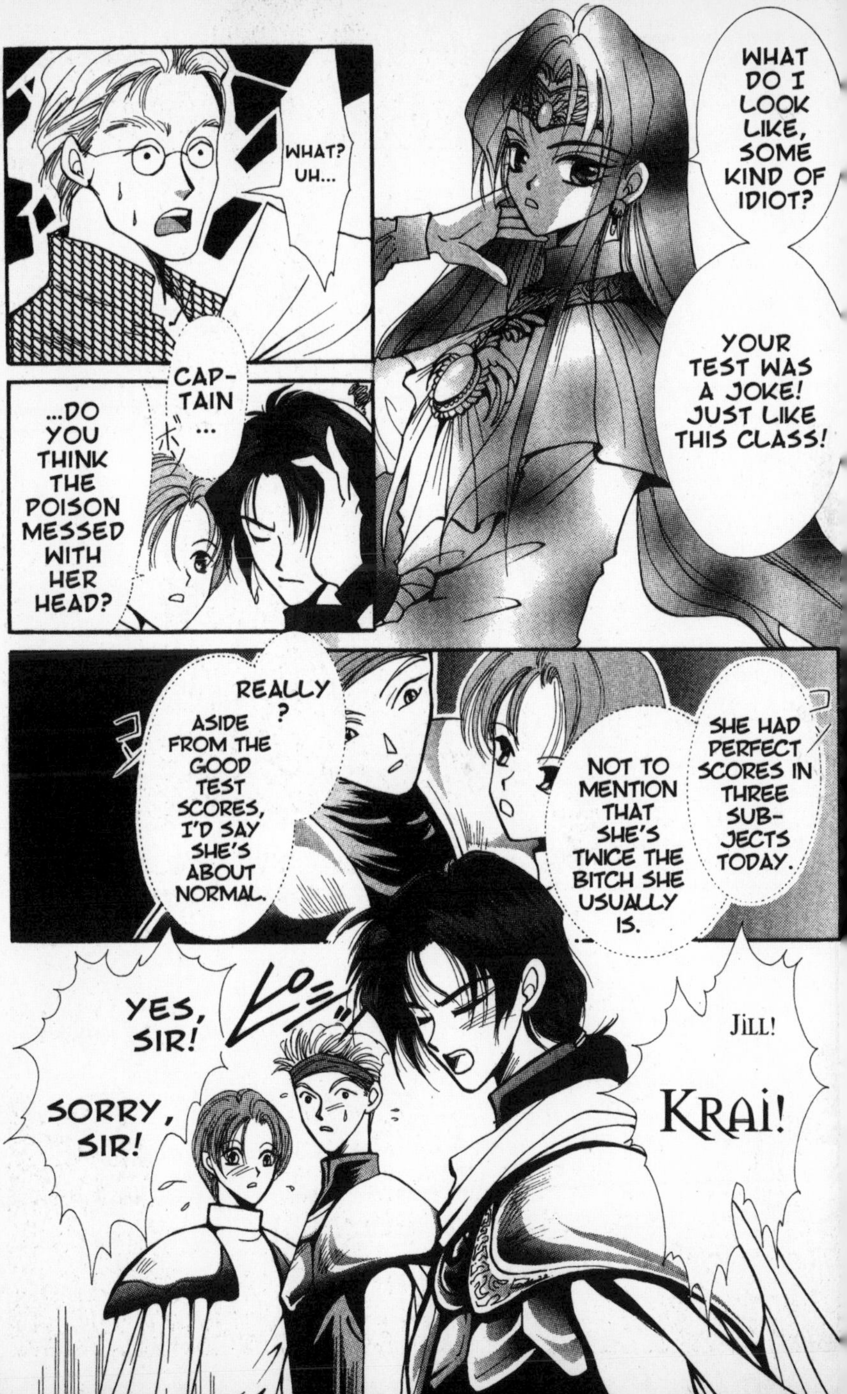
WHAT DO I LOOK LIKE, SOME KIND OF IDIOT?
YOUR TEST WAS A JOKE! JUST LIKE THIS CLASS!
WHAT? UH...
CAPTAIN...
...DO YOU THINK THE POISON MESSED WITH HER HEAD?
SHE HAD PERFECT SCORES IN THREE SUBJECTS TODAY.
NOT TO MENTION THAT SHE'S TWICE THE BITCH SHE USUALLY IS.
REALLY?
ASIDE FROM THE GOOD TEST SCORES, I'D SAY SHE'S ABOUT NORMAL.
JILL!
KRAI!
YES, SIR!
SORRY, SIR!

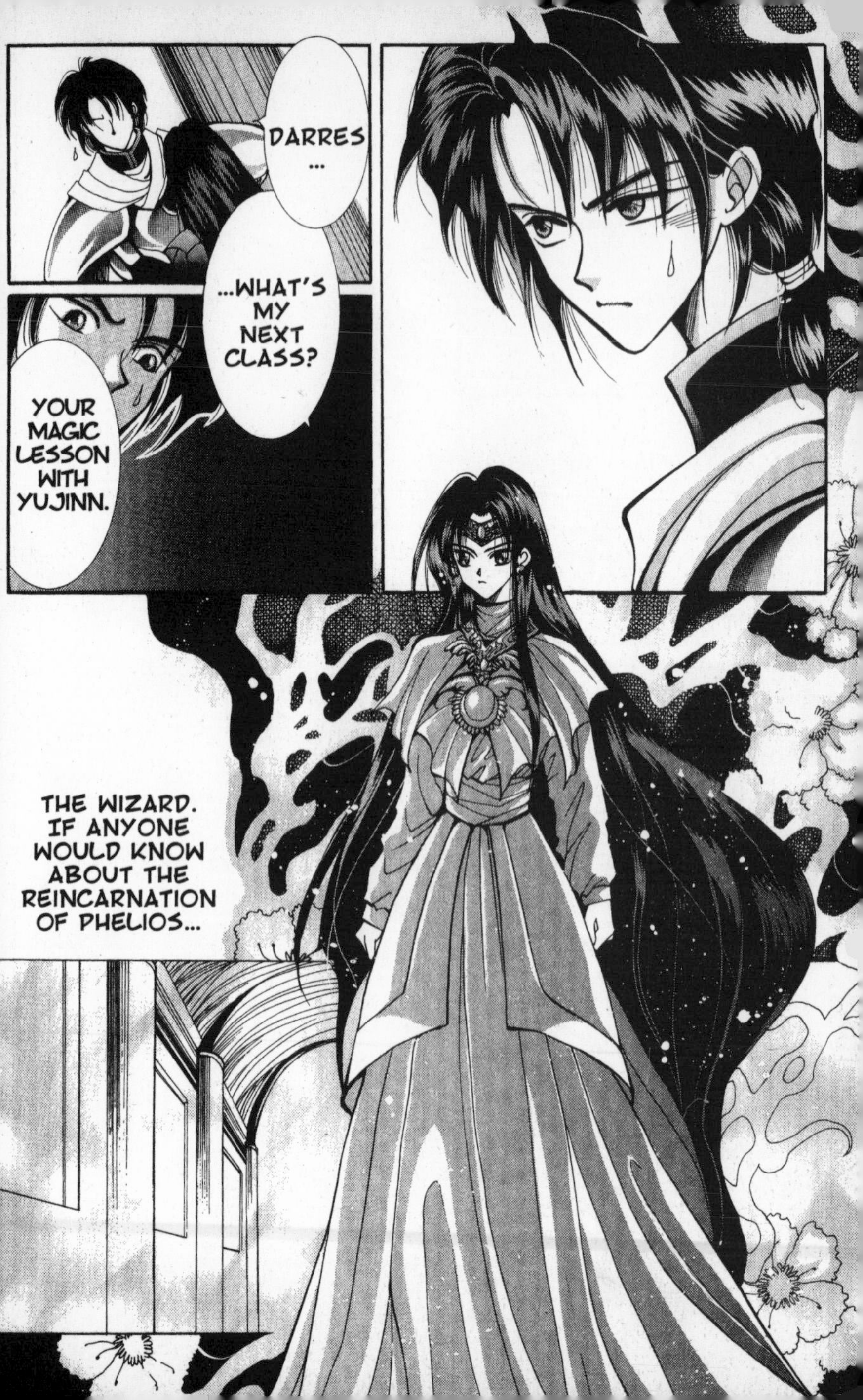
DARRES ...
...WHAT'S MY NEXT CLASS?
YOUR MAGIC LESSON WITH YUJINN.
THE WIZARD. IF ANYONE WOULD KNOW ABOUT THE REINCARNATION OF PHELIOS...

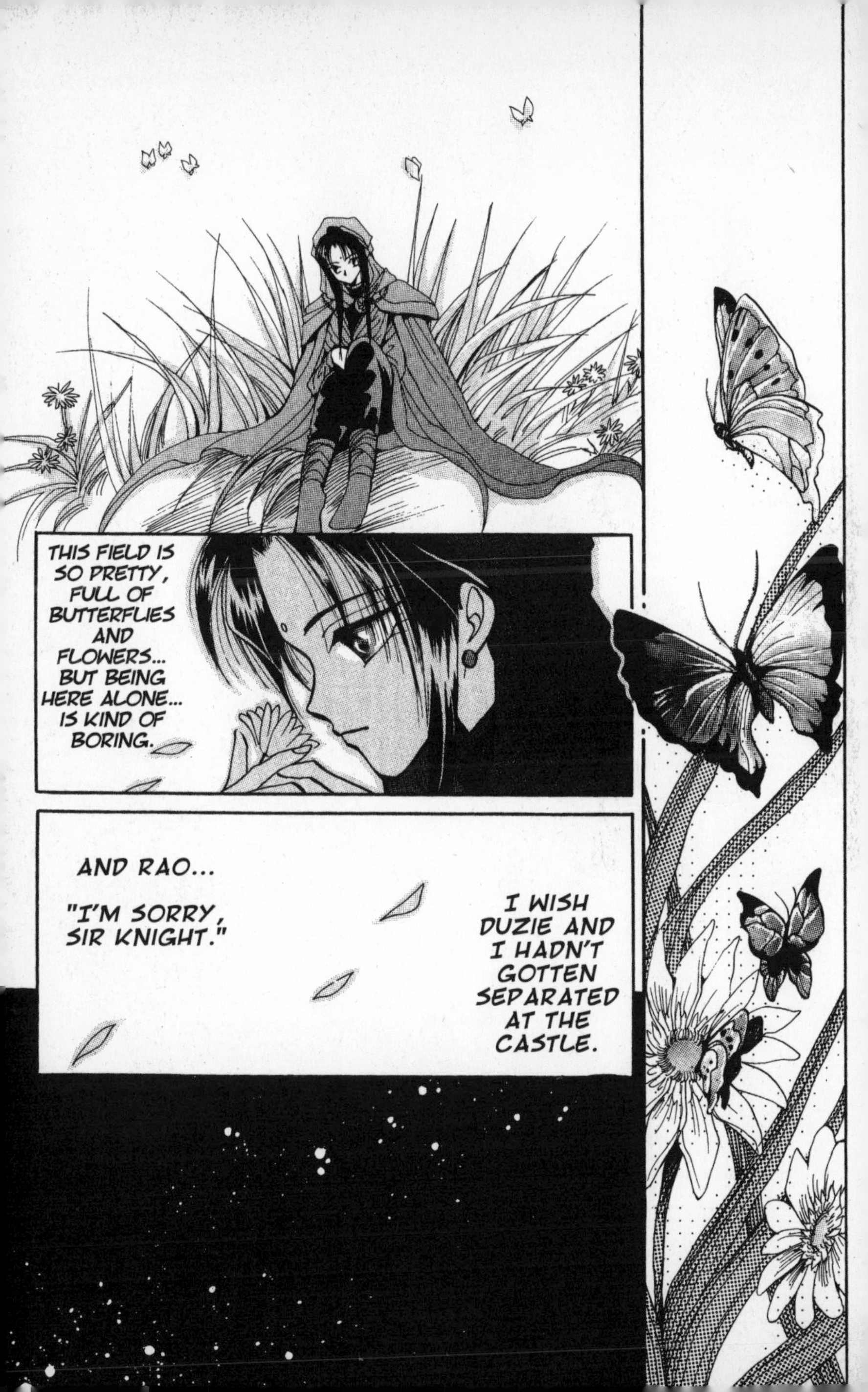
THIS FIELD IS SO PRETTY, FULL OF BUTTERFLIES AND FLOWERS... BUT BEING HERE ALONE... IS KIND OF BORING.
I WISH DUZIE AND I HADN'T GOTTEN SEPARATED AT THE CASTLE.
AND RAO...
"I'M SORRY, SIR KNIGHT."

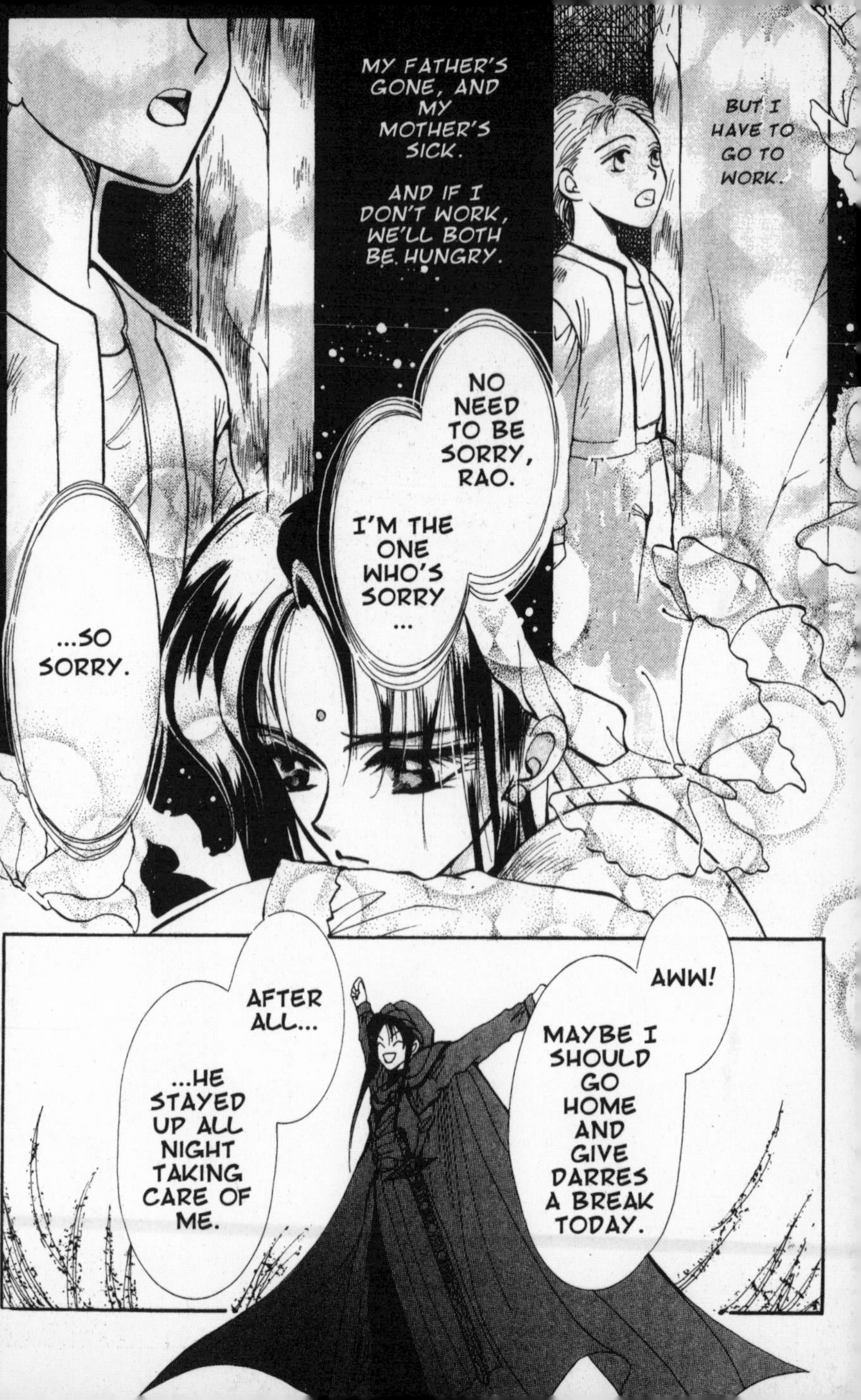
BUT I HAVE TO GO TO WORK.
MY FATHER'S GONE, AND MY MOTHER'S SICK.
AND IF I DON'T WORK, WE'LL BOTH BE HUNGRY.
NO NEED TO BE SORRY, RAO.
I'M THE ONE WHO'S SORRY ...
...SO SORRY.
AWW!
MAYBE I SHOULD GO HOME AND GIVE DARRES A BREAK TODAY.
AFTER ALL...
...HE STAYED UP ALL NIGHT TAKING CARE OF ME.

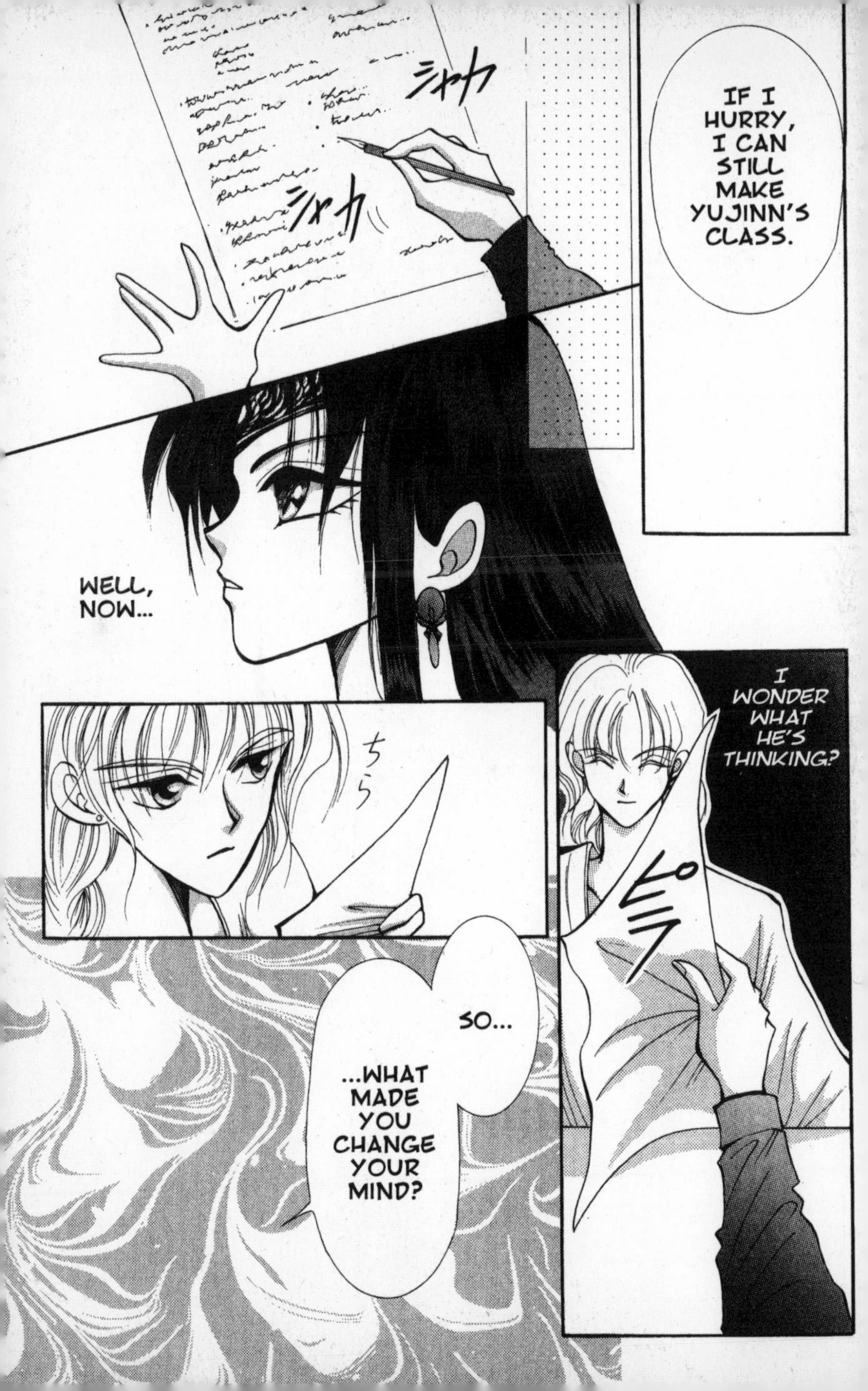
IF I HURRY, I CAN STILL MAKE YUJINN'S CLASS.
シャカ
シャカ
WELL, NOW...
I WONDER WHAT HE'S THINKING?
ペラ
ちら
SO...
...WHAT MADE YOU CHANGE YOUR MIND?

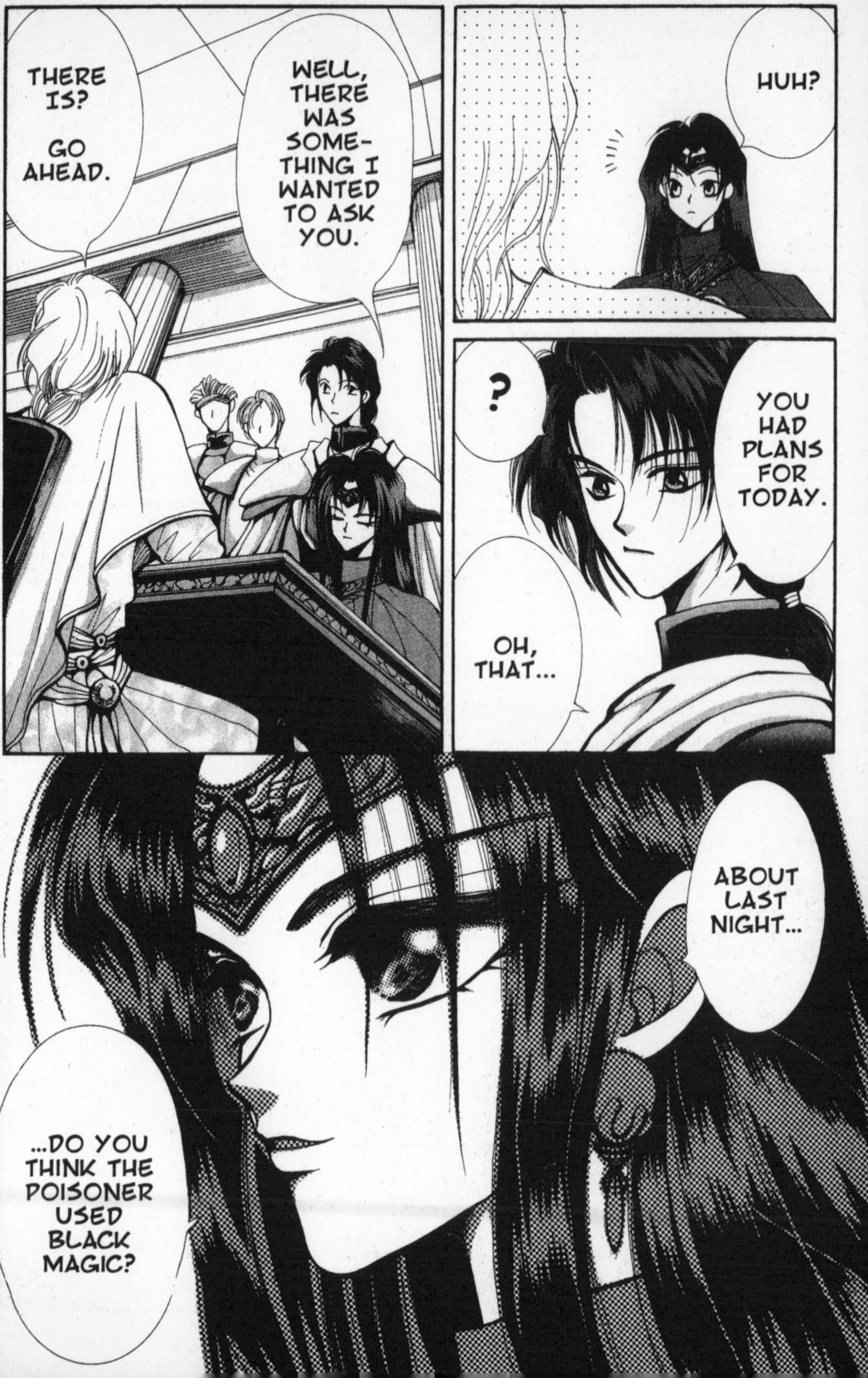
HUH?
YOU HAD PLANS FOR TODAY.
?
OH, THAT...
WELL, THERE WAS SOME-THING I WANTED TO ASK YOU.
THERE IS? GO AHEAD.
ABOUT LAST NIGHT...
...DO YOU THINK THE POISONER USED BLACK MAGIC?

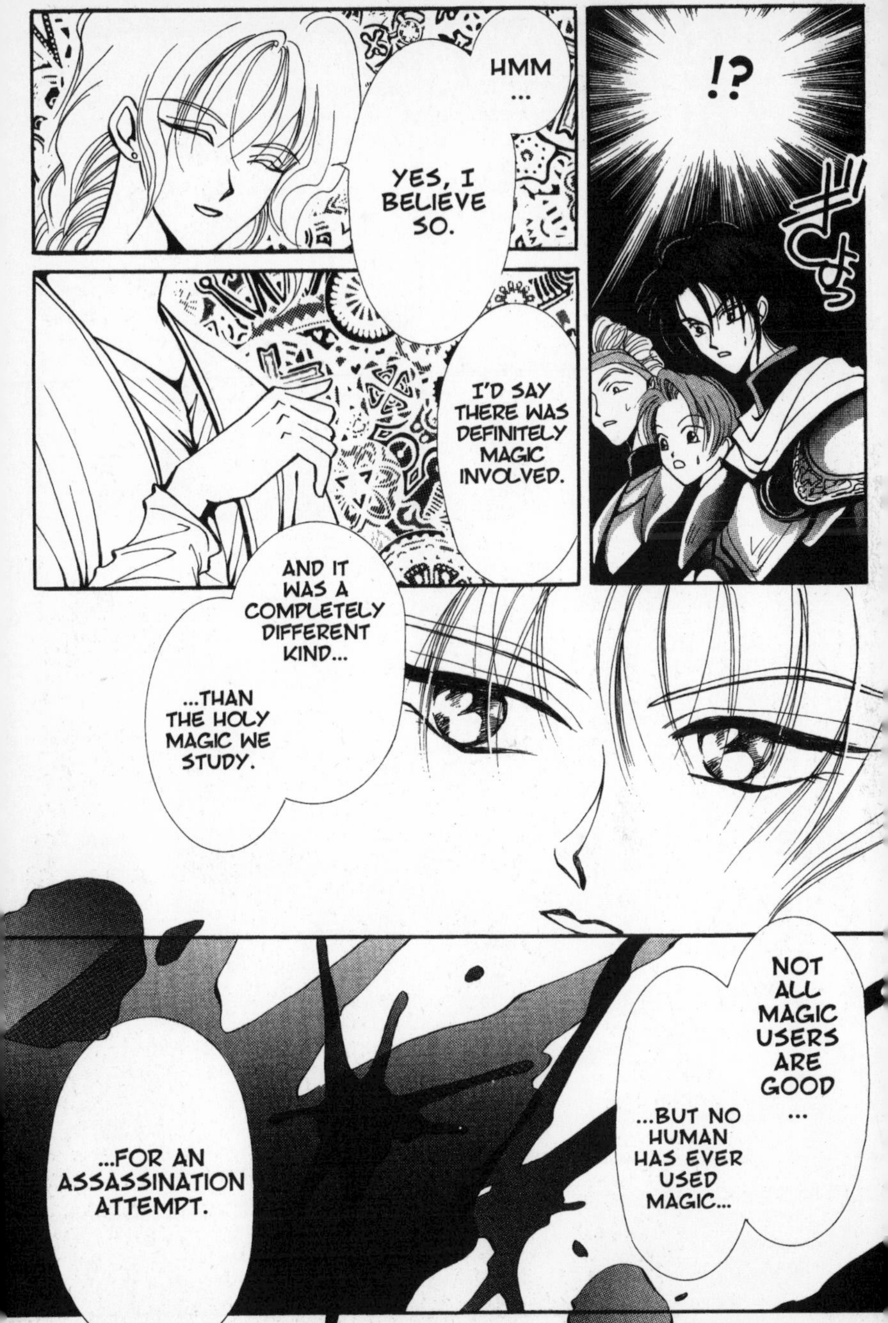
!?
HMM ...
YES, I BELIEVE SO.
I'D SAY THERE WAS DEFINITELY MAGIC INVOLVED.
AND IT WAS A COMPLETELY DIFFERENT KIND...
...THAN THE HOLY MAGIC WE STUDY.
NOT ALL MAGIC USERS ARE GOOD ...
...BUT NO HUMAN HAS EVER USED MAGIC...
...FOR AN ASSASSINATION ATTEMPT.

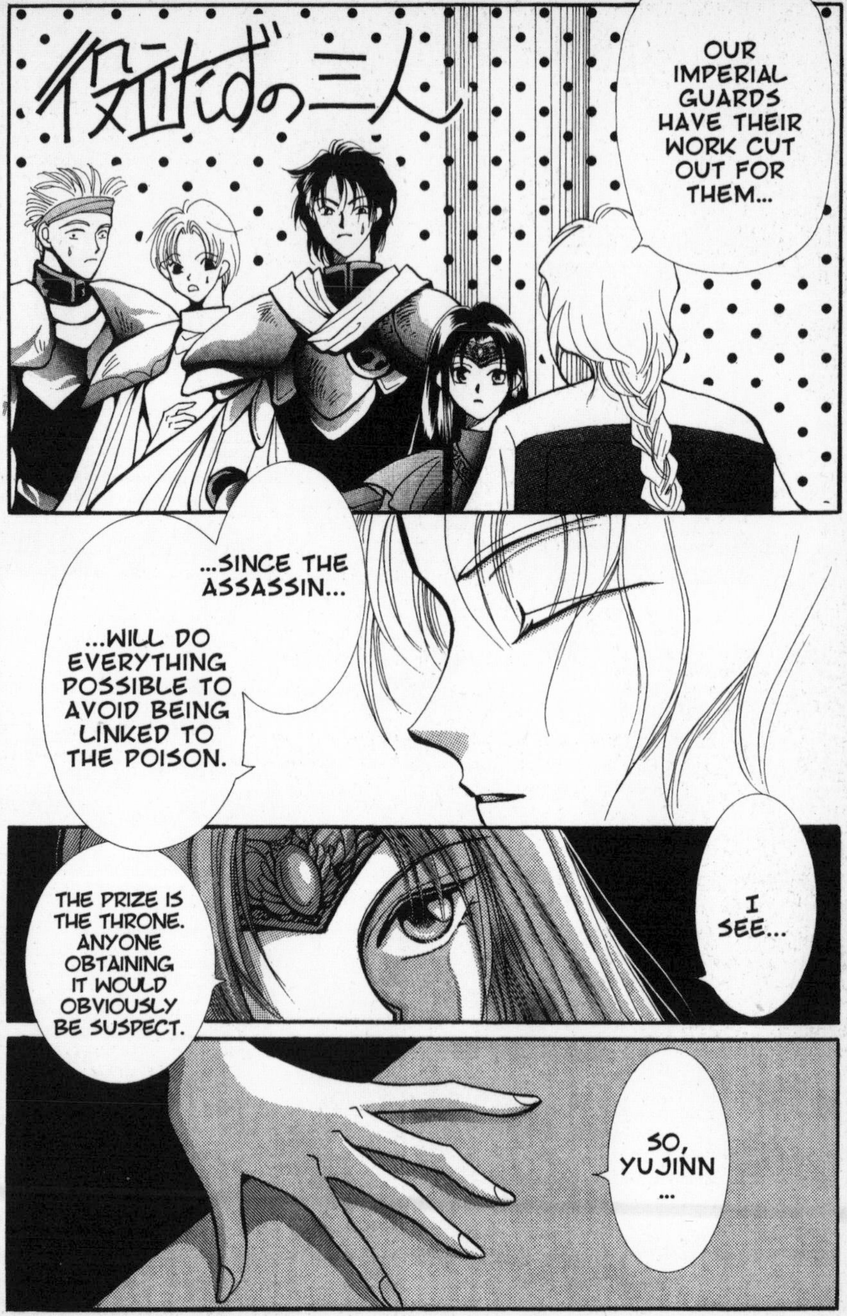
OUR IMPERIAL GUARDS HAVE THEIR WORK CUT OUT FOR THEM...
役立たずの三人
...SINCE THE ASSASSIN...
...WILL DO EVERYTHING POSSIBLE TO AVOID BEING LINKED TO THE POISON.
I SEE...
THE PRIZE IS THE THRONE. ANYONE OBTAINING IT WOULD OBVIOUSLY BE SUSPECT.
SO, YUJINN ...

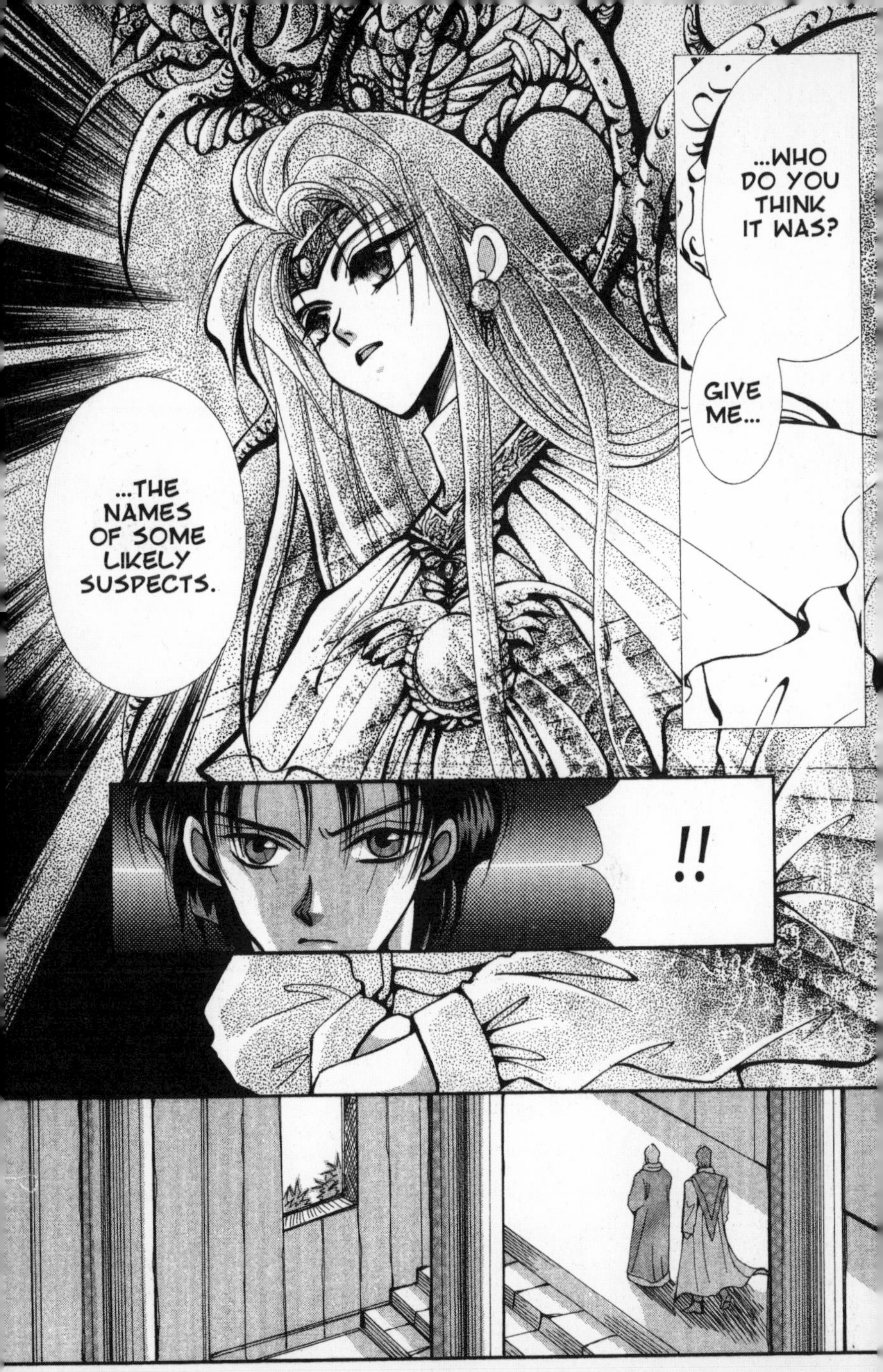
...WHO DO YOU THINK IT WAS?
GIVE ME...
...THE NAMES OF SOME LIKELY SUSPECTS.
!!

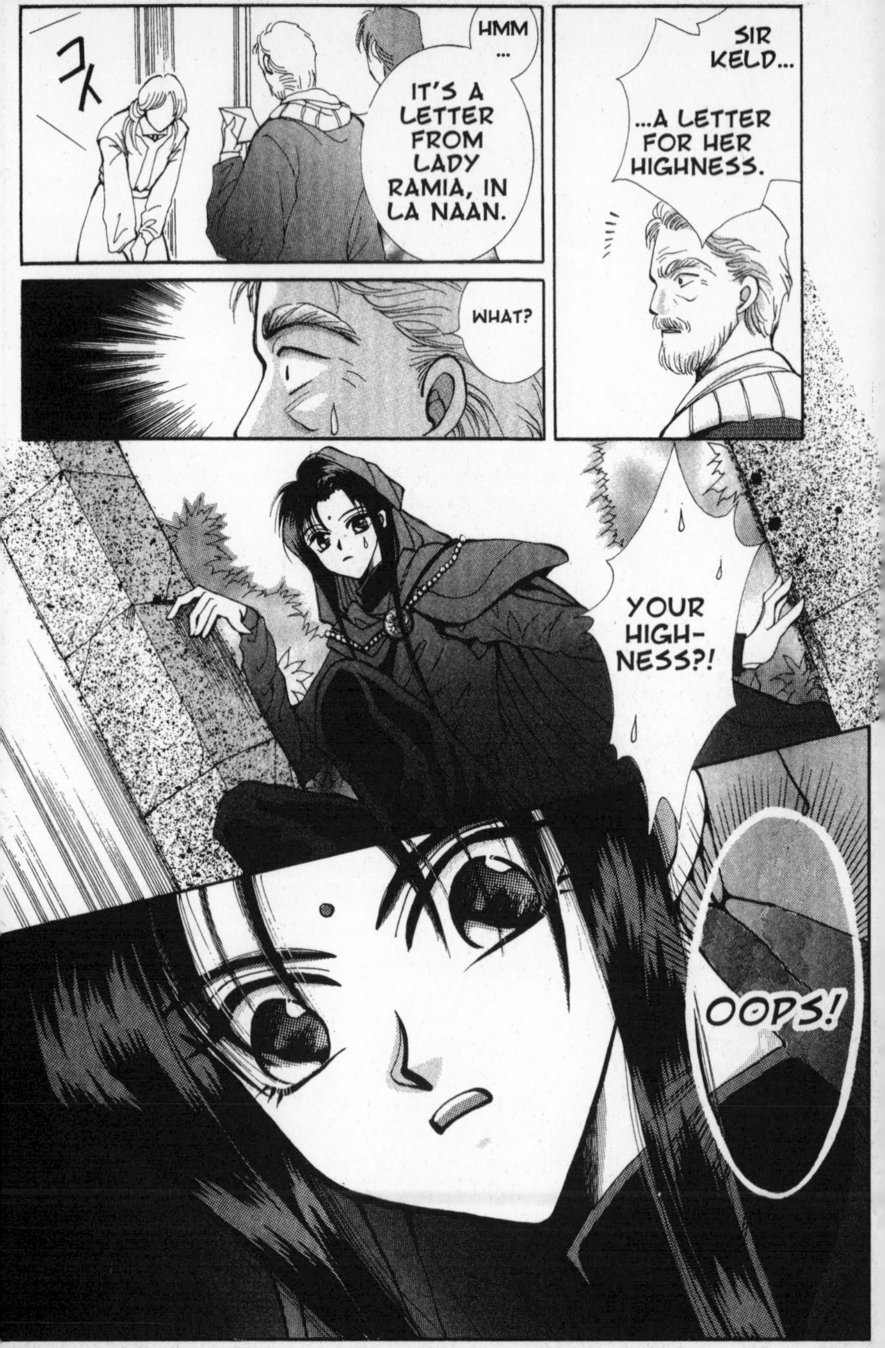
SIR KELD...
...A LETTER FOR HER HIGHNESS.
コト
HMM ...
IT'S A LETTER FROM LADY RAMIA, IN LA NAAN.
WHAT?
YOUR HIGH-NESS?!
OOPS!

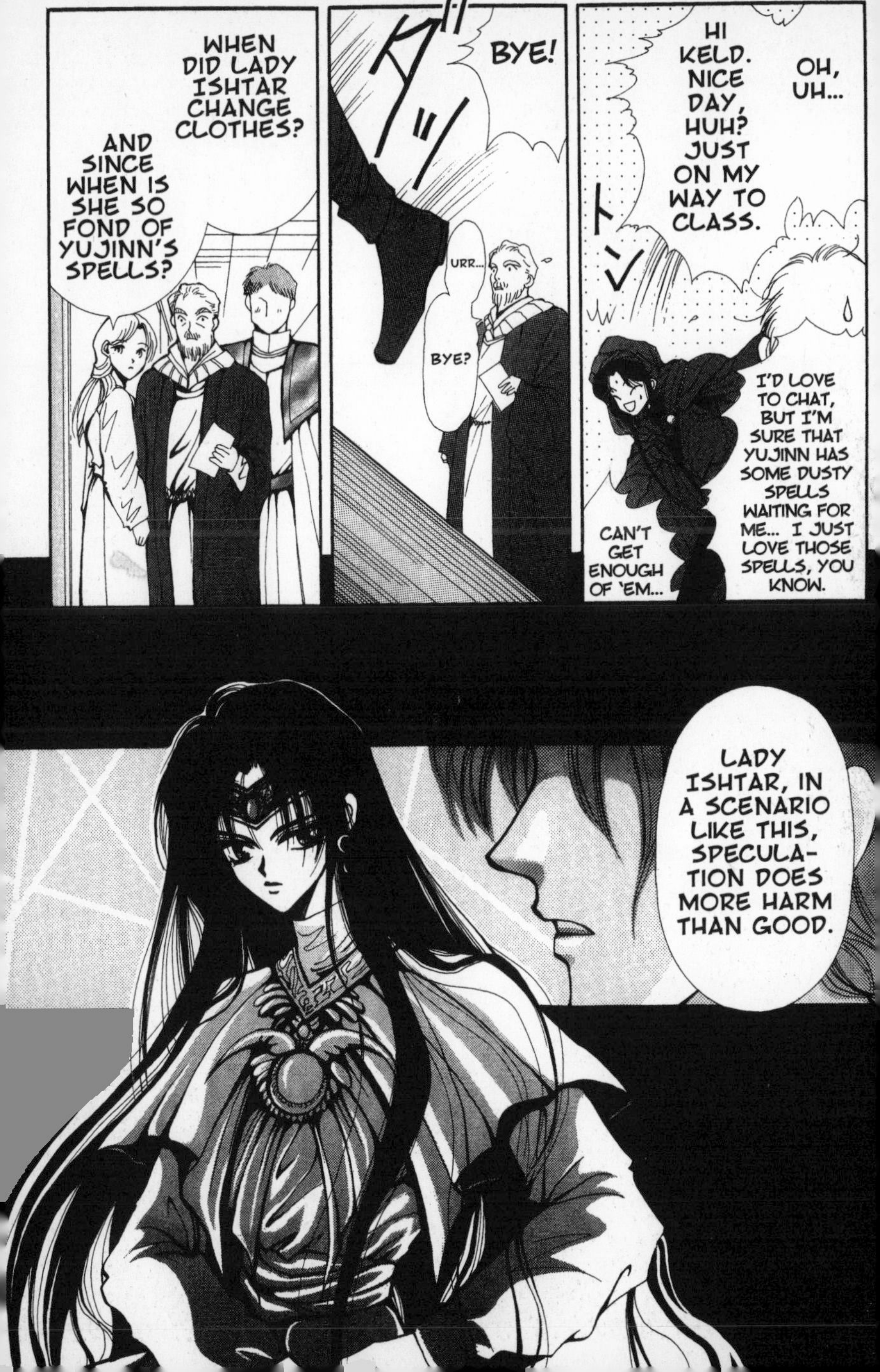
OH, UH...
HI KELD. NICE DAY, HUH? JUST ON MY WAY TO CLASS.
I'D LOVE TO CHAT, BUT I'M SURE THAT YUJINN HAS SOME DUSTY SPELLS WAITING FOR ME... I JUST LOVE THOSE SPELLS, YOU KNOW.
CAN'T GET ENOUGH OF 'EM...
BYE!
URR...
BYE?
WHEN DID LADY ISHTAR CHANGE CLOTHES?
AND SINCE WHEN IS SHE SO FOND OF YUJINN'S SPELLS?
LADY ISHTAR, IN A SCENARIO LIKE THIS, SPECULA-TION DOES MORE HARM THAN GOOD.

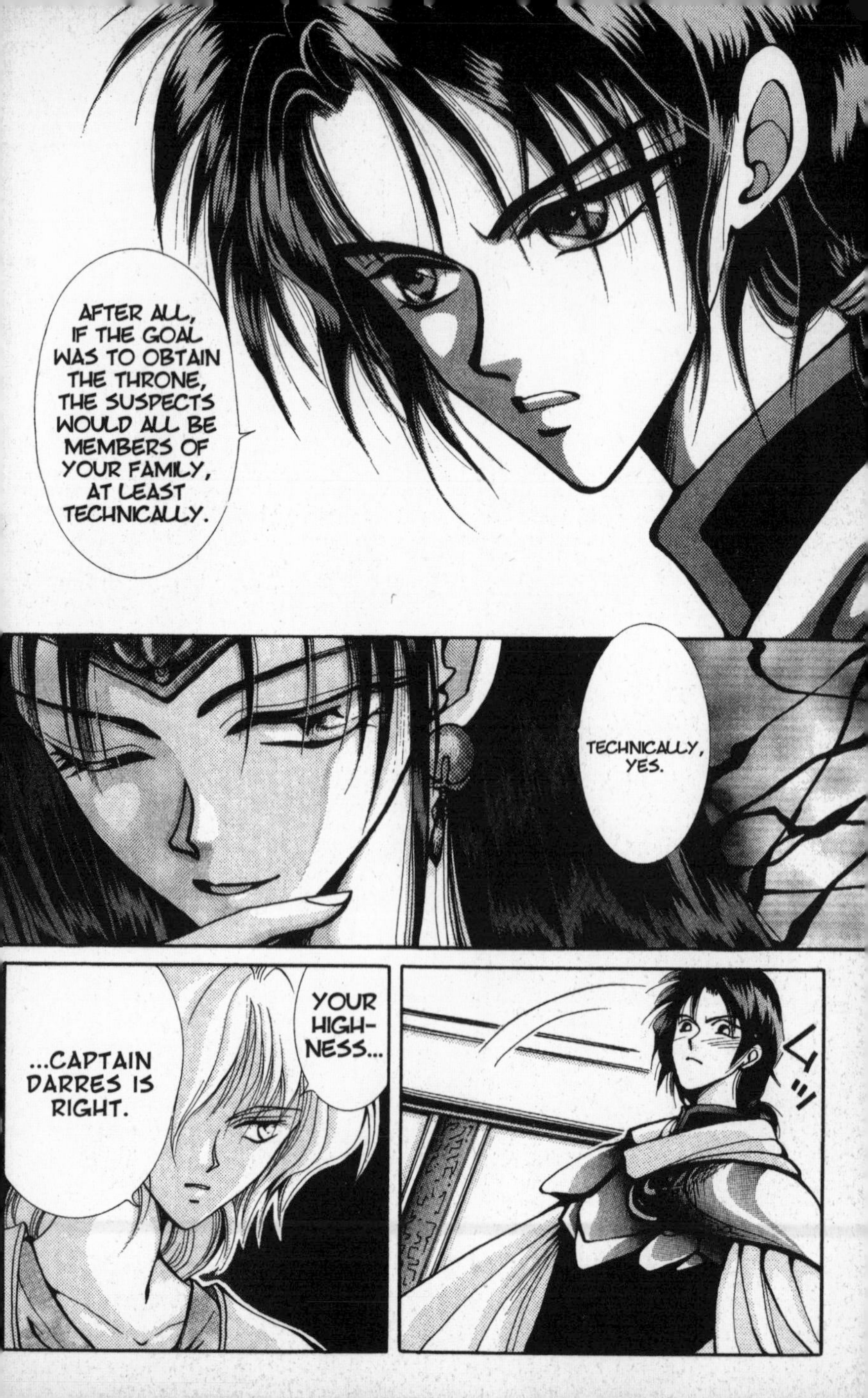
AFTER ALL, IF THE GOAL WAS TO OBTAIN THE THRONE, THE SUSPECTS WOULD ALL BE MEMBERS OF YOUR FAMILY, AT LEAST TECHNICALLY.
TECHNICALLY, YES.
ムッ
YOUR HIGH-NESS...
...CAPTAIN DARRES IS RIGHT.

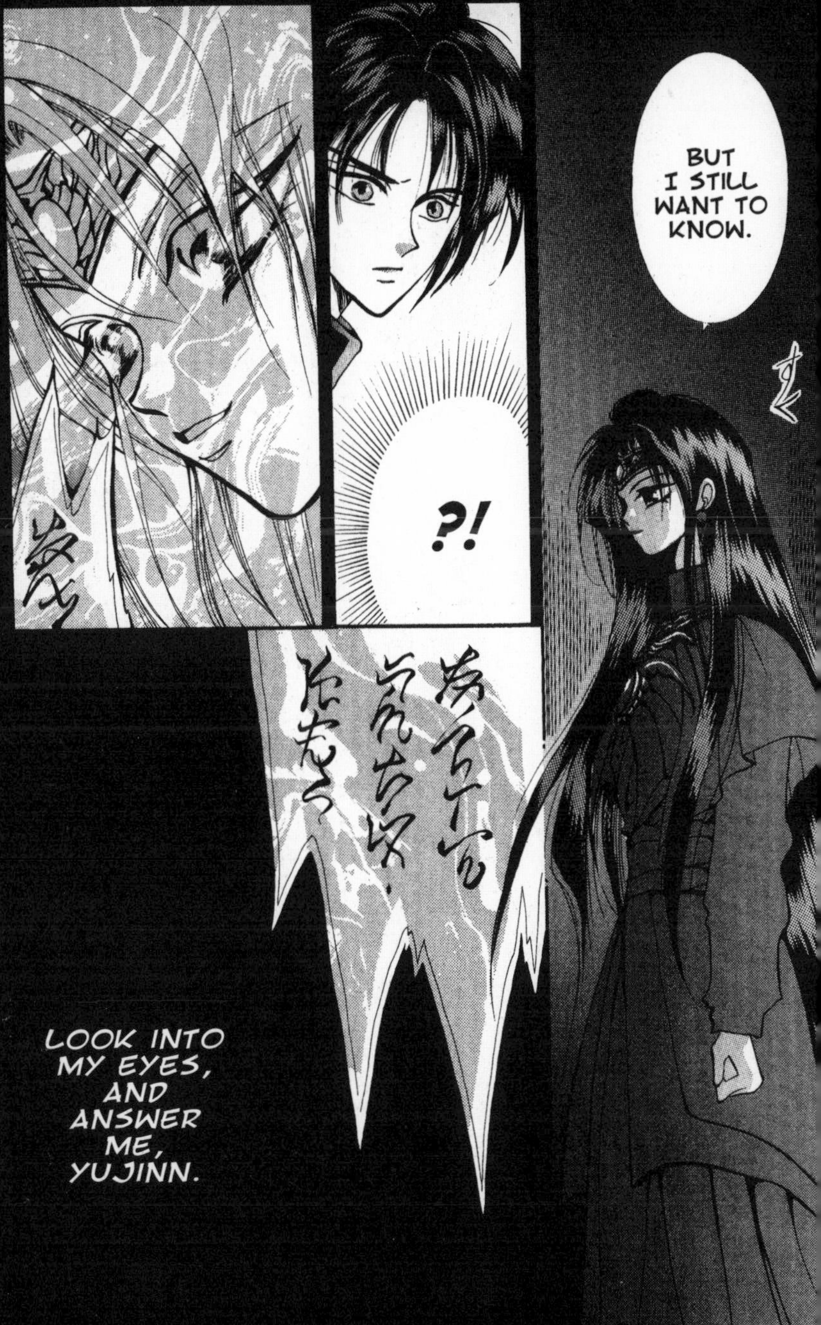
BUT I STILL WANT TO KNOW.
?!
LOOK INTO MY EYES, AND ANSWER ME, YUJINN.

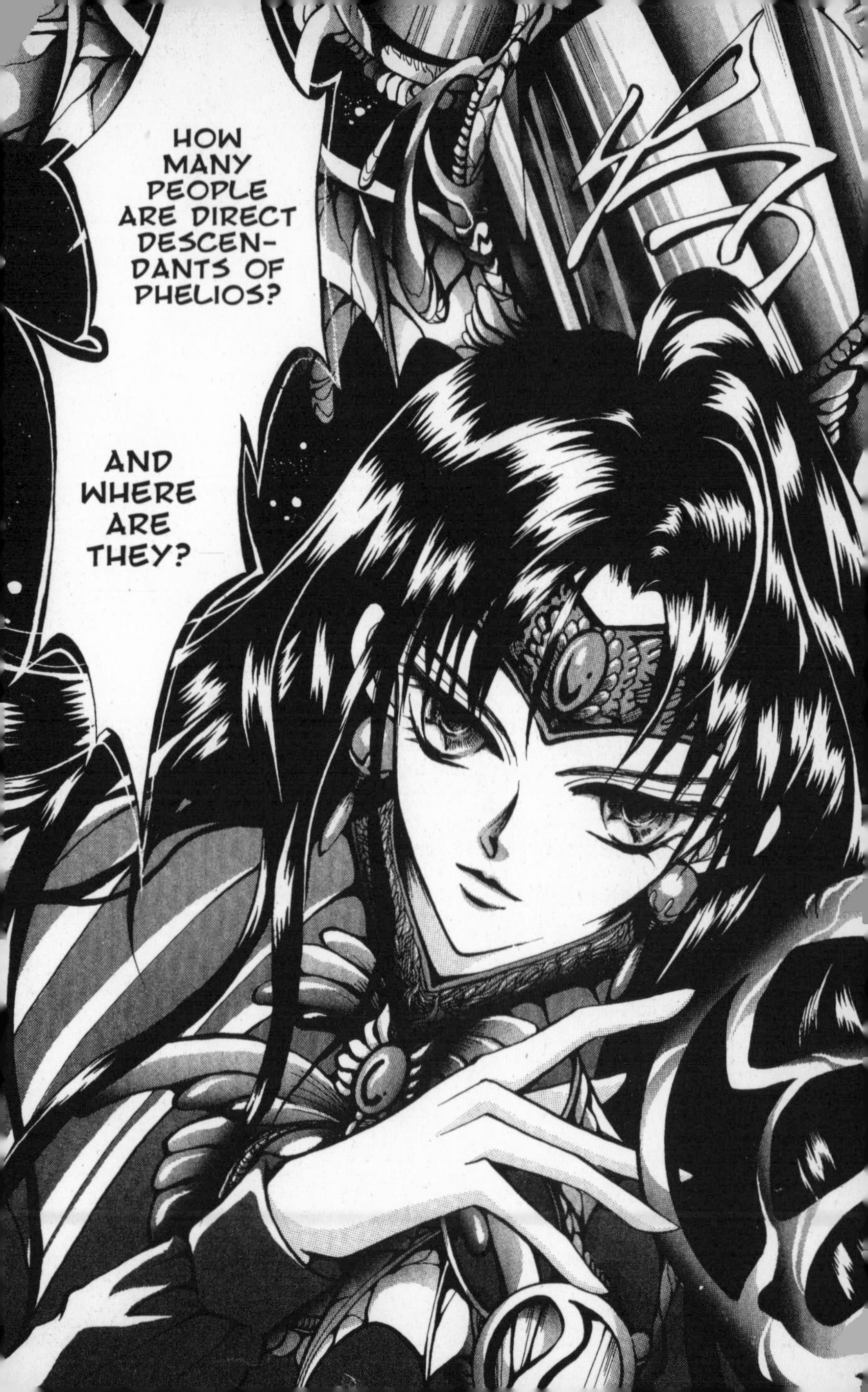
HOW MANY PEOPLE ARE DIRECT DESCEN-DANTS OF PHELIOS?
AND WHERE ARE THEY?

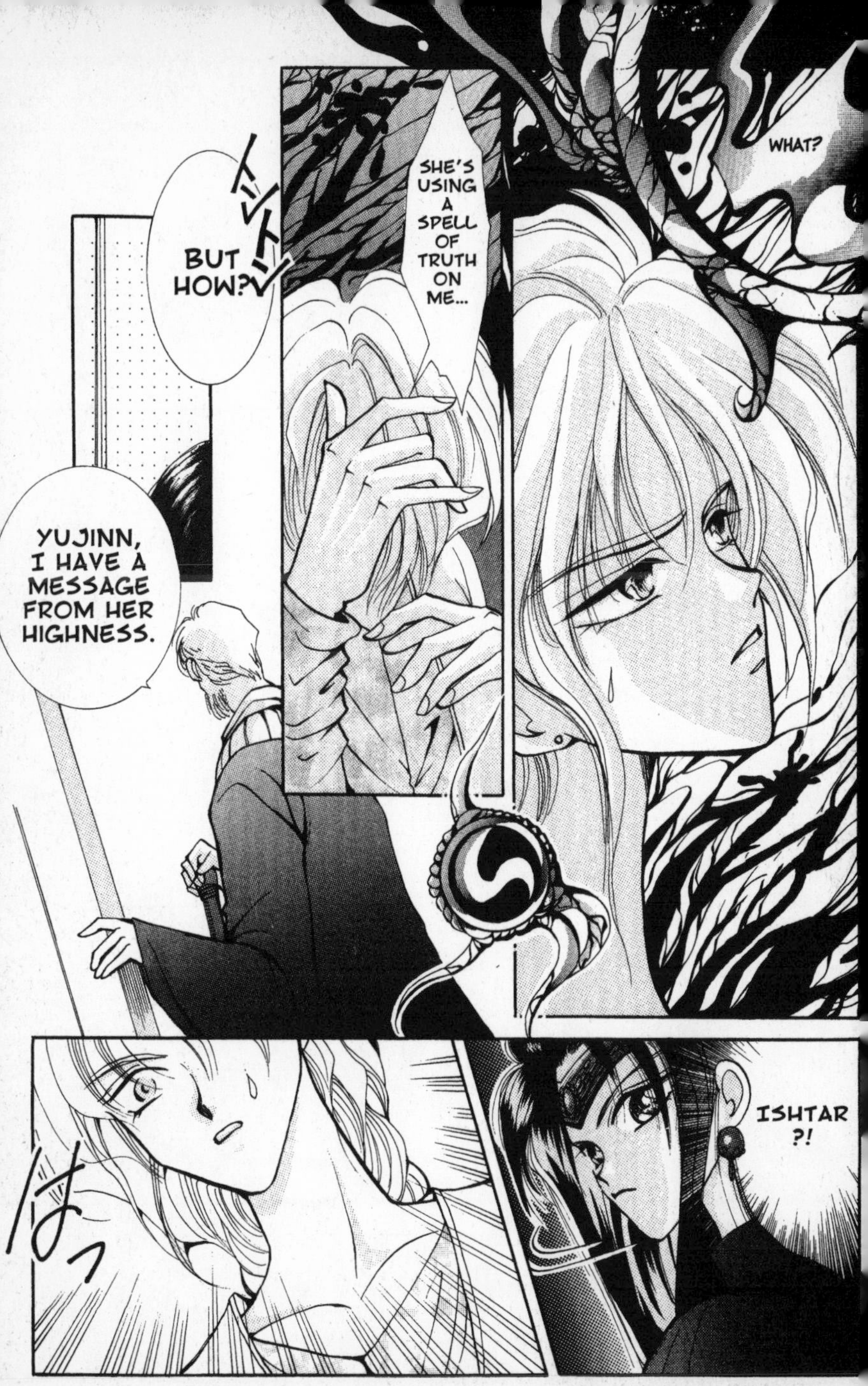

WHAT?
SHE'S USING A SPELL OF TRUTH ON ME...
トントン
BUT HOW?
YUJINN, I HAVE A MESSAGE FROM HER HIGHNESS.
ISHTAR ?!
はっ

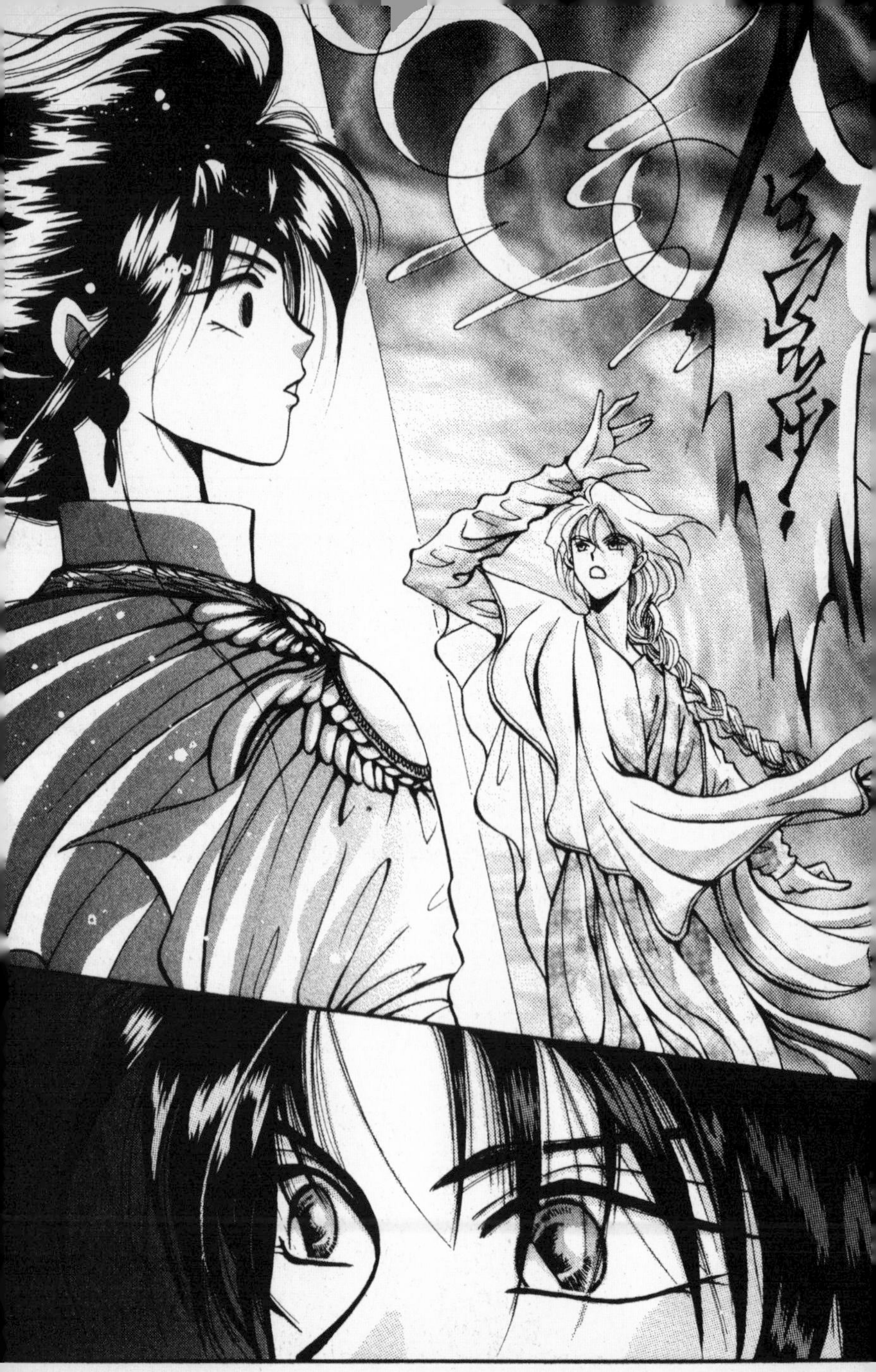

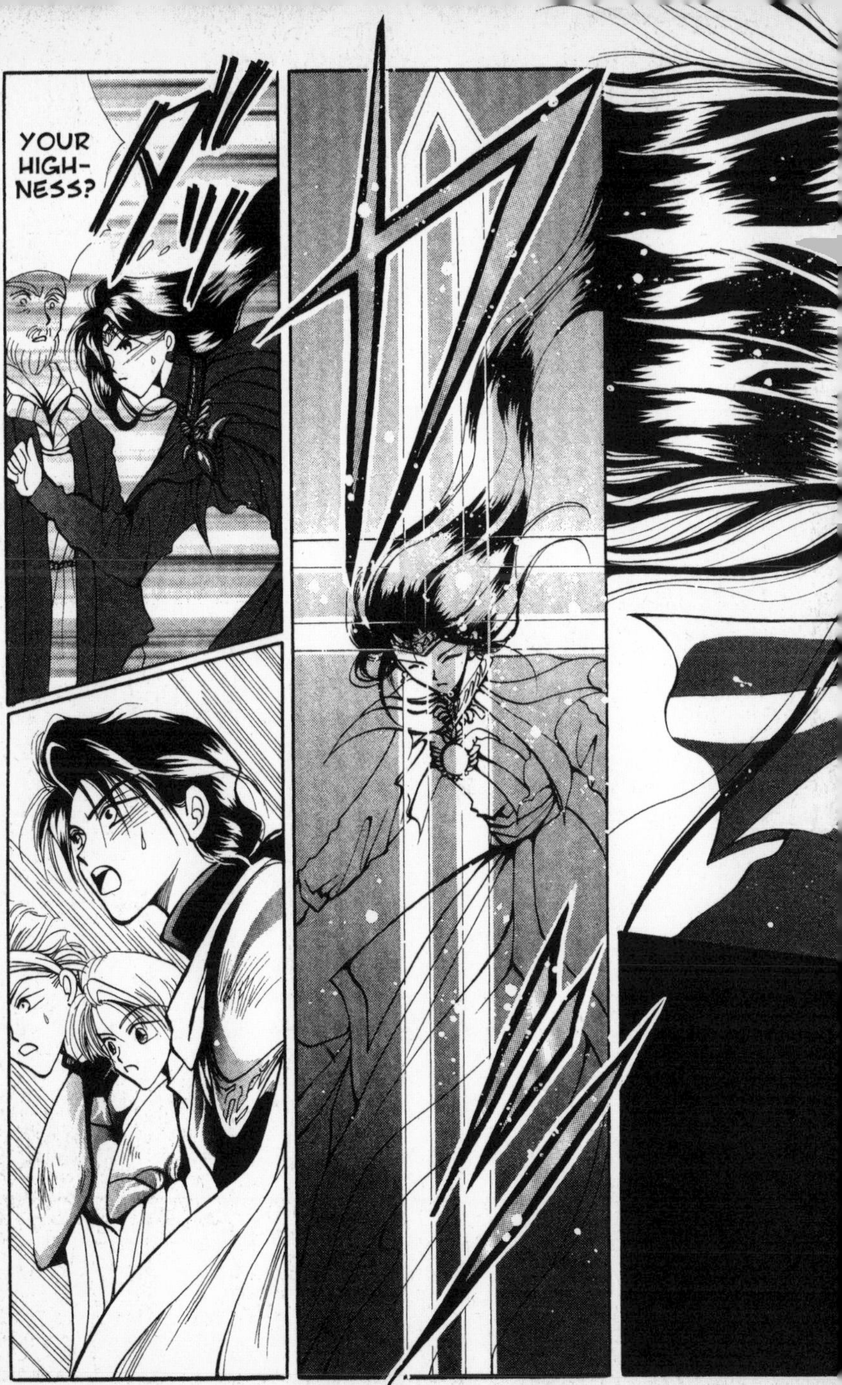
YOUR HIGH-NESS?

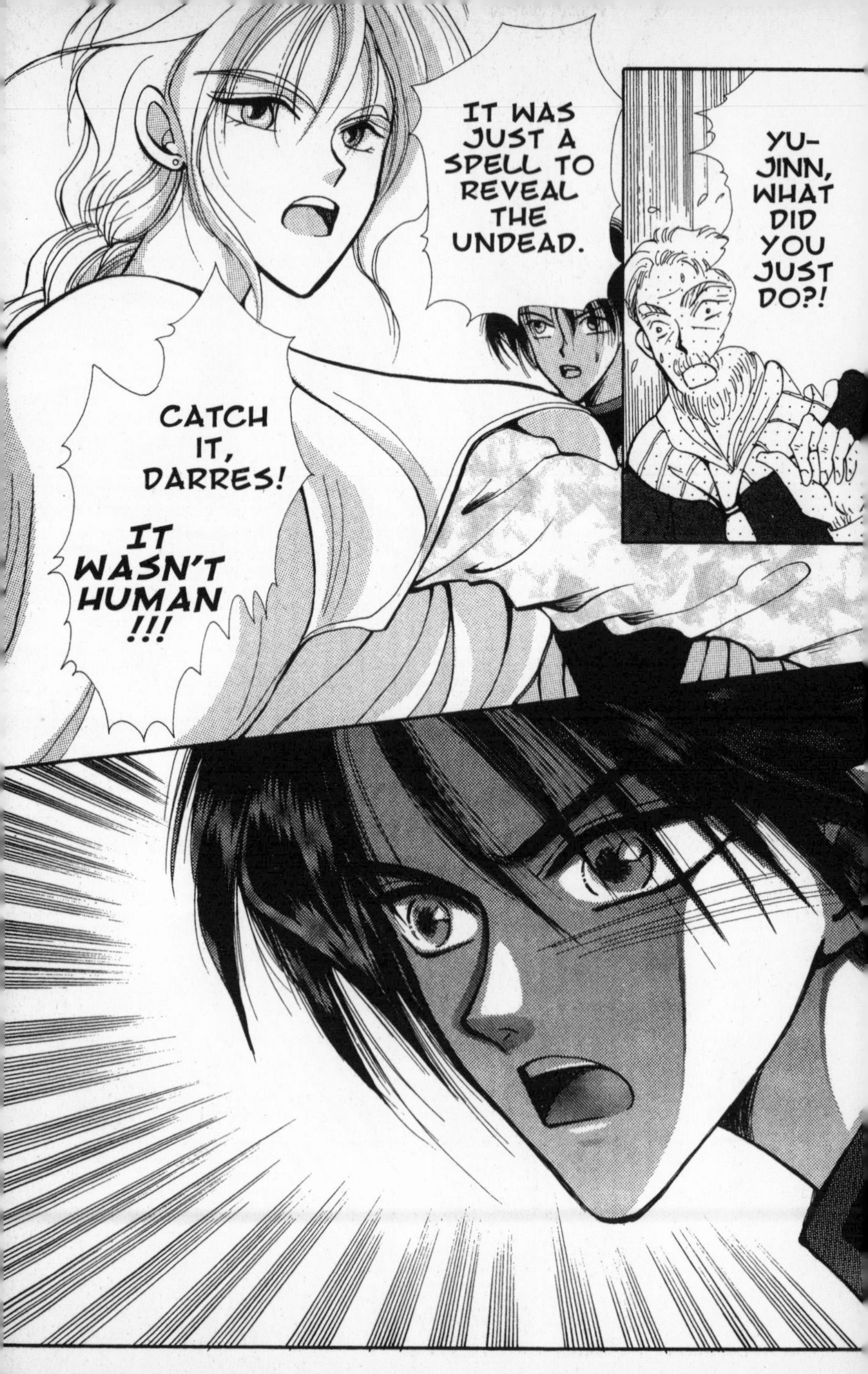
YU-JINN, WHAT DID YOU JUST DO?!
IT WAS JUST A SPELL TO REVEAL THE UNDEAD.
CATCH IT, DARRES!
IT WASN'T HUMAN!!!

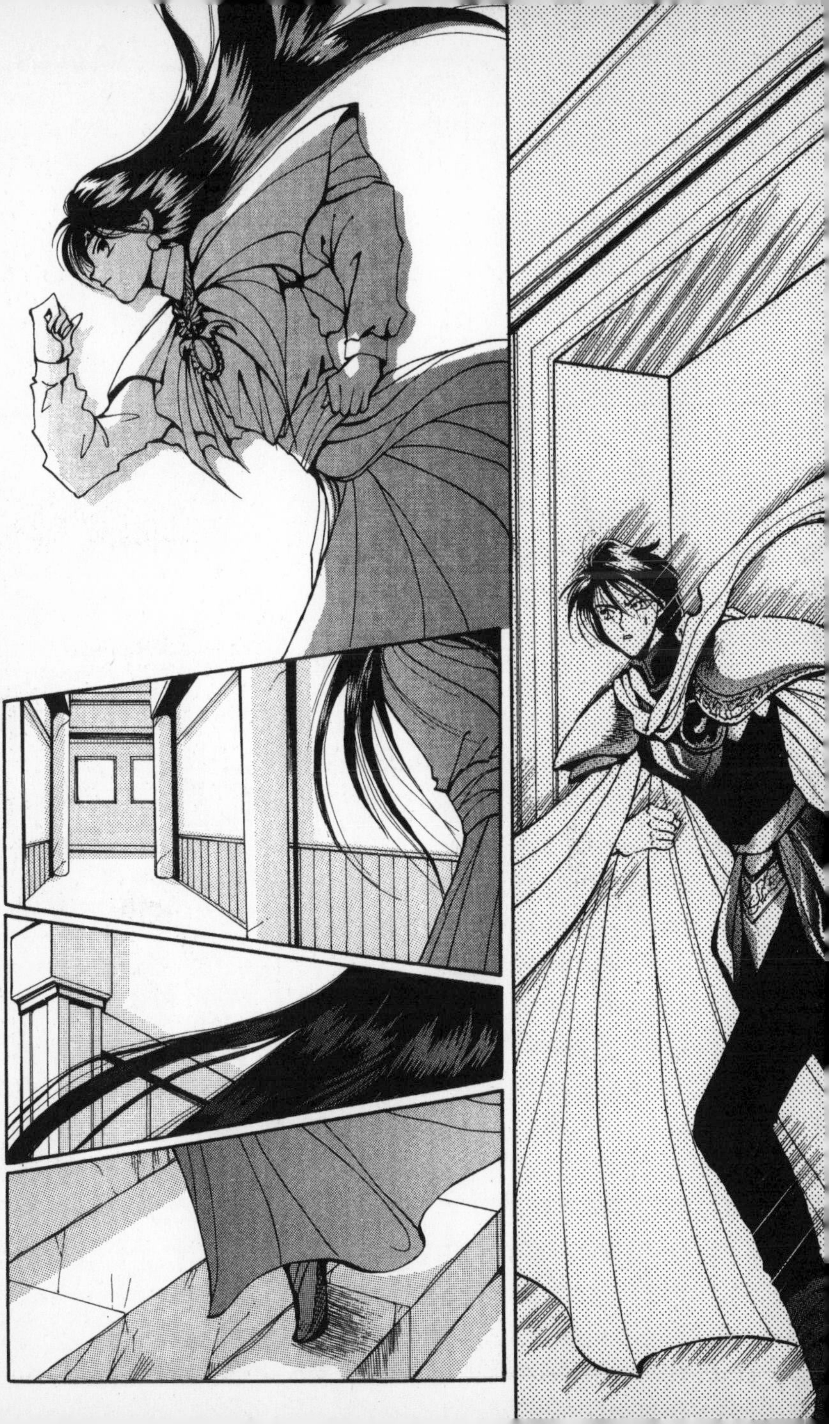

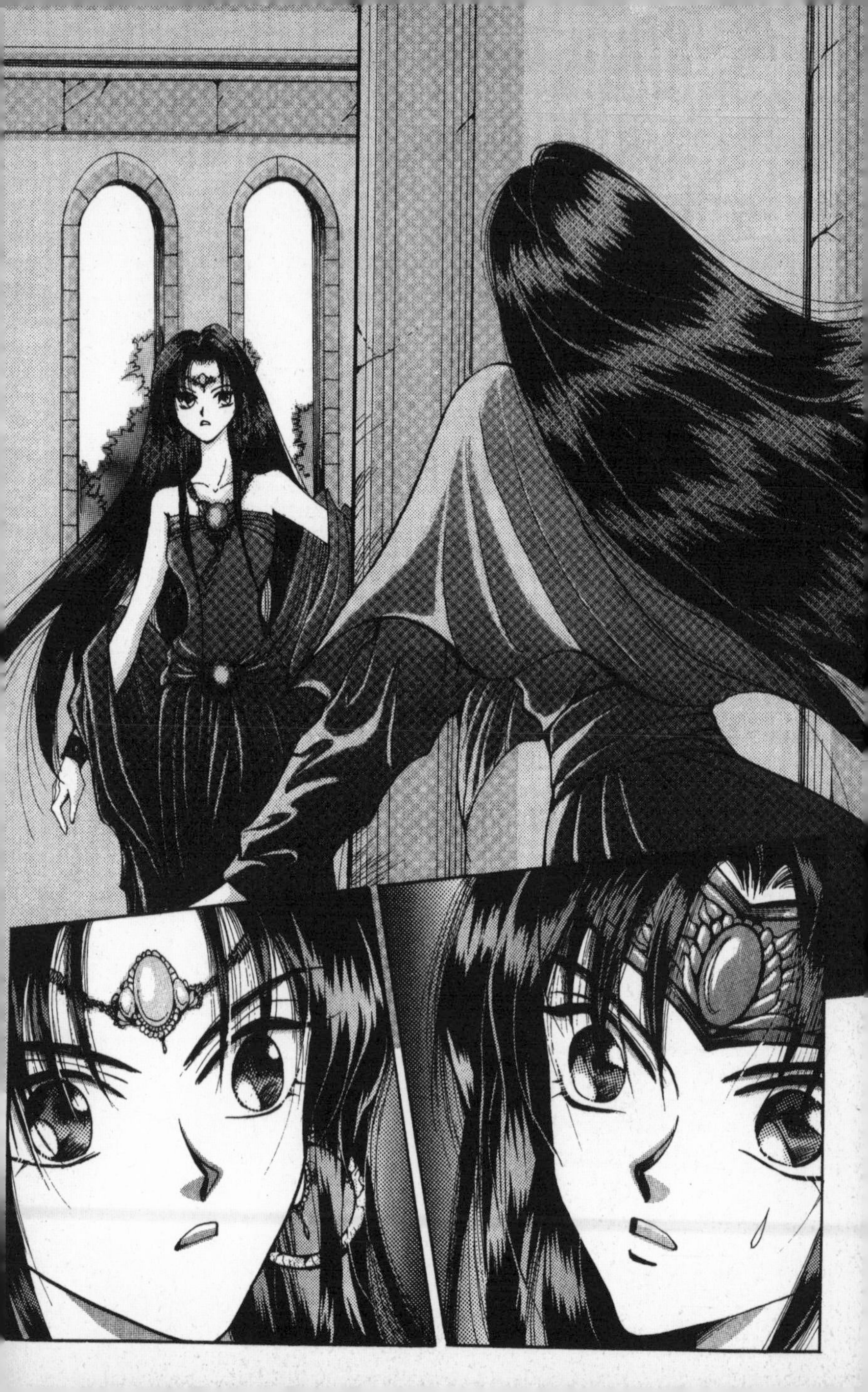

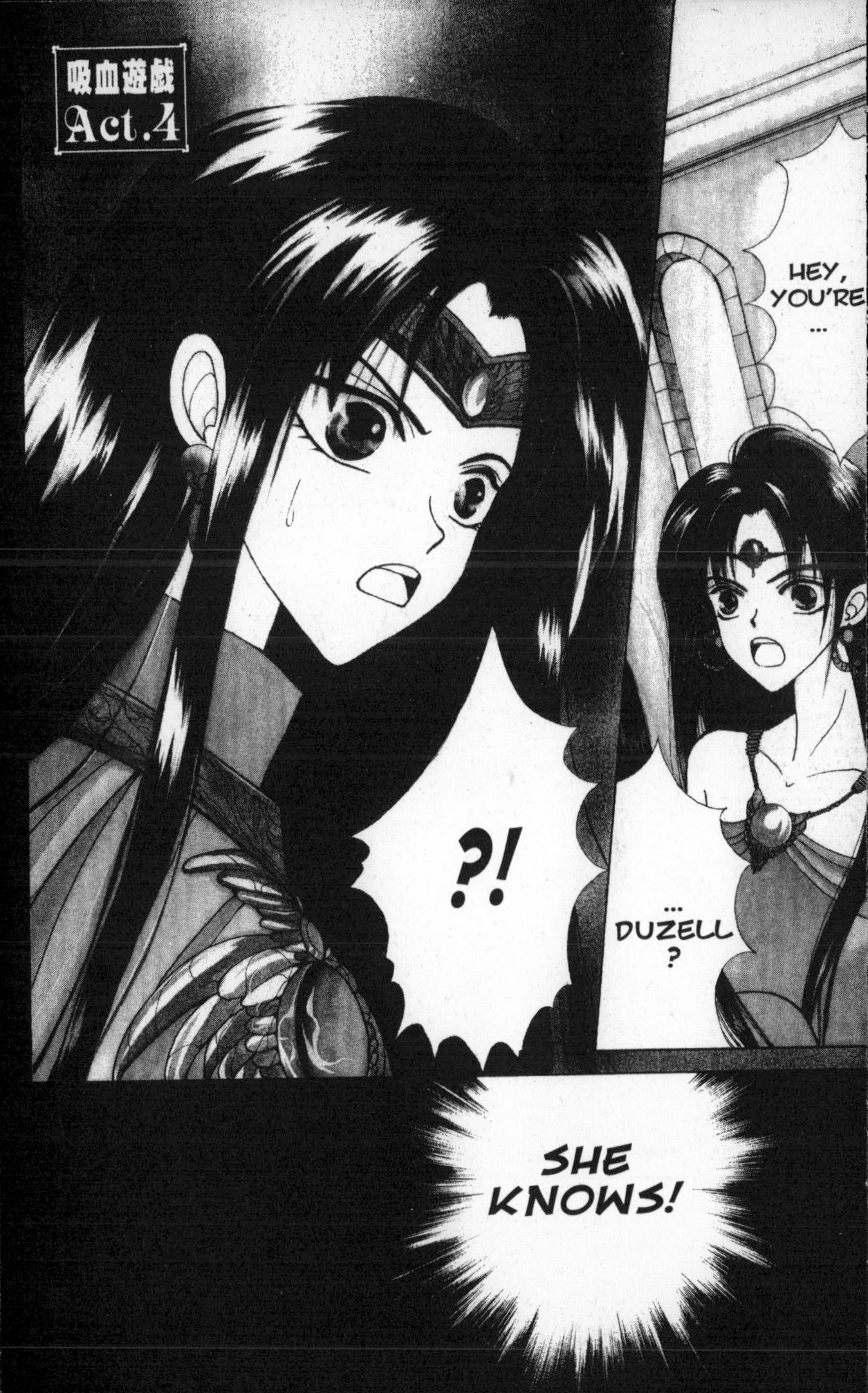

吸血遊戯
Act.4
HEY, YOU'RE ...
?!
... DUZELL ?
SHE KNOWS!

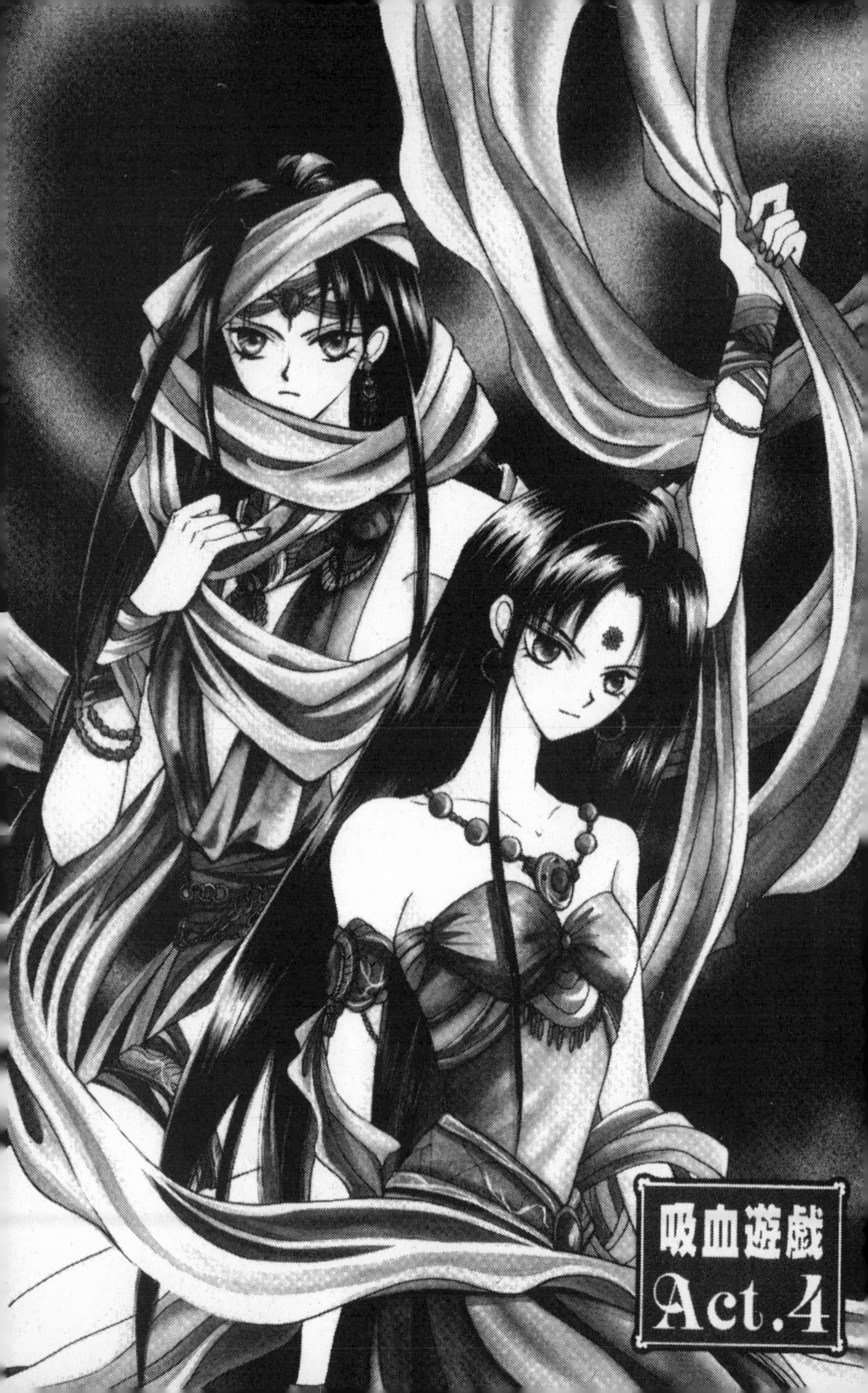
吸血遊戯
Act.4

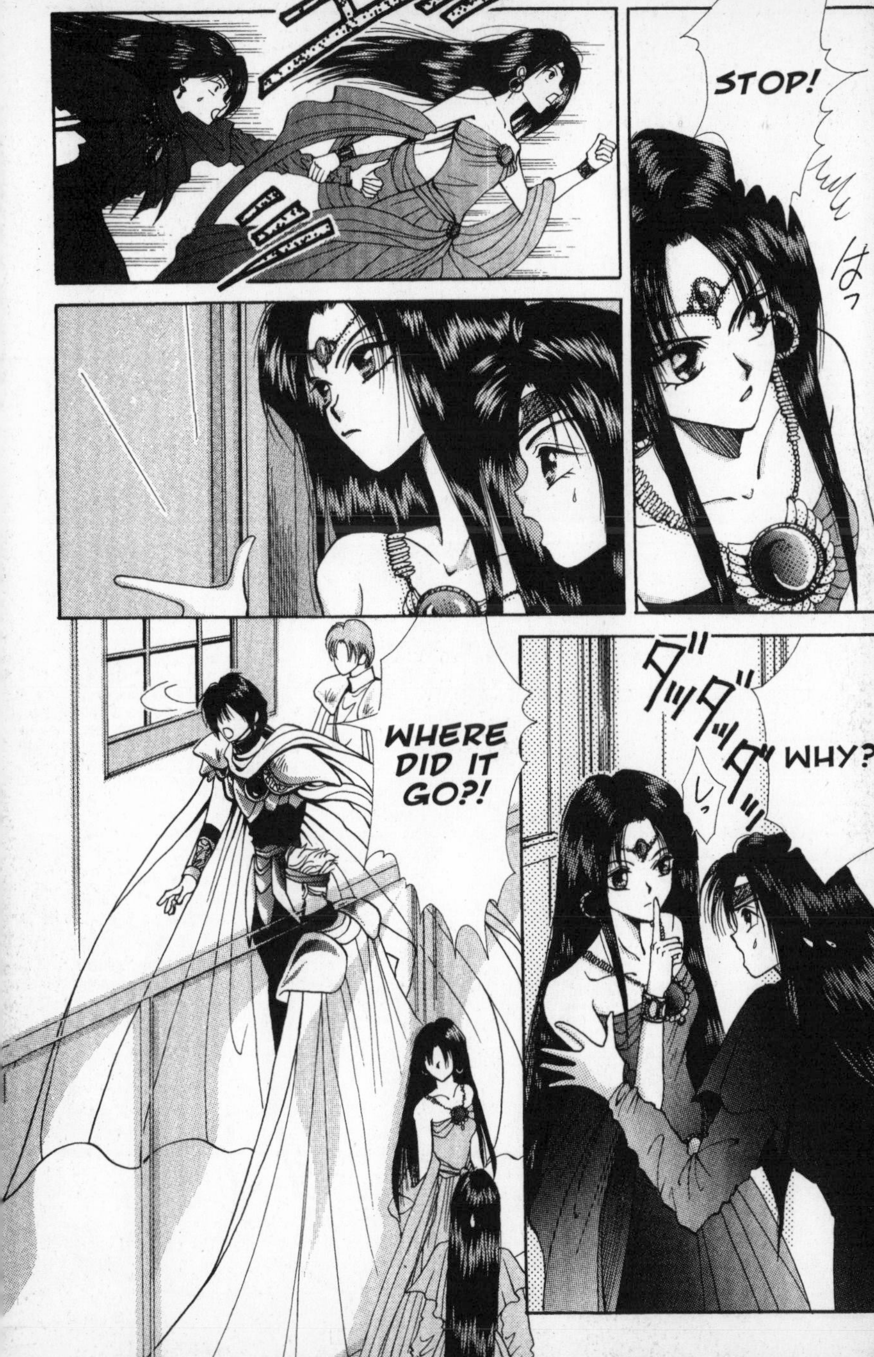
STOP!
はっ
ダッダッダッ
WHY?
しっ
WHERE DID IT GO?!

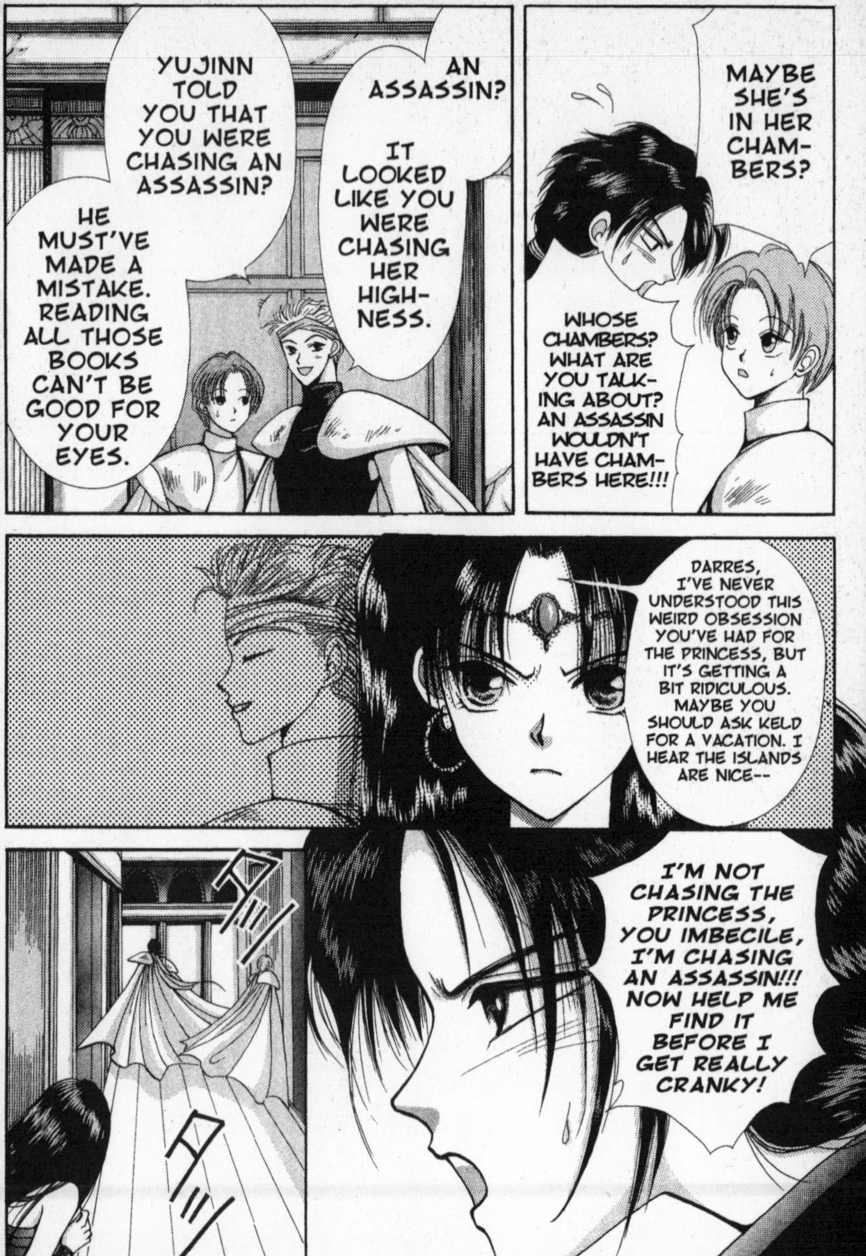
MAYBE SHE'S IN HER CHAMBERS?
WHOSE CHAMBERS? WHAT ARE YOU TALKING ABOUT? AN ASSASSIN WOULDN'T HAVE CHAMBERS HERE!!!
AN ASSASSIN?
IT LOOKED LIKE YOU WERE CHASING HER HIGHNESS.
YUJINN TOLD YOU THAT YOU WERE CHASING AN ASSASSIN?
HE MUST'VE MADE A MISTAKE. READING ALL THOSE BOOKS CAN'T BE GOOD FOR YOUR EYES.
DARRES, I'VE NEVER UNDERSTOOD THIS WEIRD OBSESSION YOU'VE HAD FOR THE PRINCESS, BUT IT'S GETTING A BIT RIDICULOUS. MAYBE YOU SHOULD ASK KELD FOR A VACATION. I HEAR THE ISLANDS ARE NICE--
I'M NOT CHASING THE PRINCESS, YOU IMBECILE, I'M CHASING AN ASSASSIN!!! NOW HELP ME FIND IT BEFORE I GET REALLY CRANKY!

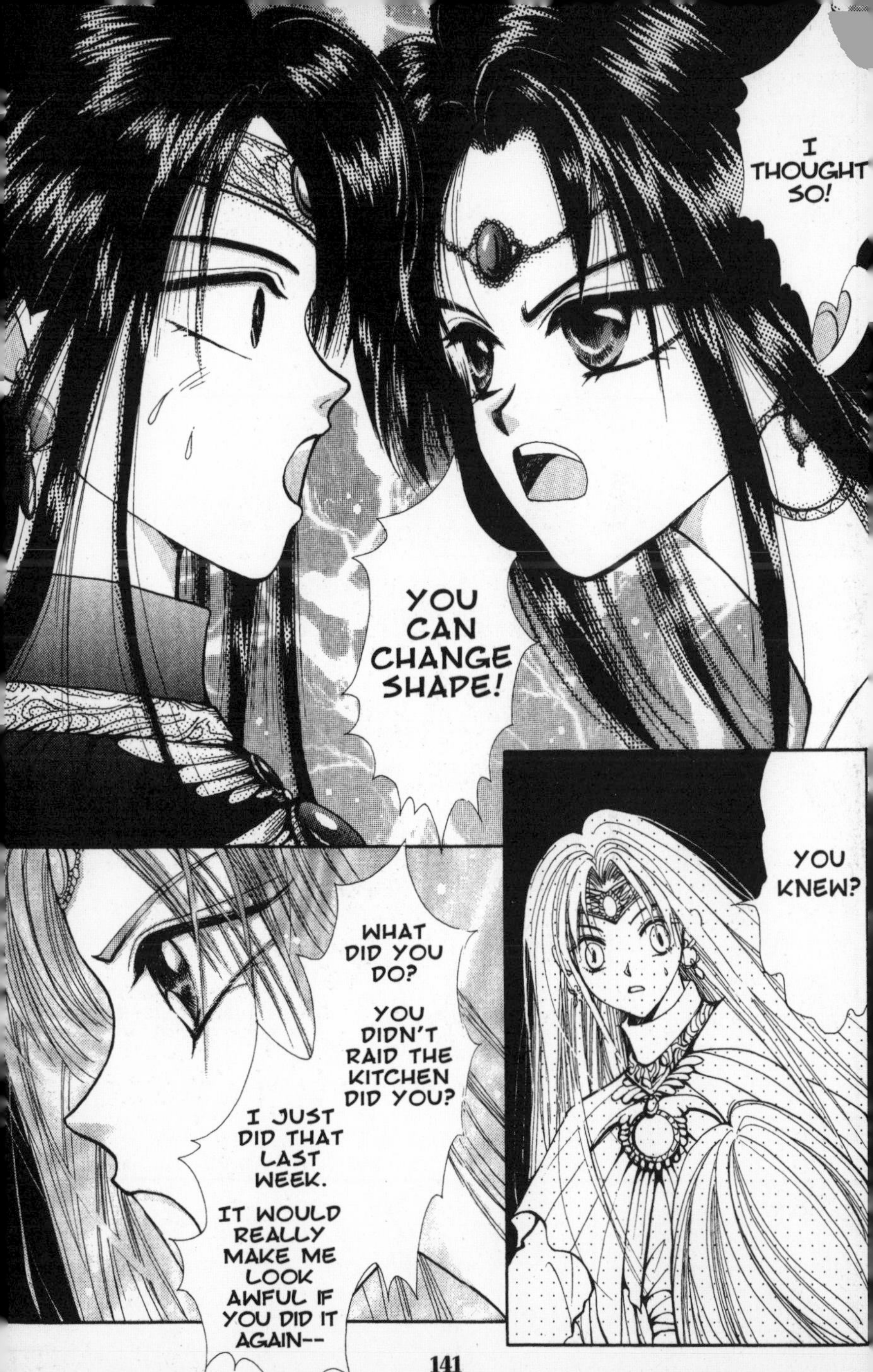
I THOUGHT SO!
YOU CAN CHANGE SHAPE!
YOU KNEW?
WHAT DID YOU DO?
YOU DIDN'T RAID THE KITCHEN DID YOU?
I JUST DID THAT LAST WEEK.
IT WOULD REALLY MAKE ME LOOK AWFUL IF YOU DID IT AGAIN--

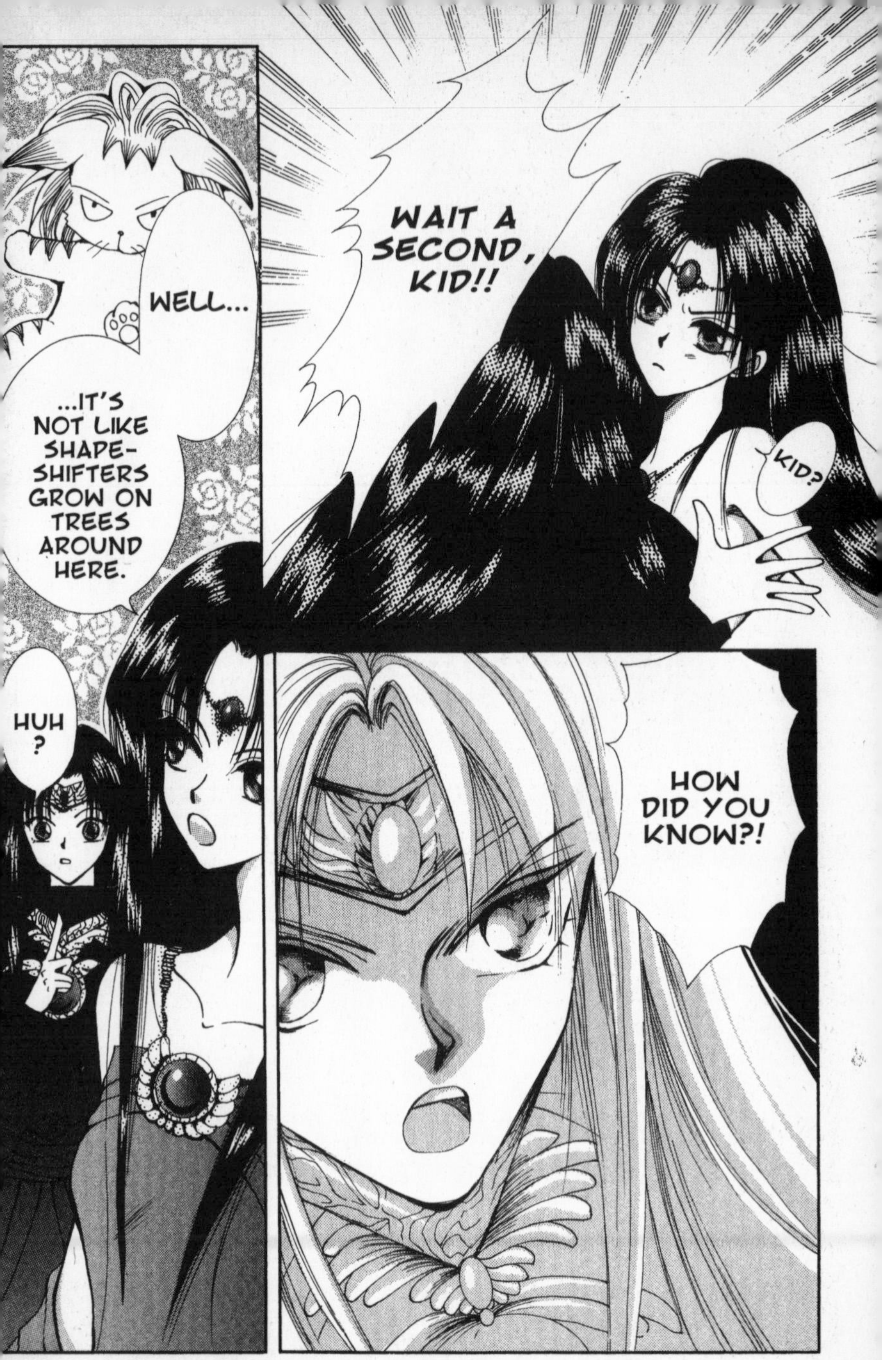
WAIT A SECOND, KID!!
KID?
HOW DID YOU KNOW?!
WELL...
...IT'S NOT LIKE SHAPE-SHIFTERS GROW ON TREES AROUND HERE.
HUH?

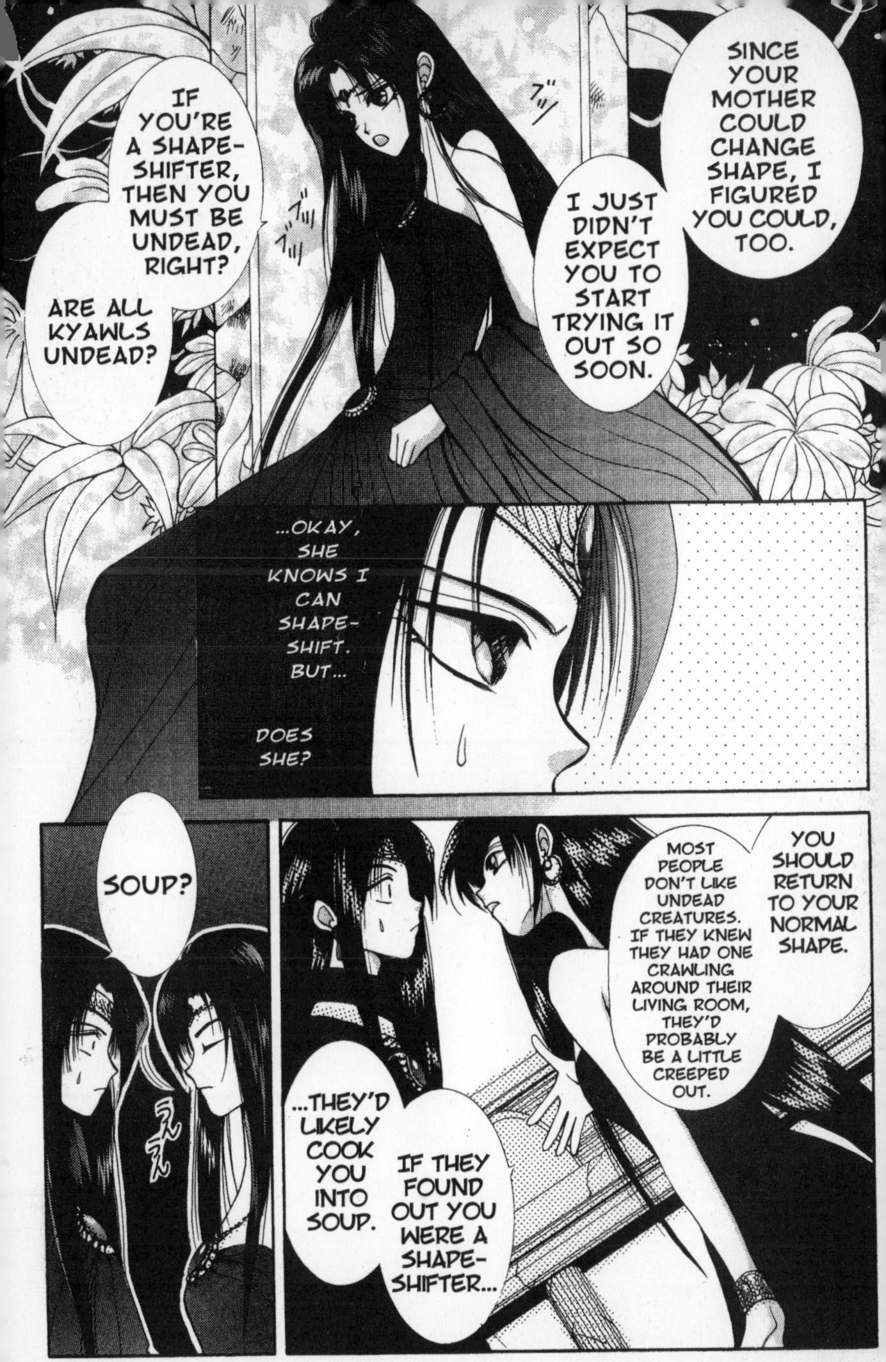
SINCE YOUR MOTHER COULD CHANGE SHAPE, I FIGURED YOU COULD, TOO.
I JUST DIDN'T EXPECT YOU TO START TRYING IT OUT SO SOON.
IF YOU'RE A SHAPE-SHIFTER, THEN YOU MUST BE UNDEAD, RIGHT?
ARE ALL KYAWLS UNDEAD?
...OKAY, SHE KNOWS I CAN SHAPE-SHIFT. BUT...
DOES SHE?
YOU SHOULD RETURN TO YOUR NORMAL SHAPE.
MOST PEOPLE DON'T LIKE UNDEAD CREATURES. IF THEY KNEW THEY HAD ONE CRAWLING AROUND THEIR LIVING ROOM, THEY'D PROBABLY BE A LITTLE CREEPED OUT.
IF THEY FOUND OUT YOU WERE A SHAPE-SHIFTER...
...THEY'D LIKELY COOK YOU INTO SOUP.
SOUP?

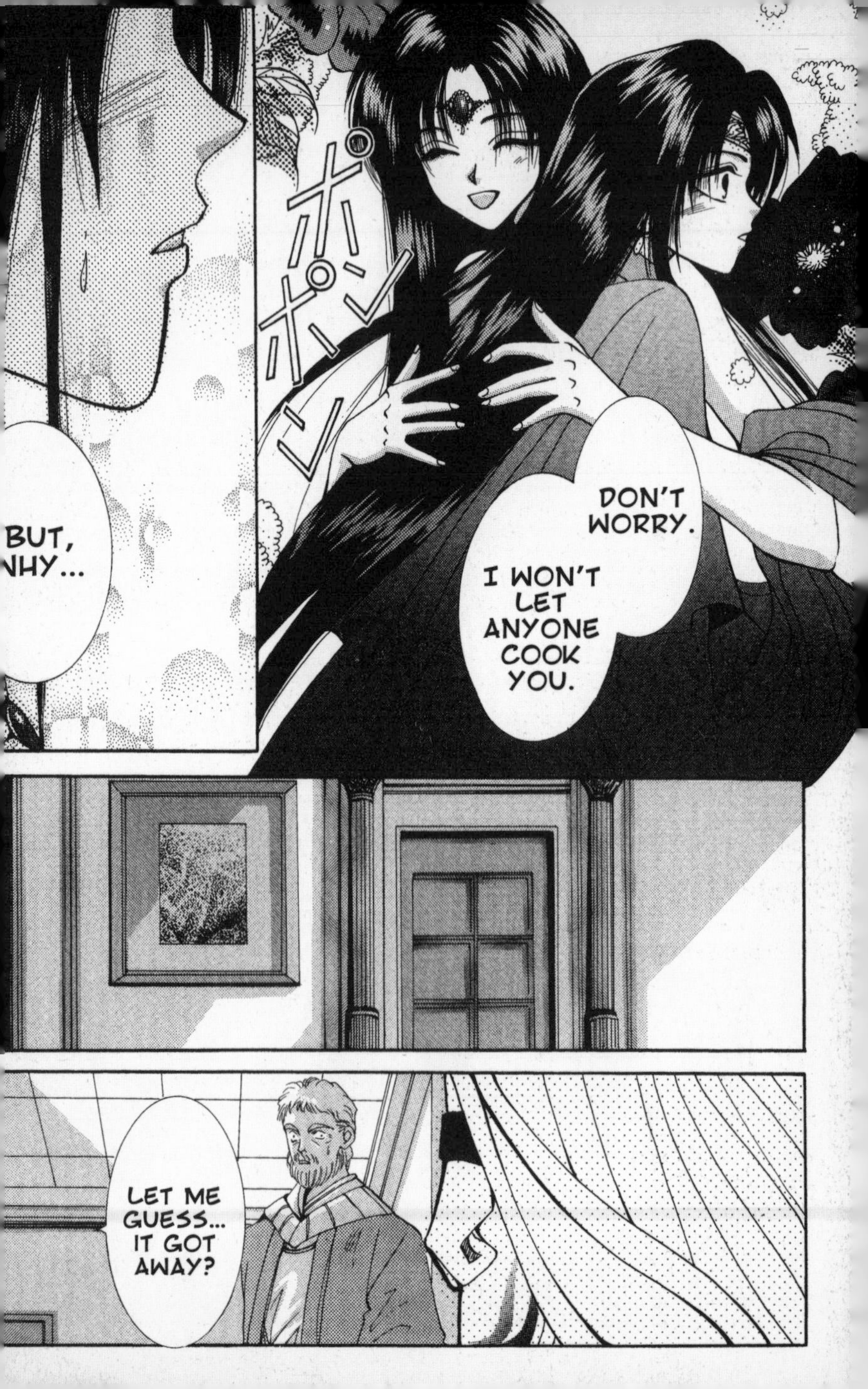
ポンポン
DON'T WORRY.
I WON'T LET ANYONE COOK YOU.
BUT, WHY...
LET ME GUESS... IT GOT AWAY?

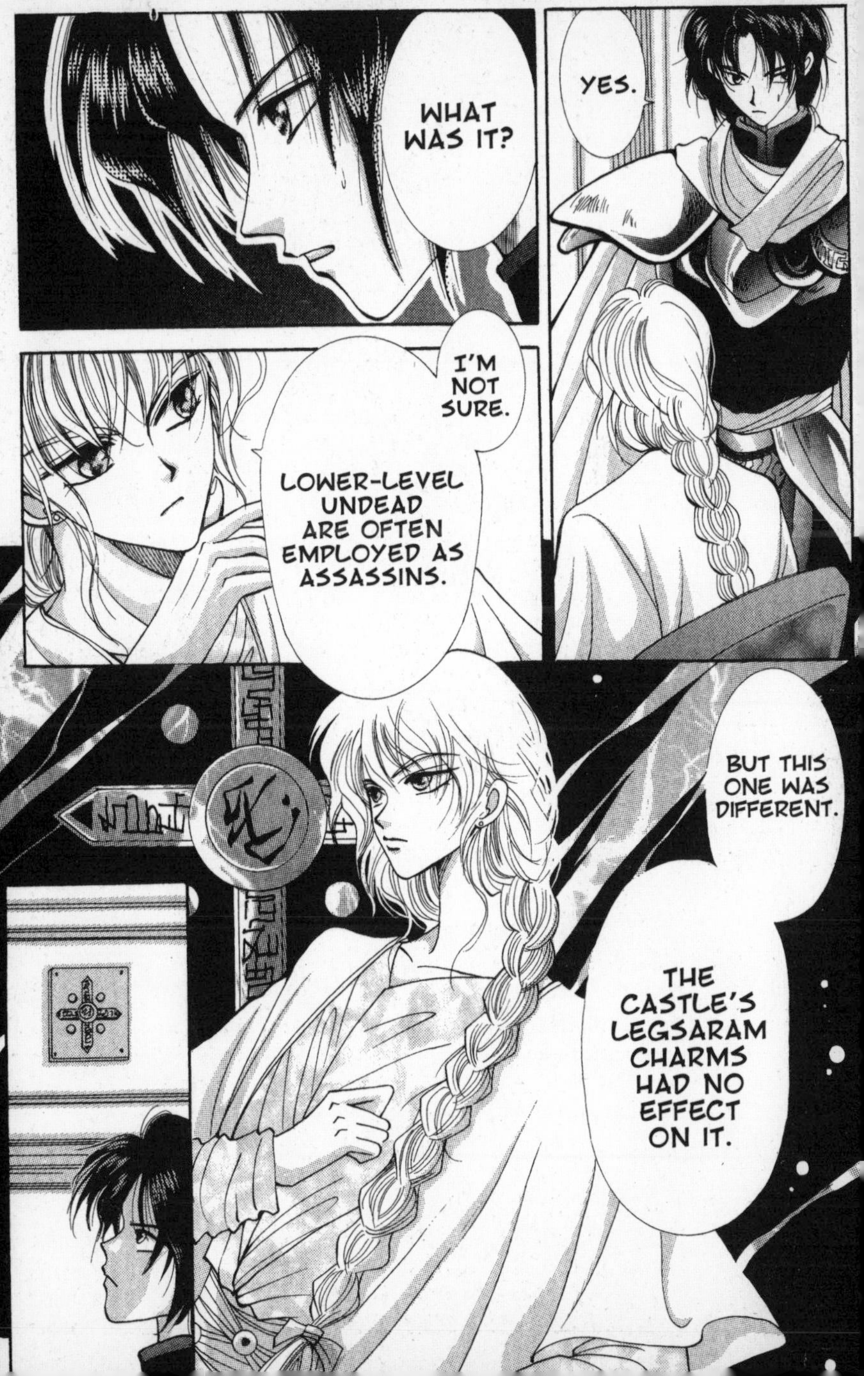
YES.
WHAT WAS IT?
I'M NOT SURE.
LOWER-LEVEL UNDEAD ARE OFTEN EMPLOYED AS ASSASSINS.
BUT THIS ONE WAS DIFFERENT.
THE CASTLE'S LEGSARAM CHARMS HAD NO EFFECT ON IT.

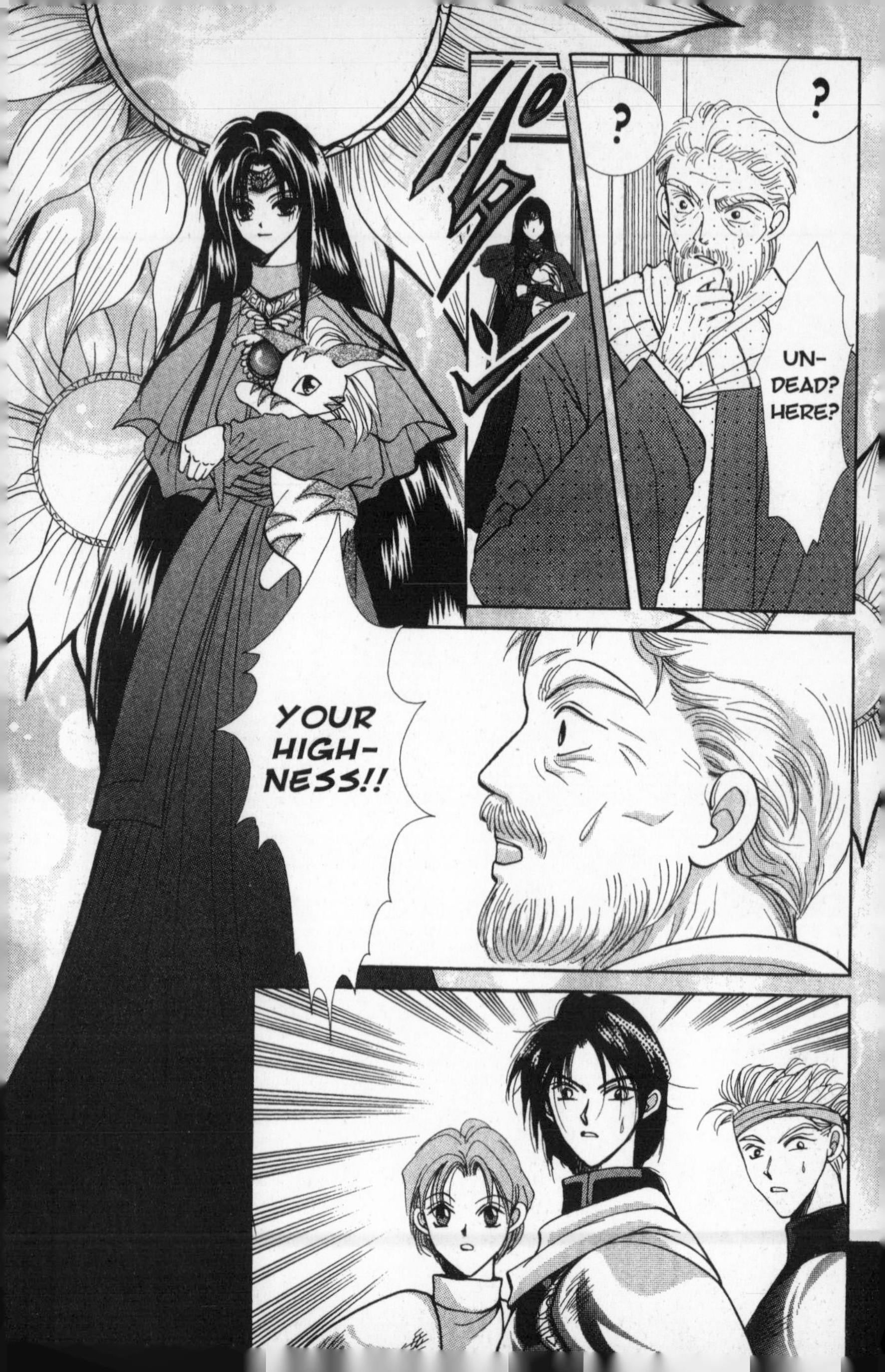
?
?
UN-DEAD? HERE?
YOUR HIGH-NESS!!

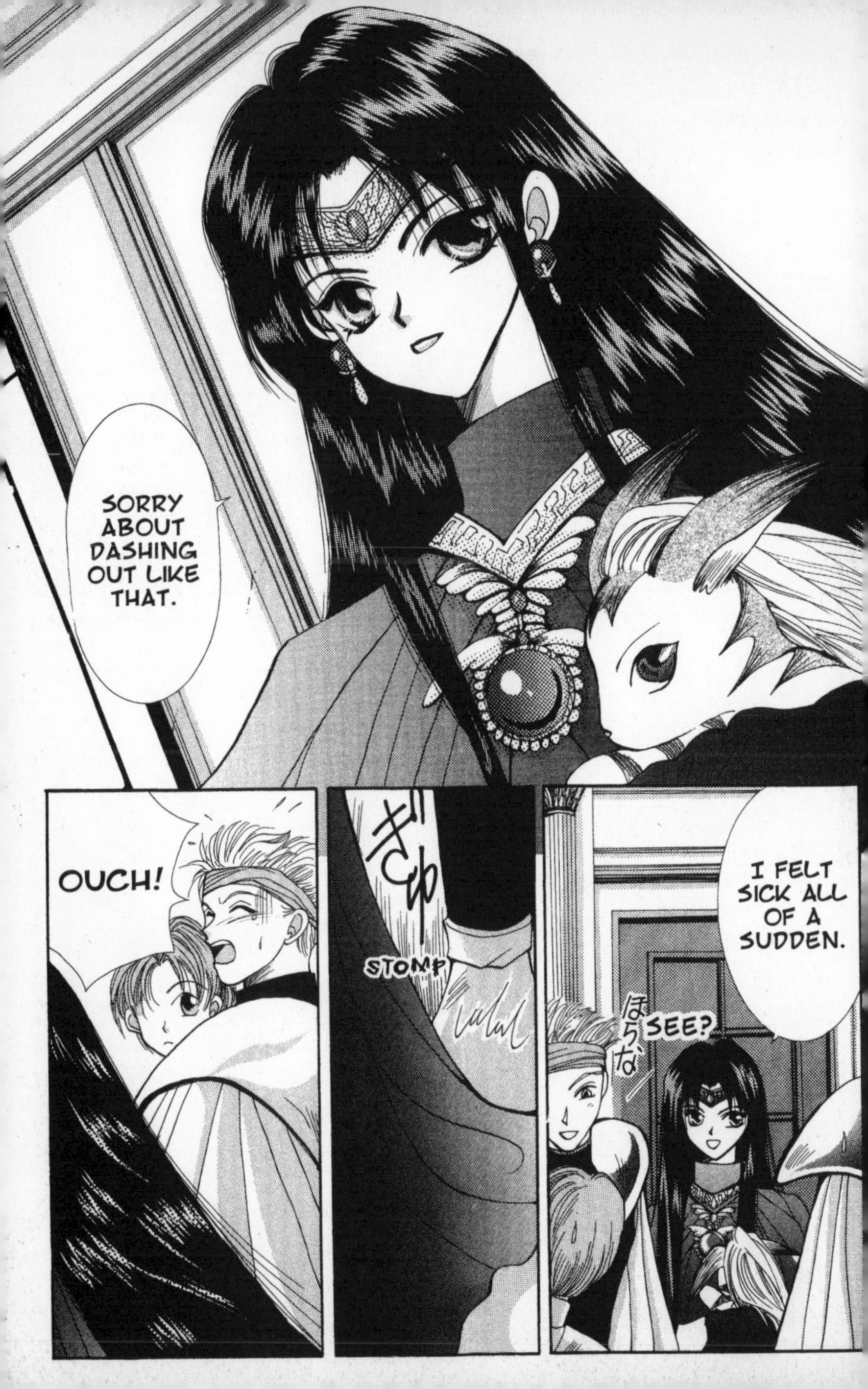
SORRY ABOUT DASHING OUT LIKE THAT.
I FELT SICK ALL OF A SUDDEN.
ほらな
SEE?
ぎゅ
STOMP
OUCH!

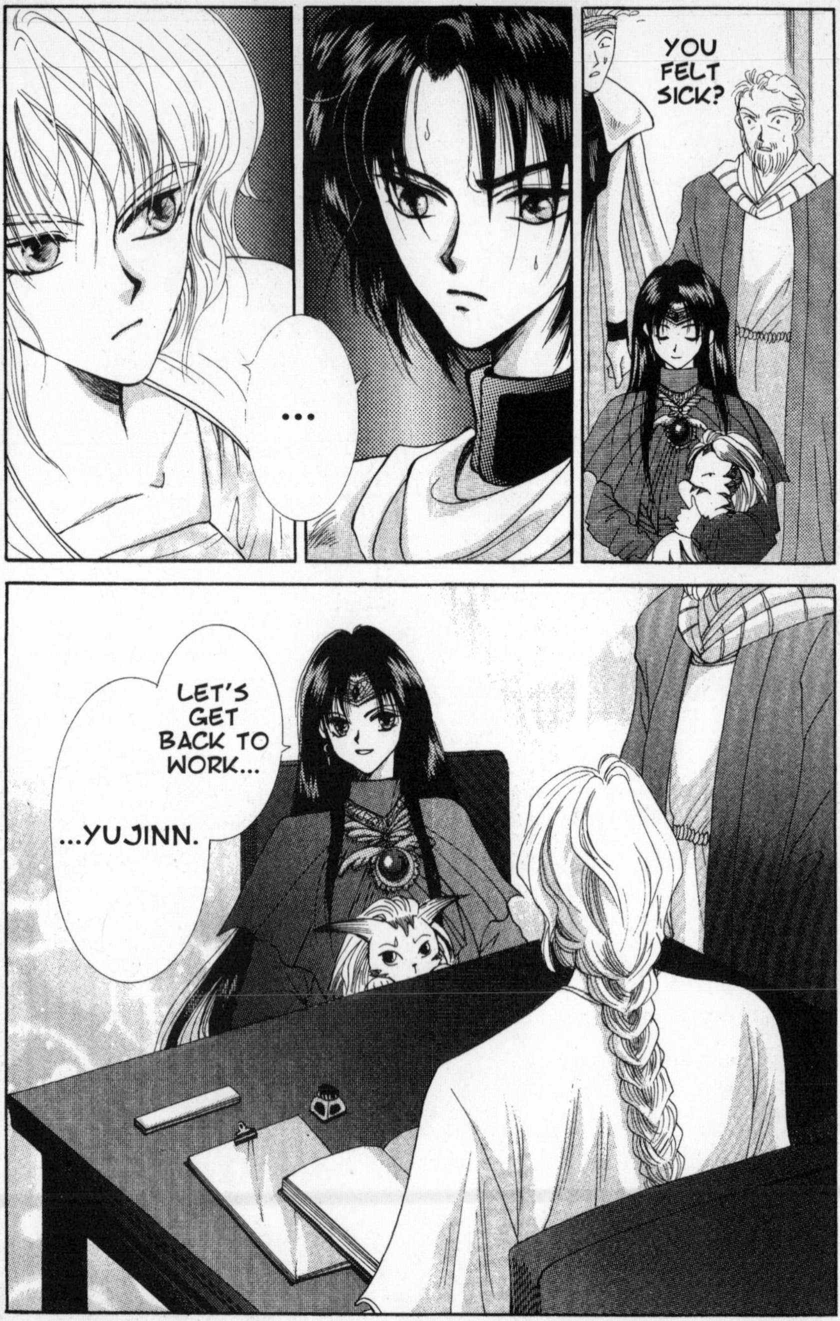
YOU FELT SICK?
...
LET'S GET BACK TO WORK...
...YUJINN.

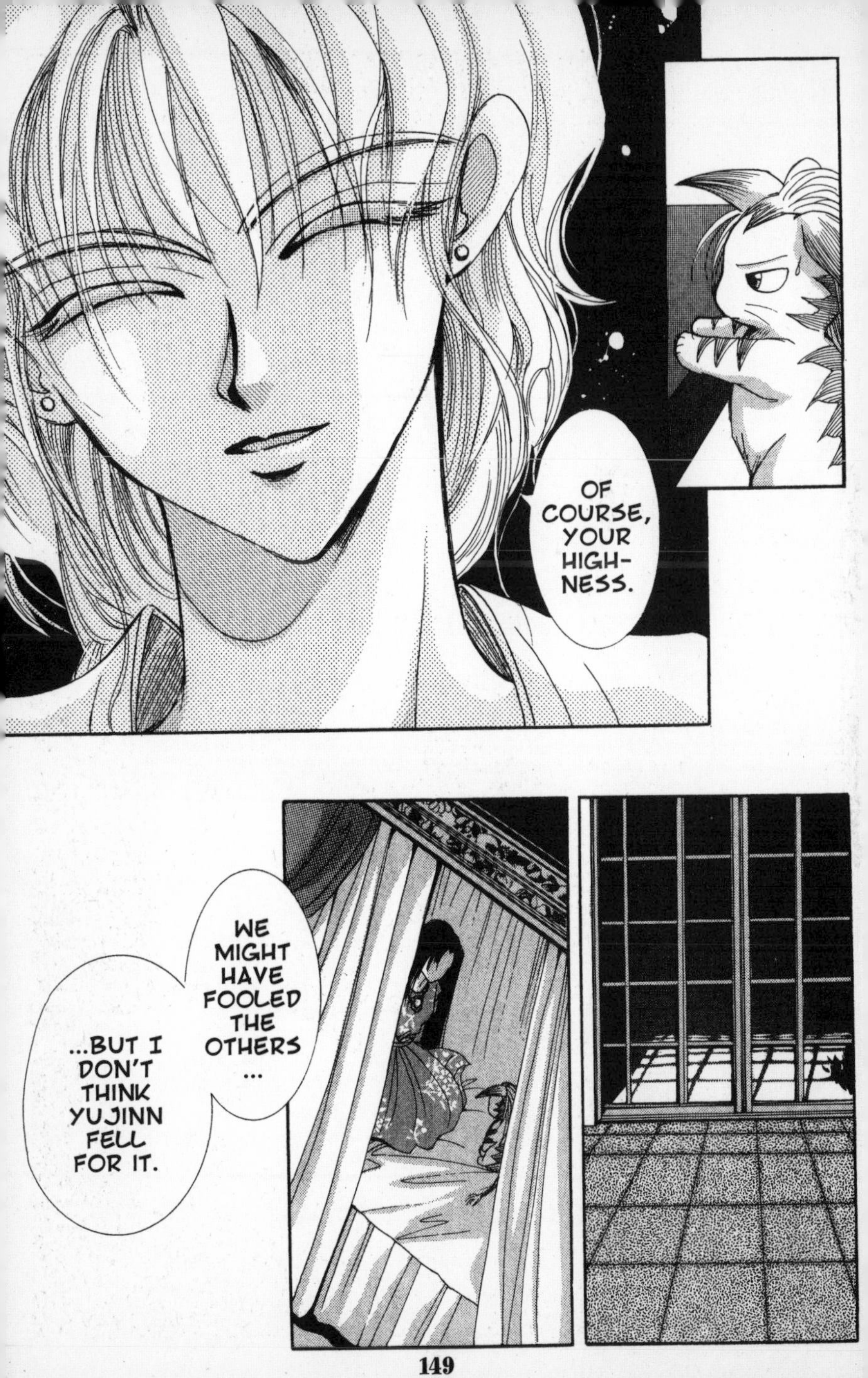
OF COURSE, YOUR HIGHNESS.
WE MIGHT HAVE FOOLED THE OTHERS...
...BUT I DON'T THINK YUJINN FELL FOR IT.

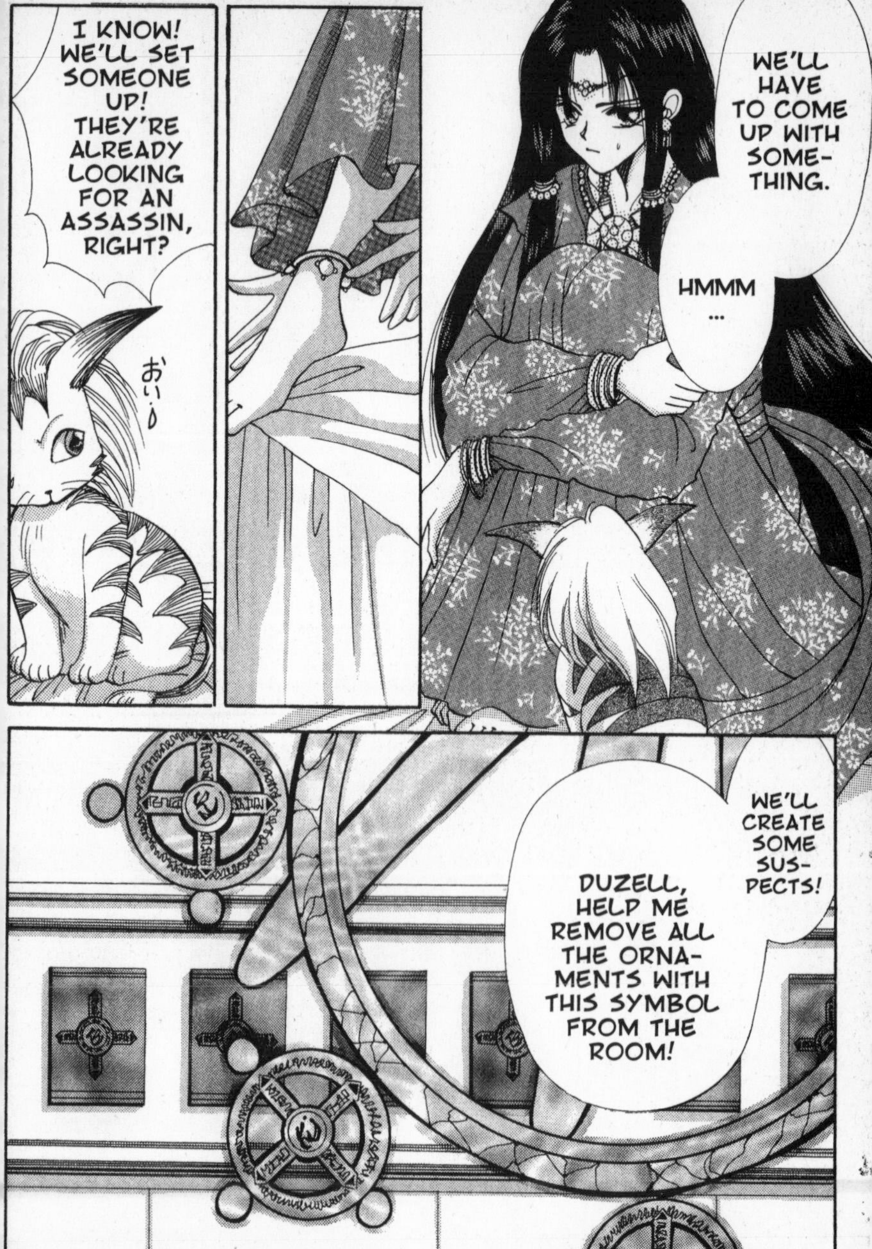
WE'LL HAVE TO COME UP WITH SOME-THING.
HMMM ...
I KNOW! WE'LL SET SOMEONE UP! THEY'RE ALREADY LOOKING FOR AN ASSASSIN, RIGHT?
おい。
WE'LL CREATE SOME SUS-PECTS!
DUZELL, HELP ME REMOVE ALL THE ORNA-MENTS WITH THIS SYMBOL FROM THE ROOM!

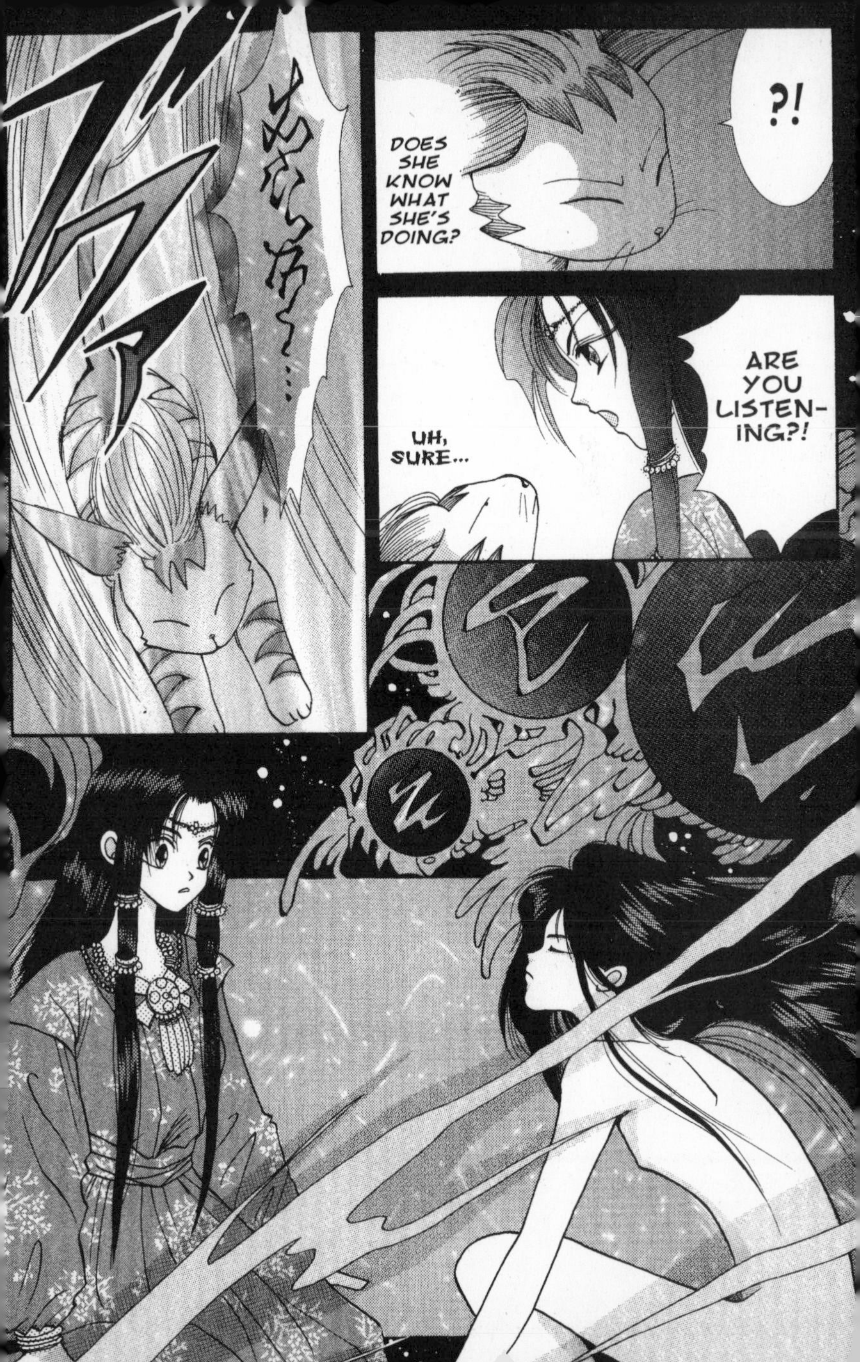
?!
DOES SHE KNOW WHAT SHE'S DOING?
ARE YOU LISTENING?!
UH, SURE...

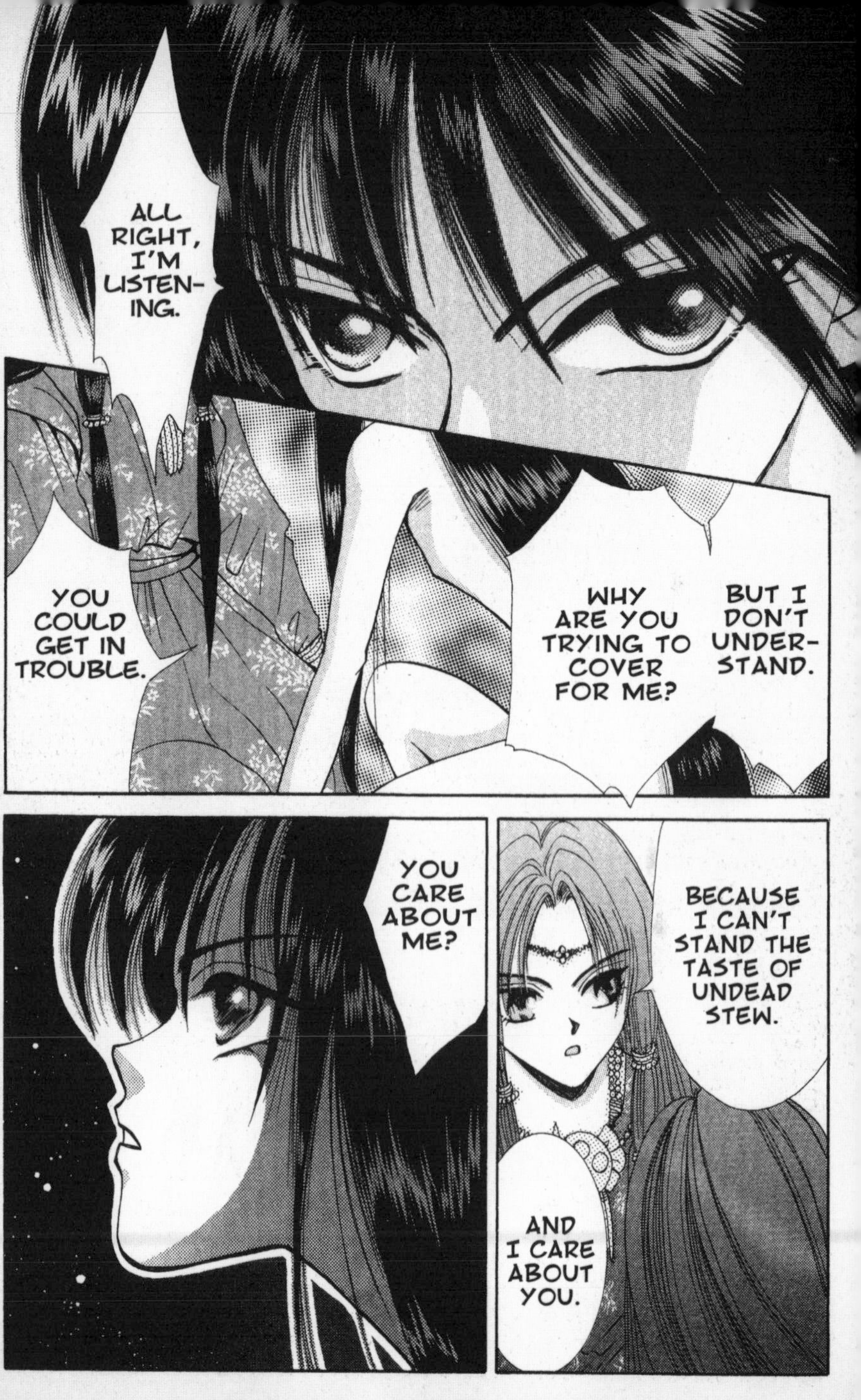
ALL RIGHT, I'M LISTENING.
BUT I DON'T UNDERSTAND.
WHY ARE YOU TRYING TO COVER FOR ME?
YOU COULD GET IN TROUBLE.
BECAUSE I CAN'T STAND THE TASTE OF UNDEAD STEW.
AND I CARE ABOUT YOU.
YOU CARE ABOUT ME?

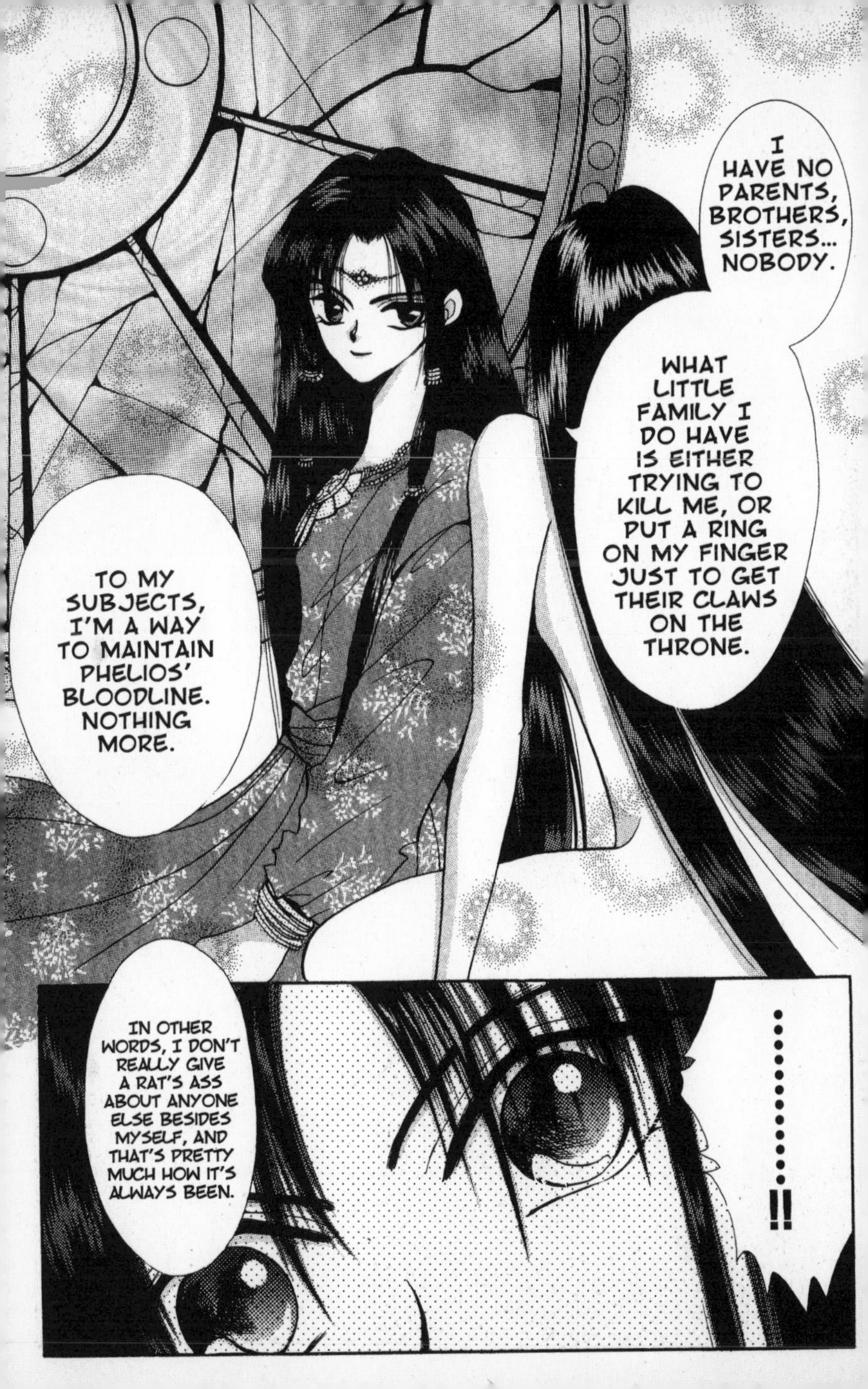
I HAVE NO PARENTS, BROTHERS, SISTERS... NOBODY.
WHAT LITTLE FAMILY I DO HAVE IS EITHER TRYING TO KILL ME, OR PUT A RING ON MY FINGER JUST TO GET THEIR CLAWS ON THE THRONE.
TO MY SUBJECTS, I'M A WAY TO MAINTAIN PHELIOS' BLOODLINE. NOTHING MORE.
IN OTHER WORDS, I DON'T REALLY GIVE A RAT'S ASS ABOUT ANYONE ELSE BESIDES MYSELF, AND THAT'S PRETTY MUCH HOW IT'S ALWAYS BEEN.
..........!!

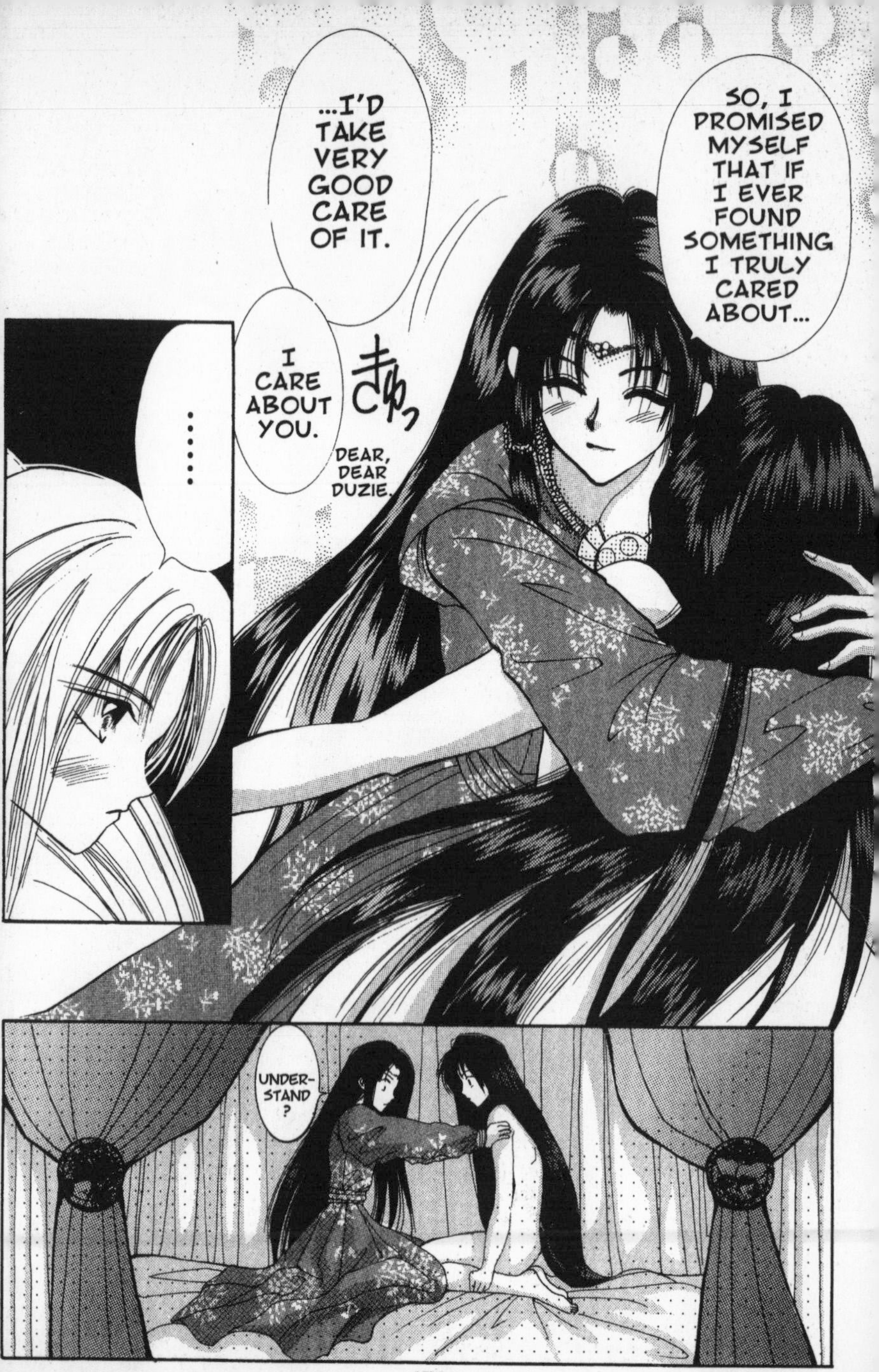
SO, I PROMISED MYSELF THAT IF I EVER FOUND SOMETHING I TRULY CARED ABOUT...
...I'D TAKE VERY GOOD CARE OF IT.
I CARE ABOUT YOU.
きゅっ
DEAR, DEAR DUZIE.
.....
UNDER-STAND?

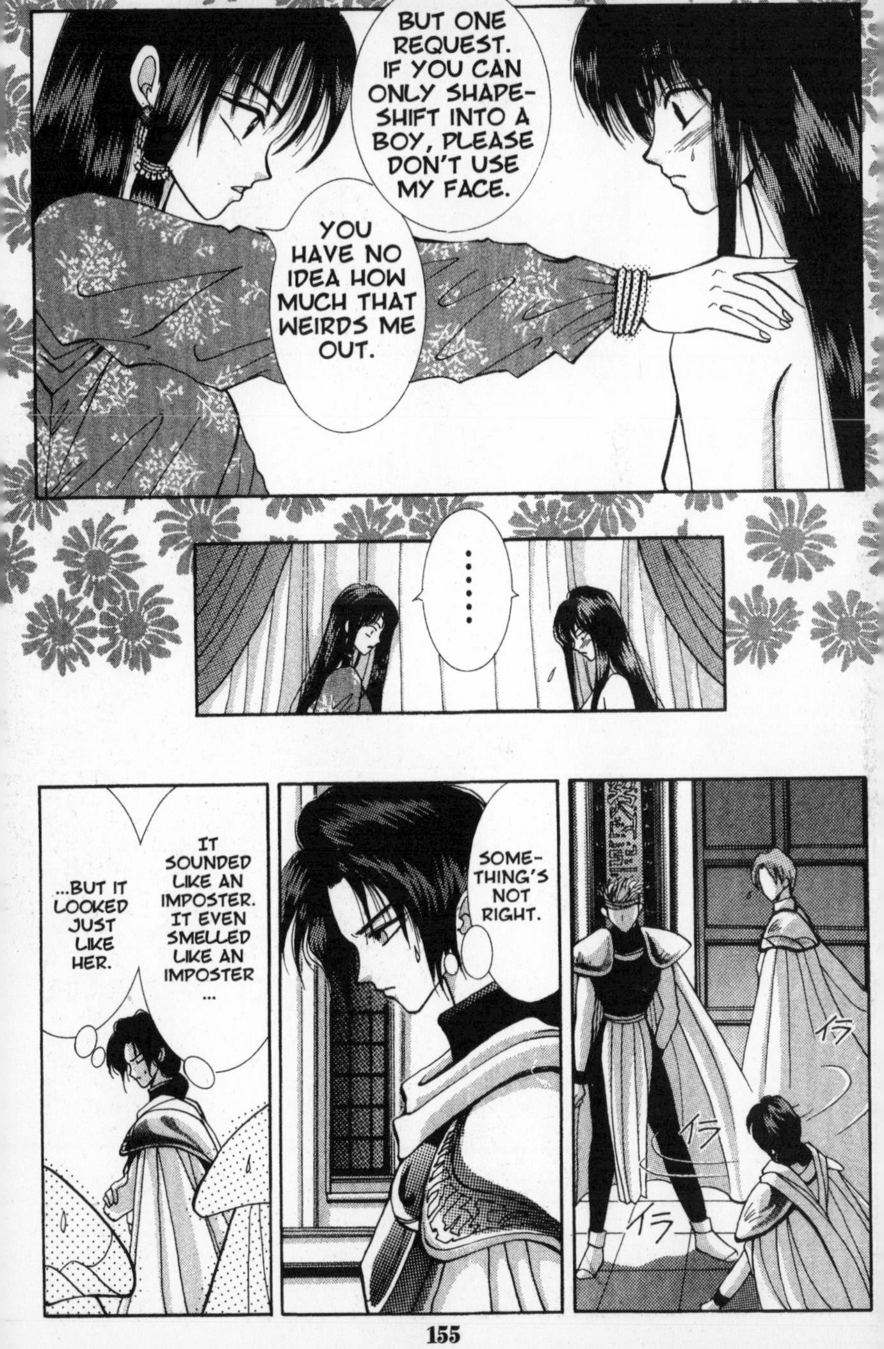
BUT ONE REQUEST. IF YOU CAN ONLY SHAPE-SHIFT INTO A BOY, PLEASE DON'T USE MY FACE.
YOU HAVE NO IDEA HOW MUCH THAT WEIRDS ME OUT.
......
イラ
イラ
イラ
SOME-THING'S NOT RIGHT.
IT SOUNDED LIKE AN IMPOSTER. IT EVEN SMELLED LIKE AN IMPOSTER ...
...BUT IT LOOKED JUST LIKE HER.

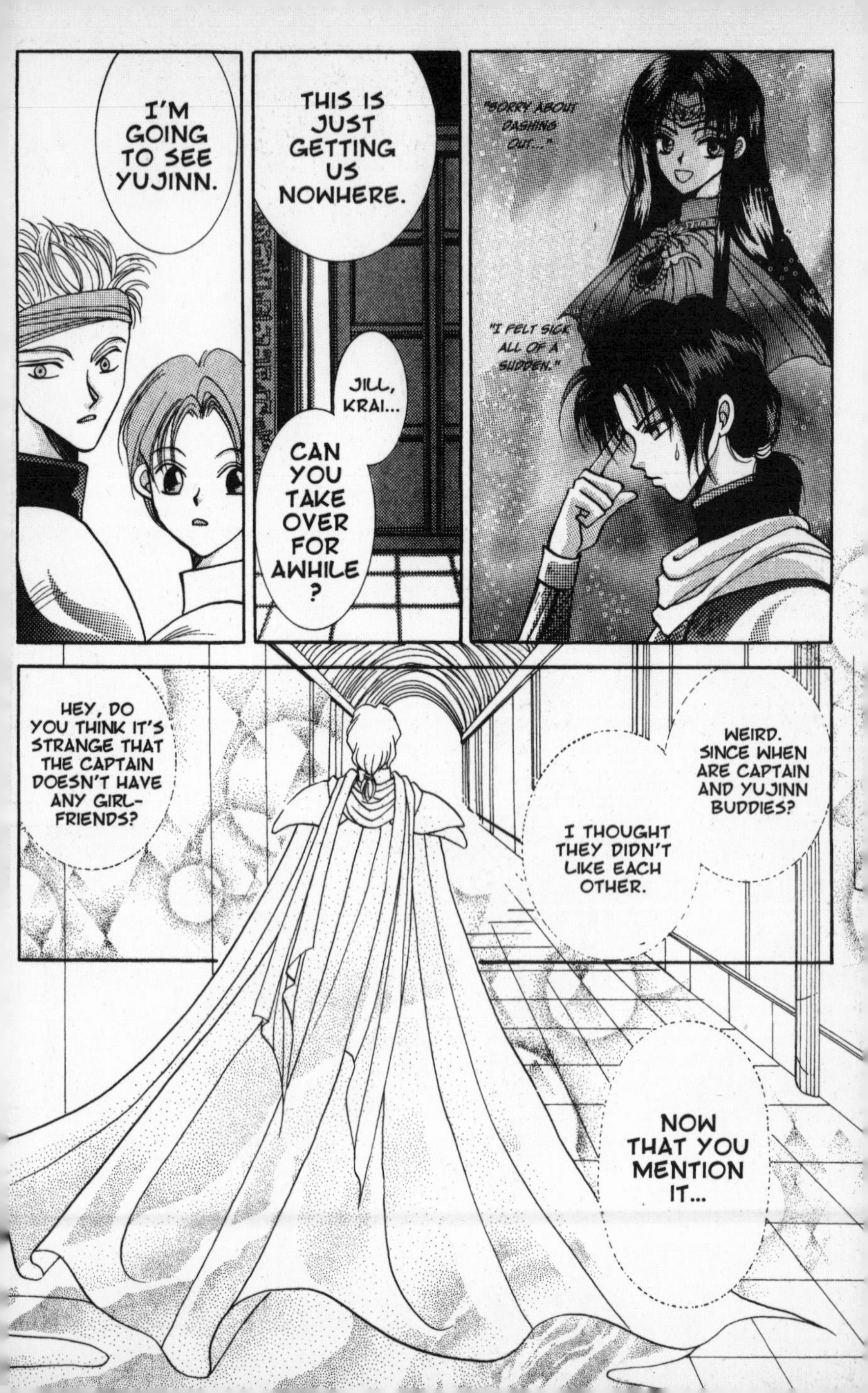
"SORRY ABOUT DASHING OUT..."
"I FELT SICK ALL OF A SUDDEN."
THIS IS JUST GETTING US NOWHERE.
JILL, KRAI...
CAN YOU TAKE OVER FOR AWHILE?
I'M GOING TO SEE YUJINN.
WEIRD. SINCE WHEN ARE CAPTAIN AND YUJINN BUDDIES?
I THOUGHT THEY DIDN'T LIKE EACH OTHER.
HEY, DO YOU THINK IT'S STRANGE THAT THE CAPTAIN DOESN'T HAVE ANY GIRL-FRIENDS?
NOW THAT YOU MENTION IT...

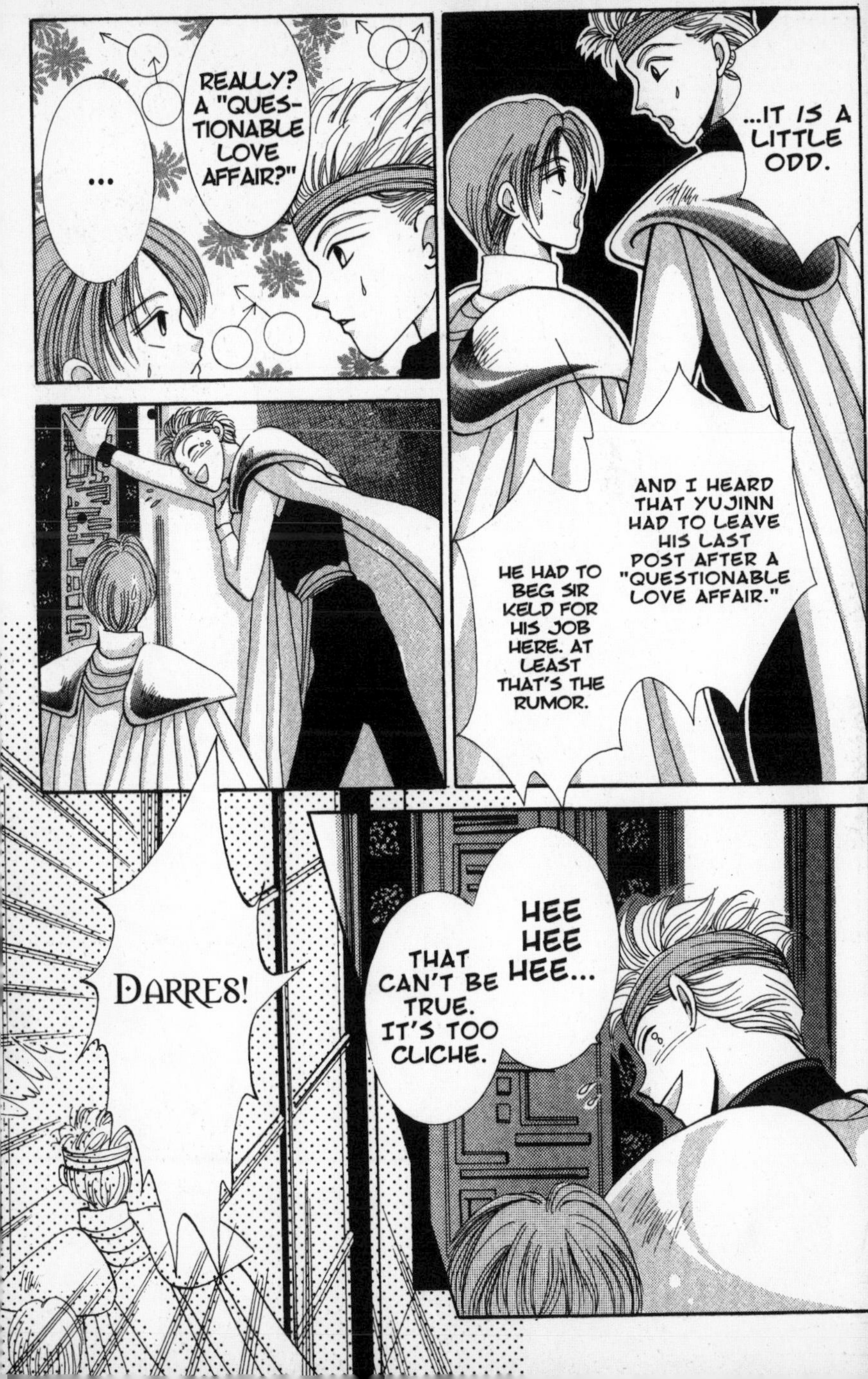
...IT IS A LITTLE ODD.
REALLY? A "QUES-TIONABLE LOVE AFFAIR?"
...
AND I HEARD THAT YUJINN HAD TO LEAVE HIS LAST POST AFTER A "QUESTIONABLE LOVE AFFAIR."
HE HAD TO BEG SIR KELD FOR HIS JOB HERE. AT LEAST THAT'S THE RUMOR.
HEE HEE HEE...
THAT CAN'T BE TRUE. IT'S TOO CLICHE.
DARRES!

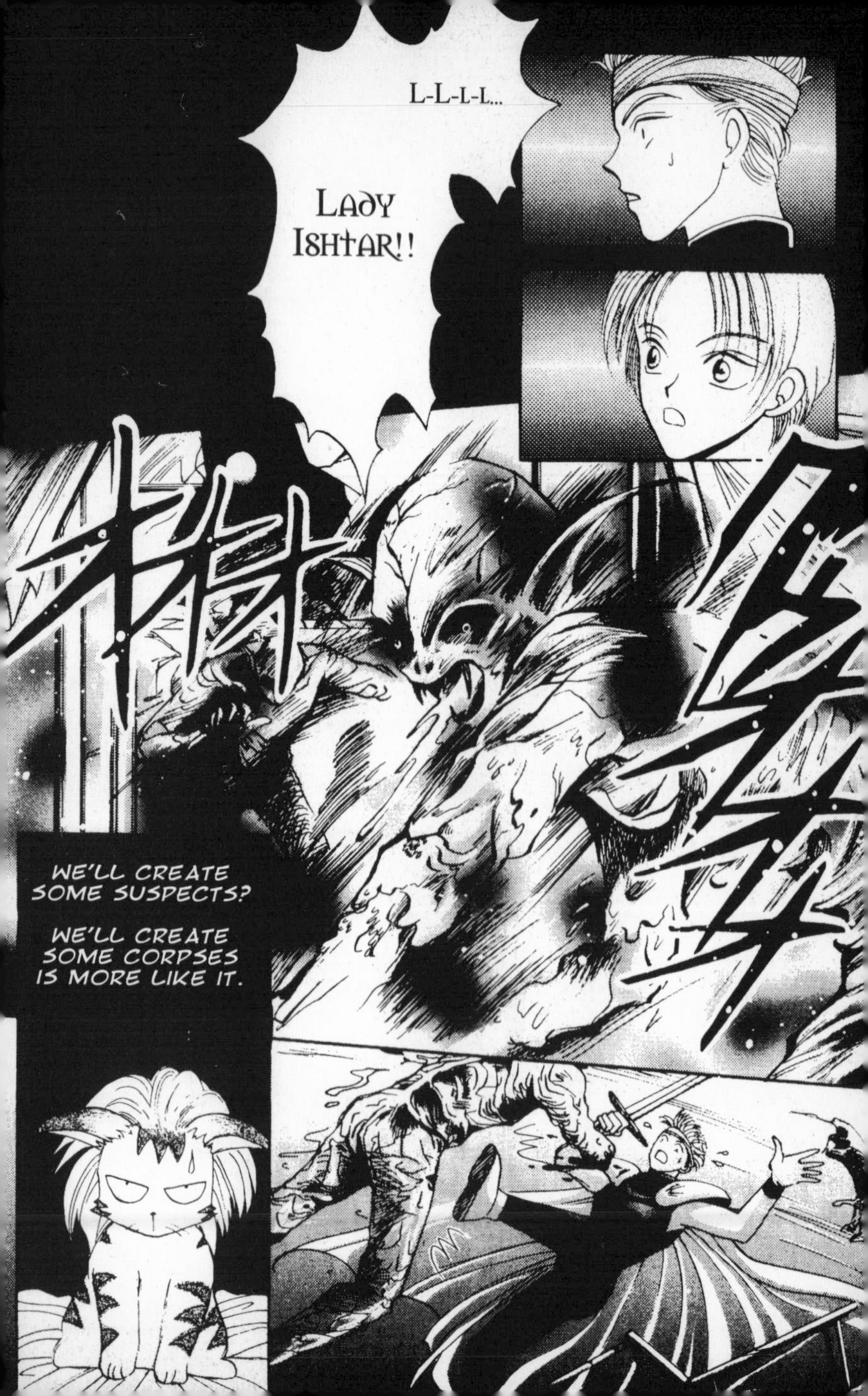

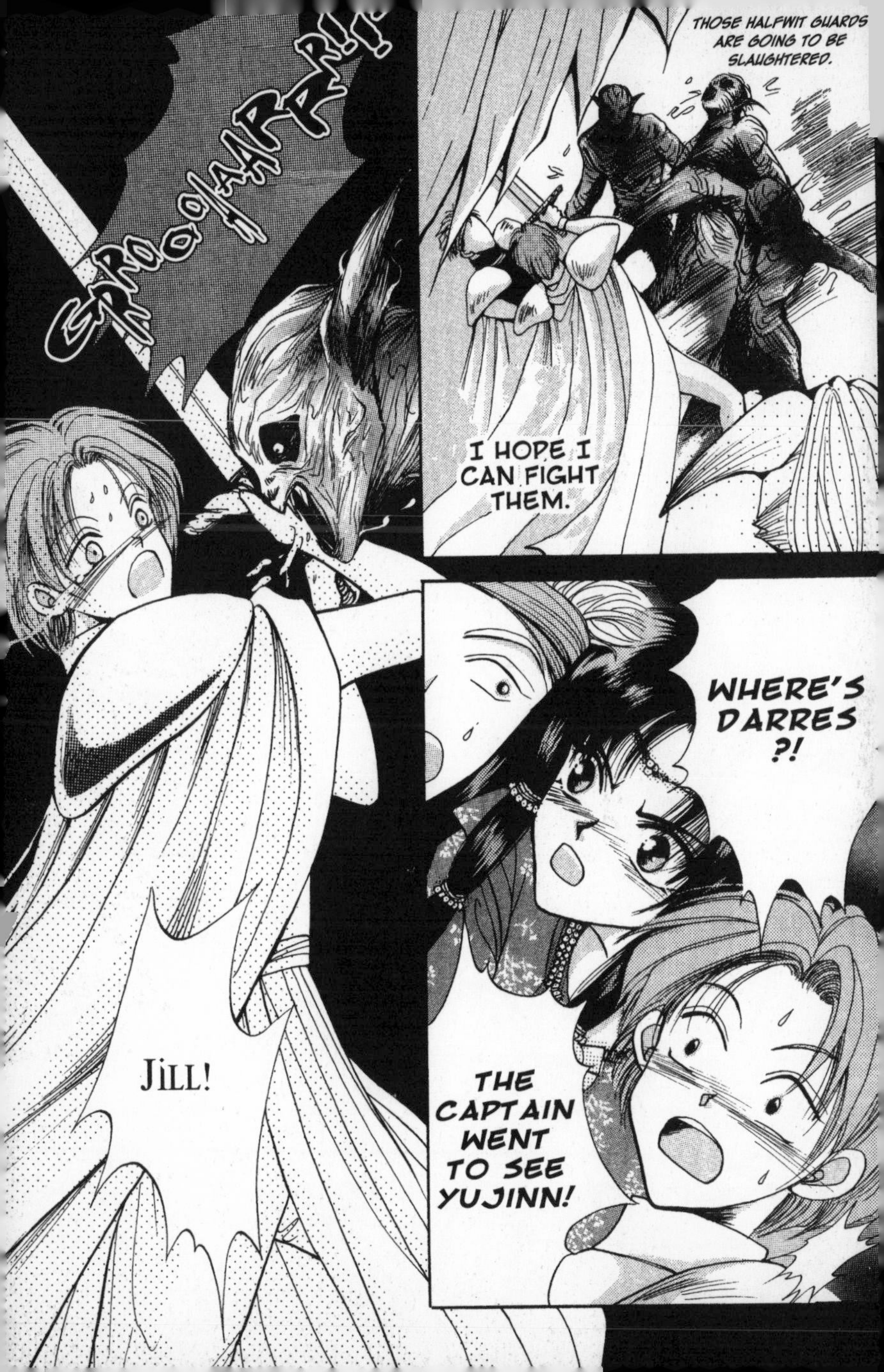
THOSE HALFWIT GUARDS ARE GOING TO BE SLAUGHTERED.
I HOPE I CAN FIGHT THEM.
WHERE'S DARRES ?!
THE CAPTAIN WENT TO SEE YUJINN!
GROOOAARR!!
JILL!

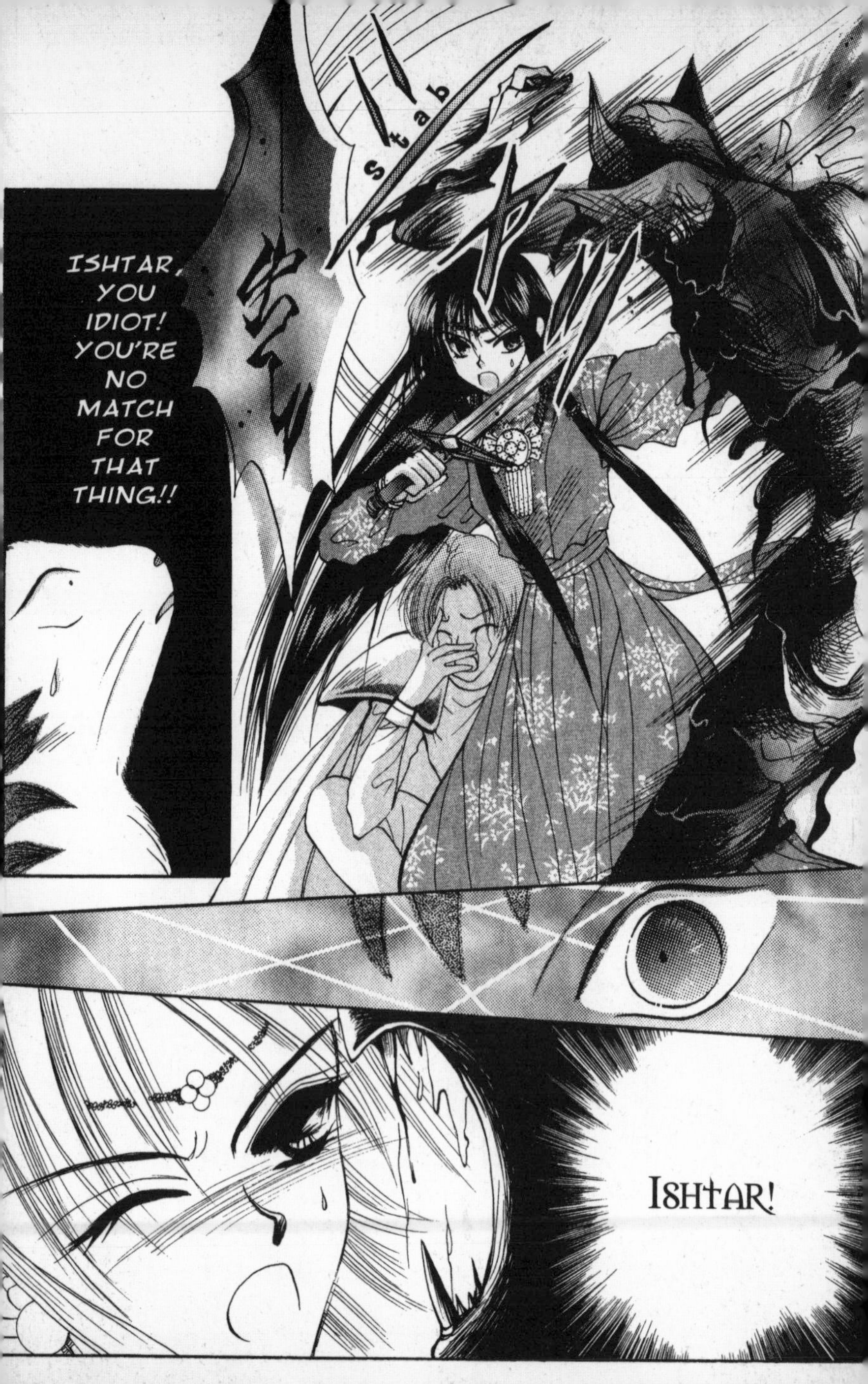
Stab
ISHTAR, YOU IDIOT! YOU'RE NO MATCH FOR THAT THING!!
ISHTAR!

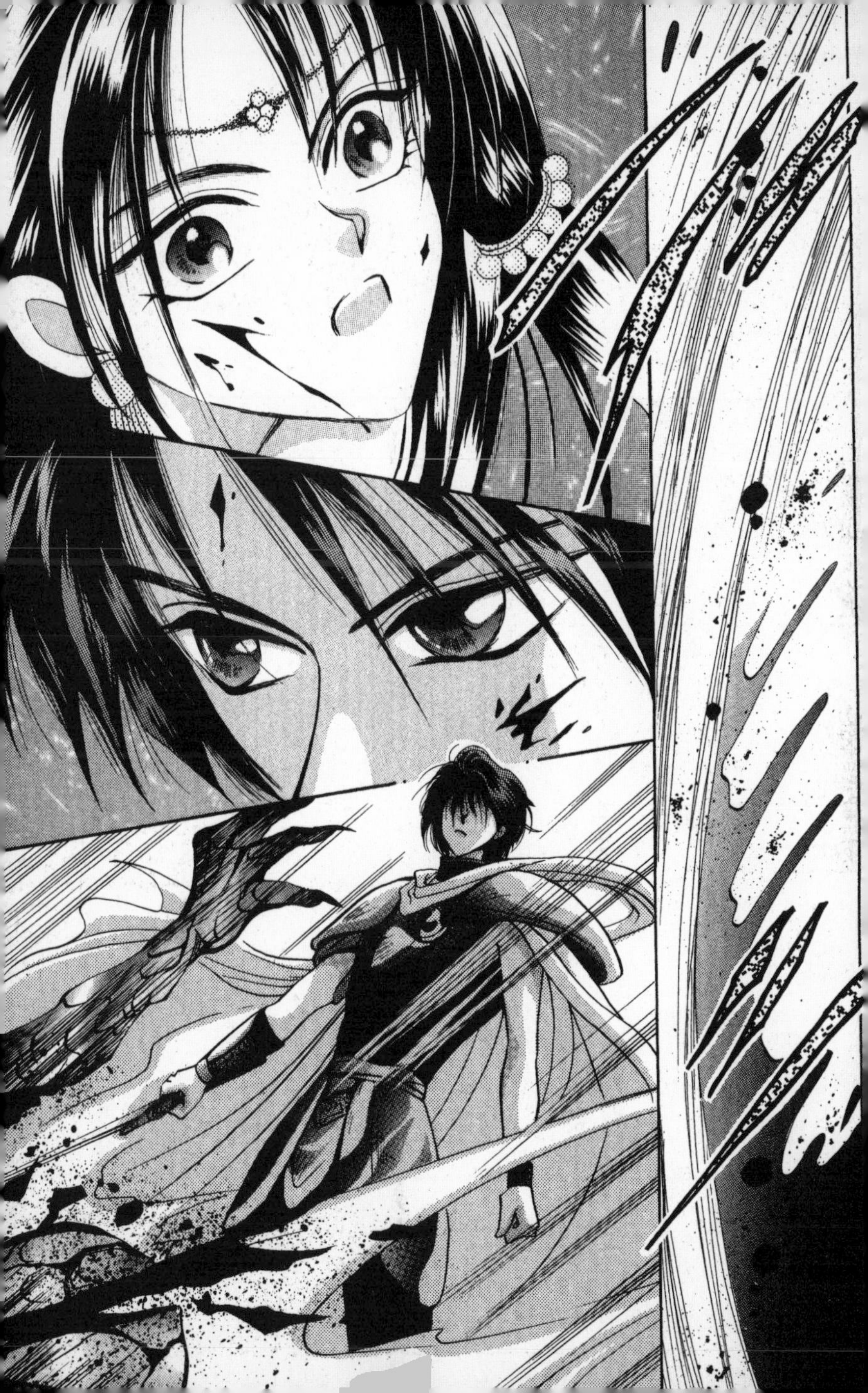

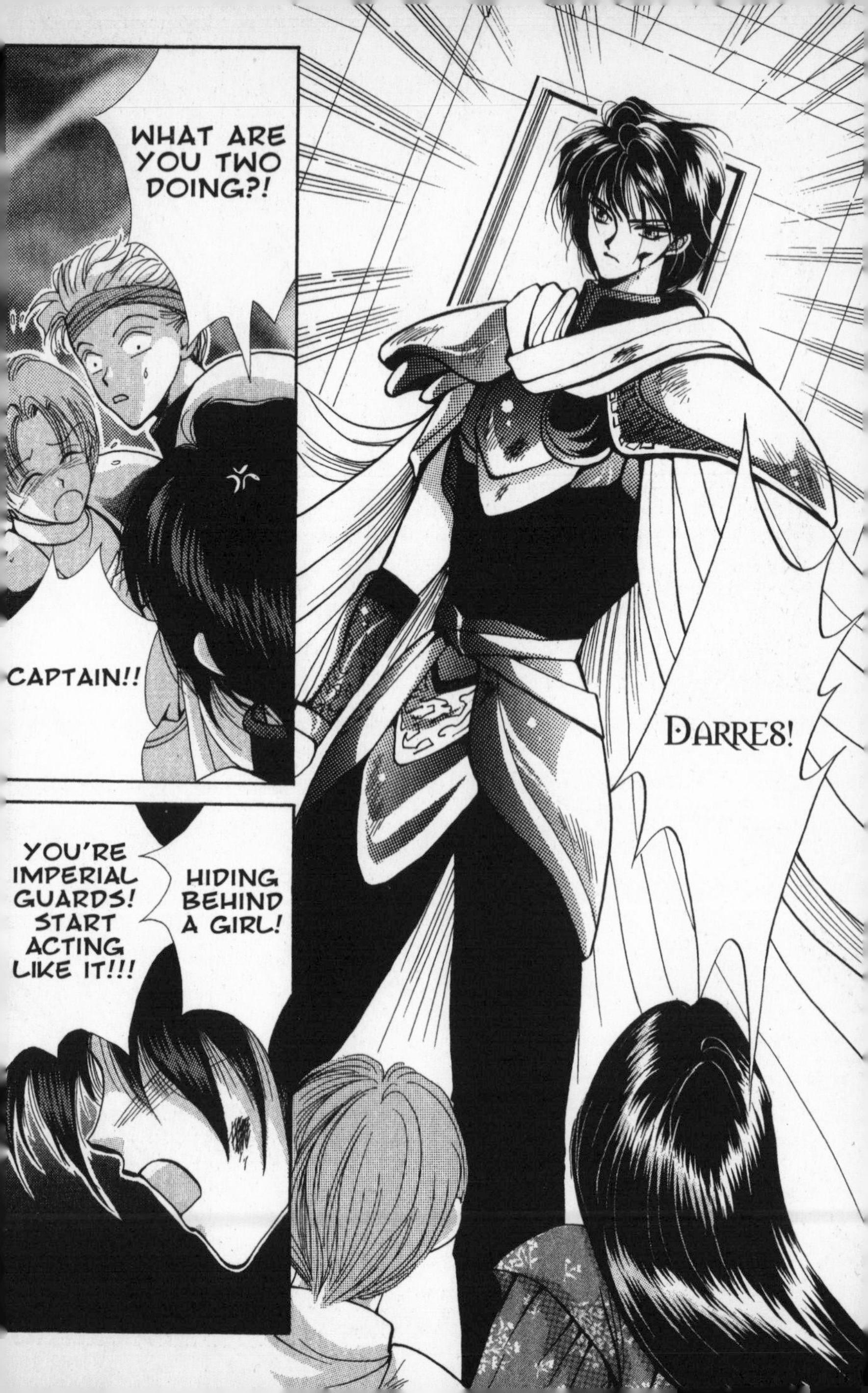
DARRES!
WHAT ARE YOU TWO DOING?!
CAPTAIN!!
HIDING BEHIND A GIRL!
YOU'RE IMPERIAL GUARDS! START ACTING LIKE IT!!!

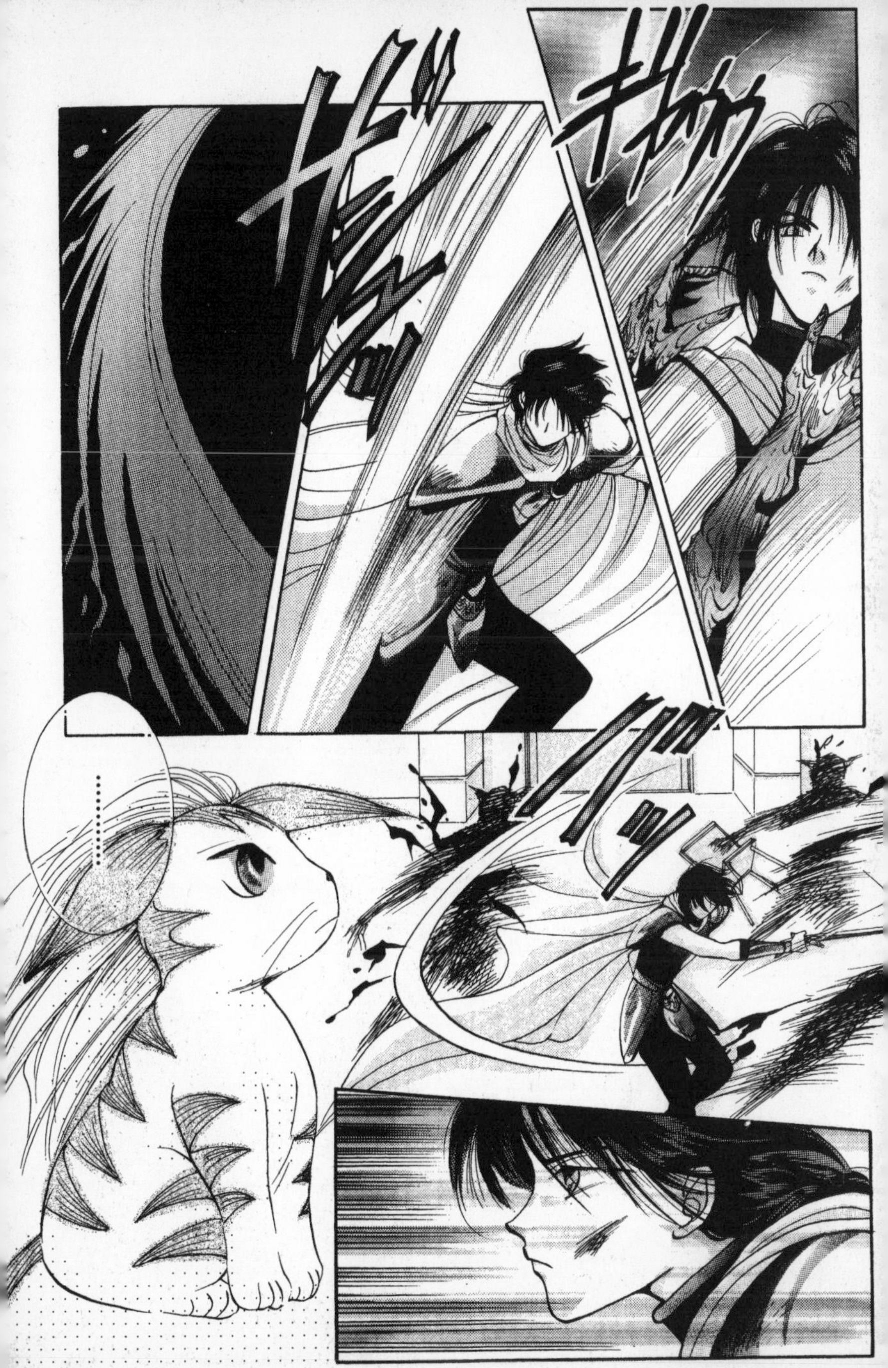
……

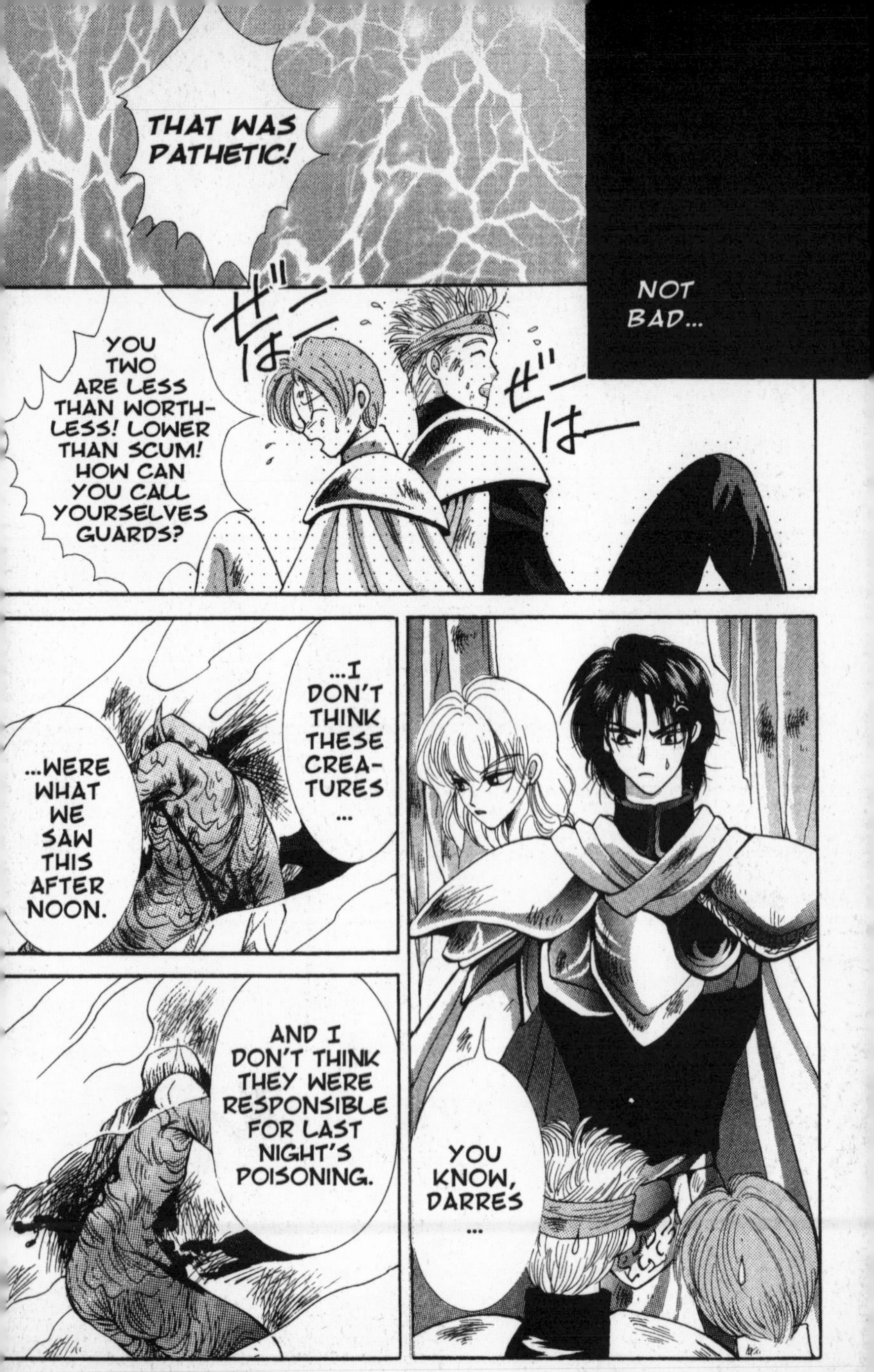
NOT BAD...
THAT WAS PATHETIC!
ぜーはー
ぜーはー
YOU TWO ARE LESS THAN WORTHLESS! LOWER THAN SCUM! HOW CAN YOU CALL YOURSELVES GUARDS?
YOU KNOW, DARRES ...
...I DON'T THINK THESE CREATURES ...
...WERE WHAT WE SAW THIS AFTERNOON.
AND I DON'T THINK THEY WERE RESPONSIBLE FOR LAST NIGHT'S POISONING.

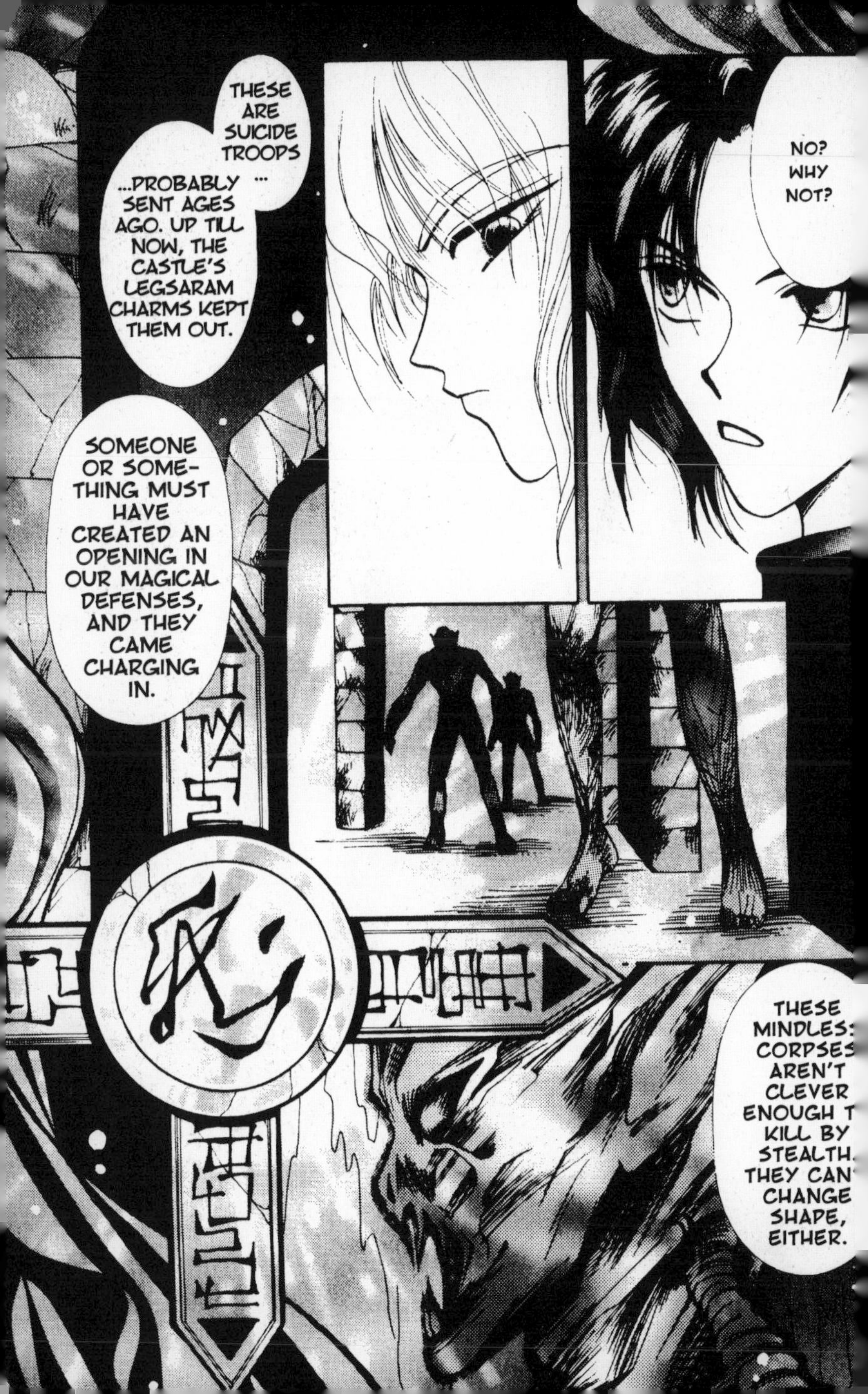
NO? WHY NOT?
THESE ARE SUICIDE TROOPS ...
...PROBABLY SENT AGES AGO. UP TILL NOW, THE CASTLE'S LEGSARAM CHARMS KEPT THEM OUT.
SOMEONE OR SOME-THING MUST HAVE CREATED AN OPENING IN OUR MAGICAL DEFENSES, AND THEY CAME CHARGING IN.
THESE MINDLES CORPSES AREN'T CLEVER ENOUGH T KILL BY STEALTH. THEY CAN CHANGE SHAPE, EITHER.

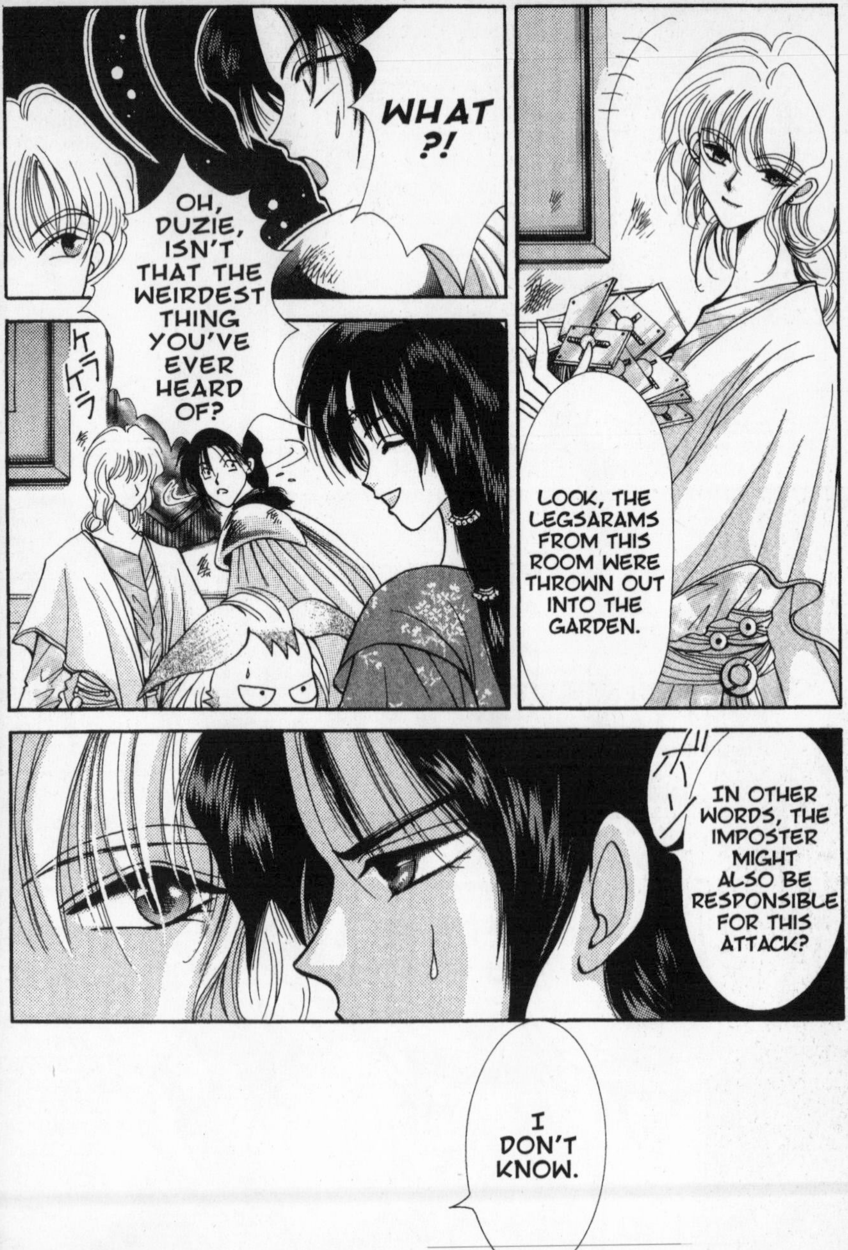

LOOK, THE LEGSARAMS FROM THIS ROOM WERE THROWN OUT INTO THE GARDEN.
WHAT?!
OH, DUZIE, ISN'T THAT THE WEIRDEST THING YOU'VE EVER HEARD OF?
ケラケラ
IN OTHER WORDS, THE IMPOSTER MIGHT ALSO BE RESPONSIBLE FOR THIS ATTACK?
I DON'T KNOW.

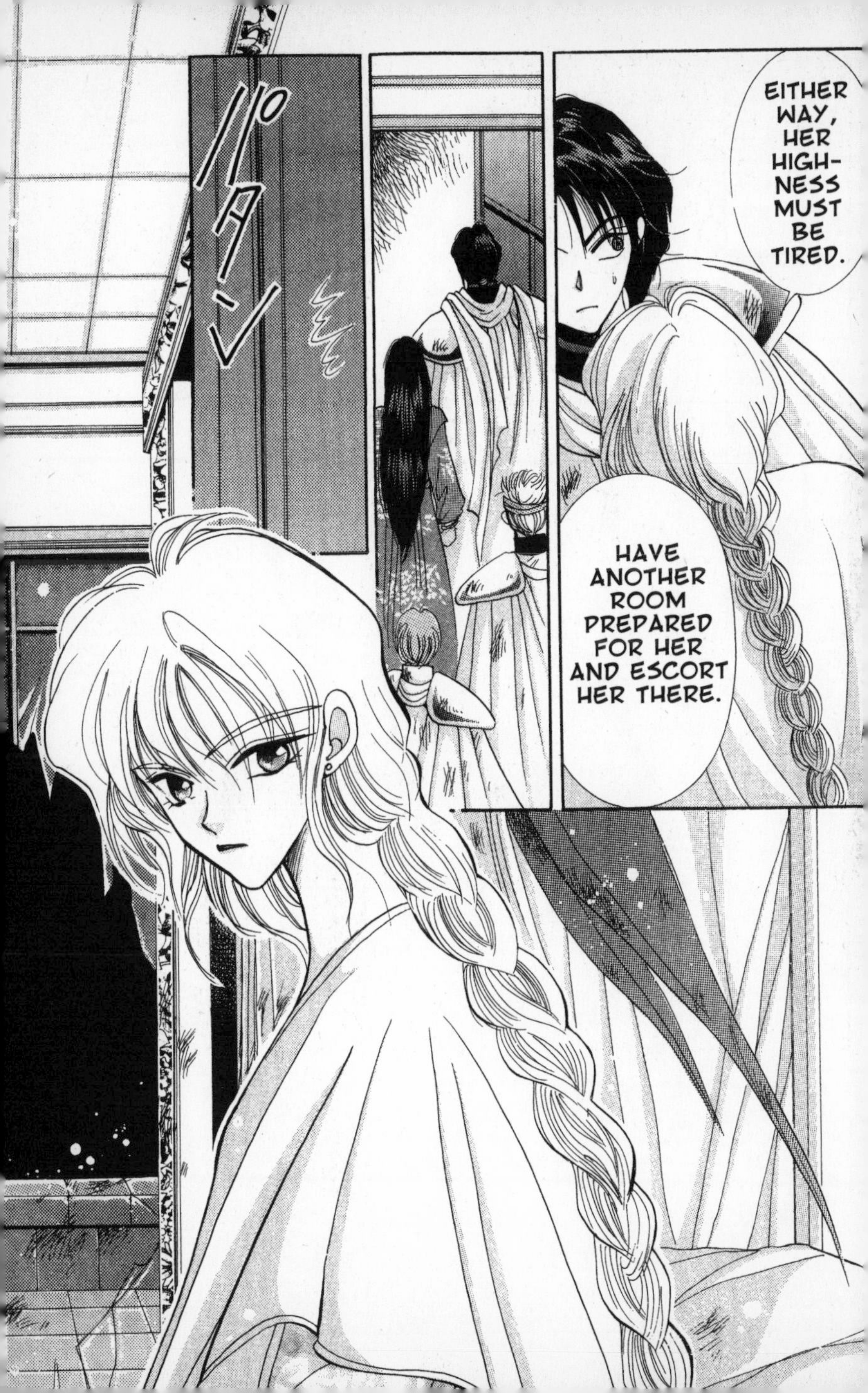
EITHER WAY, HER HIGHNESS MUST BE TIRED.
HAVE ANOTHER ROOM PREPARED FOR HER AND ESCORT HER THERE.
パタン

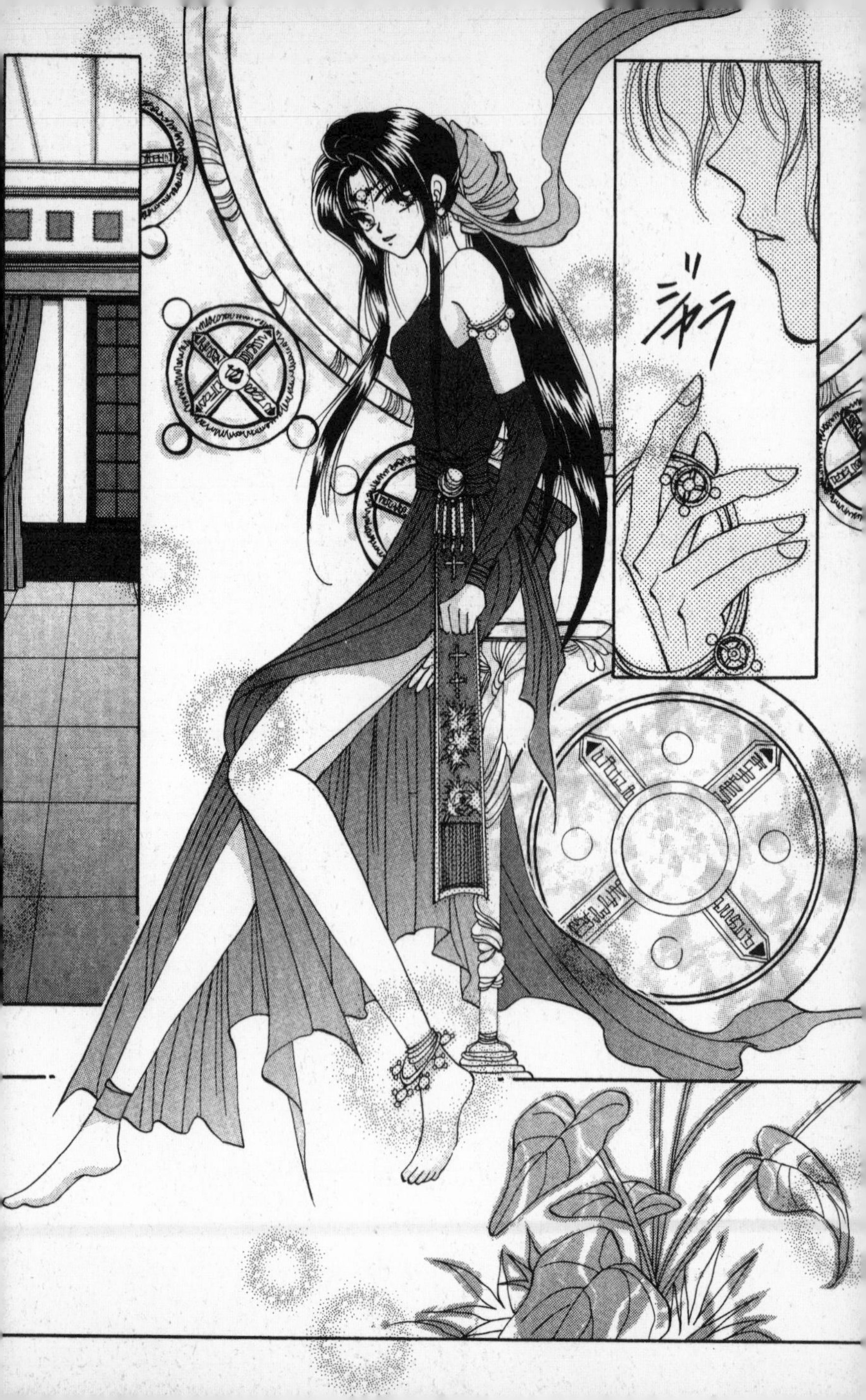
ジャラ

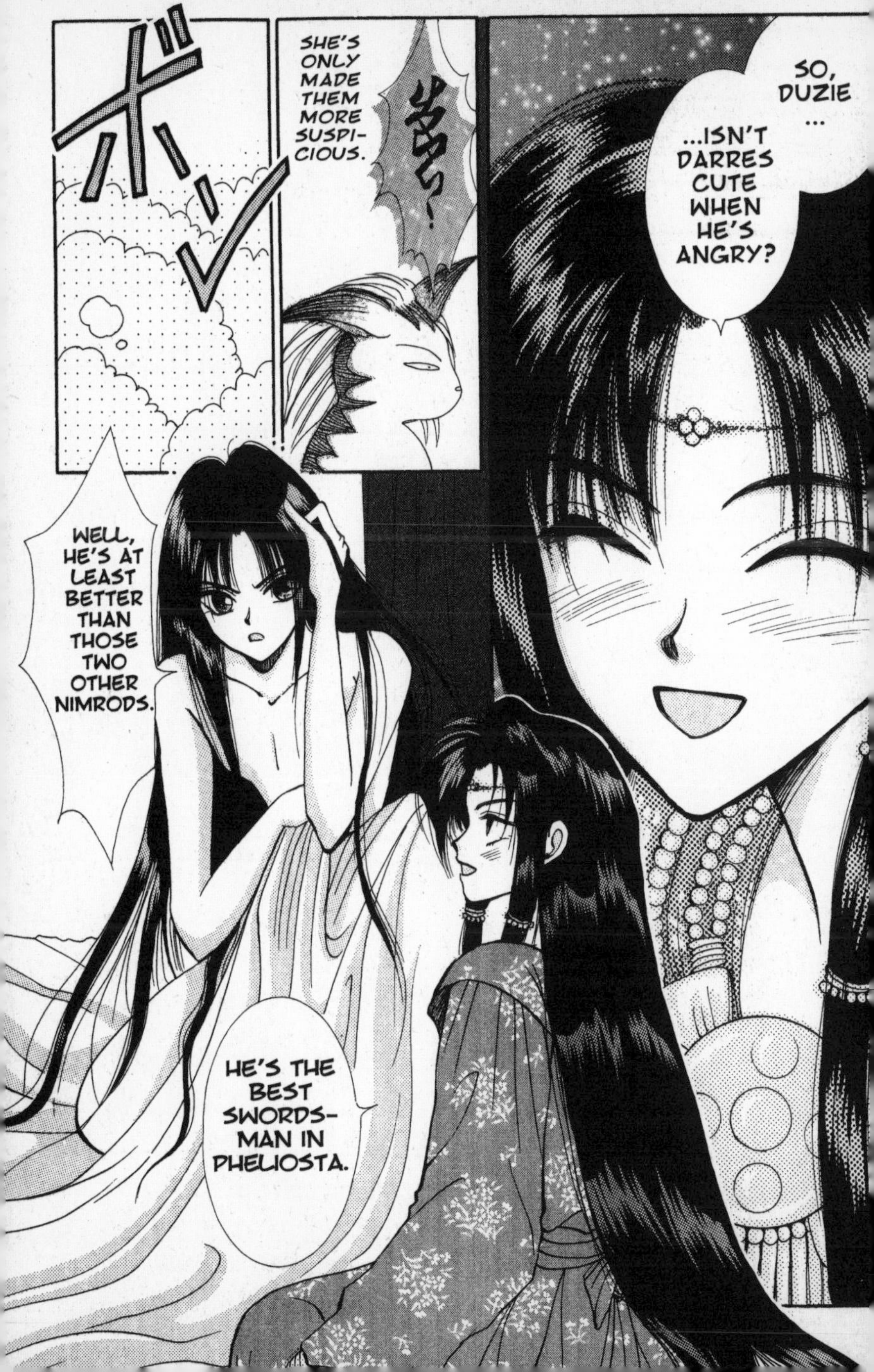
SO, DUZIE ...
...ISN'T DARRES CUTE WHEN HE'S ANGRY?
SHE'S ONLY MADE THEM MORE SUSPICIOUS.
ボッ
WELL, HE'S AT LEAST BETTER THAN THOSE TWO OTHER NIMRODS.
HE'S THE BEST SWORDSMAN IN PHELIOSTA.

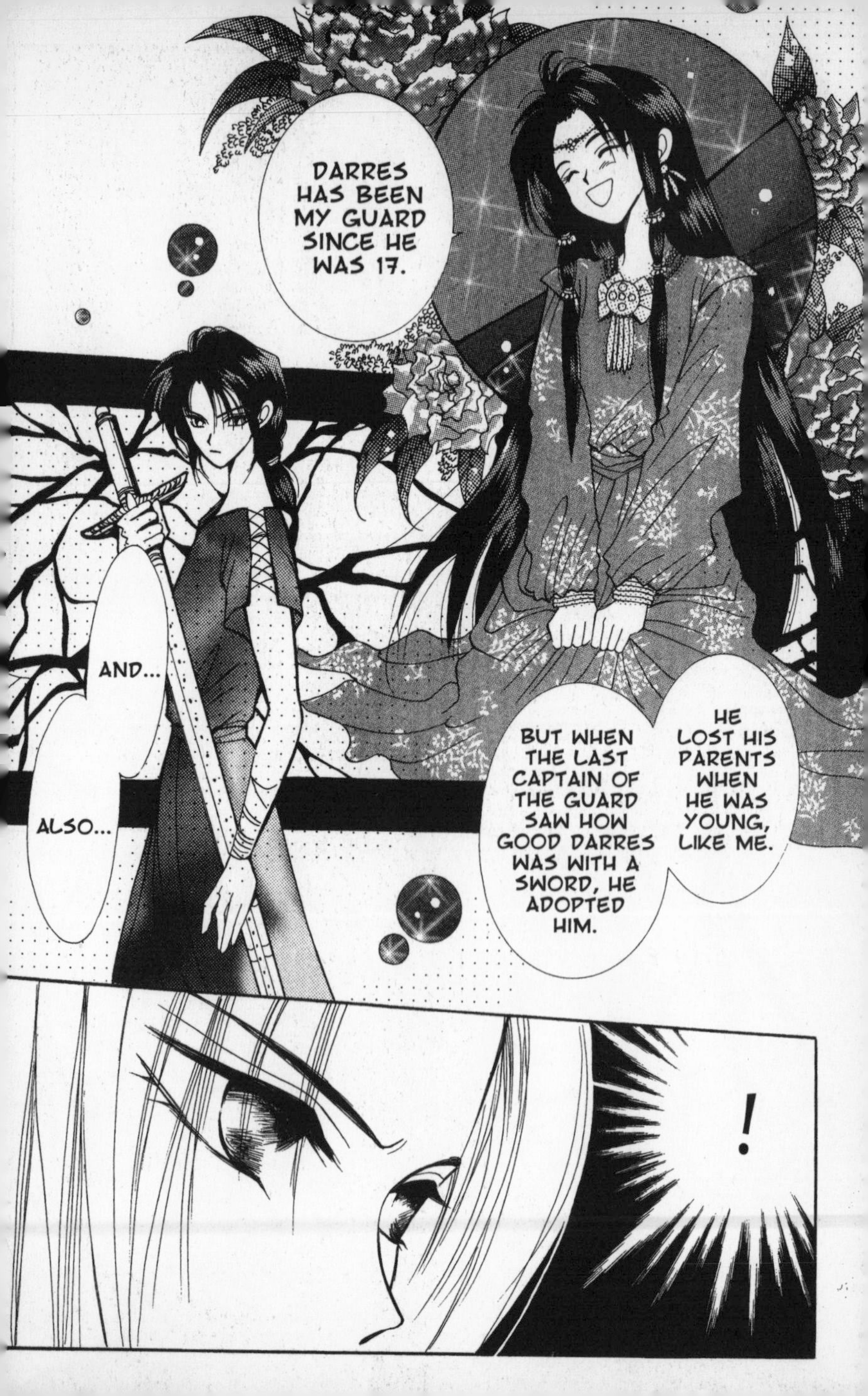
DARRES HAS BEEN MY GUARD SINCE HE WAS 17.
HE LOST HIS PARENTS WHEN HE WAS YOUNG, LIKE ME.
BUT WHEN THE LAST CAPTAIN OF THE GUARD SAW HOW GOOD DARRES WAS WITH A SWORD, HE ADOPTED HIM.
AND... ALSO...
!

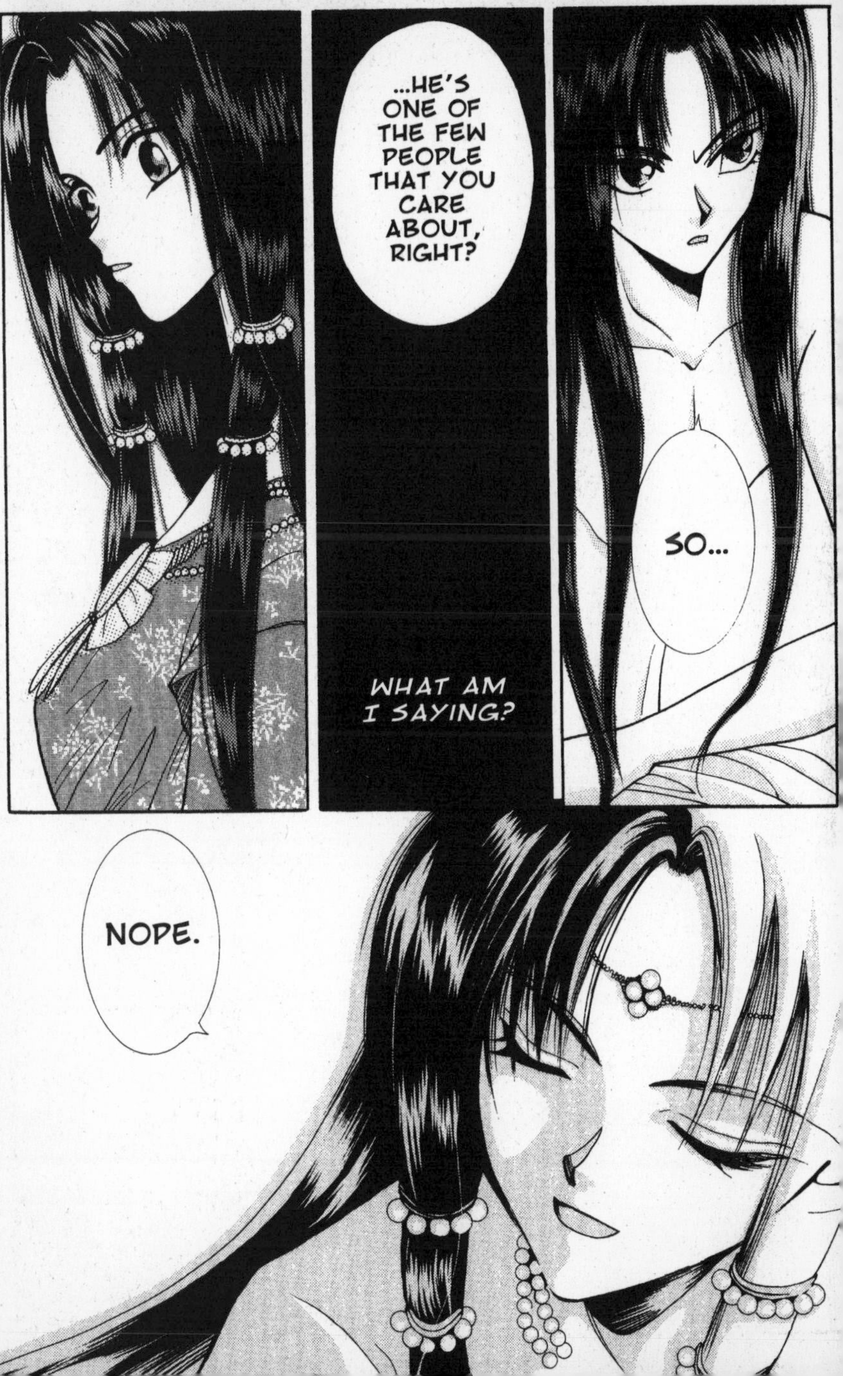
SO...
...HE'S ONE OF THE FEW PEOPLE THAT YOU CARE ABOUT, RIGHT?
WHAT AM I SAYING?
NOPE.

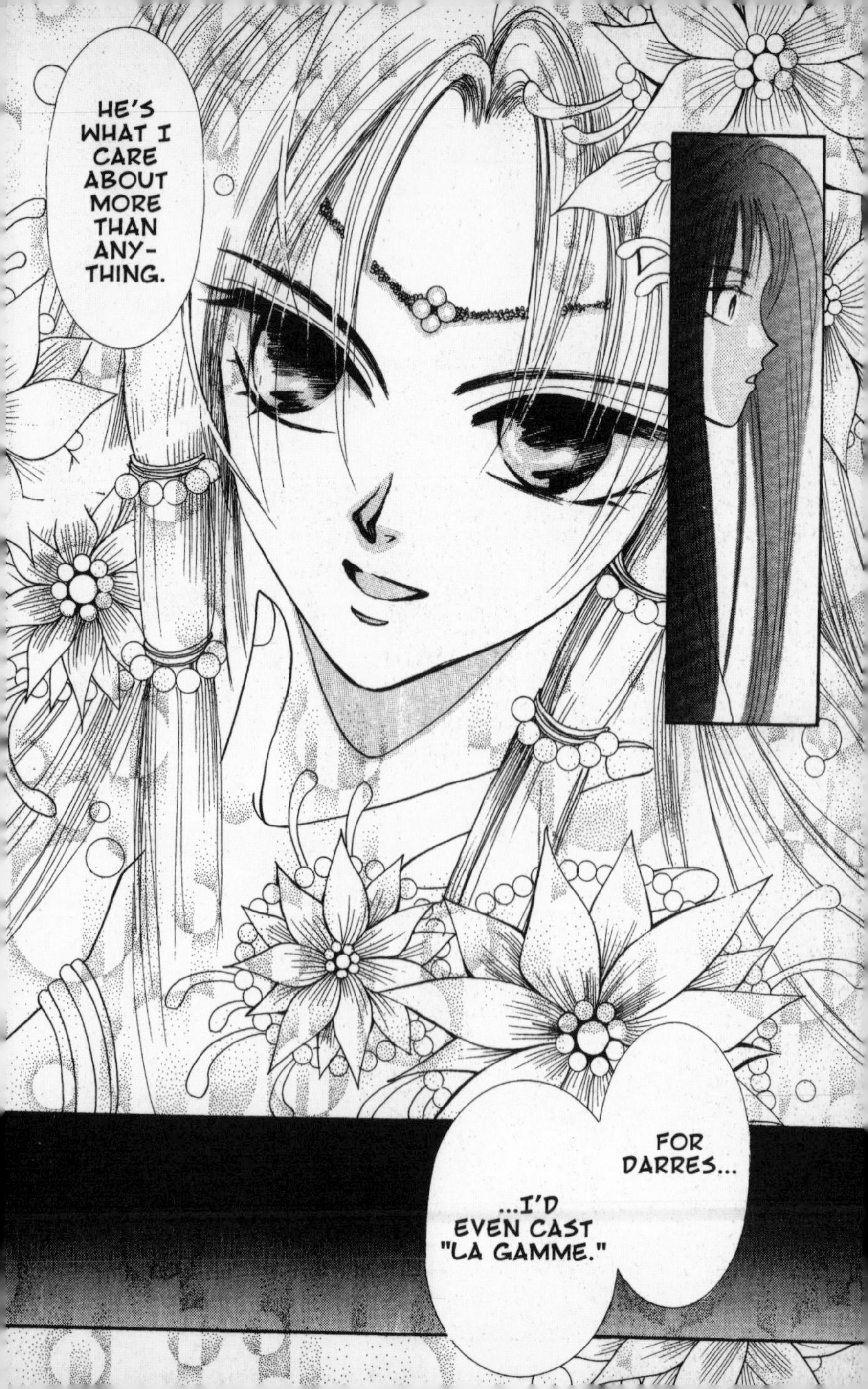
HE'S WHAT I CARE ABOUT MORE THAN ANY-THING.
FOR DARRES...
...I'D EVEN CAST "LA GAMME."

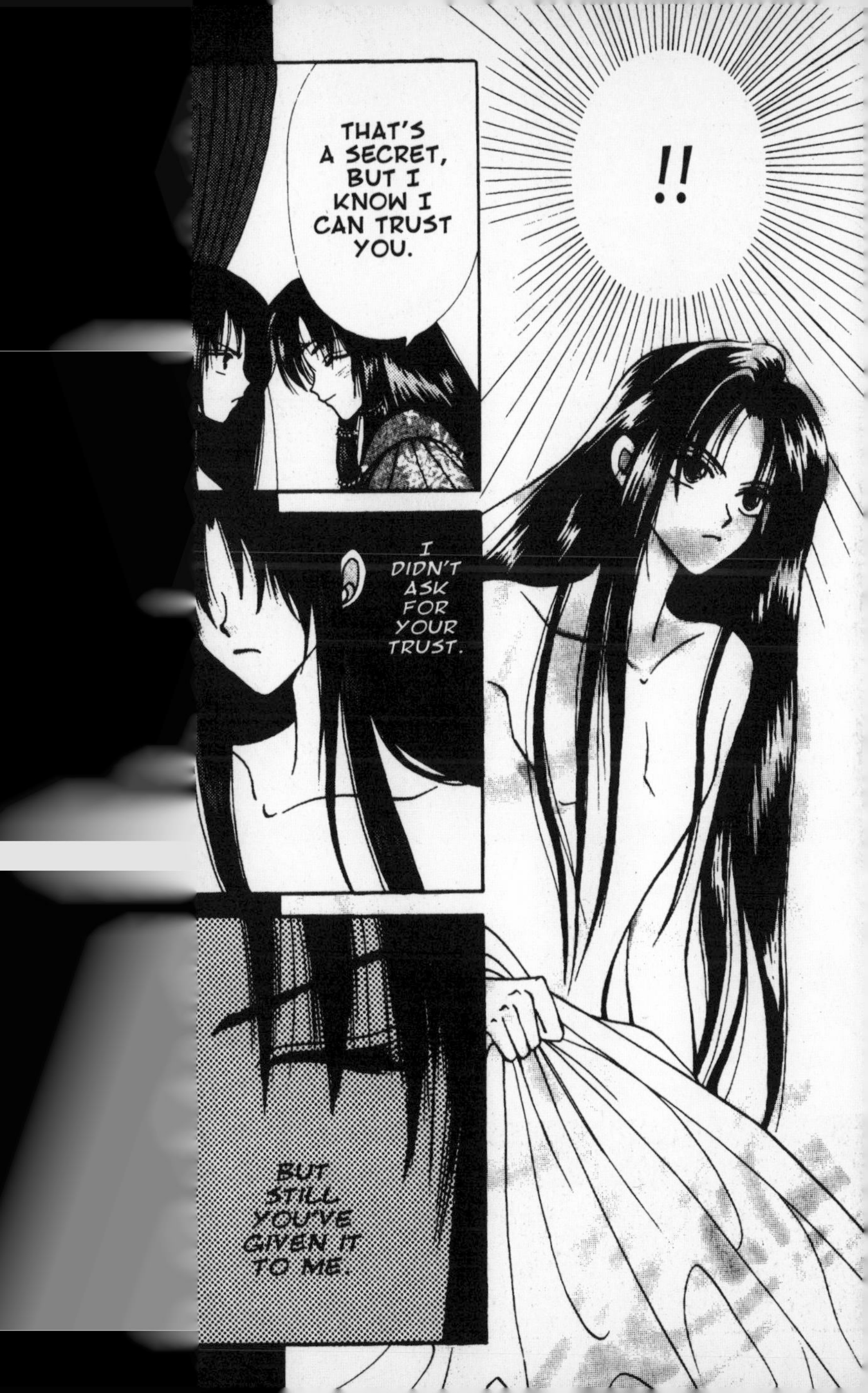
!!
THAT'S A SECRET, BUT I KNOW I CAN TRUST YOU.
I DIDN'T ASK FOR YOUR TRUST.
BUT STILL YOU'VE GIVEN IT TO ME.

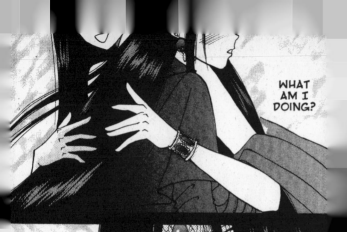

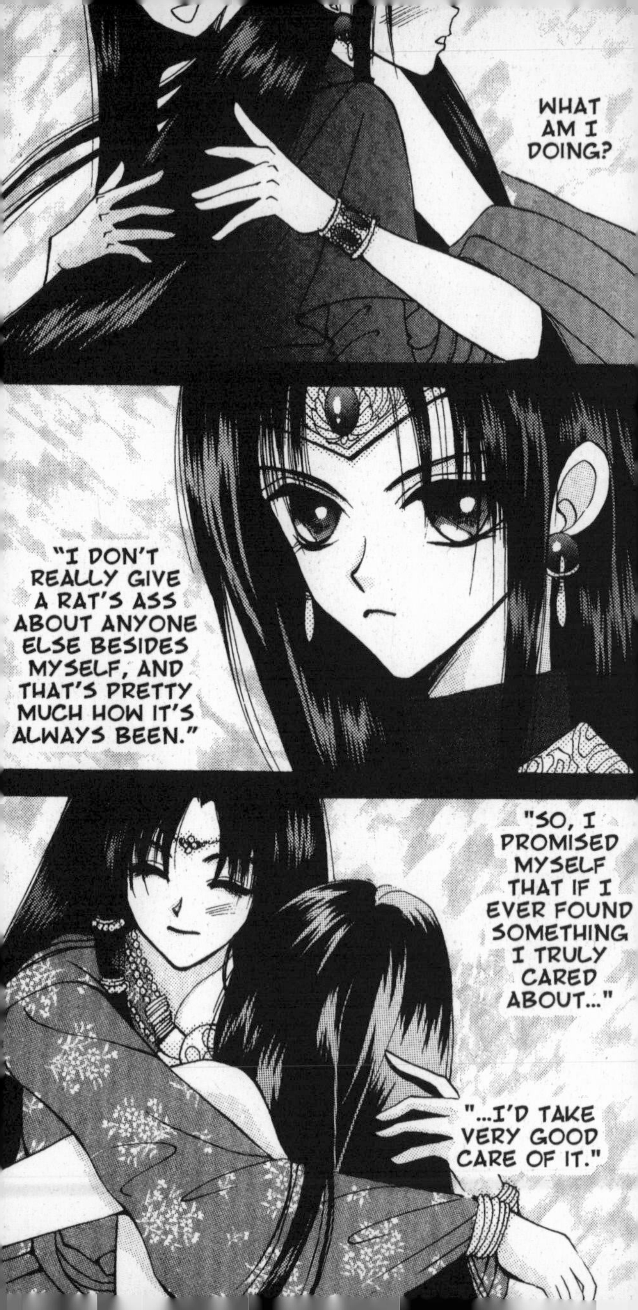
WHAT AM I DOING?
"I DON'T REALLY GIVE A RAT'S ASS ABOUT ANYONE ELSE BESIDES MYSELF, AND THAT'S PRETTY MUCH HOW IT'S ALWAYS BEEN."
"SO, I PROMISED MYSELF THAT IF I EVER FOUND SOMETHING I TRULY CARED ABOUT..."
"...I'D TAKE VERY GOOD CARE OF IT."

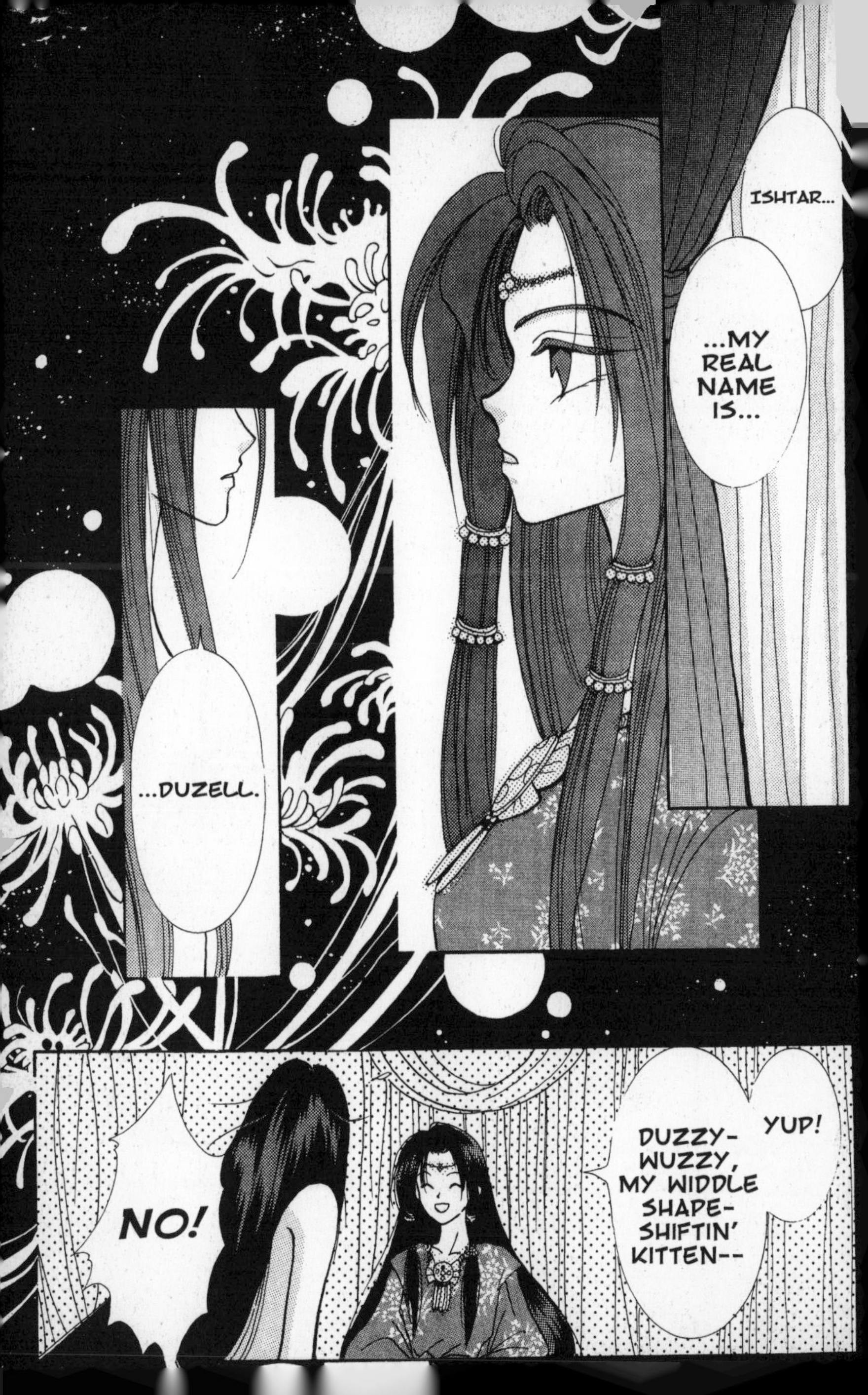
ISHTAR...
...MY REAL NAME IS...
...DUZELL.
YUP!
DUZZY-WUZZY, MY WIDDLE SHAPE-SHIFTIN' KITTEN--
NO!

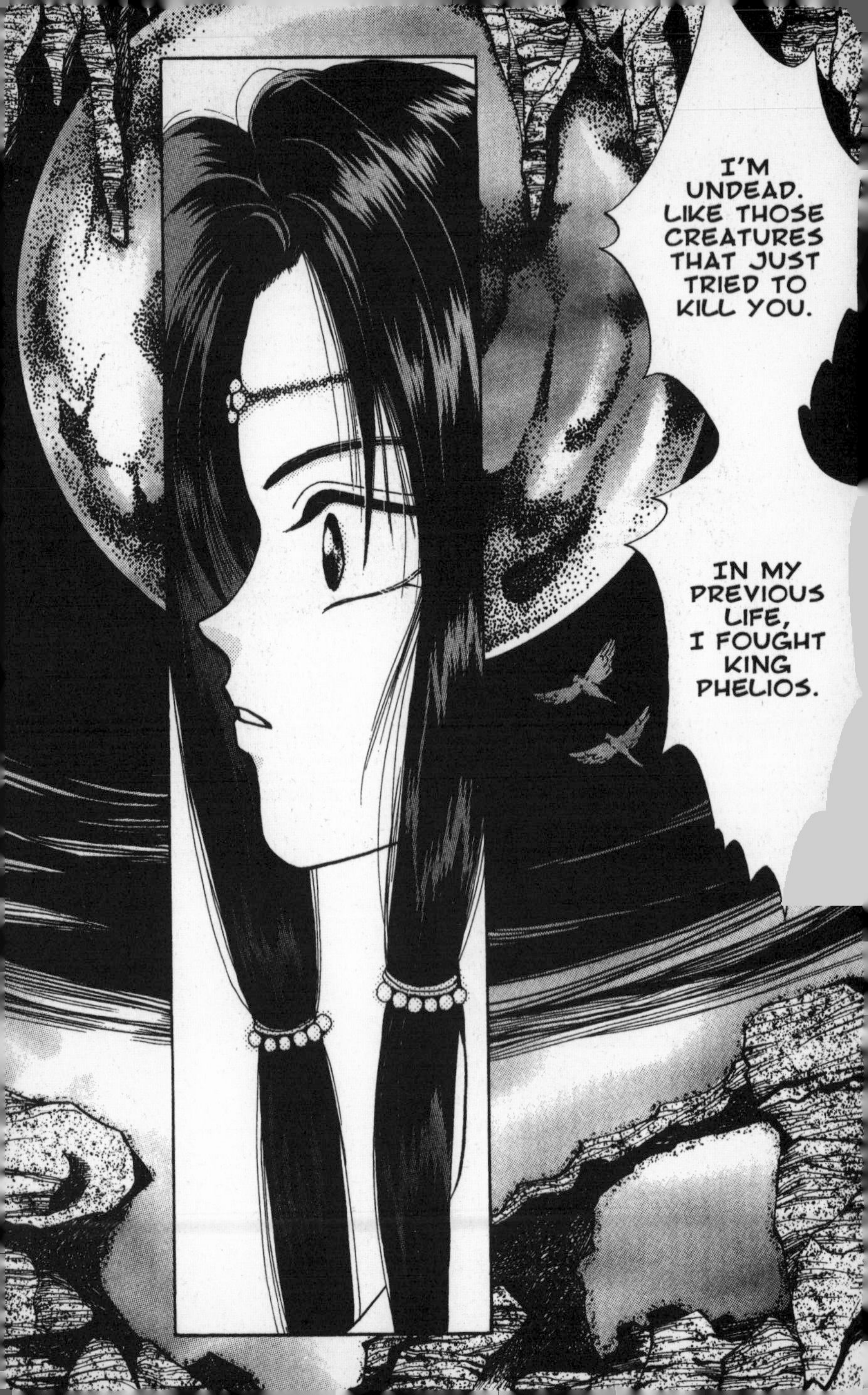
I'M UNDEAD. LIKE THOSE CREATURES THAT JUST TRIED TO KILL YOU.
IN MY PREVIOUS LIFE, I FOUGHT KING PHELIOS.

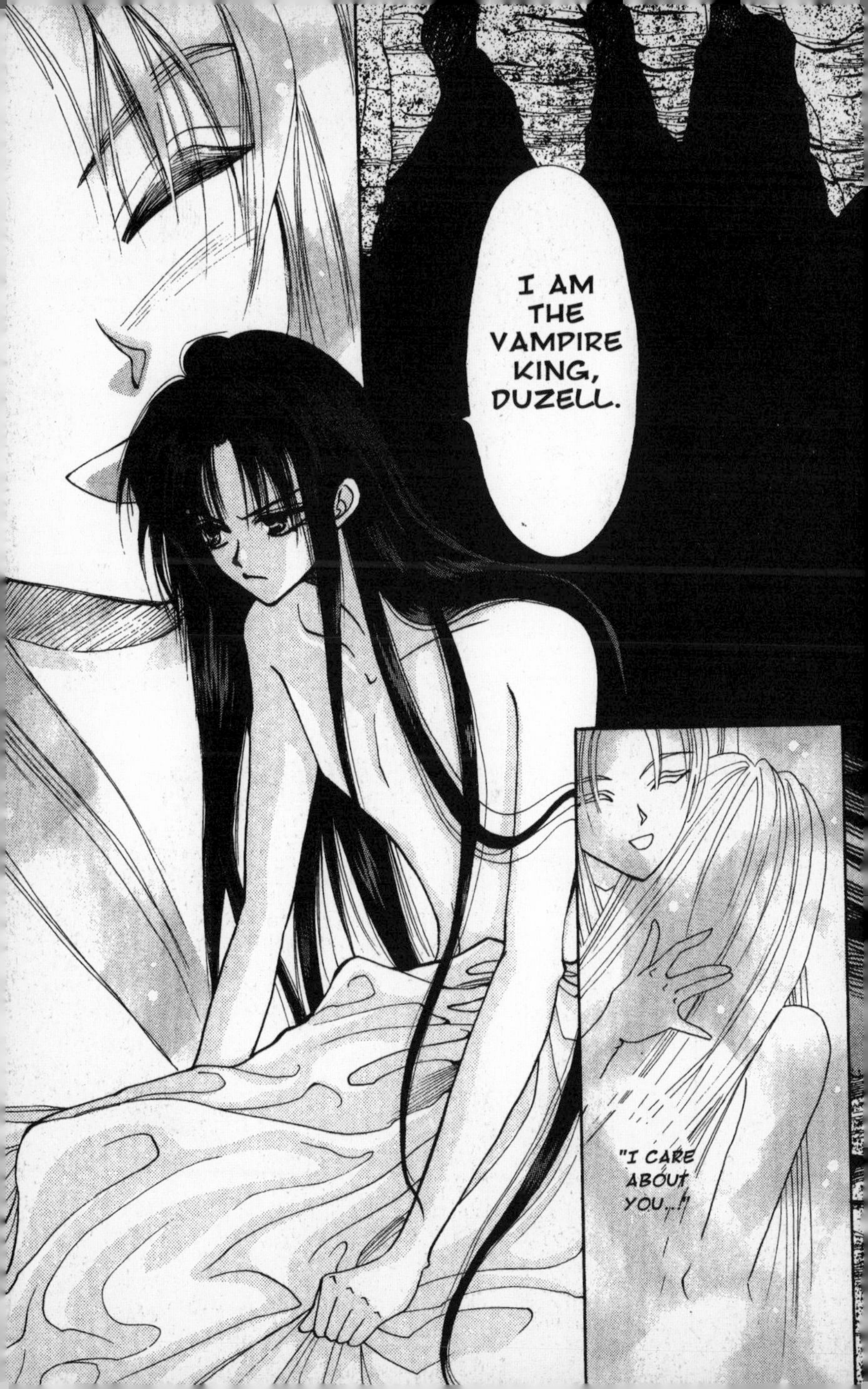
I AM THE VAMPIRE KING, DUZELL.
"I CARE ABOUT YOU...!"

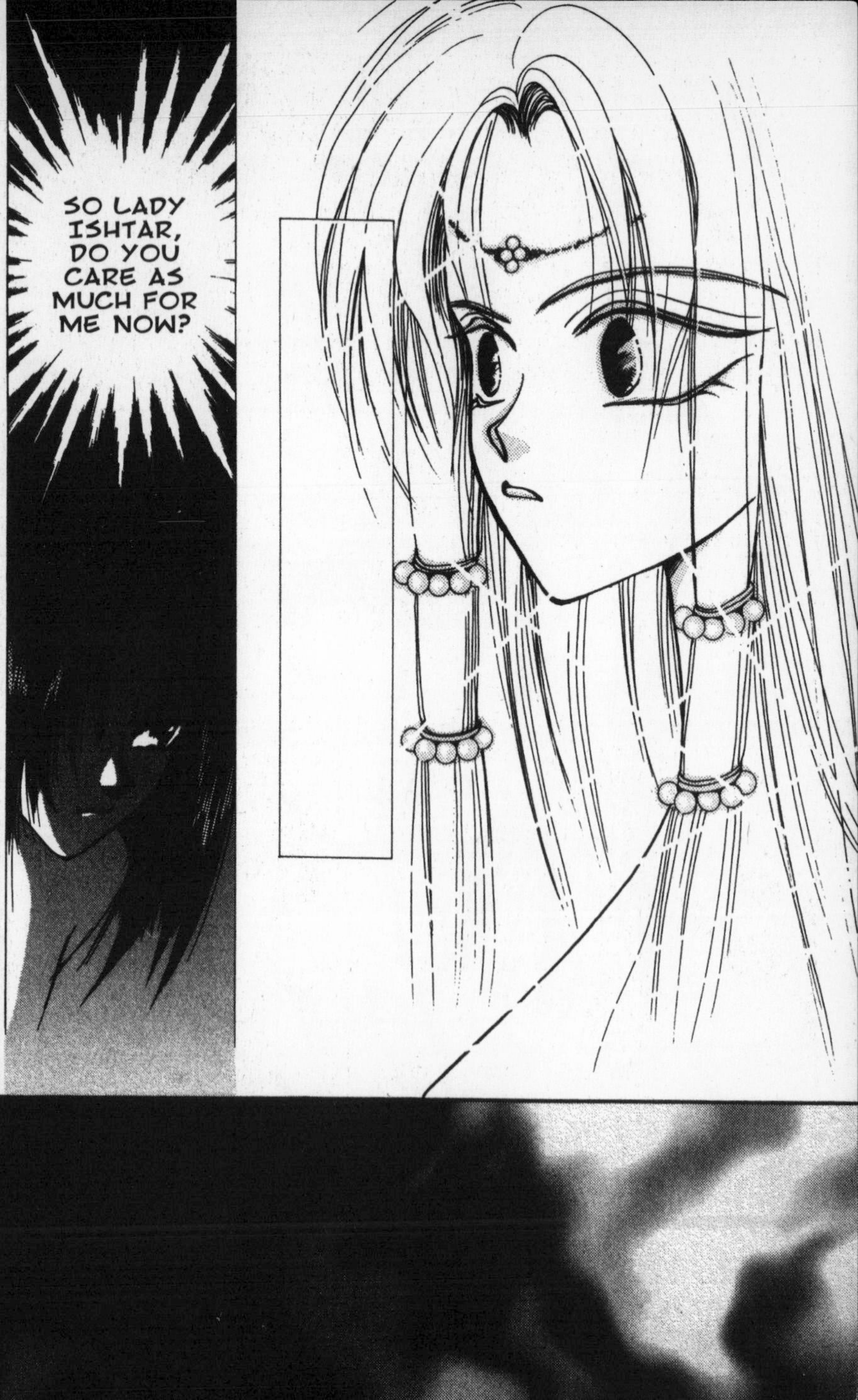
SO LADY ISHTAR, DO YOU CARE AS MUCH FOR ME NOW?

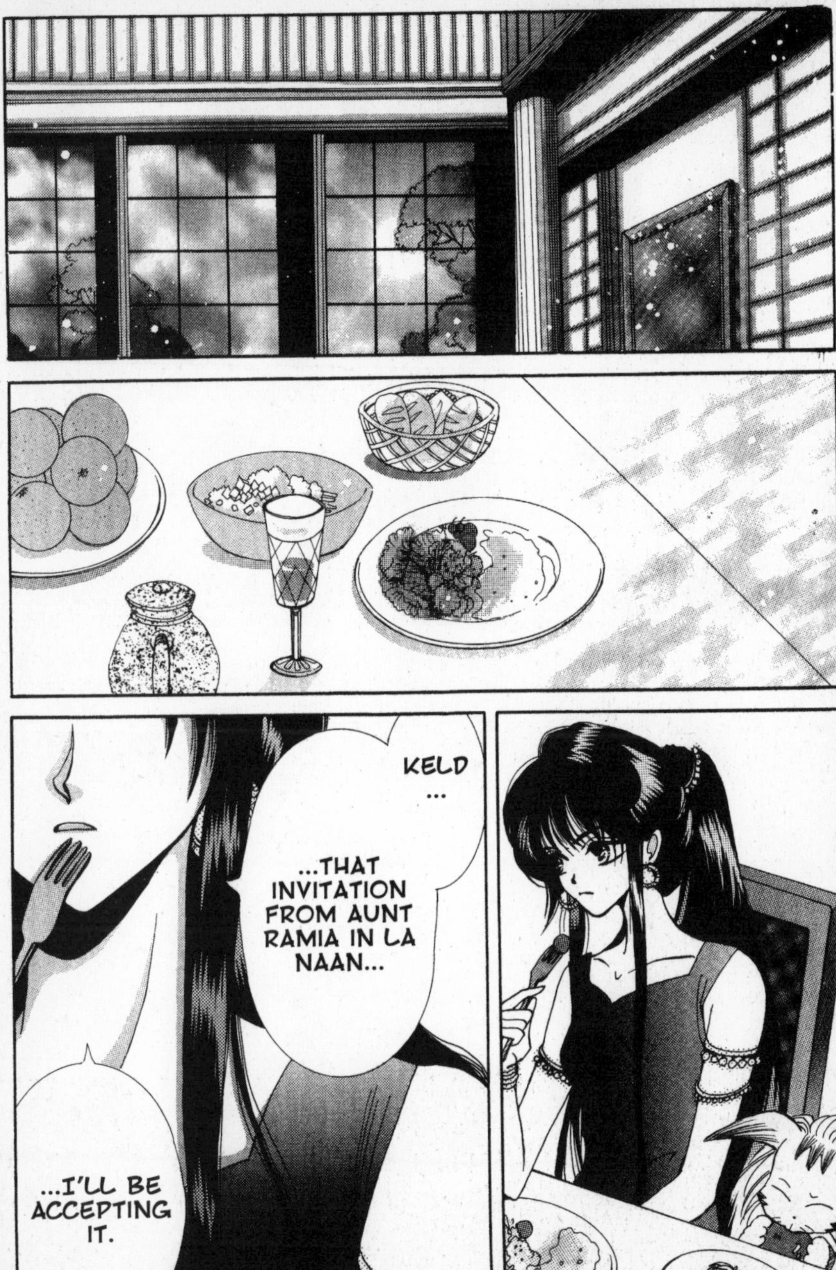
KELD ...
...THAT INVITATION FROM AUNT RAMIA IN LA NAAN...
...I'LL BE ACCEPTING IT.

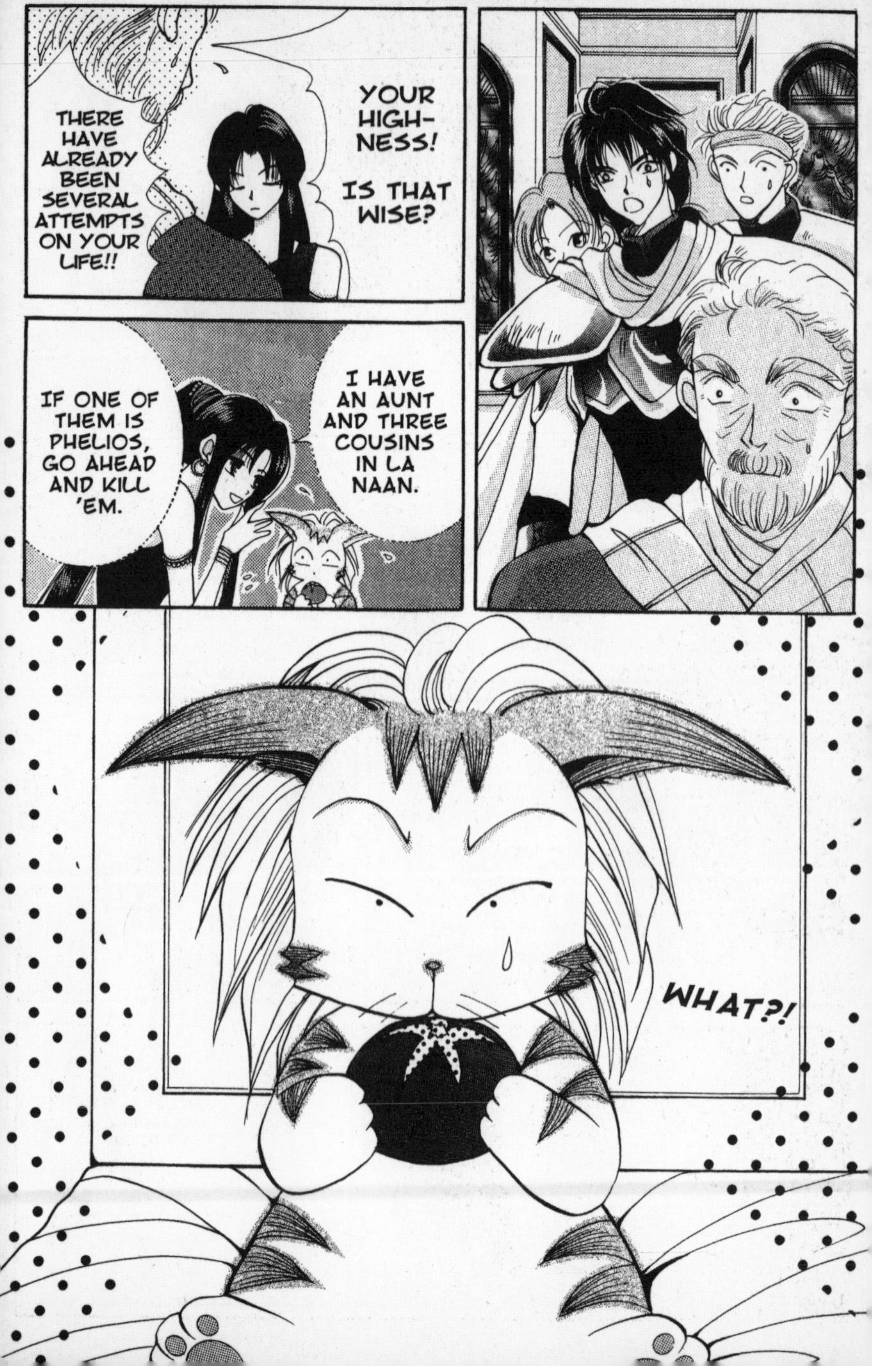
YOUR HIGHNESS! IS THAT WISE?
THERE HAVE ALREADY BEEN SEVERAL ATTEMPTS ON YOUR LIFE!!
I HAVE AN AUNT AND THREE COUSINS IN LA NAAN.
IF ONE OF THEM IS PHELIOS, GO AHEAD AND KILL 'EM.
WHAT?!

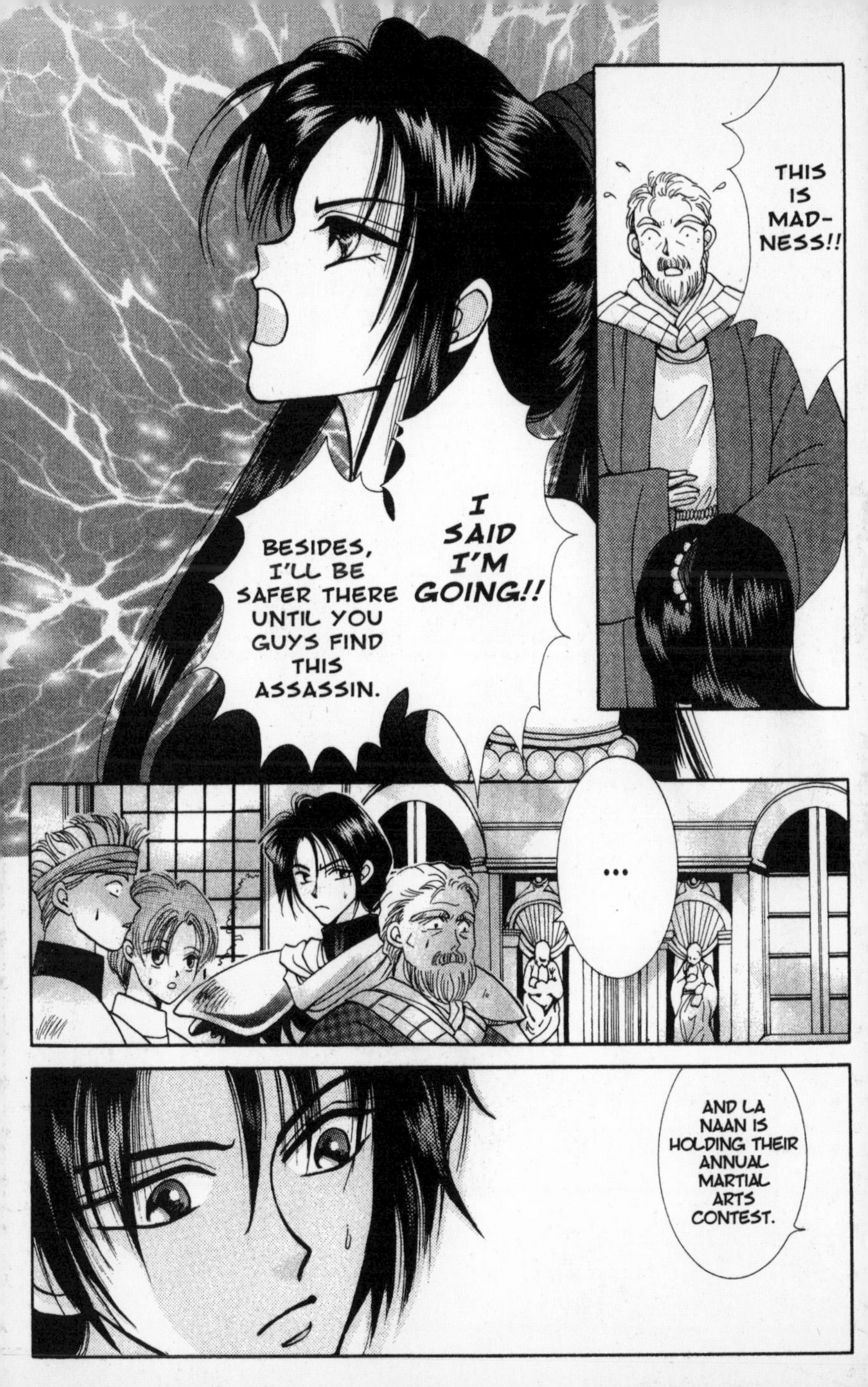
THIS IS MAD-NESS!!
I SAID I'M GOING!!
BESIDES, I'LL BE SAFER THERE UNTIL YOU GUYS FIND THIS ASSASSIN.
...
AND LA NAAN IS HOLDING THEIR ANNUAL MARTIAL ARTS CONTEST.

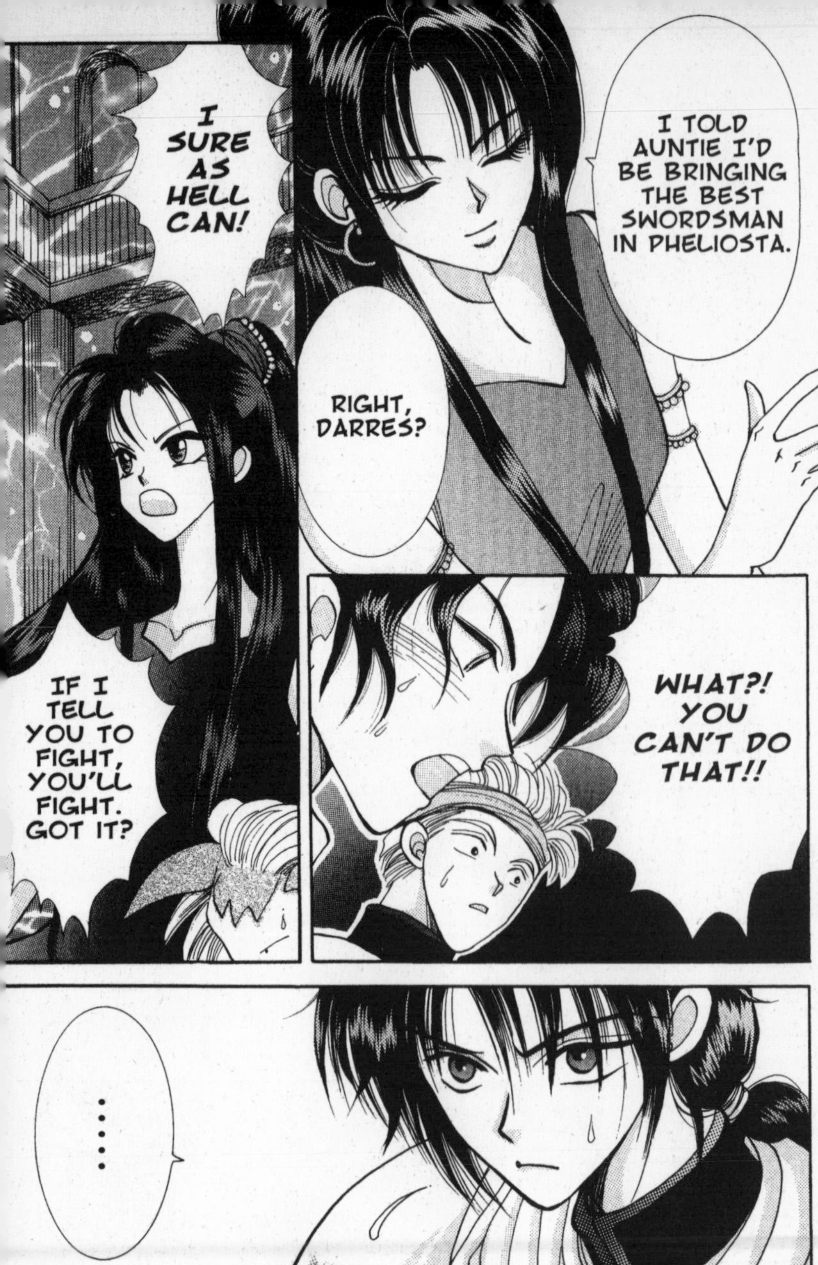
I TOLD AUNTIE I'D BE BRINGING THE BEST SWORDSMAN IN PHELIOSTA.
RIGHT, DARRES?
WHAT?! YOU CAN'T DO THAT!!
I SURE AS HELL CAN!
IF I TELL YOU TO FIGHT, YOU'LL FIGHT. GOT IT?
.....

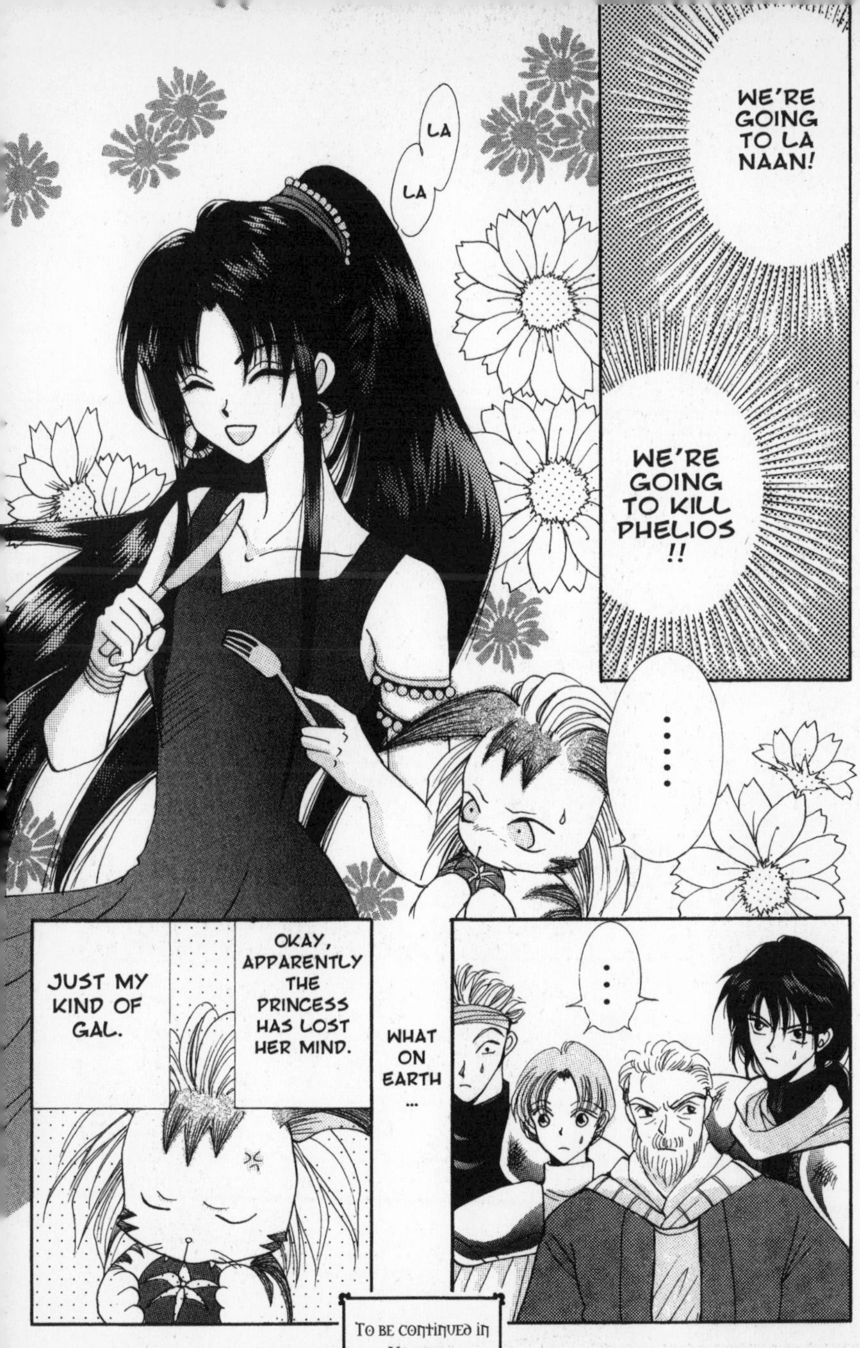
WE'RE GOING TO LA NAAN!
WE'RE GOING TO KILL PHELIOS!!
LA
LA
.....
...
WHAT ON EARTH ...
OKAY, APPARENTLY THE PRINCESS HAS LOST HER MIND.
JUST MY KIND OF GAL.

To be continued in Volume 2

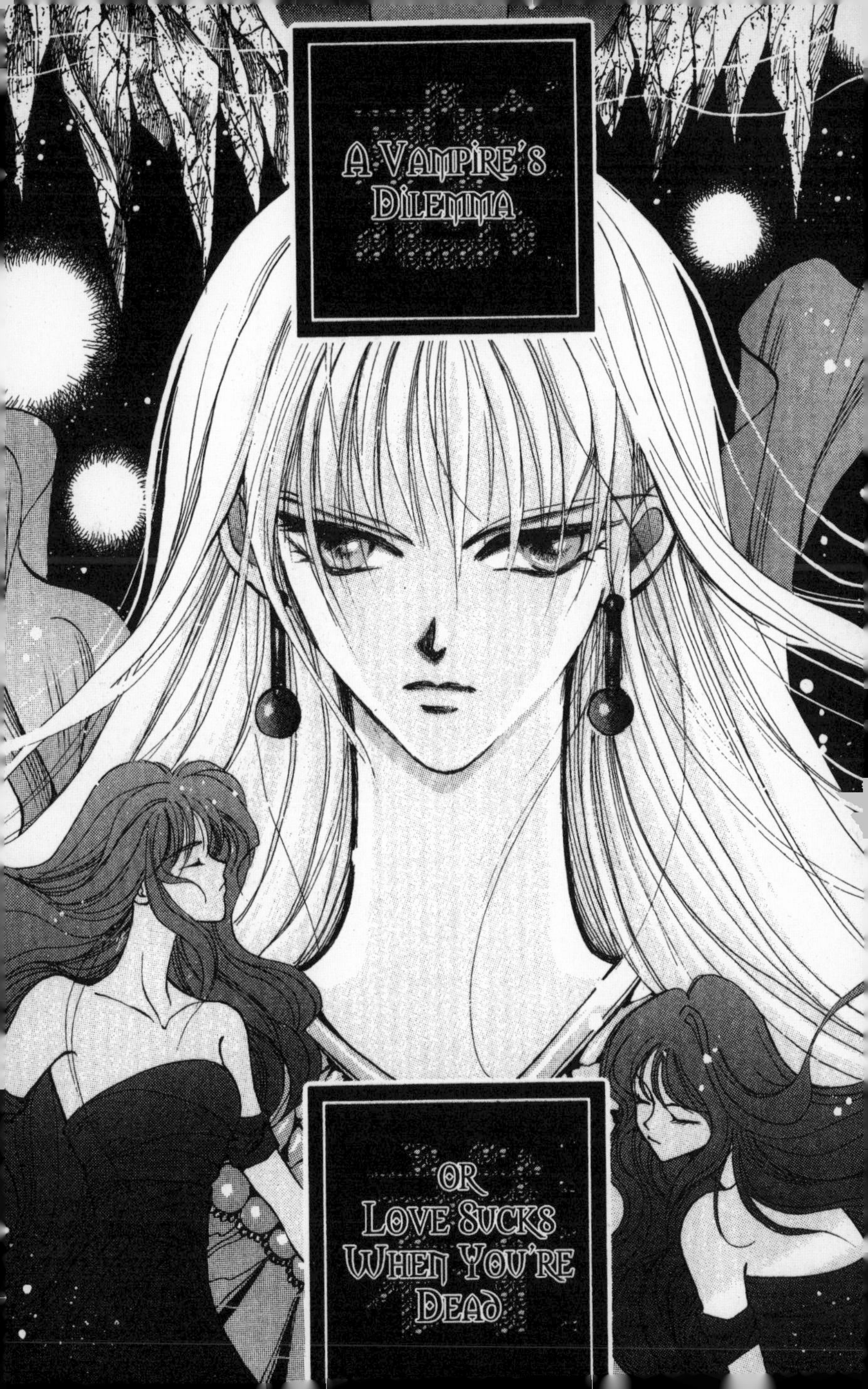
A Vampire's Dilemma
or
Love Sucks When You're Dead

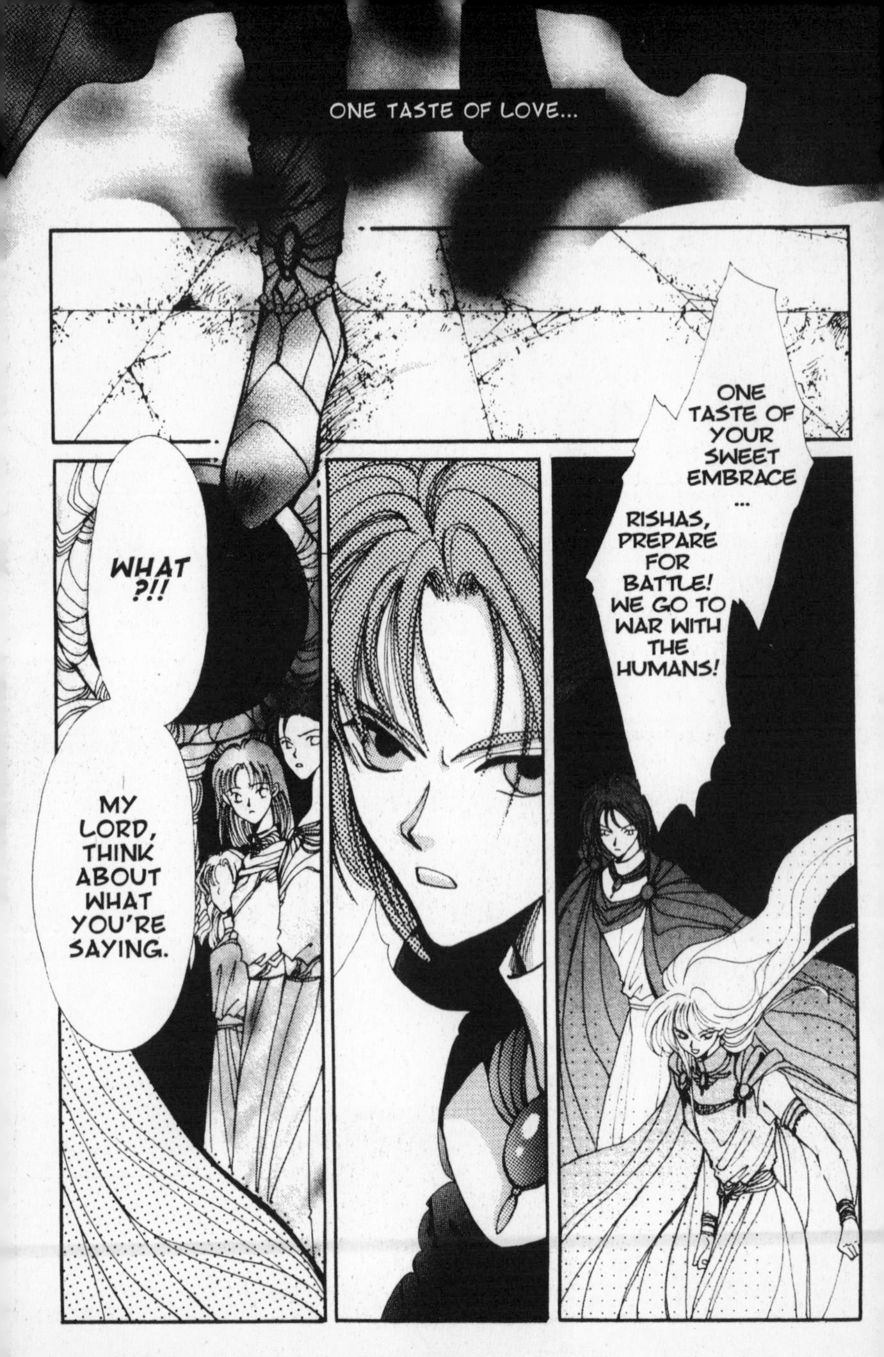
ONE TASTE OF LOVE...
ONE TASTE OF YOUR SWEET EMBRACE...
RISHAS, PREPARE FOR BATTLE! WE GO TO WAR WITH THE HUMANS!
WHAT?!!
MY LORD, THINK ABOUT WHAT YOU'RE SAYING.

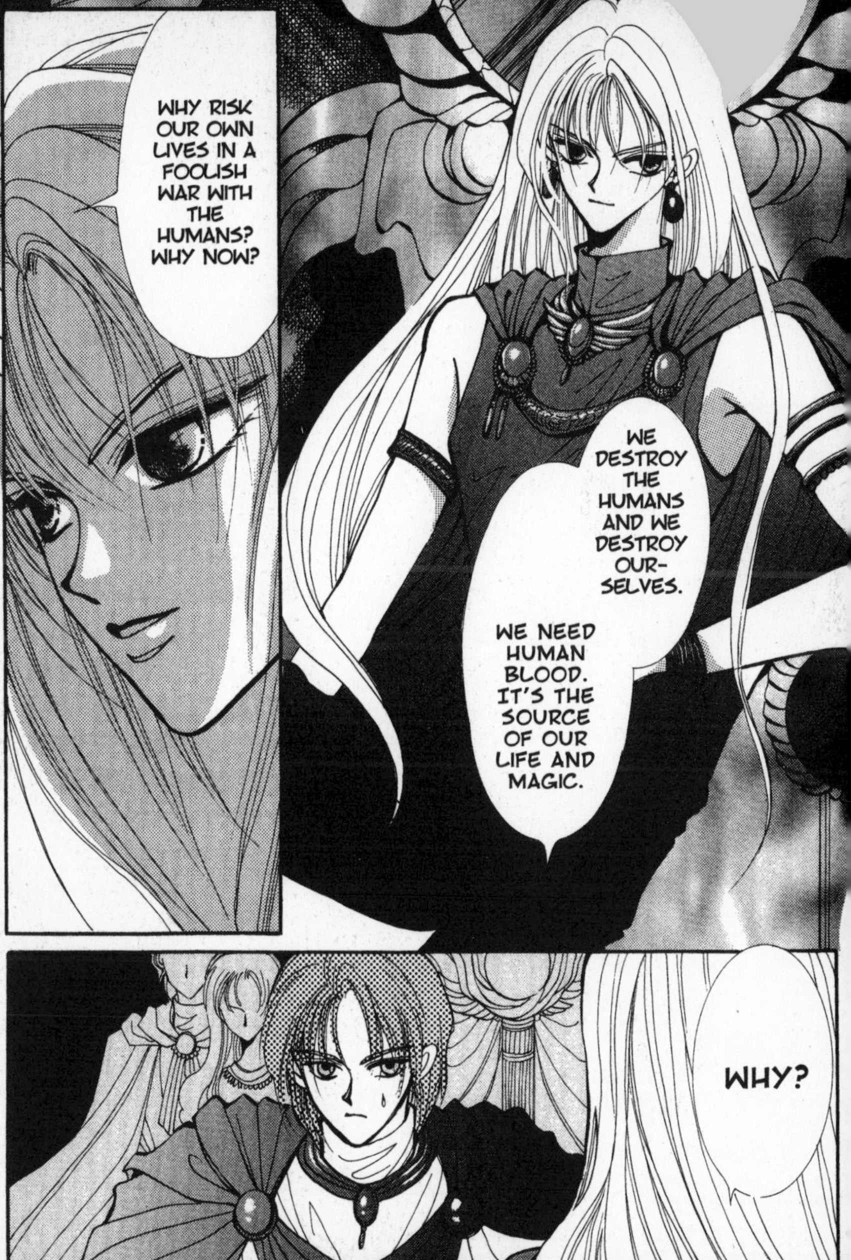
WE DESTROY THE HUMANS AND WE DESTROY OUR-SELVES.
WE NEED HUMAN BLOOD. IT'S THE SOURCE OF OUR LIFE AND MAGIC.
WHY RISK OUR OWN LIVES IN A FOOLISH WAR WITH THE HUMANS? WHY NOW?
WHY?

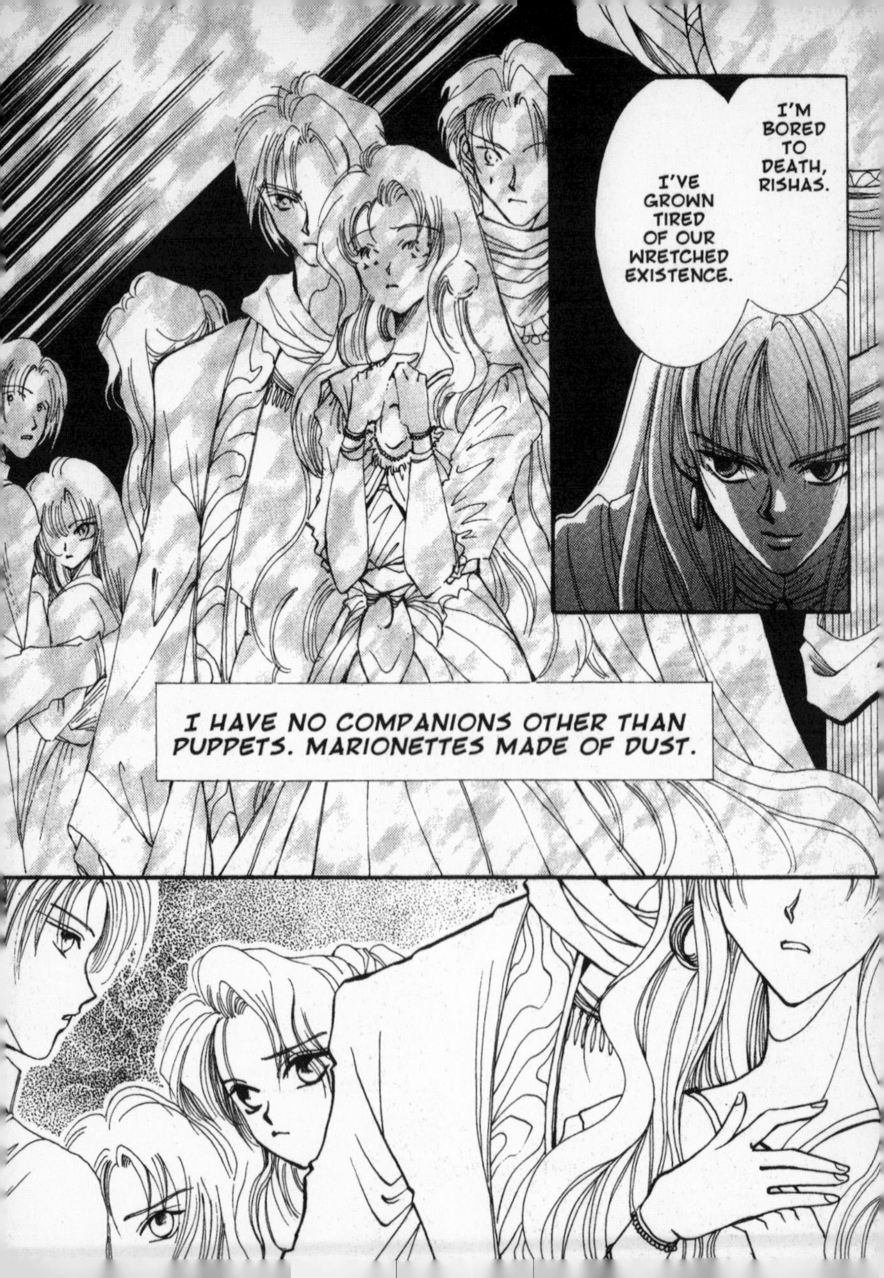
I'M BORED TO DEATH, RISHAS.
I'VE GROWN TIRED OF OUR WRETCHED EXISTENCE.
I HAVE NO COMPANIONS OTHER THAN PUPPETS. MARIONETTES MADE OF DUST.

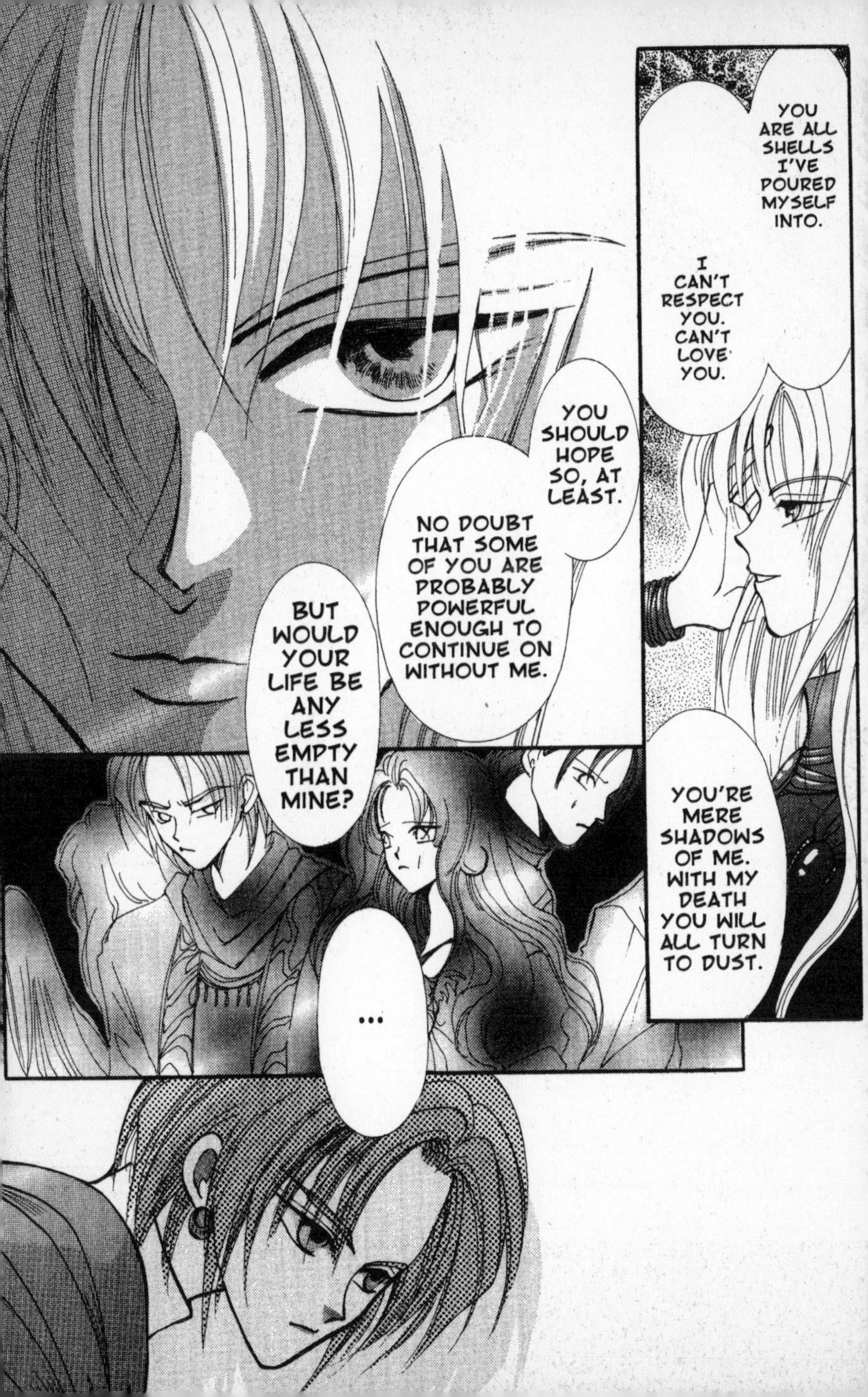
YOU ARE ALL SHELLS I'VE POURED MYSELF INTO.
I CAN'T RESPECT YOU. CAN'T LOVE YOU.
YOU'RE MERE SHADOWS OF ME. WITH MY DEATH YOU WILL ALL TURN TO DUST.
YOU SHOULD HOPE SO, AT LEAST.
NO DOUBT THAT SOME OF YOU ARE PROBABLY POWERFUL ENOUGH TO CONTINUE ON WITHOUT ME.
BUT WOULD YOUR LIFE BE ANY LESS EMPTY THAN MINE?
...

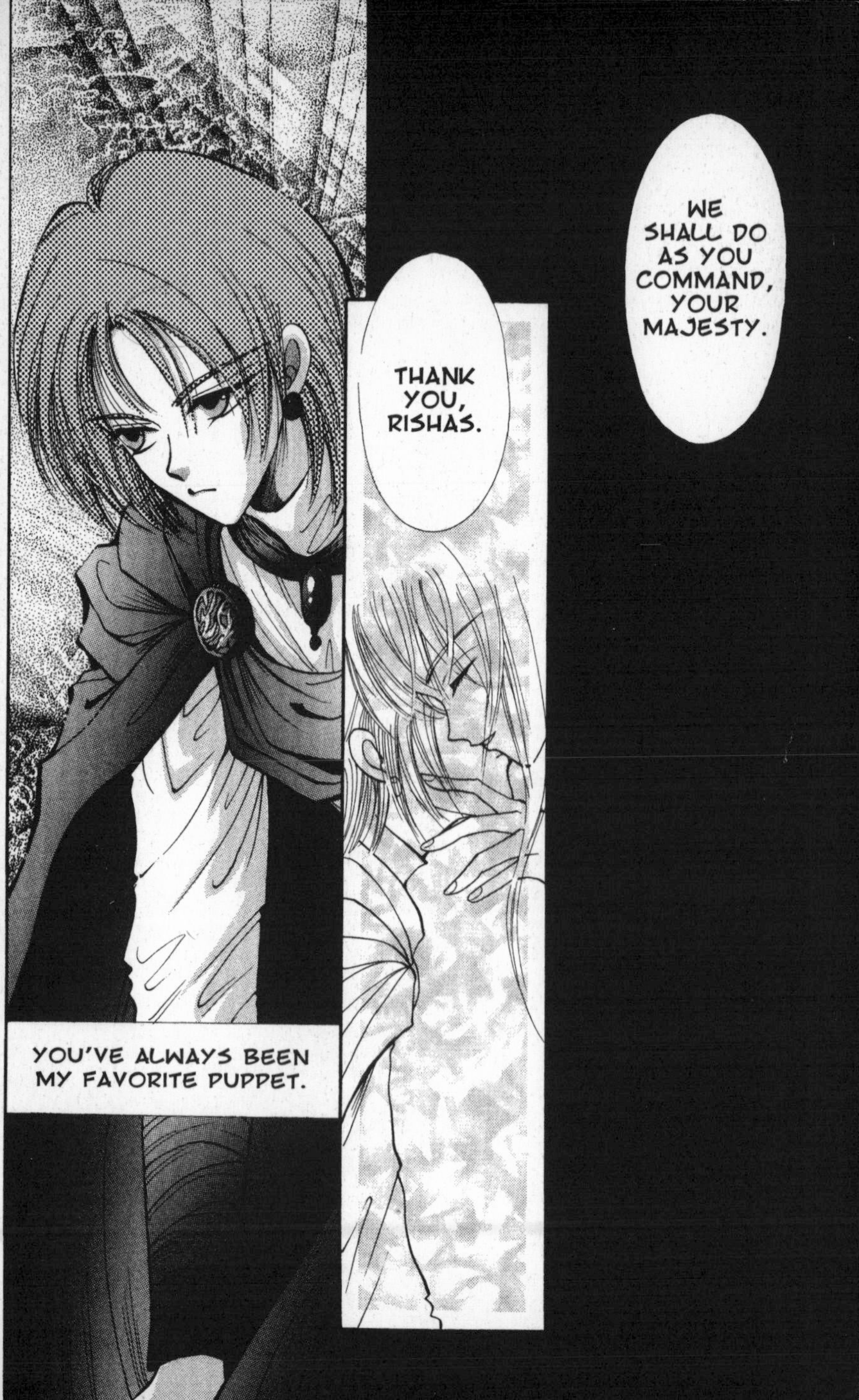
WE SHALL DO AS YOU COMMAND, YOUR MAJESTY.
THANK YOU, RISHAS.
YOU'VE ALWAYS BEEN MY FAVORITE PUPPET.

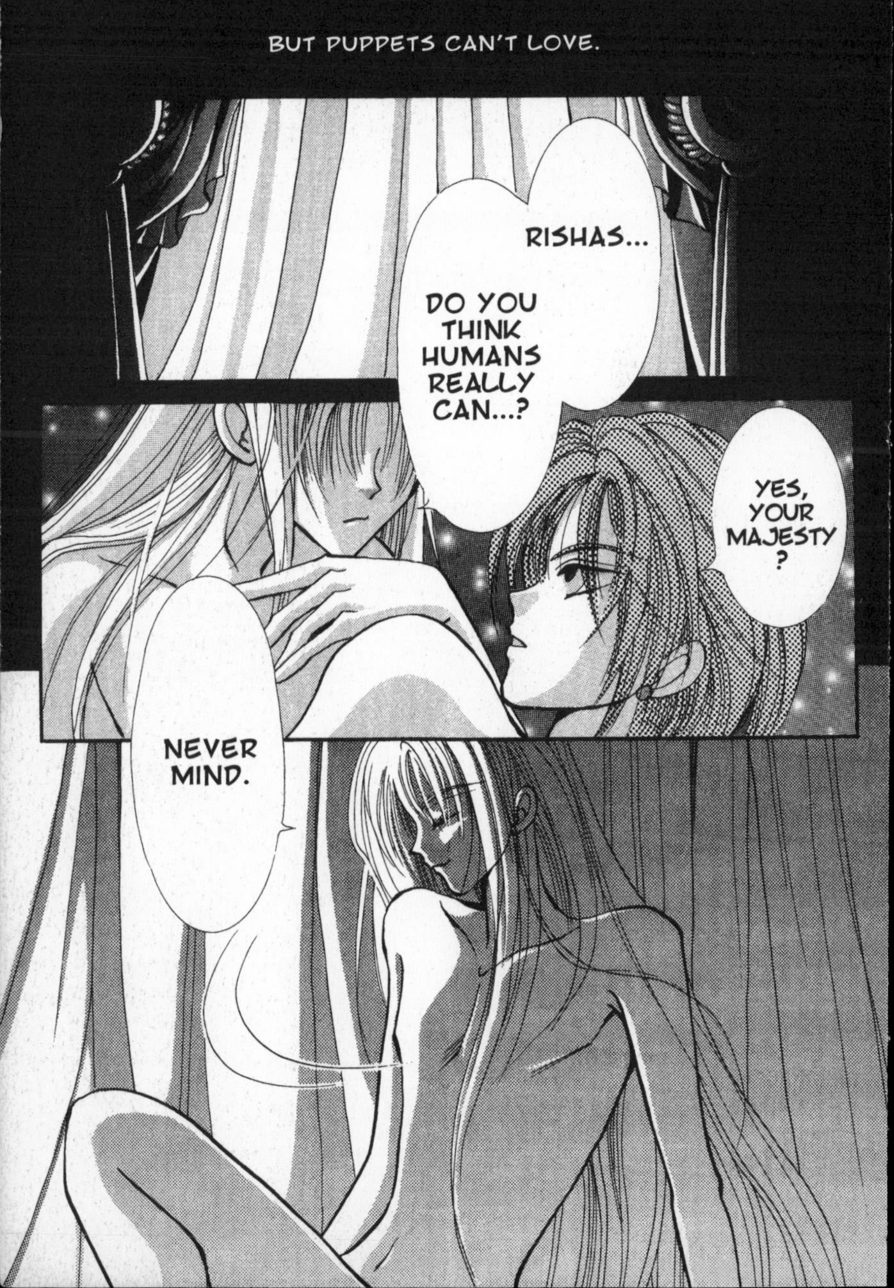
BUT PUPPETS CAN'T LOVE.
RISHAS...
DO YOU THINK HUMANS REALLY CAN...?
YES, YOUR MAJESTY?
NEVER MIND.

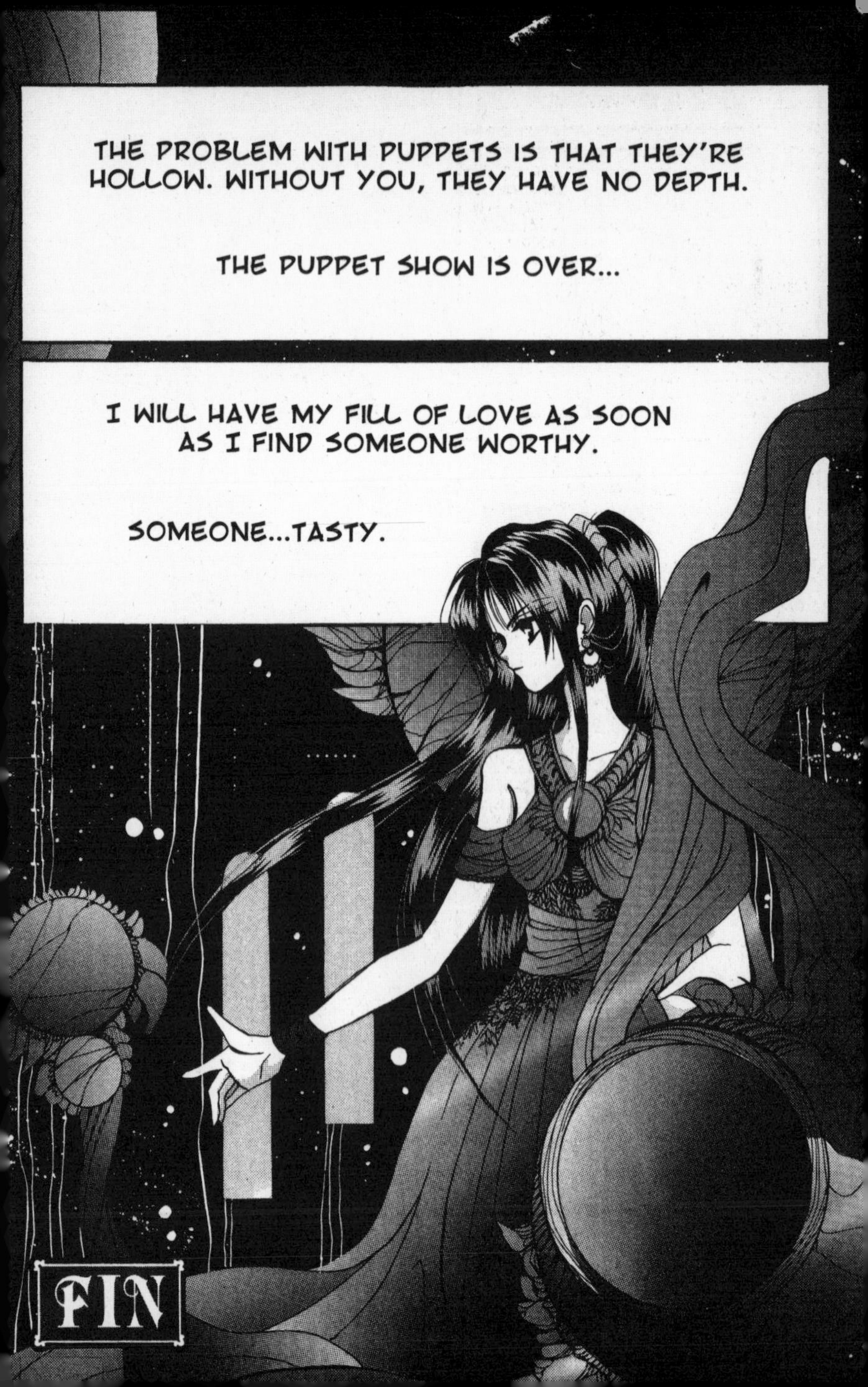
THE PROBLEM WITH PUPPETS IS THAT THEY'RE HOLLOW. WITHOUT YOU, THEY HAVE NO DEPTH.
THE PUPPET SHOW IS OVER...
I WILL HAVE MY FILL OF LOVE AS SOON AS I FIND SOMEONE WORTHY.
SOMEONE...TASTY.
FIN

AFTERWARD

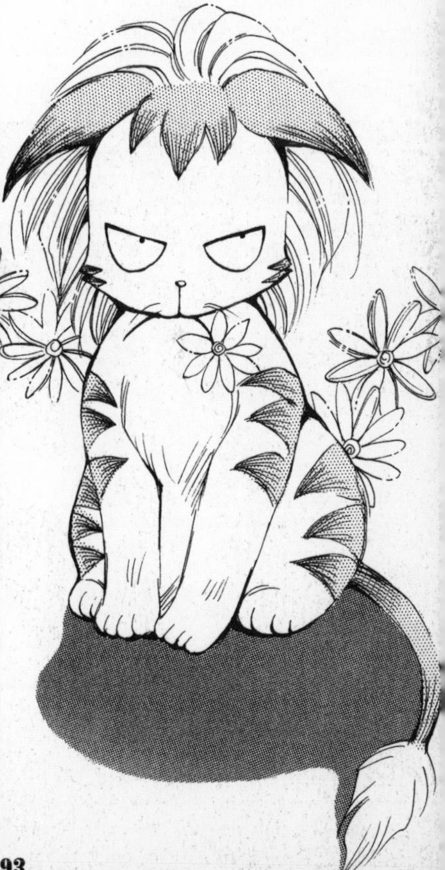

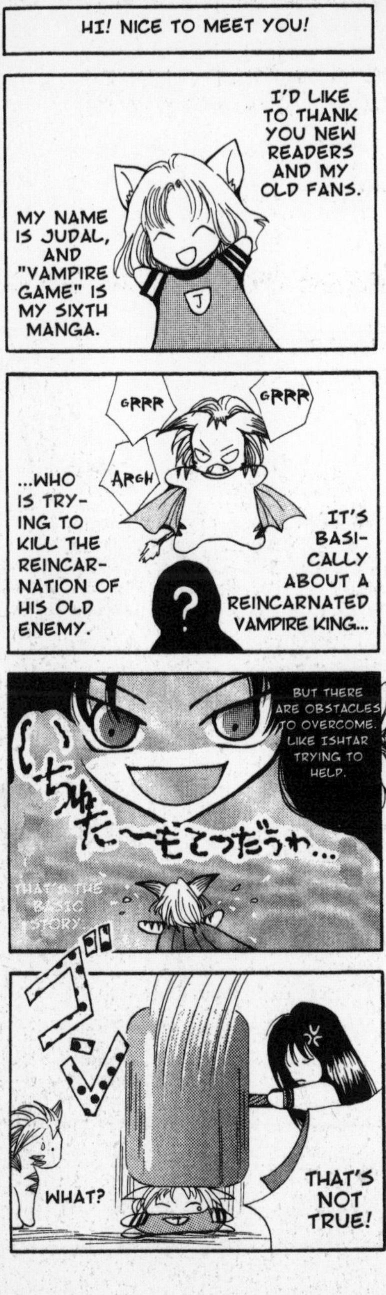
HI! NICE TO MEET YOU!
I'D LIKE TO THANK YOU NEW READERS AND MY OLD FANS.
MY NAME IS JUDAL, AND "VAMPIRE GAME" IS MY SIXTH MANGA.
GRRR
GRRR
ARGH
IT'S BASICALLY ABOUT A REINCARNATED VAMPIRE KING...
...WHO IS TRYING TO KILL THE REINCARNATION OF HIS OLD ENEMY.
BUT THERE ARE OBSTACLES TO OVERCOME. LIKE ISHTAR TRYING TO HELP.
THAT'S THE BASIC STORY.
THAT'S NOT TRUE!
WHAT?

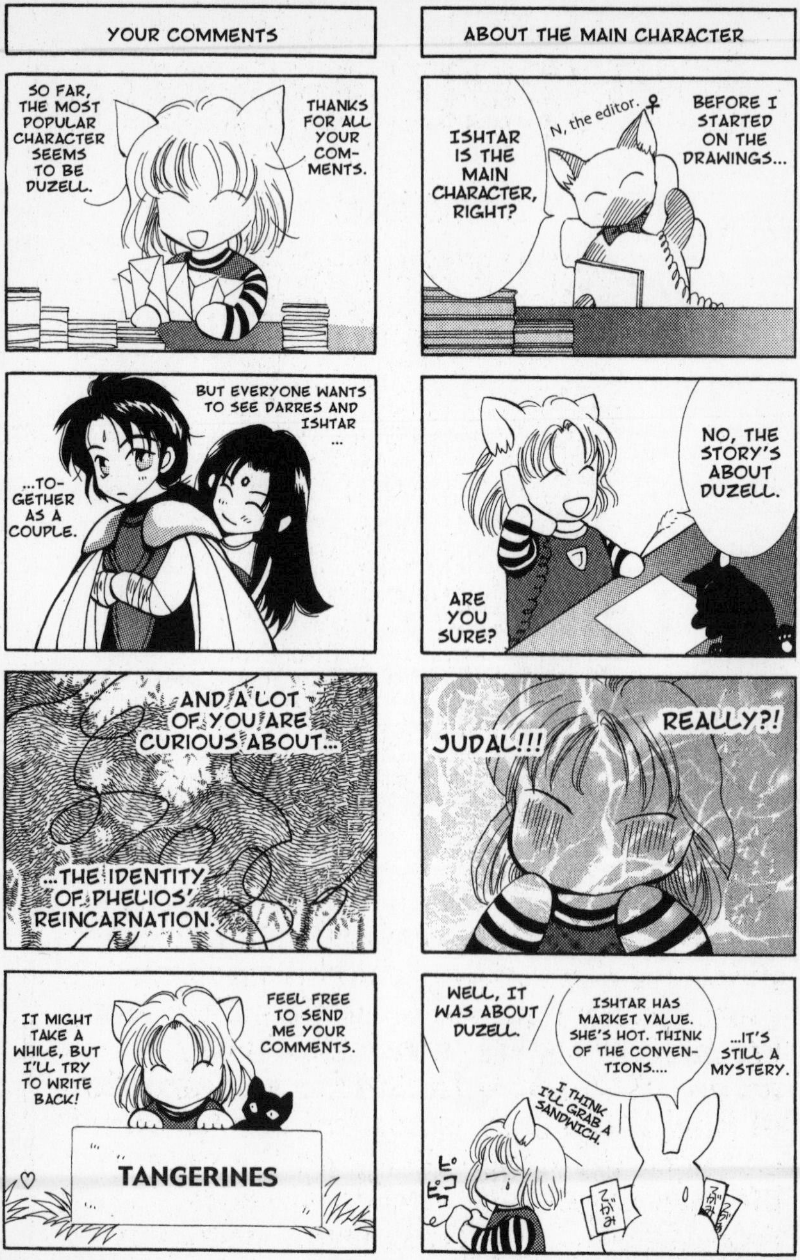
ABOUT THE MAIN CHARACTER
BEFORE I STARTED ON THE DRAWINGS...
N, the editor.
ISHTAR IS THE MAIN CHARACTER, RIGHT?
NO, THE STORY'S ABOUT DUZELL.
ARE YOU SURE?
REALLY?!
JUDAL!!!
...IT'S STILL A MYSTERY.
ISHTAR HAS MARKET VALUE. SHE'S HOT. THINK OF THE CONVENTIONS....
WELL, IT WAS ABOUT DUZELL.
I THINK I'LL GRAB A SANDWICH.
YOUR COMMENTS
THANKS FOR ALL YOUR COMMENTS.
SO FAR, THE MOST POPULAR CHARACTER SEEMS TO BE DUZELL.
BUT EVERYONE WANTS TO SEE DARRES AND ISHTAR ...
...TOGETHER AS A COUPLE.
AND A LOT OF YOU ARE CURIOUS ABOUT...
...THE IDENTITY OF PHELIOS' REINCARNATION.
FEEL FREE TO SEND ME YOUR COMMENTS.
IT MIGHT TAKE A WHILE, BUT I'LL TRY TO WRITE BACK!
TANGERINES

VAMPIRE GAME

Next issue...

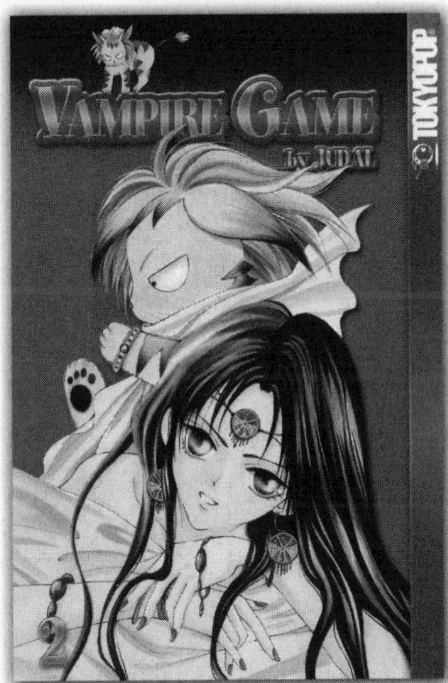
VAMPIRE GAME
by JUDAL
TOKYOPOP
2

So Ishtar is off to visit her aunt in La Naan, ostensibly to see a warriors' competition in which her three strong cousins and her gaurdian, Darres, will be participating. But her motives are far more mischievous in nature. If Duzell is to find the reincarnation of King Phelios, he needs to taste his blood, and what better way to lap up the juice of life than from the floor of a warriors' competition... especially when matrimony is the prize.

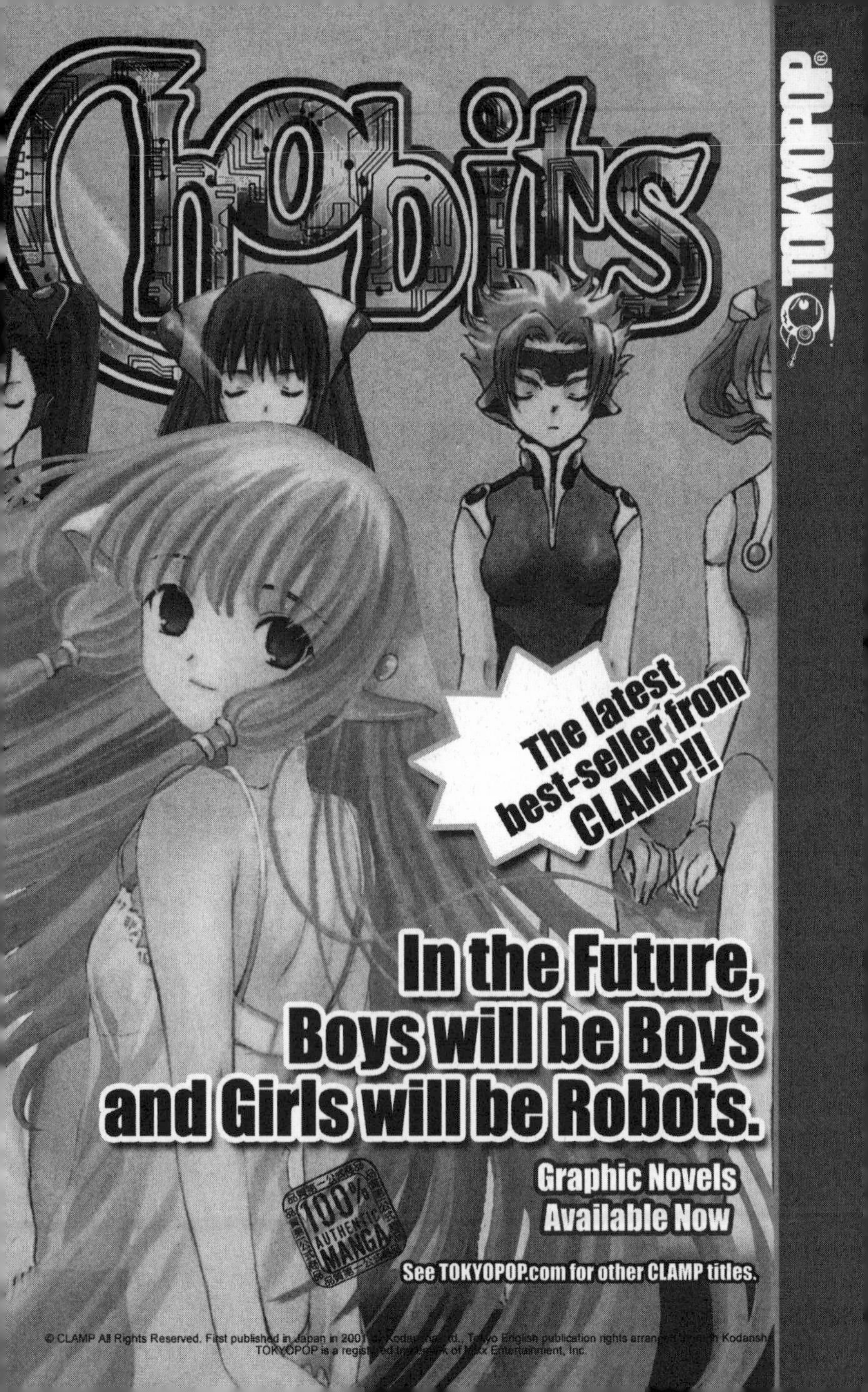
Chobits
TOKYOPOP
The latest best-seller from CLAMP!!
In the Future, Boys will be Boys and Girls will be Robots.
Graphic Novels Available Now
100% AUTHENTIC MANGA
See TOKYOPOP.com for other CLAMP titles.
© CLAMP All Rights Reserved. First published in Japan in 2001
Tokyo English publication rights
Kodansha
TOKYOPOP is a regis
Entertainment, Inc.

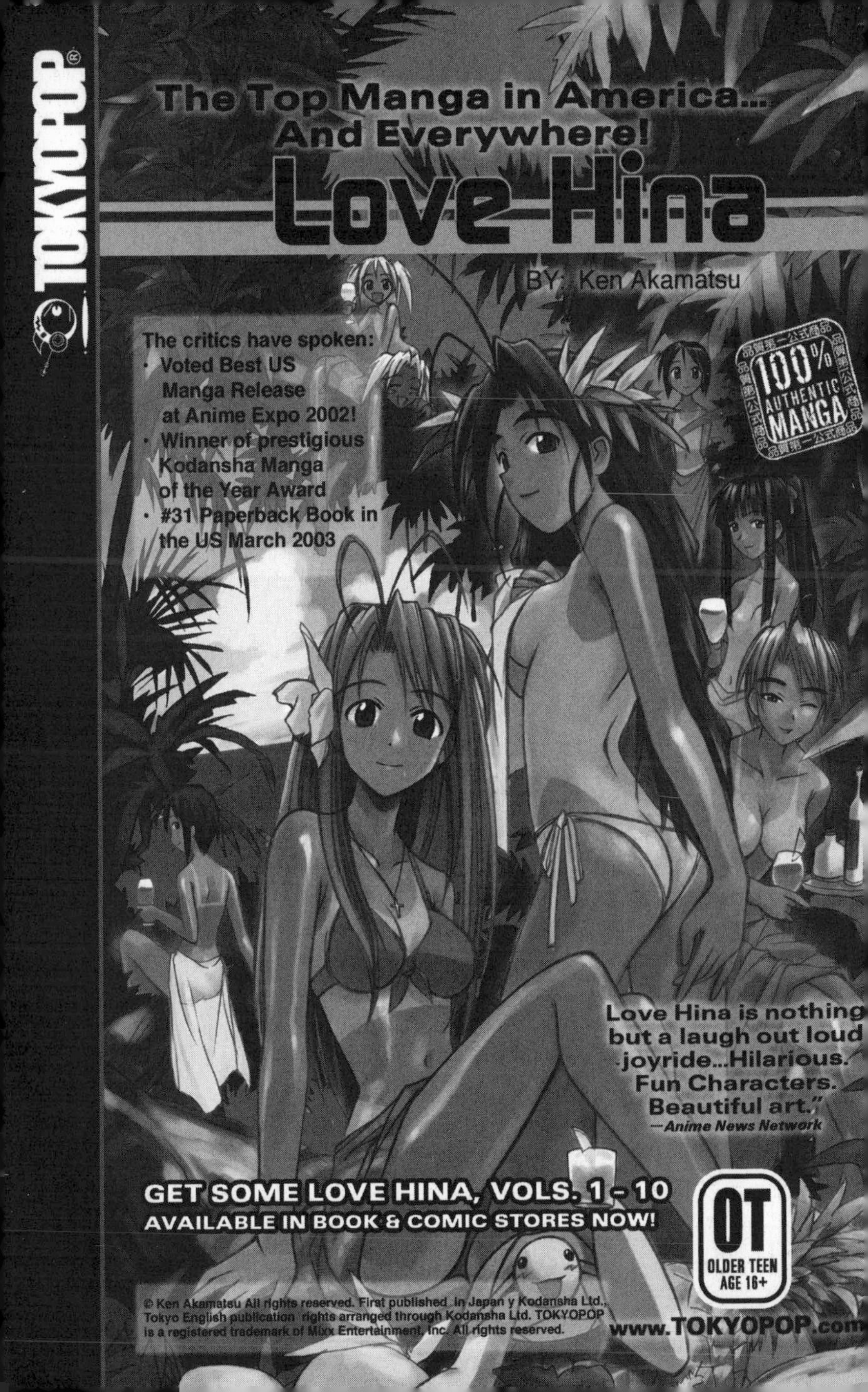
TOKYOPOP®
The Top Manga in America...
And Everywhere!
Love Hina
BY: Ken Akamatsu
The critics have spoken:
· Voted Best US Manga Release at Anime Expo 2002!
· Winner of prestigious Kodansha Manga of the Year Award
· #31 Paperback Book in the US March 2003
100% AUTHENTIC MANGA
"Love Hina is nothing but a laugh out loud joyride...Hilarious. Fun Characters. Beautiful art."
—Anime News Network
GET SOME LOVE HINA, VOLS. 1 - 10
AVAILABLE IN BOOK & COMIC STORES NOW!
OT
OLDER TEEN AGE 16+
© Ken Akamatsu All rights reserved. First published in Japan y Kodansha Ltd., Tokyo English publication rights arranged through Kodansha Ltd. TOKYOPOP is a registered trademark of Mixx Entertainment, Inc. All rights reserved.
www.TOKYOPOP.com

STOP!

This is the back of the book.
You wouldn't want to spoil a great ending!

This book is printed "manga-style," in the authentic Japanese right-to-left format. Since none of the artwork has been flipped or altered, readers get to experience the story just as the creator intended. You've been asking for it, so TOKYOPOP® delivered: authentic, hot-off-the-press, and far more fun!

DIRECTIONS

If this is your first time reading manga-style, here's a quick guide to help you understand how it works.

It's easy... just start in the top right panel and follow the numbers. Have fun, and look for more 100% authentic manga from TOKYOPOP®!